PRAISE FOR
PREMONITIONS

"One half heist and one half damn good urban fantasy, *Premonitions* has it all."
—Seanan McGuire, *New York Times* bestselling author of *Sparrow Hill Road*

"The development of the three women's relationships will keep readers coming back to this gritty series."
Publishers Weekly

"A sterling urban fantasy debut with a great cast of characters. . . . The action is nonstop and extremely well plotted. Like a cross between the TV show *Leverage* and Jim Butcher's Dresden Files books, this series is off to a terrific start."
—*Library Journal*

"Dark, gritty, and utterly captivating! . . . Jamie Schultz breathes new life into the urban fantasy genre, giving readers a whole new take on what happens when crime lords and denizens of Hell collide. *Premonitions* is a wild ride."
—Fresh Fiction

"Definitely unique. . . . I really enjoyed [Schultz's] voice and unique world setup."
—Smexy Books

"An amazing debut from Jamie Schultz. It's got everything you could ask for in a novel that blends a high-stakes caper with supernatural abilities. It's a little bit of *The Italian Job* . . . mixed in with a lot of grit, unpredictable alliances, and some truly scary individuals."
—Team Tynga's Reviews

Also by Jamie Schultz

Premonitions

SPLINTERED

An Arcane Underworld Novel

Jamie Schultz

A ROC BOOK

ROC
Published by the Penguin Group
Penguin Group (USA) LLC, 375 Hudson Street,
New York, New York 10014

USA | Canada |UK | Ireland | Australia | New Zealand | India | South Africa | China
penguin.com
A Penguin Random House Company

First published by Roc, an imprint of New American Library,
a division of Penguin Group (USA) LLC

First Printing, July 2015

 REGISTERED TRADEMARK — MARCA REGISTRADA

ISBN 978-0-451-46745-4

Printed in the United States of America
10   9   8   7   6   5   4   3   2   1

For Jenny

ACKNOWLEDGMENTS

It's easy to carry around the impression that an author is some sort of creative island. We get an idea, spend a bunch of time rooting around in our own skulls looking for interesting bits to place in proximity to the idea and hoping they'll leap to one another like magnets, and then pound out thousands of words at a keyboard while sucking down too much caffeine and grunting at anybody whose orbit passes through our general vicinity. Or maybe that last bit is specific to me. In any case, nothing could be further from the truth. An author isn't an island, and books don't happen in a vacuum. There's a veritable army involved, from the people who help work out the creative kinks to the tireless publishing folks to the people that make our lives work on a daily basis. I don't have enough space—or even a good enough memory—to thank all of the people who helped make this book happen, but here's a start.

Huge thanks to:

Evan Grantham-Brown, of course. I sometimes tell other writers that you don't necessarily need a critique group to help you work your craft. You need a single person who gets your work and can be candid with you on its shortcomings. Evan has been that guy for me for a long damn time.

Janet Sked and Conrad Zero, for additional feedback and criticism. I said above that you need a single person, but having an embarrassment of riches in that department ain't a bad thing, either.

Jessica Wade, who has a wonderful talent for pointing out exactly which crud needs to be cleared out, which elements need to be shored up, which excesses need to be reined in, and where a story just plain isn't getting the job done. I don't know if "saving the author from himself" is explicitly in an editor's job description, but it should be.

Lindsay Ribar, for helping get this book out into the world and for helping me navigate a new and unfamiliar world while she did so.

And my wife, Jenny, for not only putting up with me writing at all kinds of weird hours but for actively encouraging that sort of behavior.

Chapter 1

"I hate this," Anna said. She twisted her body to look out the back window of the parked car. Street mostly dark, nobody moving. A pair of headlights swung by and vanished as somebody made a wrong turn onto the street and then turned right back around. "I hate every damn thing about it."

Nail didn't say anything from the driver's seat, but he scowled. She heard the sandpapery sound as he ran a hand over his shaved head, and she could feel the annoyance radiating from him. It wasn't hard to imagine what he was thinking. Something along the lines of *I heard you the first six times*. She turned to face forward again, held still for almost ten seconds, and then started monkeying around with the car's side mirror. She caught a glimpse of the side of Genevieve's face, watching out the window from the seat behind her, just a line highlighting the profile of her cheek and a small arc of metal gleaming above the shadow of her eye socket.

"What time you got?" she asked.

Nail made a slight, skeptical smile and raised his eyebrows. "One forty." A long pause, and then, with a smirk playing around the corners of his mouth: "One forty-one."

"Not funny."

"The hell it ain't. I never seen you with nerves like this."

"I never fuckin' kidnapped nobody before, neither."

He shrugged. She wasn't sure if he was conceding the point or indicating that it wasn't really a big deal. *You think you know a guy . . .*

He was right, though. She couldn't remember the last time she'd been so jittery. Ten years, maybe, back when she and Karyn had first gotten into their bizarre line of work, swiping items of usually dubious occult value from their so-called rightful owners. Maybe the first job, the first time she'd found herself standing in a stranger's house at night, wondering, hey, what if they were actually home? And armed? Maybe not even then. Her heart raced like she'd downed a pot of coffee, and the acid-burning sensation in her gut wasn't too dissimilar, either.

The fatigue wasn't helping. She hadn't had a good night's sleep in weeks, not since the disaster at Enoch Sobell's office after the last job. There had been a showdown — gunfire and magic, a demonic creature summoned by the cult known as the Brotherhood of Zagam, and once the bodies had been cleared away, Anna's little four-person crew found itself in a sort of indentured servitude to Sobell.

And Karyn, Anna's friend and partner-in-crime for over a decade, had been put out of commission, wandering her weird interior world of visions from displaced times.

Helping Karyn, however she could, was job one, but Sobell's demands never stopped, and Anna was in no place to tell him to go fuck himself. But the current mission had now dragged on for weeks, diverting attention from Anna's real job. She just wanted to get it over with, however horrible it was.

"Van Horn's taking his time," Anna said.

Nail nodded. "Yeah."

She checked the side mirror. Still nothing. No movement of any kind. There was an empty lot, overgrown with high weeds and strewn with bricks and other construction debris. Then a body shop, closed down with metal shutters at this time of night. Past that, Bobby Chu's party shack, a big metal building that pulsed with bass. Lights flashed through the seams, extending multicolored fingers out through the windows of the cars that crowded around.

"What's he doing here?" Anna asked.

"Depends what he needs, I guess," Nail said.

"I guess." Still, it wasn't quite in pattern. They'd found Van Horn and his creepy entourage three nights ago, and this was by far the lowest the group had crawled down the socioeconomic ladder. The last few nights, Van Horn had been visiting well-off criminals who were plugged into the occult underworld in some way or other—one of them had, in fact, given Sobell the tip that had led the crew to Van Horn. Bobby was plugged in, but not with the grade of crook that Van Horn or Sobell trafficked with. More like the kind of scum that grew on the rocks at the bottom of the lake.

I hate this, Anna thought, again, but at least this time she kept herself from singing that refrain aloud and aggravating Nail and Gen with it once more. Bad enough that Sobell had them doing every odd shit job under the sun, but it was escalating. She'd thought she'd drawn a sharp line when he told her to act as a bagman—just this one time, and then it's back to business as usual, she'd said, her voice stripped down to a cold steel edge. He'd pretended to hear, or maybe she'd read agreement where none had existed, and then sent her out again the following week. The week after that, it had been another "pickup job," except she knew it wasn't, not really, not when Sobell had said, "Far be it from me to instruct you in the finer points of your business, but I strongly suggest you bring that big fellow, Nail, along. For the ride, as it were." And the pickup job had turned into a beatdown when Ernesto "Spaz" Rivera chose to live up to his nickname. He'd been short on the cash, but rather than talk it out he'd gone for intimidation, which rapidly turned into violence. Nail hadn't actually been necessary. Pepper spray, it turned out, was more than adequate for the likes of Spaz Rivera. That wasn't the last beatdown, either, and there had been a couple of other unsavory demands sprinkled in as well. It had barely come as a shock when Sobell upped the stakes to kidnapping.

"I shoulda told him to fuck right off," Anna muttered.

"Who the hell are they?" Nail said. Anna followed his pointing finger to the barrels and tubs stacked against the side of the body shop. "I don't . . . huh." No, there *was* somebody there. Hard to see in the shadows thrown by the streetlight, but there were at least a couple of people lurking among the trash. As she watched, one peeked around the corner at Bobby's place.

"Here comes Van Horn," Genevieve said.

Anna checked the side mirror. Van Horn and his crew were leaving Bobby's place, throwing long dancing shadows as, bizarrely, they jumped and spun and collided with one another. Somebody fell down hard, and the first sounds of the group reached the car—laughter, high and hysterical. Seconds later, the whole group erupted in the same sort of frenetic, desperate laughter as well, making an eerie chorus that grabbed Anna's spine at the base and twisted.

There was a ripple of motion to Anna's left as Nail actually shuddered.

"You okay, tough guy?" Genevieve asked.

He nodded. Anna studied his face for a moment, then slid down in her seat and resumed watching the mirror. It looked like the same drill out there as the last several nights. Van Horn walked in the middle, head down, fedora pulled low, hands in the pockets of his pin-striped slacks. He wasn't close enough for her to see his face or hear him well, but if the past nights were representative, he was either grinning like a fool or whistling an eerie music-box-sounding tune. Around him, a shifting, spinning cloud of chaos. Maybe half a dozen men and half a dozen women, and a more motley assortment couldn't easily be imagined. Two of them looked like Genevieve's crowd—lots of black, trench coats despite the scorching heat of August in Los Angeles, and lots of piercings. The others, not so much. There was a skinny black kid in a basketball jersey. An old white guy with a mustache, wearing a black suit. He'd look like a slimeball attorney, if only he weren't capering and shouting and stumbling down the street without any shoes on. A twentysomething hippie in what appeared to be a tie-dyed muumuu, tossing invisible handfuls of something at the group and laughing.

It looked as though the membership had dwindled again. Seemed that every day, one or two of Van Horn's entourage disappeared. There had been fifteen or so to start with. Genevieve had joked that maybe the missing ones had been eaten by the others, and nobody had laughed. Anna had wondered if she and the crew could just wait until nobody was left and Van Horn was alone, but she eventually decided there was no guarantee that would ever happen, and Sobell was not a terribly patient man.

The mob got closer, and the shouting got louder, and Anna slid farther down into her seat. Even Nail did his level best to make himself small. They hadn't been noticed before, but Anna couldn't help feeling that, if Van Horn's deranged entourage ever did pay them any attention, a bad scene would follow.

In the mirror, Anna saw the lawyer stop. He weaved unsteadily on his feet, waved his hands in the air, then pointed at a trash bin that had fallen over in the mouth of an alley.

The trash ignited.

"Oh, shit," Genevieve said.

Van Horn spun on the lawyer and, in a sudden move totally unlike the easygoing, down-on-his-luck businessman he'd seemed to Anna all week, clouted the other man viciously on the side of the head, shouting something Anna couldn't make out. The lawyer rocked, then fell back, tensed and half crouched, and Anna could have sworn he was about to spring on Van Horn. She had the sudden crazy impression the man was about to attack Van Horn with his teeth, and then the rest of the entourage formed up, standing to Van Horn's left and right. The lawyer's body went limp, submissive, all trace of a fight gone. He laughed. Even from here, Anna could tell he was playing it off like a joke. *Hey, sorry, man. Just got carried away.* That kind of thing.

Van Horn's entourage wasn't placated. They began spreading in a semicircle around the lawyer.

"They're gonna kill him," Genevieve whispered.

Anna thought she was right. The hippie chick's face was contorted in a crazy sort of zeal that was visible even from here, eyes avid and gleaming with red and blue light from the party shack, and the Goth kids had curled their hands into fists. No, not fists, but claws. A brief crazy thought ran through her mind. *Call 911.* The lawyer was undoubtedly an asshole, but he didn't deserve this. Whatever was about to happen, it was going to be *awful*.

The lawyer evidently reached the same conclusion. His strength deserted him, and his legs gave out. He fell to the asphalt.

The semicircle closed around him. Anna stopped breathing, her chest locked tight in horrified anticipation. It didn't matter if she called 911 or not. Nobody could get here in time. And yeah, she was armed, but the guy about to get himself killed had started a fire in a trash can from forty feet away. Who knew what the others were capable of?

The whole group paused, coiling to launch themselves on the prone lawyer, and then Van Horn stepped inside the circle and extended a hand to the man. The others held where they were, seeming to tremble with the strain of it.

Sudden movement pulled Anna's attention from the reconciliation as the guys behind the body shop stepped out. There were four that Anna could see. Before she could say anything, they opened fire.

The man—kid, really, one of the Goths—on Van Horn's left went down first, shot in the back. The others dropped to the pavement, spreading out and staying low behind the row of cars. One of them began laughing hysterically.

Another barrage of shots sounded. They went wild, shattering glass and punching holes in car doors, but if they hit anybody, Anna couldn't tell.

The remaining Goth kid stood. A blade shone under the light, and he slashed it down his palm. Sparks flew as a bullet *spanged* off the car in front of him.

He flicked his hand at one of the shooters. Drops of blood flew from his fingertips, and the man was flung backward, slamming into a pile of fenders. Nearby, another barrel went up in flames. The kid in the basketball jersey uttered some strange words and tore a piece of paper in half, and a shower of rocks skittered across the sidewalk and pounded into the group's attackers.

"Go!" Van Horn said.

Anna thought it was a sign to run, but it turned out to be anything but—the mob of ten or eleven stormed over and around the cars, charging the group by the body shop. After that, confusion in the darkness. There was noise and shouting, the sound of running feet.

Less than a minute later, Van Horn and his entourage emerged. They scurried for a van and a busted-looking old station wagon, got in among shouts and crazed laughter, and a few moments later, pulled out.

They left the Goth kid's body in the street.

"Follow them," Anna said.

Nail started the car. "Ain't gotta ask twice."

Van Horn and his entourage drove an erratic, circuitous route, probably assuming *somebody* was following them at this point, but they ended up back at the same place they'd ended up the last couple of nights—an abandoned meatpacking plant at the end of a very quiet tenement block. Nail pulled the car up a short way at the other end of the street and watched them get out and then file into the building.

He turned off the car and killed the lights. The three of them waited wordlessly in the vehicle. An hour passed. Anna played with the button on the glove compartment and wished for a cigarette. Nobody else showed up, and nobody came out of the building.

"Where's that leave us?" Genevieve asked finally.

Nail grunted. "Same as before. He doesn't go out alone, he doesn't stay in alone. Either we grab him on the street and risk being killed or seen, or we go in."

"And just risk being killed."

"Any idea who those other guys were?" Anna asked. "Seems like we aren't the only ones gunning for him. Sobell got somebody else on this, you think?"

"Doubt it," Nail said. "Not if he's so concerned about taking him alive. Which probably means we got even less time than we thought."

"We scope the place tomorrow, then," Anna said. "When they're out doing . . . whatever."

It was action, anyway. Motion in some direction. That didn't make her feel any better.

Anna jolted awake, heart pounding and breath coming panicky and shallow, but Genevieve was there, close, hand on her shoulder, hip touching her hip. Ready with soothing words in the darkness. "It's all right; it's okay. Shhh. It's just a bad dream."

"Jesus Christ," Anna said. She sat up and pushed the blanket away. Her T-shirt was glued to her body with sweat, her hair greasy and gross and hanging down in her eyes in wet tangles. "Jesus fucking Christ."

"It'll be all right," Genevieve said. She moved her hand to the back of Anna's neck, kneading as though pushing on the flesh would somehow purge the fear. "Really."

"What time is it?"

"I don't know. Four or five in the morning, I guess."

So she'd gotten, what? An hour of sleep? Two? This was exhausting. "Did I scream?"

A pause. "Only a little."

Anna grunted with disgust. She brushed the hair away from her face and stared into the blackness of the room. The room was entirely dark, and she figured that was just as well. The cinder block walls were oppressive, and she was convinced the pile of debris in the corner concealed a nest of wriggling, squirming creatures of some kind. Better not to see it . . . though now that she was listening, was there movement over there? A tiny piece of plasterboard sliding down the pile as some creeping creature pushed its nose out of its den?

You're imagining that, she thought, but she grabbed for her phone anyway and flipped on the light.

Genevieve held up an arm, squinting. "A little warning would've been nice." She looked worn down, too, in disturbing contrast to her usual energy. Genevieve had two arms tattooed in full, colorful sleeves, a shock of pink hair at the base of which blond roots had begun to show, over a dozen piercings in her ears and more in her tongue, lips, eyebrows, and nose, and she had an upbeat swagger about her that seemed impenetrable most of the time. Not tonight, though—she was peevish and tired, like Anna. Couldn't really blame her.

Anna turned the phone so that it threw its fragile, diffuse beam of light toward the pile of stuff in the corner. Nothing moved. She swept the light around the room. A backpack and some basic camping equipment lay over by the wall. Near Genevieve's sleeping bag, a stack of Genevieve's paperwork—occult stuff, notes and fragile old documents covered in cryptic scrawling. Anna found that stuff almost as creepy as the pile in the corner, but in the circles they traveled, having somebody with a little occult know-how was as necessary as lockpicks and police scanners, and Genevieve was among the best Anna had worked with.

She moved the light back to the pile in the corner. Still nothing moving, and she wondered if that was because there was really nothing in there after all or because it was too smart to move in the light.

"We're getting that cleaned out of here in the morning," she said.

Genevieve nodded. "Same dream?"

"Same kind of dream." *Bang bang bang bang.* Four shots, four holes in a human being. Another night spent reliving the clusterfuck at Sobell's. She'd killed a man there, or what was left of one, before the bony horror the cult had summoned up tore itself loose from the guy's carcass and attacked. The dreams were jumbled, fragmentary, and Anna no longer had a clear memory of what she'd seen and what her mind had reconstructed for her. She'd emptied an entire magazine into the bad guys; she was pretty sure that had happened. Adelaide had been there. She was *definite* on that. Hadn't seen her since, which was a major fucking problem, since Adelaide was the only one who knew how to brew or conjure up the stuff Karyn called blind, the stuff that blunted her visions and kept her most of the way in the real world. In the dream, Karyn shoved Genevieve away from the business end of a shotgun just before it went off. In the dream, the blast caught Adelaide full in the face, turning her head into red mush and fragments. It hadn't gone down quite like that in real life—Adelaide had survived, taking a few pellets instead of the whole blast—but it might as well have. Adelaide was gone, and Karyn was physically present but mentally in another time entirely, farther from Anna than if she'd been across the continent.

Now every time Anna got a few hours in the rack, instead of a stretch of blissful oblivion, she got to relive that night's violence over and over. Nobody had ever told her that the hangover off an ugly adrenaline high like that could last for weeks. Or months. There had been tough guys on the street where she grew up, before she ended up a ward of the state, hard-core gangbangers who claimed to have killed a dozen motherfuckers each. Maybe some of them had. They sure didn't act as though they'd lost any sleep over it. Maybe that was just bluster. Maybe they were wired differently.

Maybe I should just go ask them.

Genevieve tried to pull her close, but Anna held up a hand. "I'm just gonna get up," she said.

"Come on, it's late."

"And I'm done sleeping. I keep seeing his face. *Its* face. Both of them."

"Anna, he was a monster. It was a matter of survival."

"I don't feel guilty," Anna said. "I just feel *bad*."

Genevieve nodded, but it seemed perfunctory. That's what you did with the traumatized woman, right? You agreed with her, even if you didn't have the faintest clue what she was talking about. Genevieve's heart was in the right place, she supposed, but it was still all so tiring.

"I'm gonna get up." Anna stood up. No need to get dressed—they were all sleeping in their clothes anyway, awaiting the moment when everybody had to suddenly get up and run to meet Sobell, fend off a small army of Van Horn's deranged entourage, or deal with whatever other nasty surprise turned up. Maybe she didn't smell the freshest, but she wouldn't get shot trying to put on her pants, either.

"Want some company?"

"No. Thanks anyway." She bent down and kissed Genevieve on the corner of her mouth.

Concern warred briefly with exhaustion on Genevieve's face before conceding defeat. Genevieve lay back on the bedroll the two of them shared and exhaled heavily. "Okay."

Anna pulled on her beat-up old jean jacket and left the room. The main space outside, where most of the interior walls had been torn down, was dark. Just enough of the city light made its way through the broken-out windows and holes in the walls to reflect off the moldering piles of sheetrock and make the path visible. The building they were squatting in was an abandoned elementary school, half-collapsed and full of debris. As bad as Anna felt, the building made it worse. The place was familiar in layout, but disturbing and alien at the same time. She hadn't gone to school here, but schools were all the same, and hanging out in this place felt like walking through the bombed-out ruin of her childhood. She would have thought she'd feel some kind of smug satisfaction at that—her childhood had been no great shakes—but no. Instead, it was more a reminder that everything went to shit in time, as though she needed a reminder.

She knew why they were there. She got the logic of it. They were about to orchestrate a kidnapping, and you didn't want to haul the guy you'd kidnapped back to your apartment, after all. It still sucked.

Anna took the path around a pile of construction debris to the next room over in the row. Like most of the rooms, it hadn't had a door when the crew moved in. Unlike with all the other rooms but one, they'd put a door on it right away. This one was a sloppy construction of three-quarter-inch plywood with some hinges Genevieve had scrounged up from somewhere. The other was somewhat sturdier.

Using the light from her phone again, Anna found the bar that held the makeshift door shut and slid it out. The plywood's slight bow sprang back, pushing the door open for her.

Karyn was inside. Awake, unfortunately, and sitting in the corner with her knees pulled up to her chest. Her eyes didn't move toward Anna, didn't register her presence at all, even though the pupils dialed down to tiny dots as Anna moved the light over her. She was seeing another time, Anna knew, or more likely an amalgam of dozens or hundreds. Waking nightmares.

This was what Karyn had been most afraid of, back when Anna first met her. Not of going crazy, but of losing her mind in a more literal sense. The distinction was probably moot anyway. The effect was the same.

"How are you feeling?" Anna asked. She always did. Always said something. Karyn seemed to understand fragments of it sometimes, and Anna figured she must be awfully lonely in there.

If Karyn got any of it this time, she made no answer. She pulled her ponytail holder loose from her brown hair and retied it, seemingly apropos of nothing. The faint, permanent lines of anxiety in her forehead seemed deeper than usual, but that might just have been Anna, projecting her own fatigue on everything around her.

"I'll find you," Anna said. "I'll bring you back. Just hang tight." She waited a few minutes, hoping maybe Karyn would catch sight of her and say something. When Karyn remained silent, she left, barring the door once more.

"You're up early," Nail said. He sat in front of the door to the next room over, back braced against the cinder block wall. From here he was little more than a low, lumpy silhouette. If not for the orange ember of the end of his cigarette, she might not have seen him at all.

She walked over and sat next to him. He was a big guy, ex-military, still carrying most of the muscle, but she wondered if he was wearing down, too. He seemed squared away most of the time, though—boots polished, shirt tucked into his fatigue pants, clean-shaven every single day. "Any trouble?"

"Nah. Night's pretty calm."

"Wish I felt the same."

Nail took a drag from his cigarette and offered it to her. She followed suit, watching the end flare up in the darkness.

"Can't sleep?" he asked.

"What was your first clue?"

He tapped his forehead with his index finger. "Can't hide nothin' from me."

She inhaled again, burning down a third of Nail's cigarette in one long drag. Genevieve would give her a hard time, if she saw her now. *I thought you quit,* she'd say, frowning. *No,* Anna thought, suddenly confused. *Karyn would do that. Gen never knew me when I smoked.*

"You ever kill anyone?" she asked.

Nail took the cigarette back. Another brief orange flare as he inhaled. "Yeah."

No surprise there. A guy didn't tour Iraq with Marines First Recon to tickle people. She was surprised at his tone, though. Less matter-of-fact than she'd expected, a little heavier. Or maybe she was reading too much into it.

"It bother you?"

He flicked an ember onto the concrete floor. It fragmented, sending up a tiny shower of sparks. "Depends what you mean by that."

She wished she could read his face, but there wasn't enough light. "Like, you know. Insomnia."

"Bad dreams."

"Yeah."

He turned his head to look toward her. She wondered if he could see anything more than she could. Maybe it was because he couldn't that he continued.

"First guy I ever killed was because my brother's a fuckin' idiot," he said. Not what she'd expected, though by all accounts his brother was, in fact, a fuckin' idiot. "You know, he was in college? UCLA, where Dad worked maintenance. He woulda been the first on that side of the family to finish, if he'da finished."

Anna waited while Nail seemed to collect himself. She remembered his brother, DeWayne. They'd met, briefly, during the first job Nail had ever worked with her and Karyn. Nail's whole share of the take, or as near as made no difference, had gone to bailing DeWayne out of the kind of jam that usually ended with a body in a Dumpster or behind a warehouse somewhere. A whole lot of Nail's money went down that hole, she thought, though she never asked about it.

"Trouble with DeWayne," Nail continued, "is that he got more brains than sense. Everybody knows he got no sense. Always running some clever scam, always thinks he's got the angles figured . . .

"He started running sports book his second semester at college. He'd made a little pile of cash his first semester betting on that kind of shit, and he thought he'd make a whole lot more if he set himself up as the house, you know? Thing is, it took off. Started with a few guys he knew, and then a couple guys at one of the frats wanted in, and they told their friends, and so on. Before too long, there's thousands of dollars changing hands, I shit you not, and he's takin' his ten percent off the top. But that ain't quite good enough. DeWayne, he's figured all the angles, decides that the Badgers are a lock for the fuckin' Rose Bowl or some shit, so he takes the money he's supposed to be sitting on to pay the winners and he bets it himself."

"Ouch," Anna said. "He lost it, huh?"

"No, he won. Stuck his neck way out on the chopping block with other people's money, and for a goddamn miracle, he didn't get his head cut off. Won something like thirty grand."

"I don't get it."

"DeWayne's the kind of guy—let's just say he's got a knack for turning gold to shit. If everybody's got one God-given talent, that's his. The bet wasn't the problem. The problem was that he just couldn't stop himself running his mouth after. He couldn't help it. He just couldn't help it. Couldn't help flashing the cash, neither. He took care of himself, yeah, but he also put new tires on Ma's car, bought me a new computer. I swear he was talking to roofing contractors before Dad asked him where the hell the money was coming from. DeWayne told him it was a scholarship, and I don't think nobody believed that shit, but that's all we could get out of him, so it just ended with Dad telling him to spend it on school.

"Me, I knew the score. I was just too stupid to care. Far as I was concerned, DeWayne was the coolest big brother a kid could want. He let me hang with him and his boys, never tried to get rid of me. I was seventeen, hanging with college kids whenever I wanted, having a great time.

"I shoulda seen it coming, though. Whenever De-Wayne gets real nervous, real jumpy, it's because he done some shit he knows he shouldn't have, and he's waiting for it to hit the fan, and he got *real* jumpy late that spring. He didn't leave the apartment he was staying at for three days. Wouldn't go near the windows, even though it was a hundred damn degrees in there. Sent me out to get him some smokes twice, to pick up some food once.

"So what happened was some low-life wannabe connected guy running book heard about DeWayne's business from one of the frat kids, then heard about the pile of money from—well, who the fuck knows? Anybody coulda told him by that point. Anyway, he puts two and five together and thinks, 'Okay, here's some son of a bitch cutting in on my business, and now he's got a pretty good stash to fund it.' It's one thing when a guy's coordinating bets between a handful of buddies, but it's something else entirely when he's working twenty, thirty clients or more, and he's got enough dough to pay out. Starts to look like a real business, you know? So I guess he made some threats, and DeWayne told everybody that that motherfucker was toast if he messed with him, or something like that, and word got around, and DeWayne wised up and hid his ass.

"Anyway, I show up at DeWayne's on day four, and the door's kicked in. I walk in, stop in the middle of the living room when I hear yelling from the back. Begging, really. 'Jesus, Trigger, take the money, take all of it, man. I don't care.' All that kinda noise. Then some shit smashing. Then a gunshot, and the real screaming starts.

"That's what gets me moving. I grab a fork—a fuckin' *fork*, because it was lyin' on the coffee table next to a plate with some dried tomato sauce on it, and I didn't have a goddamn brain—and I run back. DeWayne's on the ground, blood squirting out of a hole in his leg, and this big dumb asshole—Trigger, I guess—is *standing* on the wound, got his heel on it, grinding away, yelling, 'You like that, motherfucker? You like that?' And he's not paying too much attention to the gun, just sort of waving it around, but for one second it's not actually pointing at nobody, and he's half-turned, and I jump on him."

Anna passed the cigarette back. Nail took it, took the last drag off it, and crushed the butt against the concrete. He exhaled heavily, and the plume of smoke took on a brief, swirling life of its own before dissipating.

"You know what it takes to kill a motherfucker with a dinner fork?"

Anna shook her head.

Another deep breath let out. "Sorriest goddamn mess you ever saw. My arm was sore for a week."

"Jesus."

"Yeah. Didn't sleep any too good for a long while after that. Then 9/11 happened, and I enlisted, and I seen a whole lot worse since."

"This where you tell me it gets better with time?"

He shrugged. "I guess you already know that." He shifted, stretching one leg out in front of him. "I knew guys in the service who got a taste for it. Power trip. Cap some guy, and you can feel like a big man for an hour, or whatever. I get that, but it ain't my thing."

"So what's your thing?'

He looked away from her, slowly surveying the wreckage around them. "When you're in a spot where you got to ice somebody, it's . . . it's like eating your vegetables. You gotta do it, no matter how bad it tastes. Bad for your health if you don't. Best get it over with quick and not think too hard on it."

Anna waited a moment to see if he had anything to add, but he stayed silent. "That's it?" she asked. "That's your expert advice on the subject?"

"It's what I got."

"I can't tell if you'd make a worse therapist or inspirational speaker."

He laughed quietly. "I imagine I'd be pretty bad at both."

"Hey, you recognize any of Van Horn's crowd?"

Nail nodded. "T-shirt and cargo pants and the lawyer-looking guy for sure. Might be others."

"From the Brotherhood. Mendelsohn's guys."

"Yeah."

That confirmed the worst of Anna's fears on the subject. Nathan Mendelsohn had run a cult known as the Brotherhood of Zagam. He'd also owned the jawbone that Sobell had hired the crew to steal, the goddamn thing that had gotten Tommy killed and come inches away from wiping out the rest of crew and even Sobell himself. Only, in the end, it had turned out that Mendelsohn had been dead awhile, and some guy named Hector had been running his cult the whole time. That guy was still around, somewhere, and so, apparently, were the remnants of the cult. Anna hated to think what they'd do if they recognized her or any of the others. The jawbone had been a precious relic of theirs, and things had gotten considerably fucked-up after the crew stole it. In the end, Genevieve had destroyed the relic in full view of Hector and others. "What's Van Horn doing with Mendelsohn's guys?"

"Sobell's all tangled up with 'em somehow. Don't surprise me none."

"No. I guess not."

They sat in companionable silence for a few minutes longer. Anna felt no fatigue coming on—she felt energized, oddly. It wasn't a good kind of energy, more that of her brain running a hundred miles an hour, but there was no chance she'd sleep. "Hey, why don't you crash out for a bit? No sense in both of us being up the rest of the night."

"Yeah, all right." He stood, knees popping, and headed down the short path to the room he'd claimed for himself.

Sunrise came slow, preceded by an uptick in the distant sound of traffic, honking horns, and sirens. Anna wondered if there was anywhere you could go in L.A. and not hear it. The city's circulatory system, as clogged and dysfunctional as it was. Omnipresent, like the blood rushing in her ears, like the sound of her own breath. It had its own rhythms, locked tighter to the clock than to the sun or the stars. Today was Thursday, and the commuters had already jammed up the 5. Must be about five thirty, then.

The sky lightened soon after, and weariness arrived with it, dragging a nice headache behind. This was life now. A few hours of sleep snatched between bone deep fatigue at the end of the day and the moment not long after when nightmares woke her up. Nights spent tracking Van Horn, and any other time that wasn't nailed down spent chasing one shitty lead after another, hoping to find someone, anyone, who could help Karyn. So far, that had been an almost laughably varied series of failures, ranging from simply disappointing to expensive and life-threatening. Dodging bullets, trading favors, and bartering for charms, occult concoctions, and spell fragments that she needed Genevieve to interpret for her. All useless so far. One so poisonous she'd had to be rushed to the emergency room for a stomach pump after testing it out on herself. Her nerves were shot. She'd lost weight, too, and as Nail was fond of telling her, she'd been built like a broom handle before.

This couldn't go on indefinitely, but she didn't see what choice she had.

Five thirty in the morning. Most of her remaining leads would likely be asleep. Fuck 'em.

She flipped open her phone and got back to work.

Chapter 2

Enoch Sobell looked up from his desk and frowned. He recognized the woman standing in front of him, but he couldn't remember from where. She was about fifty, dressed in a conservative blue suit, and her face was all creases and sharp angles, as if it had been hacked out of a stump with a machete. Her burned-in scowl and ramrod-straight bearing made him want to start humming the Marines' Hymn. She stood directly in front of his desk at the exact center, not in the least awed by the high ceiling, the dozen or so pedestals in alcoves showcasing a fraction of Sobell's collection of ancient and unusual objects, or Sobell himself.

"Has there been an election?" Sobell asked. "I seem to remember the mayor being somewhat taller. Male as well."

The woman said nothing, but he thought her scowl intensified. Call that a victory, then. "Would you care to have a seat? Perhaps I can get you something to drink?"

"The mayor is very busy."

"No drink, then?"

"He's likely to be busy for the foreseeable future."

Sobell leaned back. He tapped his fingers on the arms of his chair in a kind of low-key drumroll. His mouth tightened. "Hmm." The woman showed no signs of impatience, and he got the impression she'd stand there,

impassive, until he died of old age if she had to. "Hmm."
Well, one didn't get to his position in life without trying
to make a few friends, even if some of them were detestable. "I'm sorry. I think we've started off poorly. I'm
Enoch Sobell. I can't say I've had the pleasure of making
your acquaintance."

"Denise Watterson." She produced a business card from
her jacket pocket and offered it to him. "Trask, Hopper,
and Watterson."

"That sounds suspiciously like a law firm."

"It is."

"Pardon my thickheadedness, but you're not with the
mayor's office, are you?"

"No."

"Perhaps I'm being sued, then? Except that one
doesn't usually employ a named partner at a prestigious
law firm in the capacity of a process server. What is going
on here, if you don't mind my asking?"

"I represent Mayor Vargas's interests in a number of
areas. I have recommended to him, in light of recent
events, that he terminate all contact with you."

"You're what, then? His consigliere?"

To her credit, she didn't even blink. Tough customer.
Sobell had to respect that, even as annoying as it was.

He sighed. "Madam, I have known Ramon for fifteen
years. I've used every legal device imaginable to donate
the maximum amounts possible to his reelection cam-
paigns. You can check that. It's a matter of public record.
We have had several successful business partnerships.
You can check . . . some of that. Now I invite him over
for a couple of drinks and pleasant conversation, and he
sends a polite but none-too-friendly attorney to cut ties
with me? I find that hard to believe. Or at least in very
poor taste."

"Was that a question?"

"Has Ramon Vargas's head grown so big he won't
deign to do any of his own dirty work anymore?"

"Mr. Sobell. There was a massacre in your office

building. Nineteen bodies were carted out of here while the news cameras rolled."

"Nineteen, eh?"

"Two police officers were killed just outside."

"Perhaps if we devoted more resources to keeping down gang violence in our fair city . . ."

"Nobody, least of all you, believes this was a random act of gang violence."

"Not random, no. I was targeted for being such a staunch supporter of local law enforcement."

Still no sign of a crack. Well, she did do this for a living after all.

"There are also eyewitness accounts of a man matching your description fleeing from a firefight in East L.A."

"Slander. Who are these so-called eyewitnesses? I'll have my attorney file the appropriate defamation suits immediately. I wouldn't be caught dead in East L.A."

"I'm not here to recount the evidence or listen to all the reasons why you're innocent."

"Just to deliver a message, is that correct?"

"It is."

"Perhaps you'd like to make me an offer I can't refuse?"

He'd thought Watterson was at maximum humorlessness before, but her face hardened and a little muscle bunched at the corner of her jaw. "I hope you're not suggesting the mayor has ties to organized crime."

"Heavens no."

"Good. If you have further questions, you have my card. As I mentioned before, the mayor is extremely busy."

"Too busy to take my calls for, ah, how did you put it? 'The foreseeable future.'"

"That's correct."

"Just as well, I suppose. I've long thought he was soft on gang violence. That Henderson fellow, though, seems like just the man to clean up our increasingly violent and dangerous streets." The words were a mistake, Sobell thought as soon as he said them. Threats just made him look weak, and surely Watterson was comfortable dealing with them. That was what she would have expected. *I'm slipping.*

"Maybe you should call him," she said. With that, she left.

He sat, hands folded and his elbows on his desk, watching the closed door she'd exited through. He felt oddly . . . soiled, somehow. It was the office, he thought. The office used to be his nerve center, the place from which all his considerable power radiated out through the city and even beyond. Gresser and the Brotherhood had befouled that, Gresser when he'd moved in and taken Sobell's chair and his identity through the power of that accursed jawbone, and the Brotherhood when they'd flocked to the man and then perpetrated a slaughter here. For Watterson to come in and rub his face in it seemed to him to be practically obscene.

He reached for the phone to dial his assistant, and the light for her extension flashed on even before he touched the handset. He picked up the phone in the middle of the first ring. "Ms. Ely, excellent timing. Please send up some of the custodial staff. We're going to move my office down to the forty-eighth."

"Sir, the FBI is here. They have a search warrant."

"Excuse me?" The police had already been through the place, top to bottom, after the event Ms. Watterson had characterized as a massacre.

"A search warrant. They're demanding access immediately."

"They've waved credentials at you, then?" Sobell said, mostly to buy a few moments' thought.

"Yes, sir. Special Agent Gina Elliot. I've verified her with the Los Angeles division."

Sobell suppressed a sigh. "Splendid," he said, with all the good cheer he could fake. "Have her meet me at the bar. And can you call Erica Tran and tell her to get here as soon as possible?"

"Right away."

A dozen questions sprang to mind, but Ms. Ely would have answers to none of them. There had to be an angle here, some reason the issue had escalated to the federal level, some reason beyond the LAPD's rank incompetence that they'd need to take another swing at a basic search rather than simply going through the records from the previous search.

"Thank you, Ms. Ely."

Sobell left his office and walked toward the stairs at a leisurely pace, fretting. Special Agent Elliot, hmm? That didn't sound good. Not at all. The police were already up in his knickers enough—they tended to go a little berserk when one of their own bought the farm, so to speak. Hence contacting the mayor's office. Ramon could call them off with a phone call, but evidently Sobell was too dirty now even for Ramon Vargas to touch. Sobell supposed he ought to be angry about that, but it was mostly just vexing. That was how this worked, after all, and he'd been shut out by better men than the mayor dozens of times. Either he'd get through this and the mayor would likely find himself out of office the next time around, or he wouldn't, and the mayor would have been correct all along. Best to be a big boy and acknowledge that this was standard operating procedure. Expecting a politician to stand by you in a hurricane like this would have been like expecting a viper not to bite you when you poked it. *I knew it was a snake when I picked it up,* Sobell thought.

The most vexing thing about all this was that it was a giant distraction. The cult, the massacre in his building, the death of his most trusted lieutenant, Joe Gresser, and now the invasive probing of law enforcement—it was all a big fucking sideshow, unpleasant by-products generated on the way to achieving his real goal. The jawbone had been a catalyst, nothing more. The plan had been simple enough: While Mendelsohn's ridiculous cult was dealing with the patsies Sobell had sent in to steal their precious relic, they'd leave their pet demon untended, and Sobell would take the opportunity to go bargain with the creature.

It had all worked, sort of, but it had all gone more than a little sour, too. The demon hadn't been able to help him with his central problem, that of his imminent demise. By appearances, Sobell seemed a smartly dressed, fit man in his mid-forties, fifty at the oldest, with blandly handsome features and distinguished salt-and-pepper hair, but the truth was that, after centuries of magically extended life, his body was wearing out. He was dying. He was also beyond the point of being able to use magic to wring a few more years out. At bottom, magic was a deal with demons, and if you used enough of it over a long enough period, it eroded your mind or your soul—your defenses, in any case—and left you wide-open to what was, inevitably, terminal demonic possession. He'd hoped to bargain for more life, but the demon hadn't been able to help him. All it had done was point him back toward the last demon he'd bargained with, a detestable little worm called Forcas, and then give him a few weak tips on how to find the creature.

The only thread that had seemed promising from the demon's cryptic messages had been a simple image, that of a man Sobell had known years ago: Edgar Van Horn. But before Sobell had been able to follow up on any of that, the situation with the cult had exploded, and all the other dominoes he'd unheedingly kicked on the way had fallen. In the end, he'd been lucky to survive—had, in fact, taken a bullet to the head, a deep graze that still sported a crusty finger-wide scab along the right side of his forehead. Ironically enough, he'd been shot by the new leader of poor dead Nathan Mendelsohn's cult, a man named Hector Martel, who, in all likelihood, was harboring the very demon Sobell sought. But by the time Sobell had put all those pieces together, Martel had vanished, and things had gotten very complicated indeed.

That left him with Van Horn. Sobell needed to be working on the Van Horn problem and offering whatever small assistance he could to Anna Ruiz's crew, his latest reluctant allies. If there was anything worth getting dirty over, Van Horn was it. Dealing with law enforcement was simply a nuisance. A worrisome, vexing nuisance that had now ascended to an entirely new level.

He descended the spiral staircase to the forty-eighth floor. Most of this story was open, scattered structural columns the only things obscuring the view of the city through the floor-to-ceiling windows. The floor was marble, and the bar was well stocked, and all in all, it was a hell of a place to host a soiree of an evening, not that he'd felt much like partying lately. Even debauchery couldn't keep his mind off his more pressing problems for more than a few minutes. The situation was dire indeed.

He wasn't sure moving his office down here was the best idea he'd ever had, but it had to be better than leaving it where it was.

The black woman standing by the bar wore the customary dour FBI suit, and her hair, pulled back in a bun so severe it seemed to stretch the skin of her forehead, did nothing to soften her image. Sharp eyes met his gaze through rectangular lenses mounted in a pair of black designer frames. She seemed a spiritual counterpart to Sobell's earlier visitor, and he got the impressions from her stance and the set of her jaw that she was eager for a fight.

"Would you like to have a seat?" Sobell asked. "This may be a business meeting, but we can at least be civilized about it. Would you like some water? Coffee? Something with a little more kick?"

"This isn't business," she said.

Sobell smiled. "I'm Enoch Sobell."

"Special Agent Gina Elliot. FBI."

"That's what Ms. Ely tells me. How can I help you?" Sobell took a seat on the next barstool.

She brandished some paper at him. "This is a search warrant."

"So I'm given to understand." He folded his hands on

the bar and did his best to look sincere. "What is this about?"

"A lot of people died here a little while back."

"Upstairs, actually. It's all very tragic and horrible, but I think you'll find the local authorities have my complete statement on the matter. I'm not sure what else I could add."

"We think those bodies might be just the tip of the iceberg, Mr. Sobell."

"An iceberg of bodies? What a needlessly gruesome metaphor." Special Agent Elliot, Sobell was glad to see, wasn't quite the consummate stone-faced professional that Watterson was. A sort of guarded curiosity opened her face—she wasn't charmed by him, he didn't believe that for an instant, but she was interested. In him, in everything around them. Each time she moved her head or shifted position, her eyes did a quick sweep of the room, checking the walls, the corners, the ceiling. The movements carried nothing of the kind of security paranoia he might have expected—just that curiosity.

He wondered if she was here for a bribe. That didn't quite feel right, but *something* was off here. "I assure you, the police have been all up and down and through this building, and if they've found a hidden cache of corpses, they have yet to inform me about it." He cocked his head as though an idea had suddenly occurred to him. "Unless that's what you're here for."

"I'm here because your man, Joseph Gresser, appears to have had his hand in virtually every type of criminal enterprise on the books, and new ones besides."

"Again, that's no more than the LAPD has explained to me." Sobell rolled his eyes heavenward and put on his most long-suffering, martyred grimace. "Good help—tremendously difficult to find in these decadent latter days."

"Let's be real about this. Every street rat and no-account son of a bitch from Burbank to Anaheim knows Gresser wouldn't so much as unzip to piss except on your orders."

The sudden vulgarity surprised him, but he thought he knew what Elliot was about now. Taking his measure—poking at him from a few different angles to see how he jumped. He answered her avid grin with a bland smile of his own. "Oh, I highly doubt that. You see, I'll have nothing to do with no-account sons of bitches. Won't be seen on the same street as them, as it happens. Anything they claim to know about me is, what's the legal term? Hearsay, I believe. Utterly inadmissible as evidence."

Her laughter came warm and throaty, and Sobell thought it genuine. She was having fun, he realized.

"I don't need that kind of evidence," she said.

Sobell nodded. "Hence the warrant. Very well. Have at the premises. You'll find no more than the police have."

"The police," she said, very deliberately enunciating each syllable, "were looking for a different kind of evidence."

This time, her gaze stayed fixed on his face. He wondered what she hoped to find there.

She presented a sheaf of papers—the warrant, no doubt. He took it from her and set it on the bar without a glance.

"What is it you want, Agent Elliot? I'm as anxious to get this over with as you are, so if you can jump to the point, I can hopefully clear this up. I can go back to my work, and you can ransack the premises, satisfy yourself that the police missed nothing, and get back to your work."

"I'm not looking for bloodstains," Elliot said. "I'm here for documents."

"I don't follow you."

"I need you to provide company financials, documents of incorporation, minutes from board meetings, org charts, and anything else that shows company structure or income."

"I see."

"For every company in which you own a controlling interest."

"That's several companies."

"Then it will probably be a lot of documents. I also need real estate records and the location of any property you own personally or any of your companies own."

There could be no doubt now—she was enjoying this. There wouldn't be much of anything to find in the documents, Sobell thought—he was very careful about that—but the scope and the nature of the demand were alarming.

"That doesn't *seem* like the sort of thing you might need for a murder investigation, even if there is a surplus of victims by normal standards."

"Nevertheless," Elliot said.

Now he glanced toward the paperwork on the bar. "If you don't mind, I'd like to have my attorney look at this before you proceed."

"I don't think you understand, Mr. Sobell," Elliot said, her eyes positively sparkling. "This is a search warrant, bearing the signature of a federal judge. This is not a negotiation. I don't need your permission, or your attorney's permission. My people are already hauling documents and computers out of the building by the cartload."

"Already? How industrious." He started taking a mental inventory. This was the center of a legitimate business, and he was, for the most part, scrupulous about treating it as such. There shouldn't be anything for them to find, and yet he worried. "I think you're mistaken about at least one thing, though. If this isn't a negotiation, why are you talking to me? You don't need me to let you in the building, obviously, and you don't need my imprimatur of approval of your actions."

"I want your passwords. I want encryption keys. I want every last bit of knowledge you have stored away here opened up for me."

"It's been quite some time since I worked in tech support."

"Very funny."

"Just subpoena them," he said, knowing no such thing was possible. The Fifth Amendment right to refrain from incriminating yourself apparently covered giving up your passwords, a fact that he'd had more than one occasion to be grateful for. Goddamn digital world and its endless trails of ones and zeroes.

She opted, wisely, he thought, to dodge the legal argument. "If you cooperate willingly, it's possible we can make this a little easier on you."

Sobell gave her as parental a frown as he could muster. "Is it possible to cooperate unwillingly? By which I mean, is that actually cooperation, or is it something else entirely? Isn't 'cooperate willingly' a wholly redundant construction?"

Elliot said nothing, but Sobell saw her fist clench on the counter.

"You're going down, Enoch," she said. "The only question is how hard."

"I want a vodka and cranberry juice. Anything for you?" He got up, turning his back to the FBI agent, and made his way around to the end of the bar. Elliot hadn't rattled him, exactly, but it wouldn't hurt to take a moment to compose himself, either. Elliot was casting a very wide net here, and he was mildly surprised she'd managed to get a judge to sign off on it. There wasn't much to find, and the obvious legal connections could largely have been traced through public records, if with a great deal of labor. The other connections, either unobvious or illegal or both, were more concerning. Was everything clean? Had somebody, somewhere, made an injudicious note in some forgotten file? What could be traced to whom?

Perhaps the mayor knew what he was doing after all.

"Yeah," Elliot said, surprising him. "What the hell? Seven and seven."

Sobell busied himself with the glasses. Once he finished pouring the drinks, he slid Elliot's glass across the bar to her. "Cheers," he said.

His hand shook as he brought his glass to his lips. A slight tremor ran up through his elbow and through his wrist, and the surface of the liquid rippled. It worsened, and vodka slopped out, a cool kiss on the back of his hand. A wave of dizziness followed. He dropped the glass. It bounced off the edge of the sink and cracked, then fell into the metal basin and broke into four pieces. He leaned against the bar.

The FBI agent just watched.

The dizziness abated. Sobell pushed himself upright. "My apologies. Ever since I got shot in the head, I've been prone to dizzy spells." The words were calm enough, but he felt a sudden rage at his frailty. He wanted to smash something, to pick up the broken glass and grind it into somebody's face, to kick and break. His shakes had been getting worse, along with bouts of weakness, fatigue, and dizziness, and it had nothing to do with getting shot in the head. It had everything to do with the fact that he was slowly dying. He was slowly dying, his body giving out and his magic unable to stop it, and he needed to find Van Horn, and instead he was wasting his time on the ambitious pipe dreams of an FBI agent with a typically banal agenda. Stupid. He didn't have time for this.

"You'll have to excuse me," Sobell said. "This conversation has taxed me as much as I care to be taxed today. I'll leave you to your business. Best of luck."

"The passwords?"

"Oh, those." The rage swelled again, roaring with fury at being hounded, hassled with trivial stings and tiny, meaningless arrows, while Sobell's personal Rome burned. Nonetheless, he summoned up one more smile. "Kindly go fuck yourself."

After walking out on Elliot, Sobell had gone back up to his office, the damn office, and waited for his hand to stop shaking. He wasn't sure what had happened after that. He thought he'd stared at his hand until it steadied, but it was steady now, and he didn't remember when it stopped shaking. The phone was ringing now. How long had that been going on?

He picked it up. "Yes?"

"Ms. Tran is here."

Sobell looked around the room, got oriented, and checked the clock. He'd been out of it, but not for more than ten minutes or so, he thought.

"Send her in," he said.

Erica Tran, to Sobell's shock, looked tired. She'd done legal work for him in some way or another for over fifteen years, since she was barely out of law school, and he'd never seen her so much as yawn, that he could remember. She worked her fellow associates into the ground. Now, though, she looked bone-weary, at that stage where all but the tiny part of the world that has your complete focus becomes blurry and the highest-octane coffee might as well be water for all the good it does.

"Please, sit," Sobell said.

She shook her head. "If I sit, I won't get back up until tomorrow."

Another time, he might have insisted, but not today. There was too much happening now. If Erica thought she needed to keep at it, he wouldn't dissuade her.

"What have you found out?" Sobell asked.

"This is bad, Enoch."

"Everything is dire these days. A product of the terrible times in which we live."

"Did you read the search warrant?"

No, he realized abruptly, though he should have, and normally would have done so straightaway. Instead, he'd left it on the bar. He didn't like that one bit. He shook his head.

"The good news is that it's a fishing expedition. Pieces of allegations from dozens of sources tied together in a document that barely surpasses the minimum standard for a warrant, and probably wouldn't have if they'd had a less friendly judge."

"So nothing to worry about, then."

"I wouldn't say that. The warrant isn't actually related to the violence here. Not directly, anyway." She made a disgusted face and swallowed. "They're putting together a RICO case."

Sobell understood the expression on her face. He was more than a little familiar with RICO, and it was no laughing matter. It stood for Racketeer Influenced and Corrupt Organizations Act, and the neat trick it performed was essentially that of making everybody in an organization culpable for criminal activities performed on behalf of the organization, particularly the leaders. You didn't have to perform a single illegal activity yourself. If it could be shown that your organization had established a pattern of engaging in illegal activity, you were on the hook for all of it. The Mafia had been more or less wiped out by RICO.

"That's why they're following the paper trail," he said.

"Tracing connections," Erica said, nodding agreement. "Anybody they can get on the hook as working for you could become a weapon."

"It's flimsy, though," Sobell said.

"The warrant? Yes. They don't have enough for an indictment, but they put every excuse into the warrant they could think of. There are affidavits from witnesses who claim to have seen you, and still more affidavits from people who claim to have worked for you or Gresser, but they're drug addicts and felons, and many of them have some pretty outrageous claims about what else they saw, so we're probably safe there. The D.A.'s complaints about the missing camera footage from the night of the massacre made it in there, so they're using that and some other items as an excuse to take any electronic media they can. There's a lot more, mostly small stuff."

"And Gresser's records? Anything salvaged?"

She yawned. "I don't think so. They're trying, but according to my contacts, the fire got most of it and they're trying to piece the documents together from fragments of ash."

"This doesn't sound that bad so far," he said.

"I'm sorry, what?" She rubbed her eyes with thumb and forefinger, rather viciously, Sobell thought. No wonder they were so red.

"It appears to be a lot of sound and fury, signifying nothing."

"I don't see it that way."

"We've been careful," Sobell said, with some degree more confidence than he felt. "As far as I know, there shouldn't be much for them to find. They're mostly trying to annoy me, I think."

Erica lifted her head slightly. "Any of the side projects would have been handled by Gresser, right? Not you directly?"

He grinned. "On advice from counsel, yes."

"And since he's dead, it will be a lot harder to link you to any of the criminal enterprises. That helps."

"And yet you're frowning. I confess that doesn't fill me with confidence."

She bit the inside of her cheek, a sure sign she was thinking furiously. "If this adds up to an indictment, they can seize your assets. Bank accounts, real estate, the groceries in your refrigerator. Everything."

He knew. The purpose of asset seizure was, in part, to prevent the target from hiding incriminating money, but also in part to weaken his or her defense—draining funds to the point where a person couldn't even pay a decent lawyer. "I trust you'll work on credit, if worse comes to worst?"

"The RICO thing needs to be taken seriously, but it looks weak right now. Even supposing nothing new turns up, the major concern here is that the FBI has taken an interest in you."

He waved it away. "That had to be regarded as inevitable."

"No, it didn't."

"*I* regarded it as such."

"Enoch, this isn't a joke. As of right now, you're on lockdown. The FBI will have surveillance capabilities—

and likely permissions—that go well beyond the LAPD. Assume any phone you talk on is tapped, any vehicle you ride in is bugged, and that they're reading every e-mail you send or receive."

"I've assumed all that for years. It's why they don't have a case. That, and good counsel."

"Okay. Well, now is not the time to change any of that."

"That will hamper some of the side projects. My trusty lieutenant is in no condition to manage them."

Erica walked to the wall and leaned against it. Sobell was amazed she was still on her feet. It looked as if she might fall asleep where she stood. "Good. Leave them alone for a while. Stay clear of all that, and you should be fine."

Her advice was sound. He knew that. He'd made a long habit of trying to avoid any exposure to the seedier sides of his business, and it would be effortless to let them run unsupervised until things calmed down. But the thing with Van Horn ... oh no. Somebody had to handle that.

"That's not exactly an option. Not entirely, at any rate."

"What do you mean?"

"I need to meet someone," he said.

"Who?"

"Anna Ruiz."

"Absolutely not."

"She hasn't been implicated in this latest debacle. I believe the risk is acceptable."

Erica closed her eyes, a pained expression wrinkling her brow. A few moments passed, just long enough for Sobell to wonder if she'd zoned out and forgotten about him. When she spoke again, she didn't open her eyes. "I don't think it is. She's street trash, Enoch. With a rap sheet longer than the Dead Sea Scrolls."

"No convictions, though."

She opened her eyes again, squinting as though the

light in the room had become intolerable. "No, not as an adult, but she's high on the list of the last people you should be seen with right now. As far as RICO goes, they just need to establish a pattern of illegal activities. 'Pattern' for the purposes of RICO means two events in a ten-year period. If they can tie anything she does back to you, that takes care of half of the case right there." She paused. "What do you need with her?"

"I need to inquire on the status of a project. Perhaps offer some additional incentive, if motivation is flagging."

Erica's voice was heavy with suspicion. "What kind of project?"

"Personal project. Nothing to do with either the legitimate businesses or the other side projects."

"What is the nature of this project?"

"Kidnapping, if you absolutely *must* know."

That pained expression was back, and this time she rubbed her temple, too. Her lips moved slightly, probably in some kind of prayer for forbearance, or maybe just cursing him under her breath. "This is not a good idea, Enoch. I swear. In fifteen years, how many times have I told you 'No, under no circumstances should you do this'?"

"Four." He didn't even have to think to total them up. Each one had been an extremely irritating roadblock for him—but she had been proven right by subsequent events three of those times, and he'd give her the benefit of the doubt on the fourth.

"Make it five."

He looked down at his hand. It was steady now, but when would the next fit come along? And how much worse would it be? He didn't know how much time he had left, but it was surely measured in months, not years. He turned his attention back to Erica. She'd given him so much good counsel over the years, and she was almost surely right about the risks this time, too.

"Very well," he said. "You meet her."

Chapter 3

Karyn couldn't tell if she was dreaming or not. Maybe later, looking back, she'd know. Dreams had a way of relieving some of her fatigue, whereas the visions — daily life, in other words — were generally just exhausting. The other clue was that, if the events and people made some kind of sense, she was almost certainly dreaming. No such luck today.

She didn't recognize the room she was in. That was new. Before, her room had presented itself in various stages of decay or construction, various styles of decor. It had once been a hole in the earth, once a hillside, sometimes a blasted, burned ruin. Other times it changed to one of two different, other rooms, larger rooms with strange furniture and baffling appliances, and she wondered if that meant she was seeing something from the far future or simply pure nonsense.

The room was different from all that now. A little larger than it had been, smaller than the two from the future. She was sitting, though she couldn't tell on what. Earlier she had opened her eyes to see nine or ten blue-upholstered recliners jammed into the room, most of them overlapping in an extremely unsettling way, not at all like multiple photo exposures, but more like holograms: tilt your head one way, you see all of chair number one. Tilt it the other, you see all of chair number two. There wasn't enough space for all nine simultaneously, yet there they were. Her best guess was that she was seeing all of the chair's locations at the same time. It gave her a splitting headache.

The chairs were gone now. She couldn't even see the one she was sitting on, though she could feel it. That was something. The worst days were the ones when she couldn't feel things, exactly. On days like that, the chair would support her, but her senses would insist it wasn't there, and the result was a crushing cognitive dissonance that made her brain feel like a wrung-out sponge. The sensation was so awful, so disorienting, that she'd thrown up both times it happened.

Today, though, it wasn't that bad. The room looked empty. New. Unfinished. She could see the plywood decking of the floor, spattered with plaster, and the clean white sheetrock walls. People moved through it. Dozens of them. Construction workers at first, but others joined them. A woman with dyed white blond hair, leaning over blueprints with a cigarette held between two of her fingers. An entire Mexican family, speaking in excited Spanish she could barely follow. Two big men holding a third man with a bag over his head. The man with the bag over his head screamed, "I don't have your money. I don't know where it is. I don't know—I don't—" A gunshot, and Karyn flinched. A messy spray of blood spattered the white wall, then vanished. The body didn't.

Anna walked in. Another Anna walked in. A third, a fourth, a fifth. One of them, thin arms jutting out of a loose white tank top, brushed wavy dark hair out of her eyes and leaned toward Karyn.

"You doing okay in there?"

Karyn hesitated, unsure of whether this was Anna talking, or just another phantasm. She didn't know which she'd prefer. It was only after she'd gone under, after the regular world had finally drifted out of touch, that she fully appreciated how big a part of her life Anna was. It wasn't just the jobs, or the shared living situation, or the endless ways Anna helped her manage her condition. It was *everything*. A million little things, every day. Stupid anecdotes shared over breakfast at around the crack of noon, neither of them being particularly early risers. Karyn's endless jokes about the women Anna dated, and Anna's endless complaints about same. Bickering about the radio, when Anna wanted to load up goddamn Ministry for the six thousandth time, and Karyn just wanted to tune to KIIS and nod along to pop candy. The card games with the guys.

It had never consciously occurred to her before, but Anna was the one person she spoke to every single day. Karyn's mother was dead, suicide at eighteen, not long after Karyn was born — and Karyn had spent many an hour wondering about *that*, and whether her condition was hereditary. Karyn's father, whom she thought of as "the sperm donor," though his deposit had been made in a decidedly old-fashioned way, had made himself scarce even before that. Her great-aunt Florence was now in a home, and had become detached from reality in a more prosaic fashion than Karyn herself. There had been a handful of men in the last decade, but nothing even approaching anything she'd call a relationship, never anybody she felt comfortable enough with to even dream of discussing her condition.

Just Anna, and now not even that. The loneliness was as bad as not being able to see the world as it was. She and Anna had done so much together, fought their way through some unbelievable crap, and now she was cut off. The brief moments of interaction were painfully unsatisfying, rarely long enough to exchange anything meaningful before they got swamped or confused — but she kept trying.

She braced herself for the inevitable disappointment, trying to stifle the wavering flame of hope that kindled itself despite her efforts, and answered, "I — I don't really know."

"What do you mean?"

That hope grew steadier, a thin candlelight in the

blackness. "I mean, I can't tell if this is another day, or if I've finally just lost my mind."

Anna chuckled. "Well, yeah, it tastes like shit, but it'll keep you from dropping dead."

"What?"

"No, no word from him yet."

"I don't—"

A different Anna patted her on the knee. "You feeling any better?"

Karyn closed her eyes. Maybe they'd just . . . disappear. It had happened before.

"Who cares what the doctor says? You just gotta pull through this."

No luck. Worse, both Annas were talking now. Maybe others, too. It was impossible to tell.

"Nail will cut his nuts off if he screws us."

"You're going to be okay. I know you are."

"—up in Van Nuys, of all places. Three hundred bucks' worth of—"

"I hate this. Can't find Adelaide, though. She's cleared out, and nobody's saying shit. If she had suppliers, nobody's talking. I'll find them, though. For reals."

Karyn closed her eyes tighter, hoping it would shut out the endless conversation of non sequiturs, but new voices layered themselves on top. It wasn't fair. Just one minute of real conversation, just one honest exchange with her best friend, instead of this stream of nonsense, and she could hold it together.

I'm going to hold it together anyway, she thought.

From nowhere, cold metal pushed gently against her lips. She opened her eyes. Only Annas, everywhere. Then an invisible spoon pushed her mouth open, and the taste of cold breakfast cereal hit her tongue. Feeding time.

She squeezed her eyes shut even more tightly than before, but the tears escaped anyway.

Anna left Karyn's room and slumped against the make-shift plywood door, staring vacantly across the ruins in front of her. Karyn's room was one of the classrooms along the outer edge of the building, across the width of a hall from a big open space that might have been a cafeteria once and was now a wreck full of broken glass, floor tiles, and moldy acoustic ceiling panels. Much of the space must have been windows at one time, since now it was largely open, just a few columns holding up the ceiling, lined with sawtooth edges of glass. Anna could see across the space to the wide stairs leading down to the building's entry—which, she supposed, was the reason Nail liked this spot. Gold-orange rays of morning light glinted off broken bottles down there.

Anna let the cinder block wall of Karyn's room hold her up for a moment. She felt like a dishrag that had been wrung out and thrown under the sink. It had been two months since the fight in Sobell's office, two months since Karyn's last dose of the drug that kept her visions at bay. Anna wasn't sure how Karyn was holding up in there, but Anna herself wasn't doing so hot. She'd seen Karyn in bad shape before, but never this bad, never so ... disconnected. And who knew how bad it might get? Her worst fear was that one day Karyn would no longer even feel the spoon at feeding time, wouldn't know to open her mouth or to swallow, and that Anna would have to resort to an IV or a feeding tube or whatever the fuck it was you did for people who couldn't eat anymore.

Her phone vibrated. She took it from her pocket and glanced at the caller ID. It was Bobby, calling her back. She hit him up constantly for tips and rumors, and he'd had a couple of good leads for her regarding Karyn's situation. They hadn't panned out, but that wasn't his fault. She flipped the phone open.

"Hey, Bobby. Got something for me?" she asked.

"Yeah. Usual spot, forty minutes?" His voice was rough, like he'd just smoked half a pack and downed a fifth of bourbon. Given the hour, he probably had.

This is gonna be another waste of time, Anna thought, hating herself for feeling so defeated. A lead was a lead, though, and even if it was probably a waste of time, she couldn't afford to pass it up. "See you there."

She hung up and ducked into the next classroom, the temporary quarters she and Genevieve shared.

Genevieve, also enjoying a streak of insomnia, looked up from the arcane paperwork she was always shuffling. Occult research, magic prep stuff. The kind of stuff Tommy had always been fiddling with back when. It made Anna anxious.

"You all right, babe?" Genevieve asked. "You look like hell."

"Ha-ha. I gotta go do a thing. You wanna ride along?"

"Not this time. If we're gonna snatch that guy, I gotta make sure his room's secure. This is not something I can afford to fuck up, you know?"

"Yeah." Anna paused in the doorway. "Hey, any idea what Sobell wants this guy for? Looks like lots of people are looking for him, you know? Might be a good idea to know what he's into."

"No idea."

"All right. See you later."

The "usual spot" looked awful in the daylight. Usually, when Anna met Bobby Chu here, the building's interior was shrouded in darkness and fog, split with colored lights, thrumming with bass and bodies, and full of shouting, sweat, and commerce, legal and otherwise. A hyperkinetic intersection of burnouts, dope dealers, and bored suburban kids too dumb to know they were partying damn close to a line past which their families' college funds and two-car garages couldn't help them.

All that had cleared out now, the party having petered out or moved underground, and the building was revealed for itself: an empty, corrugated metal box sheltering a concrete slab. The only light now came from sunlight seeking the cracks and gaps in the metal shell. It was enough, once Anna's eyes adjusted. Bobby sat on a crate over by the table that served as the D.J.'s station, staring at his phone and wiping at the corner of his left eye. Anna walked toward him. She wrinkled her nose at the lingering smell of body odor and spilled booze, walked around a wet patch that, from the pattern, suggested a drink thrown violently to the ground, or projectile vomiting.

She stopped in front of Bobby. "So this is what's left when the party's over."

He didn't look up from his phone. "Not pretty, huh?"

"No."

He kept typing something with his right hand and wiping at his leaky eye with his left. Nothing new there— his eye had dripped for as long as Anna had known him. He laughed about it, swore that he could tell when he was about to get sick because the fluid turned cloudy. She thought there ought to be some medication for that.

After a minute or so, he stood. Sweat sheened his forehead and gave a greasy look to the sparse black stubble across his chin. It had to be ninety degrees in the building, but he still wore the same ragged brown corduroy jacket as always. The damn thing could probably run his parties for him at this point. Just stand it up in his chair and nobody would be the wiser.

"What's shakin'?" she asked.

"Know anybody that can move six keys of coke?"

This wasn't what he'd called her for, she knew. This was just his basic conversation opener—hey, I need a thing. Pissed some people off, that he treated everything as a transaction waiting to happen, but she thought it was all right. You knew where you stood with Bobby, anyway. No bullshit. "That's not my kind of business," she said.

"Didn't figure." He reached into the inside of his nasty old jacket and pulled out a piece of unlined white paper that had been folded a couple of times lengthwise. He held it out to her.

"Hope this isn't a bill," she began, but her smile faltered as she took the paper and opened it. There was a black-and-white photo of Karyn on the page. No—it wasn't a photo, she realized. A drawing, done in immaculate detail, in what looked like ink from a cheap ballpoint pen. Karyn's head and shoulders. Her face was drawn close in concentration, an expression Anna had seen her make maybe a thousand times. "What the fuck is this?"

"Yeah. Thought you might be interested in that."

"What the fuck *is* it?"

"Guy came around waving it at anybody who'd look at it. Got my attention."

"You know him?"

Bobby shook his head. "Dude definitely didn't belong here. Looked like he got lost tryin' to find his way back to prep school. I shit you not, he asked me if I thought there might be 'illicit narcotics' in use around here, and not because he wanted some. More like he thought the cops were going to kick in the door any moment."

"I don't get it."

"Not a friend of yours, then?"

"Doesn't sound like it."

"Tall kid, clean-cut, dressed like half of one of those traveling Mormon recruitment drives? A little spacey?"

Anna thought, but nothing clicked. "That doesn't sound like my crowd. Client, maybe, or a client's kid." *Or maybe a target, or a target's kid.* Was this somebody the crew had ripped off at some point? Maybe they'd gotten wise? But why flash a drawing instead of a photo? "So, what did he want?"

"To talk to the woman in the drawing."

"He call her by name?"

"Nope."

"Did you?"

"Fuck no," Bobby said. "Give me *some* credit. I just told him to leave the picture with me, and maybe I could hook him up."

Anna shifted her weight. "I don't like this."

"Looks weird to me, too. You can see why I called."

"He was just wandering around, showing this to everyone in the place?"

Bobby nodded. His phone buzzed, but he thumbed the call to voice mail. "I asked around, but nobody ever saw him around here before."

Anna didn't know what to make of it, but this didn't sound like something she could safely ignore. She got out her phone and showed Bobby a grainy photo of Van Horn. "He with this guy?"

"No. But the guy in the picture was around last night, too. Rollin' with a buncha freaks and askin' about Adelaide."

Anna felt a creeping sense of paranoia prickle the hairs on the back of her neck. One thing was a coincidence, but two . . . Somebody looking for Karyn, and somebody else for Adelaide? That felt less like coincidence and more like sharks circling in the water. "Yeah?" she asked cautiously.

"Yeah."

"You have anything for him?"

"I'd give it to you first if I had anything. You know that."

She nodded.

"I got nothing new, or at least nobody's saying anything," Bobby said. "Far as the usual suspects are concerned, Adelaide is smoke. Poof."

"Nothing? Not even a tiny lead?" She sounded desperate, she knew, and she hated that—but she *was* desperate.

"Davy's tip didn't pan out?"

"Davy's tip cost me twenty thousand dollars and almost got me shot in the head."

"Ouch. Sorry 'bout that."

"Nothing else?"

"No. Wish there was. Seems like there's a lot of noise out there about her—I could make a lot of money, if I knew anything. I didn't know she was such a big deal."

Anna frowned. "She's not, that I know of. Except to me, and maybe a handful of other people." She'd been working with the Brotherhood, though. Maybe they'd gotten all the use out of her they could. Maybe she was in a hole somewhere. Poor Adelaide. "You get a number off the Mormon?"

"No. No name, either."

"Well, if he comes back around, tell him I want to meet him. Maybe I can help him out with his problem." *Or not.* "That everything?" she asked.

"Yeah."

Anna pulled a roll of bills from her pocket and peeled five hundred bucks off. "Here. Keep me posted. Anything you hear about Adelaide, or this new guy. Or the old guy," she added, after a moment's hesitation. "His name's Van Horn. Edgar Van Horn. You hear anything, you come to me first, okay?"

He took the money. "I'm happy to keep taking your money, but you know you don't have to do this. I'd tell you this stuff anyway."

"I know you would, Bobby. But I'm in a spot where I can take care of my friends for once. I'm gonna do it."

He wiped at his eye. Anna pretended it was because he was touched.

Chapter 4

"You sure about this?" Nail asked.

Anna pulled out a cigarette, crumbled it into pieces, and dropped the pieces. "I don't have any better ideas. You?"

"Nada."

She waited as the sun went down, trying to shake the paranoia that had been with her ever since meeting Bobby. This stretch of street wasn't abandoned, not exactly, but neither did folks hang out in front of their doorsteps past eight at night. The last few nights either she, Nail, or Genevieve had come down here watching Van Horn and his entourage, and nobody else had stirred. Lights went out early in the graffiti-tagged tenements just down the street behind, and they never came on at all in the boarded-up meat-processing plant ahead. Other than a brief appearance by the sorriest-looking dog Anna had ever seen, 'long about day three, Van Horn and company were the only things moving out here after ten or so. Even the rats had better places to be.

The three of them were down here together now — Anna, Nail, and Genevieve. Anna hated leaving Karyn alone, but they were shorthanded, and there was no good way to do this without taking some risk. Leaving Karyn by herself for a few hours seemed like the least bad alternative in a field of shitty options.

She and Genevieve got out of the car. Nail stayed put. He'd run spotting duty, tailing Van Horn and company and making sure Anna and Genevieve had ample warning if they decided to come back. Anna and Genevieve ducked into an alley with a decent view of the packing plant and settled in to wait.

The streetlights flicked on, and soon after, the sun retired for the night. Not ten minutes later, the doors to the plant swung open and Van Horn's traveling revel came out. They came out through the gate in the fence and walked up the street, laughing and staggering. One cut loose with a bloodcurdling scream, apparently just for the hell of it. The group came closer, closer, until finally it drew abreast of the car, only forty feet or so away across the street, their laughter raucous and grating. Anna mentally clamped down on a rising tide of revulsion that threatened to sweep her away, to cause her to jump back in the car, twist the key in the ignition, and stomp on Nail's foot if she had to to reach the gas. They were just people, she thought, but if you saw them in a bus station, you'd come back and catch a bus tomorrow rather than get in a confined space with them. If a couple of them stood on the sidewalk, you'd go a block out of your way rather than even cross the street. If they cornered you in a dark place alone, you might just shoot yourself rather than . . . Rather than what? Genevieve's un-joke about them eating their own sprang to mind. It had never seemed less funny.

They piled into their vehicles and took off. Nail waited a moment, waved one time at Anna, and rolled out after them. Two sets of taillights disappeared around the corner, then a third.

"You ready?" Anna asked. She didn't know that she was ready herself, but as the ostensible leader of this mess, she had to either pretend to be or straight-up call the whole thing off.

"Let's get this shit over with," Genevieve said.

They stepped out of the alley. Contrary to ten years'

habit from breaking into homes and other buildings, Anna cast a nervous look up the street. Still nobody.

"Come on," she said. With Genevieve close behind, she headed across the street. The floodlights around the old meat-processing plant had long since gone dark, and the streetlights out front had been destroyed. Approaching the building was like descending into a black cave with light and life receding at every step. Anna imagined she could smell the ancient stink of blood and offal, and never mind that the plant must have been closed for nearly a decade. That shit would never go away, not completely. She had a grim suspicion that that was part of why Van Horn and company had chosen this spot to settle in.

They reached the big double doors without incident. The nearest streetlight might as well have been some outer planet for all the light it cast here. Everything was reduced to simple shapes in grayscale, clearest at the edges of vision or where occluding the distant yellow spots along the sidewalk.

Genevieve walked in front of the door, the black of her clothing barely distinct against the lighter gray of the doors. She moved to one side, mumbling under her breath and making passes in the air with her hands. She paused, fiddled with something Anna couldn't see, and then tossed a burning scrap of paper into the air. Anna flinched and glanced down the street, but nothing moved. When she turned back, Gen was studying patterns in the smoke as the paper fluttered to the ground. After it burned up, she moved to the other door and repeated the whole process. Then she looked up and shrugged. "Clean," she whispered. "I think."

Anna waited, listening intently. This street was eerily quiet, the only sound a distant roar of traffic that reminded her of a radio tuned to static. She couldn't see the highway from here, though. Just had to assume it still existed out there, and she wasn't trapped in a quiet bubble in a world that had turned to raw noise.

She shook her head. *Thinking all kinds of weird things tonight.* She turned her attention back to the plant. A light tug on the door got her nowhere. Either it was locked, or somebody had barred it from the inside. She got out her lock picks and prayed for the former.

A moment later, she pulled the door open.

Nobody sent up the alarm. Anna and Genevieve went in, pulling the door shut behind them. Anna got out a pair of the night-vision goggles they'd used on the last gig and held them to her face. Everything here was a roughly uniform temperature, and nothing human-sized showed up in the goggles. She put them away and got out a flashlight.

Most of the building's interior was an open space, a vast floor under high ceilings like some kind of gruesome meat-processing cathedral. Small holes dotted the floor where equipment had once been secured, but most of it was gone now. A few bulky conglomerations of angle iron and metal piping still loomed here and there, apparently too big to move and too inconvenient to disassemble and sell for scrap. Along the outer edges of the floor were several walled-off areas that had presumably once held offices, meeting rooms, and bathrooms.

"Room to room?" Genevieve asked.

"Yeah." It didn't look as though the entourage was sleeping on the open floor, which was a good thing. That meant Van Horn might have a room, which in turn meant they might be able to get to him without eleven of his closest friends getting involved.

She opened the nearest door. The smell boiling out of it made her eyes water, and Genevieve gagged and covered her mouth and nose with her hand. "Aw, Jesus."

Anna shone the flashlight into the room, got a quick look, and shut the door. "That would be the latrine," she whispered.

"My God."

They kept moving. The next room was entirely empty except for a bedroll stuffed into a corner. Anna moved the beam of the flashlight over the floor. Spotless. Nothing in here, except—

"Whoa."

She shone the light on the far wall and walked closer. The entire wall had been covered in arcane-looking glyphs and symbols, written in red ballpoint pen, with letters about as tall as those you'd see on notebook paper.

"What the hell is this?" Anna asked.

Genevieve came close, inspecting the writing. "Gibberish. I mean, it *looks* like some kind of heavy-duty crazy-ass sorcery, but I don't recognize any of this. It's meaningless, I think."

That sounded good, but as Anna backed up, from certain angles it looked as though the words crowded together or spread out in the beam of her flashlight, making dark and light spots, and Anna could swear the patterns were depicting a face in there, screaming.

"Let's get out of here."

The next few rooms weren't much better. One had a pile of blankets, like a nest, with thousands of toothpick-sized splinters of wood scattered everywhere around it. Part of a wooden chair lay on the floor, and it was obvious that it was the source of at least some of the splinters, as if somebody with a mean nervous habit had spent hours picking the chair apart. Judging by the amount, they'd gone through the whole dining set before getting to that last chair. Anna pretended not to see the dry dots of spattered blood on the floor, or the rust-dark ends of many of the toothpicks, though she thought she'd be seeing them in her dreams later. They found another room they couldn't even walk in—the floor was covered inches deep with the morbid latticework of tiny animal skeletons, thousands of them. A fourth room contained two bedrolls, a pair of beat-up tennis shoes, and two sets of clothing, a man's suit and a woman's summer dress, laid out flat against the wall and pinned there like dead butterflies.

"This place is like a museum for the creepy," Gene-vieve said.

Anna didn't say anything.

The next room was near the middle of the row, and relief washed over Anna as she opened the door. "Van Horn's," she said. "Got to be."

"If only because it looks like an actual human being might sleep here, yeah."

It was more than that, though. There was a rust-stained mattress on the floor, a couple of candles and a dog-eared copy of a coverless paperback sitting on a small crate, and a hook on the wall from which a ratty pin-striped suit hung. "Must be his spare," Anna said, shaking her head in disbelief.

"He's warded this room," Genevieve said, pointing at the glyphs on the lintel and the walls. "To keep people from finding him."

"Apparently, it ain't working."

They didn't bother with the rest of the rooms, just took a quick look around to fix the layout in Anna's mind and make sure there was nothing they'd over-looked. The search turned up a side door that was much closer to Van Horn's room than the front door. On the way out, Anna blocked the latch and put a rock in front of the door on the outside to keep it from swinging open. Easy, quiet way back in.

Anna checked her watch. Eleven o'clock. Time to set-tle in and wait for Nail.

Headlights lit the street, jolting Anna from half sleep into wakefulness. She'd been dreaming, she thought. Dream-ing of the screaming face in the room they'd found in the processing plant. In her dream, it had been as though the face were trapped behind the words rather than made of them, pleading with her to let it out, and she'd found her-self wishing she'd done something. Punched a hole in the plasterboard. Scratched some words out. Something. She sat up and peered out of the alley.

Van Horn and his entourage parked and got out. There was considerably less revelry this time than on previous nights. Anna checked her watch. Twelve thirty. They were early, too. They didn't make much fuss as they disappeared back into the building, and they didn't dawdle, either.

Wonder what happened.

Nail rolled up a few minutes later, and Anna and Genevieve got up to meet him.

"What's going on?" Anna asked.

"Van Horn is spooked. Jumping at shadows since last night. I swear, a car door slams and he jumps about four feet. Can't say I blame him—I swear, somebody besides me was following him at some point. I think some of his creeps are spoiling for a fight, but Van Horn won't have it. They stopped at a couple places—nobody I know— and didn't stay long before he just called it a night."

"Anybody follow him here?"

"Besides me? I don't think so. Won't be too many more outings like this, though, and you bet your ass somebody will."

"So we take him tonight, then," Anna said.

"Guess so."

She gave him a quick rundown on their trip inside, and then an argument broke out about who would go in. They went back and forth for the better part of an hour about this before Anna finally offered a grudging agreement. Nail was clearly the best equipped for this kind of bullshit, and he would need Genevieve to scope out the area in case Van Horn had laid any traps of a magical nature. Anna couldn't replace either of them. She tried to convince them that they should all go together, but that didn't fly, either. If Van Horn slipped out the front, or worse, Van Horn's new enemies showed up, they needed somebody on lookout. Nail also insisted that if things went bad, it would be helpful to have somebody who wasn't pinned down with everyone else. Or somebody who could get help.

"This sucks," Anna said, but in the end she agreed.

They waited until well after the time of Van Horn's usual return, hoping things would settle down by then. Anna shredded half a pack of cigarettes into a pile of brown and white curls by the curb and dozed intermittently.

Around four in the morning, Nail pulled three headsets out of his satchel and passed them out, keeping one for himself. Anna clipped the radio to her belt and made sure the earpiece was secure. "Check."

"Read you," Nail said, his voice doubling up in the earpiece and from in front of her.

Genevieve nodded. "Me, too."

"All right," Anna said. "Be careful."

"No sweat. We'll be out in five." They crossed the street and approached the front of the building. Anna stopped at the front. Nail took his gun from his waistband and, without further ceremony, crept around the side. Genevieve cast a quick grin Anna's way and followed.

I fucking *hate this,* Anna thought.

She waited. A stray dog sniffed the alley across the way, but nobody else was out. The tenements were locked down, blinds drawn, only a couple with light leaking through. The neighborhood had a quiet, grim feel to it, and Anna wondered if the presence of Van Horn and company had cast a pall over the street, or if it had always been like this. It took a certain level of poverty and desperation to live in the constant stink of a meat-processing plant. She imagined a lot of old people here. Sixty-year-old men in long coats the color of mud puddles, sour-faced and carrying groceries in sagging plastic bags. Apartments rancid with the smell of cat piss. Busybodies watching windows but never exchanging words with one another.

The dog, a mangy thing from what looked like the bloodline of a really ugly strain of German shepherd, lay down next to a bulging black trash bag and curled up to sleep. Nothing else moved. Anna watched the dog, then turned her attention back to the meat-processing plant's door behind her, then glanced back down the street. She fought the urge to tap her foot. How long had it been? Nail and Genevieve had to be close by now, right? They knew the room. There was nothing complicated about it. Why was this taking so long?

No sound from the radio. No sound from anywhere, save the distant river of traffic. Anna leaned against the building's front door, pressing her ear to the steel. She imagined Nail edging past the gantrylike structures of metal, Genevieve close behind, each step an agonizing exercise in patience and dread as they crept toward Van Horn's room. Faint light coming from the small, smashed-out windows high in the walls would throw distorted yellow-orange rectangles on the ceiling above, providing only the weakest illumination.

Surely the entourage didn't keep a watch of any kind, or there would have been a shout before now. And it was unthinkable that they could have taken Nail by surprise, taken him down fast enough to keep him from getting off a few shots. Silence was good, Anna thought. Silence meant no trouble.

Wishful thinking, she chided herself. If only Karyn were here. Karyn would *know.* She probably would have known from the second that Genevieve and Nail entered the building whether or not this was a good idea, whether it would work out, or whether they were in serious danger. She'd know when to rush in, too. She'd know that before it happened. Give them a head start, a vital edge.

Well, she's not here. All we've got is me, a radio, and a stolen handgun. The thought was indescribably depressing.

"Shit!" Nail's voice through the radio was a rough whisper, and Anna jumped, startled. "Need help in here, A. Van Horn's room. Fast but quiet."

The words were almost a relief. She could *do* something now, anyway, rather than just sit here and worry. Even worry about what she might find was pushed aside by the need to act. If there had been something she needed to know, Nail would have told her. "Roger."

She turned the rusted door handle. It made the faintest of squeaks, a slight click, and then she pulled the door open and slipped inside.

It was darker in here, but not much. The windows let in some light that the building had blocked from Anna's view, and flickering orange light spilled out from under one of the doors a ways down. Van Horn's room. Anna pulled out her gun, trying to ignore the cold sweat that beaded up on her forehead and between her shoulder blades. The last time she'd used a pistol—no, that didn't bear thinking about. Not right now. Her dreams would remind her later anyway, and she'd probably wake Genevieve up screaming again.

In the low light, Anna saw nobody. There was just the distant flickering, and a dozen or so closed doors. She prayed they stayed closed. The nine held only fifteen rounds, and, she realized, she hadn't even thought to chamber one before coming in. Fifteen bullets seemed like a lot, but she knew better. Even if every shot hit, it could take four or five shots to stop somebody, if they were angry or psycho enough, and she thought Van Horn's entourage might top out the scales in both categories. *What happens to the missing ones? The others eat them, of course.* Of course.

She moved forward, feet stepping lightly on the concrete floor. Grit crunched softly at each step. Still, nobody heard, or at least nobody came out to have a look.

Anna wrinkled her nose as she passed the closed door to the latrine. A few steps more, and she was out of the front hallway area into the cavern of the building proper. Crosshatched shadows suggested the metal grid twenty or so feet ahead of her, and she thought briefly about going the long way around it, using it as a form of half-assed cover while she circled around to Van Horn's room. It was too sparse, though, and there were doors over on the other side, anyway.

She kept moving. Passed one door to her right. Rhythmic grunting and moaning noises issued from behind it—at least three different voices, maybe four. That was good. If only everyone were in there. She passed another door. Now that her eyes had adjusted, she saw that a faint light seeped out from under that one, too. A woman's voice droned beyond, nonsense syllables repeated at short intervals.

Two more doors, neither with any sound or light emerging from behind them, and Anna reached Van Horn's room. The door was closed, but not quite all the way. She pushed it open.

Van Horn stood in the corner of the room. He wasn't whistling now, and his smirk was gone. Anna had mistaken him for a hale fiftysomething, but up close the lines on his face and the stark shadows cast by the candles made him look more like seventy. His scraggly white goatee jumped out against the red blotches on his face, and sweat poured down the sides of his face. Probably that had something to do with the pistol Nail was pointing at his head.

Genevieve lay on the floor, unmoving.

Anna ducked into the room, shut the door behind her, and rushed to Genevieve.

"She's breathing," Nail said. He kept his voice low, but it was impossible to miss the rage in it. If Anna had been Van Horn, she'd be sweating, too. "Don't know much more than that."

Breathing, yeah. Anna checked her pulse, too, and that seemed okay. Maybe a little fast, Anna thought, but what did she know about this paramedic shit?

"Come on, babe, get up," Anna said. She shook Genevieve's shoulder to no effect. "We gotta go."

"That's, ah, not going to work," Van Horn put in.

"What did you do?" Nail asked.

"I didn't do anything. *She* entered my *sanctum sanctorum* without an invitation."

"What do you mean, it's not going to work? She's going to wake up, right?" Anna was surprised at how easy it was to keep the panic out of her voice. Mostly because anger was rapidly overtaking it. "Because if not, this kidnapping is going to turn into a murder, I swear, and—" *And Sobell can go fuck himself,* she nearly added, before good sense returned. *Jesus, where is my head today?*

"No murder!" Van Horn said.

"Keep your voice down," Nail said.

Van Horn's mouth twisted into a rictus, a parody of an attempt at a reassuring grin. "You're not here to kill me?" Nobody answered, but he continued, his voice just above a whisper. "In that case, let's just put murder aside, huh? Just, heh, put it over there in the cabinet, so to speak, and close the door. Let's, uh, let's keep that door shut, all right?"

Genevieve's breathing was even. Eyes open a slit with the whites visible, in the same mildly eerie way they were most of the time when she slept. No blood. No sign of injury. Anna looked back to Van Horn. "Talk."

"I don't—I don't really have anything. You're looking at it, all of it. Anything you want, it's yours. This crap isn't worth killing somebody over, huh? Or even kidnapping." He chuckled nervously. "Who would ransom me? I'm telling you, it's not worth it."

"Talk about *her*," Anna said.

"Oh, uh, right. With a little time, and the right tools, I can fix her right up. Scout's honor. Just, um, no murder, right?"

"No murder," Anna agreed. "At least not if you keep your mouth shut on the way out."

"The way ou—oh. Still stuck with the kidnapping, then?" He looked more glum than worried, a lonely old man being told his son wouldn't be visiting for Christmas after all.

"Yeah." Anna could hardly keep the disgust off her face. The moral calculation had always been easy in the past: Karyn needed medication; some rich assholes wanted some weird shit that belonged to some other rich assholes. No problem. Never lost an hour of sleep over it.

This, though, was some other bullshit entirely. What the hell were they even doing here? If she lost Genevieve—

No. Don't even think it. Not for a second, not one god-damn second.

"It's a deal." Van Horn made as if to step forward, hand extended, and Nail brought him up short by the simple expedient of cocking his pistol.

"How about you just keep your hands up?" Nail said. "A, you want to cover this guy? I'll get Gen."

Anna pushed to her feet and lifted her gun again. In her mind's eye, four slugs punched through a bony horror and into the body of a man who'd made one mistake too many. She exhaled, willing the image away. Her hand barely shook at all.

Van Horn turned his hands outward, displaying his empty palms up by his shoulders. "Whatever you want, we can just talk about it. I can't help you any better somewhere else than I can here."

"Walk over to the door. Open it slowly. Don't do anything stupid. I guarantee I can run you down if I have to, or I can just shoot you instead."

Van Horn gave her a pained nod and began a slow shuffle toward the door. Anna followed a few steps behind while Nail hoisted Genevieve off the floor with a grunt. Another time, she might have teased him about getting soft, but given the circumstances, and the fact that he'd had a hole shot through his torso just a couple of months back, she let it slide.

Van Horn pushed the door open but made no attempt to go through. Instead, he looked over his shoulder at Anna, a question on his face.

"Go ahead," Anna whispered. "I'll be right behind you."

He stepped into the gloom and turned left toward the front of the building. Anna followed, keeping a couple of steps behind. She'd heard somewhere that it was a bad idea to push somebody with a gun, because then they'd know where it is, and maybe they could make a grab for it or something. She had no idea if that was actually true or if she'd picked it up on some bullshit cop show, but it seemed like sound advice. Nail would probably know for sure, though maybe it didn't matter much. It wasn't like Van Horn was about to whirl around and lay her out with his wicked martial arts skills. He was older than dirt, and judging by the way he walked, his knees were shot.

Anna was barely out the door when shouting began. It came from ahead of her, a man's voice echoing in the huge building and accompanied by the flap of (bare?) feet running on the concrete. "Edgar! Edgar, come see! You'll never—"

The guy Nail called T-shirt and Cargo Pants ran out from the darkness and into the halfhearted light filtering down from the dirty, cracked windows high above, and then stopped abruptly. "What's happening?"

Anna's heart clenched like a spasming fist. *Fuck, oh fuck, oh fuck. Don't let this turn into a massacre.* Again, she thought of the jobs she'd been on where she nearly got caught—by cops, owners, lovers, gardeners, whatever. There was a little kick of adrenaline, and the world became crisper somehow, everything more clearly outlined, and then she fought or fled as necessary. Right now, though, she felt like she was going to either vomit or pass out.

Van Horn took a casual step sideways with Anna's gun trained on him the whole way. He shrugged and cast a wry glance from Anna to the man as if to say, *Would you look at this mess?*

Anna couldn't help noticing that his little sidestep took him right out of a direct line between her and T-shirt. She had a fraction of a second to watch the man's face contort in rage. Whether he was going to torch Anna, attack her with some other occult means, or simply charge, acting like a human bullet and Van Horn's shield at the same time, Anna didn't wait to see. She stepped forward and pressed the gun to the back of Van Horn's head. His chin tipped toward his chest, and he winced.

"Don't," Anna said, doing her level best to stare T-shirt down. "Whatever you're thinking about doing, don't."

The man leered at her. "You're making a big mistake."

"For what it's worth, I think you're probably right."

They watched each other. Anna could hear Van Horn's breath, raspy and wet, and beyond that, the grunting sound from before was escalating in pitch and frequency. She wondered just how crazy the man before her was. There seemed little doubt he would sacrifice himself for Van Horn. Hopefully, he was rational enough not to get Van Horn killed just because there was an interloper in the homestead.

T-shirt turned and ran away, yelling, "Help! Come help!"

"Shit," Nail said. "Side door?"

Anna grabbed the back of Van Horn's coat with her left hand. "This way, come on." Somewhere, a door banged open, and a second voice joined the man's shouting. "Come *on*," Anna said. She pulled, hard, dragging Van Horn behind her. He walked backward, stumbling, slowing them down while T-shirt rounded up an army. He tripped over his own feet once, caught himself, stumbled again.

Anna leaned against him, holding him up. "Fall, and God help me, I will shoot you and leave you for dead."

"Sorry, Gen," Nail said. Awkwardly, wincing at the pain in his side, he hoisted Genevieve up over one shoulder like a big heavy sack and readied his gun with his free hand. "Aw, hell."

Anna glanced back. The side door was still fifty feet away, and between her and it stood the kid with the basketball jersey. The lawyer stepped out from a dark doorway just past him, from the room with the clothes pinned to the wall, if Anna remembered right.

She pulled on Van Horn's coat, and they started moving again. The basketball kid and the lawyer stared with hate-filled eyes. Nail did the sensible thing and gave them a wide berth. Anna's gaze darted from the basketball kid to the side door to the front. The Goth kid had come up from the front of the building, along with T-shirt, the hippie chick, two naked guys, and a woman in a fairly normal getup of jeans and a light-colored blouse, the normalcy of which was given the lie by her mad, rolling eyes. They got to about fifteen feet away and slowed, following at a speed that kept them the same distance away. T-shirt straggled a little behind, moving in a weird, shambling gait. Black rivulets ran in streams from his eyes. Blood, Anna thought.

Nobody said anything. The crazed laughter from before had vanished, and now there was only a seething hatred, awaiting an opportunity. Anna and Nail passed the basketball kid and the lawyer, each of whom rotated to watch the two of them as they went by. When the main group reached them, they simply joined the arc of the others and moved with them.

"If you hurt me, they'll tear you apart," Van Horn said, twisting his head around to try to make eye contact.

"I figured. If it comes to that, you won't be around to enjoy it."

They reached the side door. Anna backed up, holding Van Horn between her and his entourage while Nail opened the door and went out. Anna heard him go, heard him give the all-clear, but she didn't take her eyes off the group.

There was a sudden motion at the rear as T-shirt collapsed, hitting the concrete with a flat thump. Anna's heart leaped and her finger tightened on the trigger. She could feel her pulse pounding in her chest and hear it in her ears, and horror filled her as she realized how close she'd come to ventilating Van Horn's skull. She scanned the room, looking for what had dropped T-shirt. Nothing stood out. The entourage didn't even look around. Just kept moving forward, even as a pool of blood spread around the man's body.

Anna adjusted her grip on Van Horn's collar and stepped over the threshold, steeling herself. If he was going to move, it would be now. And then what? Shoot him? What choice would she have?

Perhaps he'd been thinking the same thing. There was a moment of resistance, the slightest tension as he froze in the doorway, and then he let himself be pulled through. His shoulders slumped.

The entourage followed them all the way to the car.

Chapter 5

"This ain't a negotiation," Nail said. They were back in the school, in the room Genevieve had fixed up for Van Horn. Nail hoped that shit still worked with her out of commission. He'd shot up the tires of the entourage's vehicles before leaving, but he figured that wouldn't slow them down for all that long. Outside the room, the sun would be coming up. Anna would be on the road, meeting Tran to set up a time for them to finish this shit. She'd been in bad fucking shape, shaking, with that tight-mouthed angry worried look, but they had to get this over with and Tran was expecting her.

Meanwhile, Nail just had one job to do, and he wasn't getting it done.

He squatted next to Genevieve and checked her pulse again. Even, steady. Breathing was okay, even a little color in her cheeks. She just wouldn't wake up.

Van Horn sat miserably on her other side, features cast into sharp relief by the blue-white glare of a battery-powered Coleman lantern. "I'll fix her up, you let me go, and you'll never hear of me again, I swear. I can go as far away as you want." Shit, he looked old. Liver spots along the back of his hands, his goatee with only a few threads of gray in it to darken the white. Bald head sweating nervously, now that he'd let his hat fall off. He looked like some white kid's dotty grandpa.

"I have money," he said.

"You ain't got no money."

He tried on a rueful grin. "Well, no. But I have friends who might."

"You don't have any friends."

He shrugged as if to say, *Aw, you got me.* "Acquaintances, then."

"Yeah. I bet."

The grin vanished. "You've already met one of them, haven't you? Ah, damn." His brow furrowed, creases multiplying across his forehead. "Which one? Not Nathan Mendelsohn, I hope? He *certainly* won't be paying you."

"No. He's dead."

"Like I said."

"So, who is it? It's not Gorow, or *I'd* be dead. Disraeli isn't local. Sobell thinks I'm dead."

Had Nail's expression changed? Was there a flicker of surprise across his features, or had his eyes widened slightly? He'd thought he had a better poker face than that, but Van Horn suddenly deflated. "Oh," he said, breaking eye contact with him. He stared into the corner. "It is Sobell."

"I didn't say that."

Van Horn ignored him. His face had gotten noticeably paler, even in the low light, and he chewed one corner of his mouth. "Oh, hell."

Nail couldn't leave it alone. He knew he ought to, but this thing with Sobell had Anna freaked out, and it was bugging the shit out of him, too. It was out of control. Anything he could get, any leverage at all would be helpful. "What's he want with you?"

"Nothing good, I'm sure. Vengeance, most likely."

"For what?"

Van Horn held his bound hands out to him. "Untie me?"

"Not a chance. I told you, we ain't negotiating."

"You don't have the slightest bit of leverage. If Sobell gets his hands on me, I'm a dead man. I'm having a hard time figuring out what my incentive to help your friend here is supposed to be."

"I can fuck you up pretty bad and still make sure there's enough left for Sobell."

"You should get started, then," Van Horn said. He didn't look defiant, only resigned. "I might get lucky and stroke out, which would be better than you holding me for the likes of your puppet master. Do you know he called up seven demons to skin a man one time? Seven!"

"I don't know nothin' about that."

"One is profligate enough—I mean, really. Who knows how to go about skinning a man better than a demon does? Seven is just grotesque."

"You need to be thinking about Genevieve here. Gettin' to work on that."

"No."

Nail stared at Van Horn. He was a soft, pudgy, old man, with no physical resources and no real options. He didn't look like he had any fight left in him, and he wouldn't meet Nail's eyes, but the finality of that "No" had serious weight to it. Nail couldn't figure out how pushing against it was going to get him to move any.

"I'm not kidding, old man."

"I know tough guys," Van Horn said. "Tough guys, and killers, and maniacs of all stripes. You're the first certainly, almost certainly the second, but not the third. You don't enjoy making people suffer."

"I don't enjoy a lot of things I have to do anyway."

Van Horn's mouth was soft, mealy. "Coerce me if you must, but bear in mind that I can kill her just as easily as heal her. Probably easier, under duress."

Nail dropped his gaze to his hands.

Tran looked back over her shoulder as she came into the coffee shop; Anna was sure of it. It was an abbreviated look, stopped abruptly in the middle and awkwardly played off as Tran checked her appearance in the glass door and brushed an invisible hair off her forehead.

She was actually nervous, Anna thought. Here, on her home turf, surrounded by suits and expensive shoes, looking out on the impossibly flat canyon floor of downtown, Erica Tran was shaken.

Tran let herself all the way in and walked to the counter. A few minutes later, she brought a couple of paper cups of overpriced coffee to the table.

"Black," she said. "I didn't know how you like it."

"Black's good," Anna said, reaching for the cup. Coffee was coffee. How was this place so full at six thirty in the morning? Tran must really have been worried about being overheard, if she'd expected it to be this packed.

Tran gave her a slight smile and sat. "Is it done?"

For a second, Anna thought she meant the coffee, but then she shifted gears and caught up. The job, of course. "Half-done."

"What do you mean?"

"Job ain't done until delivery. When and where?"

There it was again—a flick of the eyes toward the window. Tran's paranoia at work, or was this being recorded for posterity? Surely Tran wouldn't be laying the groundwork to fuck Anna over. Maybe lay the whole mess at the crew's feet? Anna didn't think it likely. Too much dirt would get uncovered in that event. It would be bad lawyering. "Not yet. It might be a few days before we can finish up."

"A few *days*?" Maybe it was the insomnia or the stress, but Anna's fuse burned down to nothing in an instant. The hell with Tran, and her paranoia. "I'm not sitting on a stash of antiques here, lady—this is a goddamn *human being* we're talking about."

Nobody looked up or showed the slightest interest in the conversation. A couple of guys argued about some sports event, somebody else complained loudly into her phone about something that sounded like home repair work. Tran froze, though, hands splayed on the table, cords standing out on her neck as she tensed up. "Keep your voice down, for God's sake."

"Little too much heat these days? Imagine how I feel."

"I can't do anything about that right now."

"We both know who can."

"Are you fucking kidding me?"

That was a shocker—Anna would have bet a fat pile of cash that Tran would never have let the dreaded f-word cross her lips. "I don't have time for this shit," Anna said.

"You don't have *time* for this? Do you think things just go away, Ms. Ruiz? Wait long enough, and everything bad you've done simply fades out? *It doesn't work that way.* You might not realize this, but a lot of people have to work a lot of hours to make sure you stay off the radar."

"Because it's in their best interests that I stay that way."

"Make yourself a big enough pain in the ass, and it won't be."

Whether it was the open threat itself, or just the smug look on Tran's face, Anna didn't know, but the last of her patience evaporated. Karyn and Genevieve, the two people she cared about most, were both out of commission in the service of Sobell's agenda, and now his lackey was here making *threats*? She reached out and, with her index finger, gave her oversize coffee a very deliberate shove. It toppled, sending an arc of oily-looking black coffee sloshing across the table. Tran shot to her feet, but not fast enough to avoid a slug of the stuff slopping across the bottom third of her skirt. Everybody in the room turned to look.

Anna stood. "You're a gofer," she said. "A gofer in a pretty suit. You don't get to make threats. Tell your boss he needs to hurry up and end this."

The look of hate on Tran's face as Anna shouldered past her toward the door almost made the trip worth it.

"When's the drop?" Nail asked. He sat on an overturned bucket outside the row of makeshift doors. A five-foot-wide anarchy symbol in black spray paint decorated the wall behind him. There was a surprising amount of light in here today, enough to show that the air was thick with plaster dust and worse.

Anna held up her hands in a gesture of helplessness. "They're working their shit out."

"What is that supposed to mean?"

"Means we're supposed to sit on him for a while."

"How long is a while?"

"No idea. Tell me Gen's okay," Anna said.

"She's okay. No better, though."

"Awake?"

"No."

"Van Horn?"

Nail hooked his thumb toward the third door, a heavy plywood construction that had been padlocked shut.

"No help for Gen?"

Nail shook his head.

"Did you . . . ?"

"Did I what?"

"I dunno. Get *anything* useful out of him?"

"I didn't 'get' anything out of him, one way or the other. He knows about Sobell, though."

"Knew before, or knows now?"

Nail's face was stone. "Knows now."

This was unbelievable, Anna thought. Was it possible for one single goddamn thing to go right? Just one? "You know an interrogation usually goes the other way, right?"

"I'm not about to start cutting on the motherfucker if that's what you're getting at. I'm not the fuckin' Spanish Inquisition."

"Did you think I was leaving you to make him coffee?"

"Really?" He pulled a shiny length of metal from his pocket and flicked his wrist. Butterfly knife, blade short but wicked-looking. He flipped it around and pointed the butt end toward her. "All yours."

She stared at it. Just looking at the thing made her want to wipe her hands on her pants. From beatdowns to kidnapping to torture, easy as that? "What are we gonna do if Sobell wants us to kill him?" she said, voice low. "We gotta draw a line somewhere."

"Yeah."

She gave Nail a thin smile. "You sure talked tough."

"Everybody talks tough. I've done some fucked-up shit in my time, but you know—heat of battle, and all that. This . . . This is different." He looked at his hands, as though they'd become strange to him, or maybe he was hoping for some kind of answer there.

"No shit." She kicked a short length of two-by-four against the wall, crossed her arms, and glared at the doors. Three doors. Genevieve behind door number one, Karyn behind door number two, and one Edgar Van Horn behind door number three.

"Put the knife away. Got the keys?"

Nail unlocked the padlock on Van Horn's door, and Anna went in. This room looked as though it had once been an oversize supply closet or something—maybe ten feet square, no windows. Anna slid a piece of brick in front of the door to keep it open a crack. Let a little light in.

Van Horn sat on the floor, legs stretched out in front of him, limp. A diffuse stripe of light fell across his thighs, showing the streaks of dust and grime on his pants. He looked up without much interest as Anna came in.

"I hope you'll excuse me for not getting up."

"Yeah, it's . . . It's cool." She sat cross-legged against the wall opposite him and took her trusty can of pepper spray from her pocket. Probably she could take him without it, if it came right down to it, but she might as well make sure. She set the can on the linoleum next to her. "You know about Sobell."

He worried at his lower lip with his teeth and nodded. The nod went on and on, his head tipping back and forth as if it might not stop. "I know a lot about Sobell," he said, still nodding. "He's got his hooks into your friend, doesn't he? The one with the pink hair."

For the first time, Anna had a disturbing realization, not of how far in Sobell's pocket she and the crew were, but of how much trust they had put in him. They trusted him to deal with Van Horn so much that they'd never even bothered to disguise themselves around the man. Implicitly assuming, she supposed, that either Sobell would ice Van Horn or the two men would come to an understanding some other way. Somehow Van Horn would never go to the cops, would never hunt them down. What the hell had they been thinking?

He won't go to the cops. Not this guy, with his weird crew of increasingly dead friends.

"Not exactly," Anna said cautiously.

"Not exactly not, either, I'm guessing. Genevieve's got that aura about her—she's into some very bad things, I think."

"How did you know her name?"

"I don't know. Must have heard it somewhere. Do you even know the kinds of things she's involved with?"

"Her name. Where did you hear it?"

"Has she told you she's burning her soul up like a candle? Every new parlor trick leaves her less human than before. Believe me, I know what I'm talking about."

He wasn't gloating or teasing—only tired. Anna didn't give a shit. "I'm gonna count to three, and then—"

"And then what? Mace me? Kick me to death?" Now Van Horn chuckled. "I wish you'd get on with it. I once saw Enoch peel a man like an orange. Kicking me to death would be a mercy, comparatively speaking."

"Shut up. I want to know about Genevieve, and I want to know now. What did you do to her?"

"Know what he did to deserve that? In Enoch's eyes, I mean?"

"Genevieve, dirtbag."

"Screwed up a job."

"I don't care!"

"'And then they came for me, and there was no one left to speak for me.'"

"Shut up!"

"That'll be you, one day. Or your friend. Everybody screws up eventually."

"Jesus, you think I don't know that?"

The old man held his head up, trying to meet her eyes even as she dropped her gaze to the floor. She put her hands in her lap and shook her head. Van Horn said nothing.

What a mess.

"I can help you," Van Horn said softly. His voice, low and hoarse with age and abuse, seemed to float right to her ear. "Just let me go, and I can fix Genevieve right up."

She coughed up a bitter laugh. "You're telling me to double-cross a man who you just said skins people who so much as make mistakes. What would he do to somebody who dicked him over on purpose?"

Van Horn's face was drawn and haggard, and a bleak, horror-stricken expression haunted his eyes. "You don't want to know."

Her sense of being trapped in an impossible situation was nearly suffocating. Sobell's jobs were dirty and getting dirtier, and nothing Van Horn said made her feel any better about that. Not much worse, either, given what she already knew about the man, but definitely no better. She wanted to run, hoping that maybe Sobell's forces were depleted enough that he couldn't find her—but it would be nearly impossible to do that without ditching Karyn and without giving up on finding a solution for her. And, of course, Genevieve. Even before her Sleeping Beauty affliction, she hadn't wanted to run at all. Neither did Nail, for reasons he wouldn't go into. So what to do? Keep doing what she was doing until the jobs got so heinous she couldn't do them anymore, and Sobell skinned her and everyone she cared about? Van Horn was likely not offering her any help but rather a direct route to an unusually horrific death . . . but what if he was?

"Why hasn't he come for me?" Van Horn asked. "Why didn't you take me straight to him?"

"I wouldn't get your hopes up. He's just busy, I guess."

Van Horn leaned toward her, his face a study in sincerity. "Giving me to Enoch is as good as killing me yourself—you know that? Are you ready to be a murderer?"

"I'm already a fucking murderer," she said. She wished he hadn't gone there, digging right at the spot she wanted to keep a corpse buried. He couldn't know how the showdown at Sobell's had haunted her, but he sure acted like he did. "*Not* giving you to Sobell is a good way to commit suicide."

"Information, then. Tell me what you know about him, about what he wants. I'll tell you what I know about him—which is quite substantial. There might be some way we can both come out ahead on this."

Anna hesitated. "How do you know him?" she asked.

"We go way back. I taught him a few things, when he was young. Well, younger. And then, like everyone eventually does, I disappointed him. You would not believe the lengths I went to in order to avoid paying the price for that. It started with faking my own death and got even more ridiculous from there."

"When you say you taught him a few things . . . you're not talking about things like the basics of money laundering, are you?"

Van Horn shook his head. "Unsavory things of an entirely different nature. Probably not too dissimilar from what he's teaching Genevieve."

There it was again, and another spike of fear and anger jolted through Anna's body. Before she could say anything, though, Van Horn spoke again.

"I'll give you this for free," he said. "Your friend will wake up tonight, without intervention from me or anyone else. It's a temporary effect."

She hated the hope that flared in her heart, despised it for a lie. "Bull. You have no reason to tell me that."

"Call it a gesture of good faith. When she wakes up, come see me. We can talk then."

Chapter 6

"I feel bad," Sonia said. Tears, stained with faint traces of mascara, streaked her face, yet her mouth was frozen in a wide rictus. She stood in the dusk light, dishwater gray, that came in through the old meatpacking plant's high windows. She swayed as though she might topple over. "I feel . . . really bad."

An urge, almost a compulsion, rippled through Sheila's body—she would tear out Sonia's throat with fingers and teeth and put an end to the whining, the endless fucking whining—and then it subsided, gone before Sheila could even move in that direction.

Truth be told, Sheila didn't feel that good herself. It wasn't any specific thing, no sick stomach or headache, but more a sort of general *tenuousness*. Was that even a word? She felt thin, distantly connected to the world, her body, and even her own thoughts.

"It'll be fine," Sheila said. "Get some rest. Get something to eat."

"Will we go out tonight?"

"No. I have things to work on. You probably do, too." That was one nice thing to come from Van Horn's absence—less traipsing about all over. That had been fun, in its way, and anyway she'd always gone, but her work had always been in the back of her mind. Hadn't it? That was fuzzy. In any case, she could continue uninterrupted now. She acknowledged that she was afraid as well—their enemies had taken Van Horn, and there were others who would surely see them all killed. If anything, that was more reason to stay out of sight. To keep working.

She walked to her room, past the lounging bodies of the others. They were restive, probably getting hungry. That was fine. They could go out tonight without her, if they wanted to.

She paused inside the entry to her room, looking at the far wall in the light from a gas lantern.

"That's a lot of writing," somebody said.

Sheila turned. The woman standing in her doorway was draped in a loose collection of what looked like colored sheets. Rain, that was her name. She'd been around for a while, one of the later additions to the group, though still well before everything fell apart. From the name and the shapeless hippie dresses, Sheila had originally figured her for a flake, but that hadn't seemed to be true. Rain was solid. Sturdy. *Earthy*, Sheila would have said, if she were inclined to go with the whole hippie thing.

"It's a mathematical proof." *I think.* "Mathematical" might have been stretching it, but it had a similar feel to it—a set of rules, groping toward an arrangement that somehow signified completion.

"Proving what?"

"I guess I'll know when I finish it."

"I made a sculpture out of thousands of splinters picked from a chair," Rain said. "Is that weird? I think it's supposed to be weird. I mean, I would have used to think it was weird."

"What do you want?"

"I'm hungry. Aren't you?"

"I wasn't, no." Her stomach felt neither empty nor full, but now that she thought of it, she wanted ... something. She wanted to finish this—this proof, or whatever it was, but there was another urge pulling in the opposite direction. Food. The hot wet gush of blood, salty meat tearing from the bone . . .

She kind of wanted to see her son, too.

Sheila shook her head as though to clear it. *Where did that come from?* Her son was fine. Somebody was on that job, she was sure. Her mother? Yeah, that was probably it. She must have dropped him off at Mom's before everything got weird. Good place for him, for now.

"Are you coming?"

"Yeah."

She cast a wistful glance at the wall of equations and went back out to the main room. Everyone had gathered. Van Horn was gone, but the routine was in place now. Sonia stood, weeping and grinning, in their midst.

"I wish Edgar was here," Rain said.

"Why?"

"I don't feel so great."

"I haven't felt so great for days. Van Horn didn't help."

"He used to be able to talk me through it. He knows a lot of stuff."

"Forget—"

She trailed off as she caught motion past Rain—Sonia, her knees suddenly giving out. Sheila watched her drop in slow motion, folding at the knees, then tipping backward. She watched the arc as Sonia's head whipped back into the concrete. The sound it made when it hit sent a pulse of excitement through Sheila's belly.

Sonia twitched for a few seconds and then was still.

The Chosen got up as one and gathered around her body.

Sheila's stomach growled.

After, they were too full to move. The nine of them lay around the main room in various states of torpor. Sheila lay on her side, head resting on her arm, willing her stomach to calm down. The first time she'd eaten like this, she threw up over and over again, retched until she thought she'd barf up her skeleton, until she thought her stomach would cramp and seize and draw her into a tight ball from which she'd never be able to uncoil. It had gotten easier later, but it still wasn't something her system was fully comfortable with. From the look of things, nobody else was coping with it too well, either. It reminded her of her partying days in college—there came a point when you knew, you just *knew* you shouldn't slam that next shot, but it was all so much fun you did it anyway. The excitement of drinking paled in comparison to that of *feeding*, but she liked the analogy.

"I'm worried," Rain said.

Sheila twisted her head around to see Rain, lying flat on her back behind her. Sheila rolled over. "Why?"

"How many of us were there before? Fifteen? Twenty? It was a lot more."

"Nineteen," Sheila said. She remembered them all jockeying for Belial's favor—she remembered each one as a rival, remembered sorting them in her mind, placing herself in the hierarchy. She'd come late to the game, so to speak, and she'd had a long way to climb.

She hadn't had to wait long. Kieran, Jessica, and Ernest had disappeared months ago, and Tomas and Inez had been killed in the debacle at Sobell's place. All to the good, since, other than Tomas, they'd all been closer to Belial than she was. But then Belial had vanished and the Brotherhood had scattered, and the inner circle, the Chosen, had fallen in with Van Horn. Since then, five more had died.

Barry had dropped dead two days before Van Horn was kidnapped, bleeding from every hole in his body. The kid who had inexplicably wanted to be referred to as Douche Bag bought it the next day when some crazed impulse had seized him and he'd sawed off his own left hand. Sheila wasn't even sure what kind of insanity had to take hold of a person for him to sever one of his own limbs and stay conscious through the whole ordeal, and sometimes she wished the thought didn't make her so hungry. Sometimes, though, she kind of understood. It hadn't come as much of a surprise that they'd found Douche Bag still weakly gnawing on his own severed hand when they found him. She thought he'd bled out after that, though another part of her was pretty sure that hadn't happened at all. Like maybe he could have survived after all, except that the Chosen got very hungry sometimes. Dennis had collapsed the night Van Horn was taken. Alan had killed himself more directly after Van Horn's abduction by jamming a thin metal rod into his own eye and then slamming his face into a column. He'd laughed the whole time.

Now Sonia.

"Who's next?" Rain asked. "You? Me? How long do we have?"

God, the complaining around here. The endless complaining. Worse than a faculty meeting. That didn't mean Rain didn't have a point, though, Sheila supposed, and she suddenly felt ill at ease. If she died, there would be no more magic. No more *feeding*. No sensation at all, just endless void. Endless waiting, with only the faint whispers of the rest of the damned to provide something like diversion.

Boring. So boring. Boring enough to drive you right out of your damn head.

"Maybe we can stop it," Sheila said.

"How?"

"We can do magic, Rain. There has to be some way we can use it."

"I made a glass of water float in the air last night. Without the glass—just the water, in the shape of a glass. It was cool, but . . . not very useful."

Rain was looking at her as though she expected something, but Sheila ignored her. She was already starting to get an idea. It bubbled up from somewhere down in her mind, like a corpse floating to the surface of a still pool, much of it yet unseen, but enough showing to get a sense of it.

She got up, relishing the stiffness in her limbs and the queasy feeling in her belly, and walked slowly to her room. The quiet presence of Rain behind her barely bothered her at all.

She ignored the wall full of writing and began staring at a blank wall. This was how it started—a blank mind. A *clean* mind. All her best ideas had come to her in this state, when she pushed away the clamor of half-remembered discussions and cheap thrills and let fresh thoughts rise to the surface of her mind. She exhaled, and the vague shape began to solidify.

"What are you doing?" Rain asked.

"Interrupt me again, and I will put this pen through your skull."

"Sorry."

Finding somebody was easy. She remembered that. *If you had the right stuff.* A name was good, but not usually enough. Blood, hair, tears were better. She had none of those things from Belial, and she doubted he would allow himself to be found that way in any case. He was in hiding, she had heard from Van Horn, but she didn't know where or even specifically why. They had enemies. That was all she needed to know.

Van Horn knew, though. Where *and* why.

"Go to Van Horn's bed. Bring me hairs, anything like that."

Rain ran off, leaving Sheila to contemplate. Rain would return with something, and Sheila would perform a basic seeking. She was already nearly convinced it would fail. Whoever his captors were, they weren't uninformed. She'd try anyway, because it was the easy way.

It wasn't the only way, though. She raised the pen to the wall and began sketching the outlines of the necessary diagram, in case the easy way failed. It took a few tries to get these things right, to get them fixed in her mind, but once she did she didn't make mistakes.

Rain returned a short while later and, to her credit,

waited silently in the doorway until Sheila was ready for her. She had a few short gray hairs, and a few white ones. Enough, unless Van Horn was hidden somehow.

The simple seeking took no time at all. A quick drawing, a few drops of blood, the hairs, and a short chant. Sheila held her pen suspended from a piece of string and waited for it to turn, pointing to Van Horn. It sat, inert. Sheila had expected that, but rage welled up in her anyway, and she threw the charm to the floor and kicked it into the corner, snarling.

"It didn't work," Rain said.

Sheila balled up one fist, then forced herself to relax. Rain was an insipid thing, but this had been her idea, and Sheila was now convinced it had been a good one. "No."

She went back out to the hall. Aside from her and Rain, there were seven of the Chosen left now, lying, sitting, or standing in the big open room. Raul and Deanna were fucking again, almost out of sight behind a crosshatched mess of metal framework. That was all well and good for them, but the moaning made it hard to concentrate. It was time to get to work.

Sheila sat cross-legged with her back against a shorn-off metal column. "Gather around," she said. Six of the Chosen obeyed, but Raul and Deanna couldn't seem to bring themselves to give their genitals a rest. She did her best to ignore that, though what she really wanted was to gather up the other six Chosen and show Raul and Deanna that, if they weren't part of the group, they were food.

Seven would be enough for what she needed now, though. Leave them to their rutting. Any reckoning could come later.

She stood and moved to the center of the circle of Chosen, then bent and used a piece of chalk to draw the appropriate diagram on the pavement. It was too dark to see what she was doing, but that didn't matter. This working was in her blood, and her hands moved with swift sureness. When the diagram was complete, she be-

gan a short chant, motioning for the others to join her.
They listened, then took up the chant.

She pulled a butcher knife from her satchel. It was
long and sharp, shining even in the faint light here, the
only thing for miles that seemed pure, uncorrupted by
grime and filth. She'd taken it from an apartment nearly
a week ago, reasoning that it might be useful, and by
then the owner had no more use for it.

She placed her left hand in the center of the circle,
palm against the concrete, her index finger making an L
shape with the thumb. As the chanting rose to a crescendo,
she leaned in, bearing down with all her weight, and cut
off her little finger. There was a crunch as she forced the
knife through the ligaments holding the knuckle together.
Pain, immense and blazing, tore through her skull, balanced by a pleasure almost as intense, until she thought
the two might pull her body apart.

The night coalesced around her, and she felt a strange
thickening of the air. She scrambled back from the center.

The finger vanished. A mad, exhilarating rush coursed
through Sheila's body, and the next moment, a thing,
gray and glistening, appeared in the middle of the group.
Sheila gasped, and she thought everyone gasped with
her. The creature in the center of the circle looked like
nothing so much as a freakish, giant slug. It was about
the length of a man lying down, but she thought it was
much, much heavier. It was round and fat, and its sides
quivered. It had no features to speak of—no mouth,
eyes, antennae, or anything she could see. Just a coffin-
shaped glob of gray nasty.

"Find Belial," she said.

It lifted one end of its mammoth body, and though it
had no eyes, she swore it was looking at her. A wet,
choked hissing sound escaped from it. It didn't move.

"Edgar Van Horn, then. Find Edgar Van Horn.
Please," she added softly.

It turned, its undulating body making a squishing

noise on a glistening trail of thick slime. Maurice got out of the way as the thing slid toward the door.

Sheila popped the stump of her finger in her mouth, relishing the hot blood as it ran from the wound.

I can do this nine more times, she thought. She was making some kind of noise, she realized, but she had no idea whether she was laughing or crying.

Chapter 7

Anna flicked her lighter. The flame added practically nothing to the light from the lantern, but it was something to do. Better than watching Genevieve's chest move in slow tides, better than holding her own breath while she waited for the pause after each of Genevieve's exhalations to become the next breath. Better by far than studying Gen's face. Anna had teased Genevieve at one point about how she slept with her eyes open a slit, enough to watch the iris dart around when she was dreaming. They weren't moving now, or hadn't been last time she checked, but that white crescent still glistened between her eyelids. It was goddamn creepy, and Anna didn't like being creeped out by Genevieve.

She blew out the flame. Past her lighter, a bluish blur near the lantern, Genevieve's chest rose, then fell.

Anna pursed her lips and breathed deep, shaky breaths, trying to force down a suffocating sense of impending panic. Genevieve would be okay. Would *have* to be okay. Probably it was selfish, but Anna thought she would melt right the fuck down if Gen didn't wake up. Gen's sarcastic commentary and exaggerated bravado were a little over-the-top sometimes, but a little bravado seemed called for these days, not to mention some outright mockery of the stupid shit they'd gotten themselves into. It was good for morale, Nail might have said, but

Anna thought it was more like an anchor. Fucking everything had come unglued—what else did they have to hold each other in place?

Anna missed the conversation. It was easy with Genevieve, in a way she hadn't experienced before. Had been since very their first "date," back during the jawbone job. Anna could throw up a curtain of small talk effortlessly, and often did as part of her job, but with Gen the conversation had gotten real, fast, and it had veered with dizzying speed from topics trivial to those so personal Anna couldn't believe she was talking about them. She'd thought it was a talent of Gen's until one evening at Gen's apartment, when she surprised Anna by saying much the same about her. The shock on Anna's face had been so evident that Genevieve burst into laughter. The physical attraction had been immediate, but that only went so far—as Karyn had once told her, there were almost no points for that. An attitude that was just bad enough, a little "fuck you" in her smile, and a certain swagger in a woman's bearing would get Anna's attention nearly every time. Good for fun or blowing off some steam, but who'd have thought it would turn into anything?

An indistinct voice from the next room sounded, inflection rising in a question. Karyn, talking to her phantoms again. It was the middle of the night, and Karyn was in there talking to the walls. Her body clock was a mess, rhythms adrift with no normal light or darkness to anchor them, despite Anna's attempts to at least feed her on a regular schedule. She might go to sleep anytime now, or maybe not until noon. Maybe she'd sleep sixteen hours after that. Anna just wished she'd stop talking, and then hated herself for wishing it.

Anna wasn't much for looking back, at least not past a postmortem on the most recent job to think about what got screwed up or what they could do better, but she was looking back now. What kinds of decisions had she made to end up here? Twenty-eight years old, three people in the world she truly cared about—and vice versa—and two of them lost to some bizarre occult malaise. She couldn't find the spot where it had gone wrong. There had to have been some critical choice that had led inexorably her to squatting in a condemned school with her lover comatose in front of her and her best friend in the next room talking to imaginary future people and occasionally screaming at the walls in frustration.

And, in the dark room beyond that, the guy she was going to escort to his death just as soon as she possibly could.

Sobell. That first damn job. Even that, though, wasn't so clear-cut. Would Adelaide have abandoned Karyn without the job? Anna probably never would have met Genevieve at all if they hadn't taken it. So, really, would she even make that choice differently?

That was the sort of thing Karyn was supposed to know about. Choices, and their consequences.

Anna flicked the lighter again, intentionally missing the button so that it just threw sparks.

If Genevieve doesn't wake up, I might kill Van Horn myself. There was surprisingly little feeling in the thought. More proof, as though she needed it, that she was wrung out. She slouched farther, sliding down the wall until she was nearly lying flat, her neck at an uncomfortable angle.

Minutes passed. Mercifully, Karyn fell quiet--asleep, Anna hoped. Genevieve's slow breathing wasn't audible from where Anna sat, so the night was truly quiet now. Not even the traffic bothered her here.

Like a tomb.

"Oh God," Genevieve said. "Tastes like I ate a cat box."

Anna sat up so fast it made her dizzy. She put out a hand to steady herself. "Babe, you okay?"

Genevieve rolled onto her side and groaned. "Somebody shit in my skull."

Gross, but Anna smiled anyway. "Seriously, are you all right?"

"Just scooped out my brains and . . . plop."

Anna handed her a plastic bottle, half-full of water. Gen took it, propped herself up, and downed everything that was left. Some spilled out onto her chin and cheek. She didn't even wipe it away, just tossed the bottle in the corner when she was done drinking and lay back down. A moment later she raised her left leg, put it down, then did the same with her right.

"Everything still works. We get him?"

"Yeah," Anna said. She slid down next to Genevieve and pulled her close. "We got him."

"Hey, not so tight, huh?"

Anna laughed, and something in her chest loosened fractionally, enough to let in a good, solid breath. She inhaled as deeply as she could.

The next hour passed in a slow sweet blur, the time spent alternating between Anna filling Genevieve in on the general state of things and the two of them just hanging on to each other. For once, the room was cool and comfortable, and Anna didn't think about the rats in the corner more than a couple of times.

"I'm exhausted," Genevieve said when she'd finally gotten caught up. She lay on her back, staring at the ceiling by lantern light, her fingers, warmer than usual, entwined in Anna's own. "Asleep for an entire day, and I feel like I could do go another ten hours."

"That might not be a bad idea," Anna said.

"I had the *most* fucked-up dreams. We were supposed to kill some guy, only when we got to him, it turned out he was a cheese omelet. Not even anthropomorphic— just a straight-up cheese omelet, sitting in a cast-iron pan. We were just supposed to, I dunno, finish cooking it or something. Even Freud couldn't figure that shit out."

"Hmm."

"It sounds ridiculous when I say it out loud, but it was actually *really* disturbing. Kind of hard to explain."

"I bet."

Genevieve shifted, pulling back from Anna to get a better look. "You look thoughtful. I don't like it when you look thoughtful. You only do that when you're brooding about something."

"Hmm."

"And one-syllable answers, too. Definitely a bad sign."

Anna tried on a reassuring smile. It felt humorless and awkward. "You ever think about giving it up?"

"Giving what up?"

Anna waved her hand vaguely. "All this . . . occult shit."

Genevieve laughed, then stuck out her chin and lowered her voice an octave. "Man, I'm not, like, givin' up my bike and my rock and roll and my homeboys, just cuz you want me to settle down. I'm, like, a free spirit, man. Can't put chains on me."

"It'll kill you eventually," Anna said

"So will cheese omelets. And don't think I haven't noticed the cigarette stink coming off you. You really want to go there?"

"This isn't a contest."

"Well, what is it?"

The shadows from the lantern were heavy, but Anna recognized the set of Genevieve's mouth and the slight lowering of her eyebrows. She was pissed.

"Never mind," Anna said. She sat up and shrugged on her jacket.

"Where are you going?"

"Got a deal to square up. Get some rest." She stood.

"Oh, come on," Genevieve said, sitting all the way up. "It's not like this has been my dirty little secret all along—you knew the score. This is bullshit."

Anna paused in the door, mind casting about for a comeback. There was nothing. She walked out.

Nail was on watch, but she didn't much feel like talking to him tonight. She gave him a quick nod and let herself in to Van Horn's room. *Cell. It's a cell.*

Van Horn wasn't asleep. Instead, he sat in the far corner, knees pulled up, head resting against the two walls. In the white light of her small flashlight, she saw his hat upside down on the floor next to him, as if he was hoping she'd throw a few bills in it.

"You should have tied me up," he said. "That would be the professional thing to do."

"Why bother? No weapons here, and you're outnumbered."

"You're not using your imagination. You know, I was in a situation like this once before, and I managed to draw a summoning circle in my own excrement."

"You're still here," she pointed out. "No monsters."

"Turned out the circle wasn't worth a shit."

Surprised laughter bubbled up from Anna's gut. "You proud of yourself?"

"Immensely. I spent most of today rehearsing that one."

I shouldn't be in here, she thought. *He's gonna make a few jokes, pretend to be a nice old guy who got mixed up in the wrong shit, and I'm gonna end up liking him. What happens when Sobell says time's up?*

"Have a seat," he said. "Stay a bit. The worst thing about this little dungeon you've cobbled together is that it's really, really dull."

"Genevieve is awake."

He nodded.

She wondered how much more to tell him. Exhaustion was a drag on her thoughts, though, and all she could think of was Tran's smug face. Fuck her. Fuck her and Sobell both.

She sat in the corner opposite Van Horn. She set the flashlight down next to her. It threw a fading triangle of white light across the floor, growing more diffuse until Van Horn was barely lit, a hunched bundle of shadows.

"I really thought you'd have put a bag on my head and thrown me in a van by now," he said.

"He doesn't want you yet. I guess it's a little too hot right now."

"Any idea when it's going to cool off?"

"No."

"I guess I'll count that among my blessings."

"I'm not sure what more time gets you."

His teeth glinted as he smiled. "More time. I'd've thought that was obvious."

Anna grunted agreement. "What about Genevieve? What's gonna happen to her?" Not the question she came to ask, but it was top of mind, and she wasn't sure she could concentrate on much else.

"If she's awake, she's fine. That's it. No lingering after-effects. That I know of."

"No, I mean . . . Long-term. You've been at this occult shit forever, right? What happens?"

Something gleamed in the flashlight beam--a tooth, the edge of a grin or a sneer. "You stay ahead of it as long as you can. Like you said, I've been at this forever. If she's smart, she'll be all right for a long time."

His words tapered off, rather than just ending, seeming to imply a question or some uncertainty. "And?" Anna prompted. "But?"

"But it depends how much of Sobell's dirty work he gets her to do. He uses people up. I think you might be getting some idea of that."

"He's teaching her," Anna said.

"Uh-huh."

"That's what she says."

"And she probably even believes it. Hell, he probably *is* teaching her. Doesn't mean he's not getting some benefit out of it."

"You said you'd give me some info on him. What do you want?"

"I want out of here, and a six-day head start."

Anna shook her head, belatedly realizing he couldn't see her. "You know I can't do that."

"Then, like I said, you tell me what you know, and I'll give you what I can."

"I don't know a lot."

"I'll take what I can get. You might have noticed that my negotiating position isn't so good right now."

"It started with a job that got weird on us," she began. She spun out the whole miserable story of the job with the jawbone and its aftermath, glossing over a few important details like Karyn's affliction and current situation. Van Horn listened avidly, and she thought he was actually leaning forward by the end of it. Oddly, it was kind of nice to have somebody to spill all this to, somebody who wasn't involved in it all. It felt . . . grounding. Like maybe now it would be possible to get some perspective on it.

You are losing your shit, girl.

"We've been running odd jobs and shit detail for Sobell ever since," she said, wrapping up.

Van Horn said nothing at first. He folded his arms, and Anna saw the vague shape of his head tilt back. "Interesting."

She waited. Through the wall, she heard Karyn mutter something unintelligible. Van Horn remained a dark, silent lump in the room's far corner. "And?" she prompted.

"Did you ever find out what Sobell wanted?"

"The jawbone, I told you."

"I really doubt it, young lady."

"Young lady? You're not the school principal, dude."

"Sorry. He didn't want the jawbone. I'd bet a steak dinner on it."

Anna scoffed. "He offered us two million for the damn thing."

"In the end, he paid you to destroy it. That's not consistent with the Sobell I know. When he gets fixated on something . . . let's just say he can be quite focused, and he won't usually be deterred that easily."

"*Easily?* He didn't have a lot of choice at the time."

"Who were the dead men at Mendelsohn's?"

Eight dead in a gunfight . . . She remembered Sobell's words and her own confusion at hearing them. When the job went down, only Nail had been packing—everybody else had carried Tasers and stun grenades, things like that. It had to have been the . . . the monster. The demon that had come roaring up out of Hell and torn some poor bastard apart right in front of her.

Not if it was bullets, though. Had the gunfight info been correct, or just misinformation? Tommy had caught a bullet, and Anna had no idea if the cult guy who had shot him had done so on purpose or if he'd been aiming at the demon. It didn't matter. Tommy was just as dead either way.

"I don't know," she said. "Cult guys, I guess." It was just a detail, one of many not worth exploring in the aftermath of the job. "I guess the demon got 'em."

"Mm-hmm."

"What does that mean?"

"I don't know yet. But I'm pretty sure you got conned. Played. Sobell never shows his cards. He's cagey about what he *really* wants, because if you know that, you can manipulate him. If I had to guess, I'd say you were a diversion. Classic technique—look at my hand waving on the right while I steal your wallet on the left. Probably he thought you'd be killed, but still make enough noise for him to do . . . whatever it was he really wanted to do."

"Like what?"

"Do you suppose he's stopped playing you now?"

"What did he want?"

"Do you think he'll *ever* stop playing you?"

"You're just talking to stay alive, old man."

"That doesn't mean I'm wrong."

Anna made no answer.

Chapter 8

"What's the word?" Nail asked as Genevieve got into the passenger seat. He hit the gas before she could even close the door. Downtown bothered him for reasons he could never quite put his finger on, and anyway, he had places to be. Wouldn't do anybody any good if he showed up late.

Genevieve scowled. "Fucking lawyers. She bought me a six-dollar coffee. Like I'm gonna feel fabulous about all this after she spends six bucks on me."

"So no word, then."

She tapped her fingers on the door. "No." Her voice slipped into a prim falsetto. "'Mr. Sobell is a very busy man. He is tremendously grateful to you, but it will be just a little longer before he can attend to you. I'm sure you understand.' Nyah, nyah, nyah, nyah, *nyah*."

"Attend to us? What, is he a fuckin' waiter now?"

"I don't even care anymore. I ask her what 'just a little longer' means, and she smiles the fakest smile you ever saw in your life and says, 'We'll be in touch, I assure you.'"

Nail took the car up the ramp to the 5, willing the ancient station wagon ahead of him to get moving. Who drove a station wagon these days? Why did they give hundred-year-old women drivers' licenses?

"Son of a bitch," he said. He passed the station wagon,

but that was small consolation. A thousand spears of blinding light glanced off the frozen river of traffic ahead. "How many goddamn people need to be driving around at eleven in the morning? Ain't you people got jobs?"

Genevieve chuckled humorlessly. "Nobody gets what they want today."

"Shit." He pulled in ahead of a semi and slowed the car. "So we're sittin' on Van Horn a few more days."

"That's my guess."

"Can't say I like that much." He glanced sidelong at Genevieve. "I don't think Anna's holding up too well."

"I don't think *I'm* holding up too well," Genevieve said. She smiled like it was a joke, but the smile uncurled and vanished. "No. She's not. It's not just this stupid fucking job, either. It's this stupid fucking job, the last stupid fucking job . . . Karyn." She stared out the windshield. "I hear Karyn talking sometimes. At night. Anna picked that room so we could hear her, sort of keep an eye on her.

"She has conversations, you know. Karyn, I mean. And they sound, you know, lucid. Like somebody talking on the phone. And it'll go on for ten minutes, and you sort of get lulled into this rhythm. Some words, a pause. Some words, a pause. And just when you're starting to get used to it, like maybe you can let it fade into background noise . . . The other night, after a bunch of normal-sounding bullshit about getting her water heater fixed, she says, calm as can be, 'Yeah, he cut out his own eyes.' *Cut out his own eyes.*

"So, no, Anna's not holding up too well," she said. "Not with that going on in the next room."

" 'That' is my friend you're talking about there," Nail said.

Genevieve made a pained expression and ran her hand over her head to the back of her neck. "Sorry. Shit, I'm sorry. She saved my life, you know? It's just—this is a mess."

"Yeah." He moved another lane to the left. It looked

as though it was going slightly faster, though of course it would stop as soon as he changed to it. That was life. "So, what are you gonna do about it?"

"About what? Karyn?"

"Anna."

"Just try to be there, I guess. Try to get this damn job over with."

Nail nodded. "Be a good start."

She pulled a foot up and put one of her boots on the dash. He thought about telling her to knock it off, but it was a little enough thing. He'd wipe it down later. "I don't want to fuck this up," she said quietly.

"The job?"

"Anna." She started doing that nervous thing she did, raising her hand to pull at the stud in her lip or eyebrow, but she lost steam and let it drop halfway through the motion. "You've known her longer than I have. How do I not fuck this up?"

"You kidding me? Like I know? Listen, I don't even think Anna knows. Whole time I've known her, I never seen her, you know, *with* anybody for more than a few weeks. You in uncharted territory, Gen."

"Not reassuring." She sighed. "We need to get this over with—the job, I mean. It's impossible to even fucking live while this is going on."

"Can't you get Sobell to speed things up? Thought you were tight with the man."

"Not tight enough, I guess."

"Yeah." He checked his mirror and moved one more lane to the left. Behind him, a gray sedan braked suddenly to avoid somebody cutting in to his lane. Somebody leaned on their horn. Nail felt like choking the steering wheel. The speedometer was all the way up to fifteen miles an hour now. Probably no way to avoid being late now. "I gotta make a little detour," he said. "You mind?"

"It's your ride."

They rode in silence. Genevieve put on a pair of mirrored cop sunglasses—she was wearing them ironically,

Nail assumed—and leaned her seat back. By the rhythm of her breathing, he was pretty sure she'd fallen asleep. He watched the road and tried not to swear.

On a day with decent traffic, the drive would have taken ten minutes, but it was forty-five minutes later when Nail got to his exit ramp. The gray sedan with the touchy brakes exited a couple cars behind him. Probably a coincidence—it was a big road, lots of people on it—but he still breathed a sigh of relief when he turned right and the sedan kept going straight.

Another fifteen minutes, and he pulled into the strip mall he needed to stop at.

"Sit tight," he said. Genevieve sat up, looked around, and leaned back again.

Nail grabbed a small army green satchel from the floor and got out. It was a miserably hot day in a miserable place. Every store window in the line featured heavy bars. There was a pawnshop, a payday loan place, a burger joint Nail wouldn't have eaten in at gunpoint, a dollar store, and, inexplicably, a tax preparer. That last had to be a front, he thought, but it was always damn busy around tax time. Who knew?

He headed for the payday loan shop. A shrill electronic beep shrieked from somewhere when he opened the door, and half a dozen weary-looking Mexican dudes standing in the Western Union line glanced up at him. *Must be payday,* he thought, and, even as sorry-looking as those guys were, they were peeling off as much of their check as they could to send back home to family. When he looked at it that way, he wasn't doing too much different.

He walked over to the loan desk where a kid who didn't look as if he could possibly be old enough to have graduated from high school sat shuffling some papers.

"Need to talk to your pops, Tyrell," Nail said.

"Come on."

Tyrell got up and led Nail around the desk to a door in back. The last thing Nail saw as he went in was a little guy with a huge mustache sliding a wad of bills under the bulletproof acrylic at the cashier's station. The glare off the acrylic made the inside invisible, so it looked like the man was talking to nobody.

The back office was a ten-foot-square cell of off-white linoleum squares and industrial gray walls with a desk jammed up against one of the walls. It didn't matter, Nail supposed, because Clarence never did any actual business in here. True to form, as soon as Nail walked in, Clarence stood up. He was tall enough to loom over Nail, but thin enough that it didn't seem menacing. It wouldn't even be a fight, if Nail ever got a chance to take a swing at him. That was why it never came to that—Clarence had ways of protecting himself. Today, he looked sharp in slacks and some kind of buttoned-up light blue bullshit. Nail wondered who he thought he was fooling.

"Come on back," Clarence said.

Nail followed him through the back, down a grubby hall past the bathrooms, and out through another door to the loading dock. The light was blinding out here, but at least the two men got to stand in the shade of the building. There wasn't much call for loading in and out of the payday loan place, so the trash containers were piled up over here, stinking and buzzing with flies.

"You're late."

"Maybe we can agree to overlook that this time," Nail said.

Clarence frowned. He was maybe fifty, but hard living had taken a hell of a toll on him, and the frown was an upheaval in the geography of his face that caused deep crevasses to appear, aging him further. "Maybe. Depends what you got to say."

Nail held the satchel out to him at arm's length, shoulder strap wound through his fist. It was weighty, a reminder of all the heavy shit he'd done to come up with the contents. "Eighty-five."

Clarence's eyebrows shot up, and the hills and valleys

of his visage rearranged themselves again. "The fuck'd you get eighty-five large?"

Surely he didn't expect an answer to that question. Nail just held the satchel out, saying nothing.

"That don't cover the interest," Clarence said.

"Yeah. It does."

"No. It don't." Was that a trace of a whine in his voice? "Your fool brother been in debt to me for six years, and you think eighty-five is gonna square us up?"

Eighty-five wouldn't, no, but Nail had been making payments on DeWayne's behalf now for almost the whole time. Not always on time, not always enough, but plenty. "Two forty, all in. On a hundred grand of debt, I'd say you're doin' all right."

Clarence stuck out his jaw. Nail would have liked to plant a fist on it. "Interest is a motherfucker."

"Two-forty's a damn sight more than you'd get by breakin' DeWayne's legs." *Take the money,* Nail thought. God, it would be great to get out from under this shit. And besides, his shoulder was beginning to ache.

"The fuck'd you get eighty-five large?" Clarence asked again, and Nail knew he'd go for it. He almost smiled, but that would surely screw the deal. Clarence didn't like to see anyone smiling. Nail waited wordlessly while Clarence first tried to stare him down, then made a show of doing some elaborate calculation in his head. At the end, though, he grabbed the bag.

"We're settled," Nail said. "DeWayne's free and clear."

Clarence nodded, and then, just as Nail felt his spirits lift, he shrugged. "Till he comes back for more, yeah."

That momentary satisfaction was gone, replaced with a low, pathetic rage. He was right, of course. *I could kill him,* Nail thought, not for the first time. *Break his scrawny chicken neck right now.* And DeWayne would find somebody else, maybe somebody even less flexible, and Clarence's people would be gunning for Nail, and nothing would be any better.

Nail walked back into the building, leaving Clarence holding the sack of money behind him.

He made it out to the main room just in time to see a gray sedan with tinted windows tool slowly past the front of the building. It didn't stop.

Anna's phone rang, and she had it open and at her ear before the second ring. "Bobby," she said.

"Yeah. Got a line on that guy. The one was asking about you."

"Who is he?"

"His name, believe it or not, is Guy."

"No shit?"

"That's all he'd give me. He's ... odd. Not real stable, I think."

"He say what he wants with Karyn?"

"No. Said he'd meet you, though."

Anna tapped her foot, considering. "On my terms, maybe."

"Yeah, I don't even know if that's such a great idea. He gives me a grade-A case of the creeps. You might just wanna keep your head down, let him keep looking."

"Anything specific bothering you?"

"You know those guys that show up at your door, trying to convert you? They got this vibe like, man, you just ain't heard the good news yet, and once you do, well, hell, of course you'll see it their way. That's Guy all over."

"Sounds like a real charmer. Can you get him a message?"

"Yeah. If you really need me to."

"Tell him Paco's, two o'clock. He doesn't show, that's it. He's missed his chance."

"Yeah. Okay."

The bar wasn't empty, even at two in the afternoon. A handful of motorcycles had been parked out front, and inside four heavyset bikers in Mongol jackets had laid claim to the bar and the pool table. Anna knew a couple of them. They were regulars here. Rowdy, but basically good guys if they hadn't scored any meth lately. By the look of it, they were shitfaced, still partying from the night before. That could be the only possible reason they had Megadeth cranked on the jukebox at this hour. One of them, a guy with a huge head surrounded by a nimbus of graying hair, waved at Anna as she passed, slurring something that sounded roughly like, "Yo, Anna." She waved back.

The other half dozen patrons had spread out to the corners—getting anywhere near a drunk Mongol was an opportunity to have your face caved in—and sat drinking individually. Anna had seen most of them here before as well, though she didn't know them well enough to even recall their names.

Her guy hadn't shown yet. She took a seat at the far end of the bar away from the bikers and facing the door and ordered a burger and a beer, exchanging a few words with the bartender in Spanish. With the TV going ahead and the loud chatter of the bikers to her left, this was as close as she'd gotten to relaxing in weeks.

It didn't last long. The door opened, flooding the bar with sunlight, and a man who could only be her contact stepped in. She almost gave it up right then and just walked out the back. If her good leads hadn't proven useless, she would have.

She gave the exceptional idiot now walking through the door less than two minutes to live if she didn't intervene. Bobby had warned her, but she'd thought he must be exaggerating. That would teach her. The newcomer was slender—the adjective willowy came to mind, probably ganked from one of the romance novels Karyn liked to read sometimes—just shy of six feet tall, and white as fuck. That wouldn't get him much more than the stink eye—hell, two of the Mongols were white guys—but everything else about him almost guaranteed a beating. He wore a navy blue suit for one thing, like a Bible salesman or maybe a particularly earnest College Republican. For another, his eyes were open too damn wide, as if he was just so excited to be taking in the world around him, and he had a faint, dim-witted smile. If he was a day over twenty, Anna would eat a pack of cigarettes. If he opened his mouth, the Mongols would pound him into oblivion. They were already nudging each other, and one of them asked in a slurred but very loud voice, "What the fuck?"

The man walked toward the bar, sidling past two of the hulking bikers, who were now openly gaping at him, as though a man this stupid must be the eighth wonder of the world. "Miss Ruiz!" the man said. "Robert said you'd be here."

She slipped off her barstool and headed toward him. "I don't know a Robert," she said. She met him at the bar. "And you don't need to use so many names."

The Mongols weren't even pretending to play pool anymore. One of them, a slow-moving, enormous heap of muscle, fat, and hair, began lumbering over. "This guy buggin' you?" he asked. His pool cue looked about as substantial as a pencil in his oversize paw.

"Naw, we're good, Dino."

Dino's eyebrows drew together and down, like he was having a hard time puzzling out what she meant. His gaze shifted to the kid, then back to her.

"Really. We're good."

"I want his jacket."

"C'mon, Dino. You ain't never gonna fit in that thing."

The kid was already shrugging out of it. "Not a problem," he said. He held the jacket out in one hand. "All yours."

Dino snatched it away and leaned toward the kid, glowering. He shook his head. "You dumb as fuck, kid." He turned away, though, and started back toward the pool table. "Hey! Prospect!" he yelled.

Anna headed toward the back as Dino began stuffing a somewhat smaller guy into the kid's jacket. She could hear the tearing sounds from halfway across the room.

She found a table at the rear of the room, far enough from the bar to avoid being heard and far enough from the dartboard to keep the bikers from getting any ideas for fun games. She pulled out a chair. "Have a seat," she said, pointing.

The kid held out his hand. "I'm Guy," he said.

"I figured. Sit down, Guy."

He dropped his hand to his side and sat. Anna took the chair across from him. His calm, stupid smile had returned. Just another day on this mildly interesting planet called Earth.

"Didn't think to dress down for the occasion?" she asked. "Not too smart."

"It seems fine. I'm down by a jacket, but it's just a jacket."

Looking over his shoulder, she doubted it would even be that for much longer. "You're not too concerned about keeping a low profile, are you? That worries me. Whatever it is you want, I'm not sure I want to help you."

"Robert said we can help each other. I believe him. You just have to have a little faith, is all."

"I don't do faith. I do track record. Yours sucks, in the five minutes I've seen you. The only reason I'm still sitting here is that Bobby's is pretty good. Now you tell me what you can do for me, and I'll tell you if we're gonna keep talking."

He folded his hands on the table in front of him and leaned in, giving her the impression he was trying extra hard to look sincere. "I don't really know what I can do for you."

"You're wasting my time."

"No! I mean, I saw you. In a vision. From God."

"You had me at vision. Lost me at God."

He reached into his pocket and pulled out a folded sheet of white paper. He unfolded it on the sticky surface of the table. Anna's face, rendered in near-photographic detail in what looked like blue ballpoint pen, stared up at her. Next to it was another drawing. Karyn.

"I showed it to Robert," Guy said. "He sent me to you."

"You've been flashing this around town, hoping to get lucky?"

"It wasn't luck. I've been guided."

"You draw that?" she asked.

"Yes."

"Can I see it?"

"Sure."

She reached across the table and peeled the drawing off the surface. Then she tore it into half a dozen pieces and stuffed the pieces in her pocket.

Guy's smile didn't waver. "You see? I had a vision, and now here you are."

She didn't want to give him any credit for that, but, supposing he was telling the truth, the vision thing had her attention. "Yeah, I get it. So you have visions."

He nodded emphatically.

"How do you get them to stop?"

Confusion wrinkled the smooth terrain of his forehead. "Huh?"

"How do you make the visions stop?"

"Why on earth would I want to do that?"

Anna had nothing to say. Behind Guy, the bikers had torn both sleeves off the jacket, reducing it to a ratty vest. At least they were getting something out of this.

"You can't make them stop," Anna said.

"I don't know. I've never tried."

"Jesus fucking Christ."

"Language, please."

She stood, the chair squawking against the floor as it slid out. "I wouldn't wait around here too long if I were you. Those guys might get bored."

"Wait! Wait, please." He reached out, maybe to grab her by the wrist, and she stepped back.

"Try that again, and I will break your fucking fingers."

His face fell again, dropping into a sort of contrite chagrin, eyebrows drawn together and almost meeting in an inverted V at the middle of his forehead. She wondered if he was going to cry. "I'm sorry. I'm sorry. Please, will you just listen?"

She didn't sit. "Talk."

"I can help you, I know I can. The Lord has shown me."

Anna prided herself on being able to spot a liar. It was a survival skill in her line of work. And as far as she could tell, either Junior here was utterly sincere, or he was the world's most talented natural bullshit artist. "The Lord doesn't come to this part of town," she said.

"There are—there are forces gathering. The hosts are assembling for battle."

"Hallelujah."

"I'm serious. You're already in the middle of it. That's why He sent me to you."

"You have ten seconds to say something I give a shit about."

He pulled an orange pill bottle from his pants pocket and put it on the table. For a moment, he held his fingertips to it, as though he couldn't stand to be apart from it, but then he opened his hand and leaned back. "Here."

Anna stared him down. He met her gaze without flinching. Something shifted in her peripheral vision, and she was aware of the bartender watching as he cleaned a glass. "If that's an illegal substance, I'm going to call the police," she said.

"It's not."

She sat. The light coming in through the front windows shone through the translucent bottle. Inside it, she could see something with the shape of a toothpick or a fat needle.

She took the bottle and opened it. Guy wasn't looking at her anymore—the bottle had his attention. His lips were parted, his eyes wide and gleaming.

Anna tipped the bottle upside down. A single sliver of black wood fell out onto the table. Guy seemed to be holding his breath.

"What the hell am I supposed to do with this?"

"It's a relic," Guy whispered. "A holy relic." He pulled his gaze up to hers. "It makes the visions come."

"I don't need *more—*"

"Take it to her," he said. "The Lord spoke to me. He will speak to her. He showed me."

"This is bullshit."

"Take it to her," he said again. "God will show her a true vision."

Her visions are already true, Anna thought. *This nutcase can't help her.* Nobody else had been able to, either, though. She wouldn't even be talking to this freak if she weren't desperate. "Yeah, fine. Okay. What do you want for it? A hundred bucks?"

His lips curled back and he recoiled in horror. "No!"

"Two hundred?"

"The relic isn't for sale! That's blasphemy."

"Then what are we talking about?"

He lowered his voice. "I need help, not money."

"Just a different price, is all."

A roar of laughter went up from the front of the bar. The jacket had finally given up its struggle, tearing down the middle of the back and leaving the Mongol Prospect wearing two ragged halves. He held up his arms like he'd just won a prizefight. Guy didn't even turn around.

"I don't want to talk about it like that."

"Okay, fine. What do you want for it?"

He moistened his lips. "I need you to bring her. The woman in the picture. Bring her with us. To meet someone."

Anna didn't at all care for the way his eyes refused to meet hers and his fingers fumbled with each other.

"And do what?"

A little twitch of the shoulders that suggested a shrug. "Nothing. Just talk."

"Fuck off. You're creeping me out, and I'm not going anywhere with you."

"Please." The word came out a whisper, nearly inaudible below the raucous laughter from the bikers.

"This stinks to high heaven. I'm not getting near it for a piece of wood you could have picked off a floor somewhere."

"I didn't think so." He paused, his mouth hanging open, lips slack, like his next words would be so painful his face had gone numb in anticipation of forming them. Anna could see his bottom row of teeth. Perfectly straight. "You . . . you can have that one."

"Have it. Your priceless relic, and I can just walk out of here with it?"

His lips pulled back in a pained grimace. "Yes."

"And why do I ever come back to hold up my end?"

"It burns itself down when you use it. That piece won't last long." He closed his eyes. "There's a lot more where that came from."

That was enough bait on the hook to get Anna to bite. The way she figured, she had nothing to lose. Most likely, this was a giant waste of time, like the so-called Amulet of Isis, like all the potions and concoctions she'd bought off third-rate grifters and wannabes, like every other worthless dead end she'd found over the last month or so. In that case, she'd never see this asshole again, and that would be that. If it was actually useful, though . . .

"All right," Anna said. "I'll take this. If it helps, I'll get in touch with you through Bobby. If not, you'll never hear from me again, and if I see you on the street, I'll kick your ass."

"It's a deal," Guy said. "Please be quick." He held out a hand.

Anna ignored it. She picked up the toothpick with the nails of her index finger and thumb and put it back in the pill bottle, then put the pill bottle in her pocket. She stood. "Better stick close. I was you, I wouldn't want to be left in here alone."

She headed for the door.

Chapter 9

Karyn thought she'd eaten earlier, though she remembered none of it. Her belly felt full, though, so unless *that* was the illusion, somebody had fed her. Maybe she simply didn't remember—everything was so spotty now. It wouldn't surprise her.

She had reached a point where the worst part was the boredom. Boredom, of all things! But with everything around her varying shades of unreal, there was almost nothing she could interact with. One time she'd taken a book off a shelf, thinking she'd be able to distract herself from the insanity around her for a few hours, and never mind that there had been no shelf there earlier, let alone books, and the paper grew yellow and brittle and crumbled to musty-smelling flakes before she turned the first page. Conversations with the people around her were either futile or nonsensical. It was hard to remember she wasn't *in* the future, she was just seeing it. Seeing aspects of it, anyway. And maybe the past now. Who could tell? But it was impossible to interact with the visions in any meaningful way.

On the really bad days, the days when everything seemed to take the form of a cryptic symbol, thus rendering her entire world surreal and often threatening, she slept a lot. Other times she moved through a ghost world. The only thing she could be sure of was herself,

which didn't afford much in the way of anything to keep
the mind busy. She did calisthenics sometimes, performing the first repetition of any movement very slowly, so
as to avoid braining herself on a solid object she couldn't
currently see, or otherwise doing herself injury. She was
up to three sets of thirty push-ups now, for what little
that was worth. She might lose her mind, but she'd be
healthy and fit right up until her brain threw in the towel.

Today hadn't decided yet whether it wanted to become one of the really bad days. Mostly it was recycled
images of the Latino family that would be living in this
spot five or ten years hence after this building had been
bulldozed for apartments. It was kind of like watching a
long family drama that had been chopped up and rearranged in no particular order. One moment the oldest
kid, a girl, was seven years old, and the next she was seventeen, studying over some inscrutable textbook. A moment later, her neat school uniform had been replaced
with khakis, a flannel shirt, and what looked like gang
tattoos across the back of her neck. Possible futures,
Karyn thought, even as the girl changed again.

That probably would have been okay, if not for the
truly surreal bits that kept creeping in. A small, dog-sized
dragon stalked through the room after the youngest. A
giant lifted off the ceiling and peered inside, and nobody
paid any attention. Currently, a group of very tiny people,
each about the height of a tall drinking glass, was hassling
the family cat. Karyn had no idea what the hell that was
supposed to represent, but it was mildly entertaining to
watch, kind of in the same way that watching somebody
with a poorly developed sense of self-preservation jump
his motorcycle over a dozen cars was entertaining. Perhaps "entertaining" wasn't the right word, but it was hard
to look away in any case. One of the little fellows would
run up and tweak the cat's whisker or poke it in the side,
then dodge as the cat whirled on it. Then another would
provoke the cat from the other side, causing it to spin in
that direction. It seemed like only a matter of time before

one of them was a little too slow and the cat took his head off, or maybe it would learn to ignore the second provocation entirely and run the first little guy down and eat him.

The youngest boy of the house, who evidently couldn't see the little fellows, watched the cat's leaping, spinning display and laughed.

Something sharp pricked her under the nail of her middle finger, and she jerked her hand back. She turned her hand palm-up to see. A black splinter had been wedged under the nail, and a bead of blood traced a crooked path down from the injury.

Real. Or something about it was. Pain didn't just come from nowhere, or hadn't before. Maybe this was a new, previously unglimpsed depth of her condition, or maybe something was happening.

"Is someone there?" she asked.

She heard nothing, but an image formed in her mind. Clouds in shades of blue, pink, and yellow, like a sunset in a painting by some Renaissance master. They parted, and a blazing gold light shone from them. She started to squint, then stopped herself. She wasn't *seeing* this. Half her life she'd seen visions. Had to be thousands by now. And they weren't like this. They seemed like real things, people or objects, existing in space around her, the information about them coming to her through her normal senses—usually sight, unless she'd been unmedicated for too long. They were indistinguishable from reality, which was the whole problem.

This was something else. She could still see the family's living room in all its details, and in front of her, the cat leaped after one of the gnomes, which laughed and fled. The image of the sky and the light wasn't there, though. That had bloomed directly inside her mind, planted there by some unseen hand without the usual intermediaries of her eyes and ears.

"What the hell is going on?"

The image changed to bleak desert. Hundreds of people, dressed in archaic-looking clothes, like togas and crap, trudged through the sand in the direction of a swirling column of dust or cloud in the distance. Night suddenly swept over the scene, and the cloud was replaced with a pillar of flame. Something nagged at her about that, something almost familiar . . .

The scene changed again. An arid mountainside, an old man with a long gray beard. Before him, a low scraggly tree erupted in flame.

Not a tree. A bush. A burning bush. I have gone full-on, Voices From God schizophrenic.

Then, bizarrely, the image was replaced by that of a telephone. The telephone changed to a microphone, one of the old-fashioned nineteen-forties-looking Frank Sinatra kind. It stood alone on a stage. The image point of view was from the stage, looking out at a nearly empty amphitheater. A single figure sat in the darkness out there, waiting. Abruptly, that image was gone, replaced by the drive-through menu at McDonald's. *No*, Karyn realized. *Not the menu—the intercom in front of the menu. I'm supposed to talk.*

"Um, hi?"

A man's hand, black hair prominent at the wrist, waving.

"Who are you?"

Nothing. The waving hand was gone, but nothing came in to replace it. Maybe it was her years on the street dealing with some of the shiftiest people imaginable or maybe it was just native paranoia, but that struck her as immediately suspicious. The images had been profligate and lush before, and the initial ones had been *extremely* suggestive— but not definite. Now they struck her as being almost like the "Look over here" bullshit attention-grabbing trick of a three-card monte dealer or clever pickpocket. And now, in response to the direct question, not even dissembling— flatly refusing to answer.

She waited. The splinter still stuck from her fingernail, but now she noticed that the other end of it was smoldering. And hadn't it been sharp before? Now it was a rounded nub. She wasn't sure, but she thought maybe this conversation, or whatever it was, had a pretty short time limit.

What was going on here? Had Anna finally found something that could help? Or someone? She looked at the smoldering splinter again, at the bead of blood that had run to her wrist. She had a million questions, but this smelled rotten. She wasn't asking any of them until she got an answer to the first one.

"Who are you?"

Again, nothing. The cat whirled, claws raking the air in front of one of the tiny men. A second one stabbed it in the flank with a tiny spear.

"We're done here, unless I know who I'm dealing with. One last time: who are you?"

Another image—the room she was in. Cinder block walls. Dirty plywood floor. A single door.

The back left corner of the room—not the real room, not the room she saw, but the room in her mind—began to fill with a strangely moving darkness. It wasn't the retreating of the light, like sunset creeping across the land. It was like a liquid, as though the room were balanced on one vertex, and a black, oily liquid bubbled up through the bottom point, filling a space that was bounded by four triangles—parts of the three walls, and then a black surface, held in place by some unfathomable tension. Darkness boiled and billowed off the surface, sucking more of the light from the room.

It felt . . . aware. As if it was looking back at her, with a sort of malicious curiosity that felt maddeningly familiar in some way she couldn't place. Gooseflesh rippled down the backs of her thighs, and a shiver ran through her body. It seemed that something awful crouched at the center of that darkness, waiting for her attention to wander so it could leap out and immobilize her, then devour or vivisect her at leisure. Her breath came quickly, her heart began running sprints.

It's not here. It's just in my head. That's all.

She didn't believe it for a second. There was something awful in there, something dark and horrible, burning with hate.

The darkness crept up the corner to the ceiling, extended along the edges of the room, and stopped. Waiting.

Nothing else happened.

I guess that's all the answer I'm going to get.

"What do you want?"

A new image popped into her mind: a swimmer, thrashing and floundering, out past her depth and maybe snagged on something that was pulling her down. From a boat, somebody extended a hand toward her.

The image was hard to mistake: it was an offer of help.

Bullshit. "Why?"

This time, she got a vision of Anna—almost an iconic image, plucked from Karyn's memory. Anna, standing on the courthouse steps in that raggedy-ass jean jacket she always wore, seventeen years old and bumming a cigarette. No sound accompanied the image, but Karyn knew the day like her own birthday. The day Anna had thrown in with her, offered to help. More than ten years ago. Both their lives had changed course forever that day, Karyn's away from madness, at least for a time, and Anna's in ways that maybe weren't quite as good for her.

But this wasn't Anna. She knew that. So . . .

Two more images: Nail, picking Karyn up and dusting her off after a job turned into a brawl a couple of years back. And—who the hell? A little girl, maybe ten, in a familiar schoolroom. *Raquel Huang. That's Raquel.* Her best friend in the fifth grade. Wow. She barely remembered that.

She understood now. Question: *why do you want to help me?* Answer: *I'm a friend!*

Right. Years ago she'd reached the conclusion that anybody who has to tell you they're a friend most assuredly isn't.

"What do you want?"

A jailer, opening the door to a filthy dungeon, letting the dazed inhabitant out into the sun. A surgeon, stitching up a ragged seam of hideously torn flesh. More signs of help. *I just want to help you!* Sure.

"How?"

The room again. This time, the darkness was gone, and there was nothing in the corner but dirt and cobwebs. Anna rested on her haunches in front of Karyn, studying her intently with unblinking eyes.

"I don't get it."

A vague man shape, hulking and ominous, seen through a windshield so dirty as to be almost opaque. As Karyn watched, water slopped onto the windshield and was pulled away in three swift, straight swaths, revealing the man. It was a homeless guy, sun- and windburned, with sores at the corners of his mouth—and a squeegee in hand. He grinned and gave her a thumbs-up. Then he was gone, and Anna was back, only the slight crease between her eyes betraying her interest.

Why this again? What's it . . . Oh my God.

"Anna?"

In her mind, the image-Anna's expression changed to one of surprise. Then she leaned forward. Her mouth formed a single silent word, and she extended a hand.

Karyn felt the pressure of fingertips on her knee. She reached out, saw her hand and leg in the image. With her eyes she saw only her hand, from a slightly different perspective. The effect was bewildering, the way the line of a straw submerged in water breaks, only with her hand as the straw. But her hand found Anna's, and she gave it a squeeze.

Anna's face broke into a smile, maybe the biggest Karyn had ever seen from her. A rush of words followed—all inaudible, and Anna's lips moving too fast for Karyn to even have a prayer of following.

"Hold up," Karyn said. "I can see you, sort of, but I can't hear you."

Anna held up her hand in the peace sign, or maybe for victory. She spoke with exaggerated care, forming each word slowly. It didn't matter—Karyn was no lip-reader. But the context, and some guesswork, made it pretty clear what she was saying.

"Two," Karyn said, laughing. "You're holding up two fingers."

Anna's face lit up in delighted laughter, and the image vanished. In its place, her own middle finger, the toothpick burned down to less than half.

"Okay," she said. "I get it. Your miracle cure isn't perfect, but it beats the hell out of this. I'm sure you'll do this for me out of charity, right? You'll help me out of the goodness of your heart?"

A monstrous face, eyes narrowed to gleefully mali-cious slits, and an overlarge mouth full of dagger-shaped teeth. It grinned.

"I didn't think so." It didn't take a genius to figure out that she shouldn't be dealing with this thing. To her knowledge, she'd never personally met anybody who had bartered with such a creature—other than, she supposed, every magician she'd ever met, but that situation was a little different. A direct deal? Unheard of, at least in her limited experience.

"My soul's not for sale." She wasn't even sure if she had one, but even so.

A kid grimacing and flinching away from a forkful of broccoli. A woman in a pretty dress crossing the street to avoid an overflowing sewer. Perhaps more directly, a man sniffing at a glass of blood-dark wine and pushing it away. After years of visions, many of which were nearly impossible to decipher, this game was almost fun. This group was easy enough to interpret: *do not want.*

"Then what do you want?"

There was a pause, and she thought it wasn't going to answer. Then: An engorged wood tick, head buried in the flesh beneath a dog's ear. A remora, latched onto the underside of a shark. Something thin, yellow-white, and wriggling, buried in the rich purple-red meat of a kidney or a liver. A tapeworm coiled up on itself in nauseating, segmented white loops. Karyn's stomach churned.

Parasites. Fucking parasites. "You want to . . . eat part of me?"

A young girl, rolling her eyes. Then: a bearded man with a green duffel bag, standing beside the road with his thumb out.

"You want a ride."

A slot machine, blazing light, coins overflowing from the tray at the bottom.

She wasn't even sure what giving it a ride entailed, but the parasite images were pretty suggestive. "No way."

She braced herself. She could feel the hate boiling off this thing, and it surely wouldn't like being denied. Would it kill her? Assail her with horrible images? Worse?

In her mind, she saw a puppy, bedraggled and soaking in the rain, looking in through a glass door.

In case her point wasn't clear: "Not a chance." *Here it comes—an attack, some kind of temper tantrum . . .*

An elderly man shrugging. A chubby woman with a briefcase holding out an illegible business card. A stock-broker-looking guy making that odious "call me" gesture by holding his fist to his face, thumb and pinkie extended.

The darkness slipped away, pulling in its tendrils and shrinking into the corner, like a movie of some pressurized noxious gas escaping a container, run backward and in slow motion.

She waited. No further images came. No sound. The cat lay dead on the floor, the little men dead and scattered around it, one with his head and an arm missing entirely.

The remainder of the toothpick burned away, leaving nothing but the wound.

Anna watched Karyn's eyes, but she was gone again, drawn into her strange, unknowable world. But for a few moments, it had worked. *It had worked.* That little black splinter had worked whatever magic it did, and Karyn had come back to her. Maybe there had been other visions, like Guy said—certainly Karyn had been conversing with *something*—and maybe not, but for half a minute, she had spoken to Anna. For real, not by coincidence.

Hope, real hope, not simply the grinding slog in search of finding the real thing, filled Anna, growing with an inexorable pressure. The slog? Fuck the slog. If she was on the right path, she could slog with the best of them. As long as it took.

Bobby, then. As soon as possible.

Chapter 10

"Here we go," Genevieve said. Anna reached across to the passenger seat and squeezed her hand. Four days after kidnapping Van Horn, the meet was finally going to happen. They could off-load the guy and wash their hands of this mess. What happened to him after this . . . *What happens to him after this is going to haunt me the rest of my life,* Anna thought.

Too late to cry about it now.

She turned right into an underground parking garage, trying to fight a simultaneous sense of déjà vu and claustrophobia. They'd made the drop for Gresser on the first clusterfuck of a job for Sobell in a garage like this. It wasn't even all that far away.

They had less backup this time. Nail was back at their makeshift home base, doing little more than watching Karyn and waiting. That couldn't make her feel any better about this. Not that he could have done much good this time. Last time the garage had been aboveground, so he'd at least had a clear shot. Here, not so much.

Anna took the car down four levels, all the way to the bottom. This struck her as a bad idea. There were only a few cars down here—no people right now—but this was awfully public. It was one thing to exchange a couple of boxes or bags—people who happened to glimpse the transaction would probably assume it was none of their business and get the hell out of there. Trying to exchange a box for a gagged old man in handcuffs, though, would attract the attention of even the most hardened of city dwellers. Anna had proposed a hangar she knew on a seldom-used airstrip outside town, but the lawyer said no way. Sobell didn't head out that way ever under normal circumstances, and he wasn't supposed to do anything unusual these days. That wasn't reassuring at all—it just seemed all the more likely he'd have cops following him around.

She parked at the end and looked around, immediately identifying another reason to worry about this place. There was only one way out. She'd never had much of a problem with enclosed spaces before, but this felt more like a trap. The ceilings seemed unnaturally low, the lighting poor, and the shadows cast by the support beams dark and ominous. She'd never realized just how eerie a mostly empty parking garage could be, but she fully appreciated it now.

"I don't need this shit," Anna said.

"It'll be all right. Let's just get it over with." Genevieve didn't look too confident, though.

They settled in to wait.

Erica picked Sobell up at the curb in a silver Lincoln Navigator. He let himself in and nestled a black ceramic jar between his legs. It was about a foot or so tall, wider at the top than the bottom, and heavy for its size. It might have been an urn containing the ashes of a dearly departed relative. Erica gave it a wary glance, but said nothing.

"New vehicle?" he asked.

She didn't look at him as she pressed the accelerator. "Yes."

"A trifle large, don't you think? I rather liked your old BMW."

She shrugged. When she added nothing else, Sobell turned his attention to the view out the window. It was good to be out—he hadn't left his damn office building in ten days. He lived and worked in the top two floors, and though it was dull, he didn't *need* to go out for anything in the world. If he was under surveillance, he was determined to be the most boring surveillance target the world had ever seen. He no longer spoke on the phone at all, except with his assistant, nor conversed about anything but sex, booze, and legitimate business anywhere inquisitive law enforcement personnel could conceivably pick up his voice. He was going out of his mind sitting on his thumbs while the clock ran down. He could only hope Elliot and company were also bored stiff.

"How's business?" he asked.

Erica gave him a deadpan stare. "This is my personal vehicle, Enoch. Think about that for a second."

"So business is good, then." That wasn't her point, he didn't imagine. She probably thought the car was bugged. It probably was.

"It's good enough."

She was angry, so angry that she was barely bothering to mask it beneath a veneer of civility so thin it was, in fact, transparent. He knew she didn't like being used as his personal driver, and she liked working under the scrutiny even less, but most of all she hated where they were going and the people they were going to meet. She'd been livid when he told her, and had, incredibly, initially refused to participate. He didn't blame her for trying to dissuade him— the first part of her job as his attorney was to inform him of risk. He did blame her for trying to press the issue, though. The second part of being his attorney was to shut the fuck up and do what she was told.

So, yes, she had quite the poor attitude today. She was also going to strain something in her neck as often as she checked the mirrors.

"Relax, Erica. Everything is going to be fine."

She didn't acknowledge the statement, but he thought she stopped checking the mirrors quite so much.

Five minutes later, she turned the vehicle in to a parking garage at the south end of downtown. She eased the car down the ramp inside. Four floors down, at the very bottom, an old brown Buick beater idled in one of a handful of occupied parking spaces. Sobell gestured, and Erica eased the Lincoln in next to it so that the passenger side was next to the other car.

"Wait here a moment," Sobell said. "And please stay calm."

"Wha—?"

He held a finger up to his mouth. "Shhh."

He got out, cradling the urn in his left arm. Ruiz opened her car door and had one foot out when he held up his hand.

"Ms. Ruiz, Ms. Lyle. I suggest you remain in your vehicle for a few more moments. Be sure to roll up the windows."

Ruiz scowled. "Why?"

"Exodus, chapter ten."

"What?"

He knelt and set the urn on the concrete ahead of him. Motion at the edge of his vision and the subsequent slam of a car door suggested that Ruiz had quashed her rebellious streak and followed his instructions. Good for her.

He pulled at the jar's lid. The wax cracked.

A sudden pressure threw him backward, and then the noise was everywhere.

Dear God, he thought, *I've suffered a complete failure to extrapolate.* One bug sounded like *this*, so a million or so must be loud enough to drown out his conversation and thick enough to block any cameras or recording devices. It was, but it was worse than that. The sound was beyond deafening, full of crackling and whizzing and shrieking, like standing in the middle of a raging forest fire. Like riding a tornado. Or sticking your head in a blender the size of a bus—and that was here, at the center, where the swarm was thinnest, or at least was supposed to be. He couldn't tell. All around him the bugs flew, and the world was full of the chatter of their wings and the snap of their bodies ricocheting off concrete and cars. Rows of them had settled on his arms. Some were singing their hellish mating song, while others appeared to have already paired up, and they were getting it on right on the sleeve of his Armani suit.

He stepped toward Ruiz's car, or at least the general direction of where he thought it must be, and he soon made out its shape among the locusts. As he got closer, he caught glimpses of the two women through the carpet of locusts that was beginning to cover the windshield. Ruiz wore the expression of somebody who'd eaten some suspicious seafood and wasn't sure yet if she was going to be sick. Genevieve was fascinated, craning her neck and watching through the windshield with her mouth hanging open.

He swept his arm across the driver's-side window, clearing a spot, then pointed at the back of the vehicle. Ruiz swallowed, then opened the door and rushed out into the storm. She flinched as a locust the size of So-bell's index finger bounced off her forehead. She began to yell something at him and stopped as she realized that either he wouldn't be able to hear it or a bug might fly into her open mouth.

She went back to the trunk with Sobell following closely behind. No sooner had she popped it open than it began filling with locusts. Van Horn, blindfolded and cuffed inside, failed to appreciate the situation as quickly as had Ruiz. He started shouting, and a moment later he was spitting smashed chitin and thick yellow goo out of his mouth.

Sobell and Ruiz each grabbed an arm and hauled Van Horn out. He stood unsteadily.

A hand grasped Sobell's upper arm. Erica. Good.

Sobell led the way toward the nearest vehicle he'd seen, a white Prius parked a few spaces down. They reached it without mishap, and Erica pulled a flat, thin piece of metal from her coat—an item known colloqui-

ally as a slim-jim, Sobell believed—and handed it to
Ruiz with a sharp gesture toward the car.

Ruiz did not disappoint. Sixty seconds later, they were
all in the car, Sobell and Van Horn in the back, Ruiz in
the driver's seat, and Erica in the passenger seat. It took
a try or two to get all the doors closed, but the noise
abated to something resembling tolerable once they did.
Sobell took a quick look around. Everybody seemed
whole. Locusts clung to each of them in spots, and each
of them sported dozens of tiny cuts and scratches, but
that seemed pretty minor, all things considered.

"What the hell was that?" Ruiz asked.

"Biblical plague. I've had it in a bottle for nigh on
forty years. Poetic, don't you agree?" He wasn't going to
add that it was also deeply irritating. An entire biblical
plague, and he'd had to blow it for a few moments of
private time. Granted, he was prepared to blow through
every last item in his stash that he'd collected over the
years, if it meant staying alive, but that didn't mean it
wasn't annoying.

"You . . . unleashed a plague of locusts on Los Angeles?"

"It's not as bad as it sounds. Places were a lot smaller
in biblical times. I imagine the locusts will denude every
tree and shrub for a few city blocks, but it isn't as though
the local crops will suffer. Now, if you'll leave us for a
moment, I need to talk to Mr. Van Horn."

"When I drop off the goods, I get paid."

"I expect I'll have more instructions for you shortly.
When I issue them, you will receive payment. It's not as
though I'm going to stiff you and run off, is it? I don't
have the car keys."

The incredulous look on Ruiz's face told him what
she thought of that—probably something along the lines
of *You just unleashed a giant swarm of locusts from a jar,
and I'm supposed to believe that a lack of car keys is going to slow you down?*—but she didn't argue. She sighed
and pushed the door open, heading back out into the

swarm. The noise screamed in, then dropped back to tolerable levels abruptly when she slammed the door.

He reached over and pushed the blindfold up to Van Horn's forehead, grimacing at the touch of the man's sweaty skin.

"Edgar," Sobell said.

Van Horn swallowed. "Enoch."

"You have reparations to pay."

"I'll pay them," he said, almost before Sobell had finished speaking.

"How do you propose to do that, Edgar? Some things cannot be undone. Most things, in fact, cannot be undone."

"Anything you want. I swear. *Anything.*"

Had Van Horn always been so pathetic? Sobell had once looked to him as, well, if not a teacher, then at least a fairly experienced colleague who could help Sobell unlock the secrets of the universe. Now he seemed just a scared old man, and the only secret he was able to unlock was the one that lay behind the final door. No great skill, that. The trick was keeping *that* door shut.

"That's a start," Sobell said.

"What can I do? What do you need?"

Here was the rub. It was all well and good to follow the demon's directions and find Van Horn, but what next? How much should he share with the man? It wasn't safe to share *anything* with the old fraud, but Sobell was at the point where some risks must be taken. Hard to believe this shriveled husk could help, but what else did he have?

"A woman with serpents for arms. Thirteen vultures circling a stone slab. A man named Hector and a demon named Forcas. And blood."

"I don't understand."

"What do you know about any of those things?"

Van Horn blinked. His gaze darted around the car, from the front seat to Erica to the still-swarming locusts outside, and back. "I—I don't know. In conjunction with what?"

"I need help," Sobell said. True enough, though admitting it galled him.

Van Horn paused in his frantic search of the car and studied Sobell's face. His creased brow furrowed further. "You don't look well, Enoch."

Sobell waited.

"You were in the news recently. Trouble?"

"Not the kind I need help with."

"Why did you open that jar? I remember when we found that thing. You don't crack something like that open for a little private time."

Generally, I'd agree with you.

"Not normally, anyway," Van Horn said. "I can only think of one reason you, of all people, wouldn't opt for more subtle magic."

"Aside from my natural flair for the dramatic?"

Van Horn lowered his voice, until it was just audible above the muted buzzing of the locusts. "How long do you have?"

"Who the fuck knows?" Sobell snapped. Then, more calmly: "Longer than you, if that's the extent of your aid."

Anger flashed across Van Horn's face, looking as out of place as a machine gun in the hands of a ballerina. A retort paused on his lips and then he visibly got control of himself. "We were friends once, Enoch. Can't you just let it go? Let *me* go? For old times' sake?"

"Attempting to play on my sentiment is beneath you, not to mention profoundly futile. You of all people should know that."

Van Horn looked at his hands. He clanked his cuffs together nervously. Without looking up, he whispered something.

"I didn't get that," Sobell said.

Van Horn closed his eyes and then, with an effort that looked as though he was summoning every ounce of his tiny amount of courage, faced Sobell. "Yes, I can help you."

Relief flooded Sobell's body, releasing tension from places he didn't know he'd been tense. It wasn't that Van Horn had decided to cooperate—Sobell had been prepared to make sure he cooperated, by whatever means necessary—but that he could help at all. Until that moment, Sobell had nursed a nagging fear that maybe Van Horn truly wouldn't be able to do anything for him.

"You got your ... directions from a demon, yes?"

Sobell nodded.

"Yeah." Van Horn paused for a moment, looking at the bugs bouncing off the glass. "You need another demon to help you along."

"Very astute."

"I know how to get to Hector. Forcas. Whatever it's calling itself."

Thank whatever passes for God. "And?"

"You're not the only one hunting it, you know."

"I'd imagine it's made a lot of enemies. Demons have a way about them. How do I find it?"

"The woman with snakes for arms. That's Mona Gorow."

Sobell mused on this a moment. "Oh."

"Yes, indeed. Why is it you seem to have had a falling-out with everybody?"

"And she's got my answer?"

"Not exactly." Van Horn pulled at his mustache, and his eyes were wide. The face of a man contemplating a dangerous action, wondering if he should take the next step forward—wondering if he's capable of it. "I shouldn't even be talking about this. I could be—I could be killed."

Making the threat aloud would be pointless. Sobell just waited.

"She's got something in her possession I might be able to use to find Hector. A tooth."

"If she has one of his teeth, she should be able to find him herself."

"You'd better hope not. If she finds him, she'll kill him. Then where will you be?"

Fucked. Hector would be dead, and Forcas would be kicked back to the abyss, or wherever demons spent their spare time. The only way to get to it then would be conjuration, and it would be insane to attempt that in his current precarious state. Wouldn't Forcas love that, though? It'd be like leaving the welcome mat out for it. Move in and own Enoch Sobell for a while. The thought made him queasy.

"She's got a small army, Enoch. She hates Forcas with a passion, and she's been making my life miserable just for being vaguely associated. Get the tooth, for sure, but don't dare leave her alive."

"Why does she hate it so much?"

"She's in thrall to one of its enemies. I'm not really sure which one. Baphomet, maybe."

Sobell laughed. Of course. By the time he was done, he was going to piss off every demon in creation.

"I see." There seemed to be only one way to proceed, in that case. "Erica, will you kindly go retrieve Ms. Ruiz for me?"

"What are you going to do to me?" Van Horn asked.

"Remand you into the custody of your captors. I have work to do."

"Enoch, please, I can help you. Don't—don't do something we'll regret. You *know* I can help you."

Sobell looked into Van Horn's wet eyes, masking his revulsion at the little crescents of pink revealed by the man's sagging eyelids. "That might be true. But you've already screwed me once, Edgar. It'll be safer for both of us if you stay with Ms. Ruiz and company for now.

"And you'd better pray your tip works out. I might not have much time left, but even if I don't get this situation in hand, I have more than enough time to make a lot of people suffer a great deal before I go."

Erica returned with Ruiz. Ruiz did a poor job of masking her dismay when Sobell asked her to take Van Horn back to the vehicle and return, but she seemed relieved when he laid out the next job for her. It was simple enough, and certainly something in her area of expertise, so perhaps he shouldn't have been surprised.

Her dismay returned when he asked her to bring Genevieve over and leave them. It didn't rise to the level of insubordination, but he made note of it. Best to keep an eye on these things.

Genevieve sat in Van Horn's former spot, and Erica sat in front, facing forward, pretending to have no part in the proceedings.

"I've given Ms. Ruiz an assignment for you all," Sobell said. "Theft of a simple object. She'll brief you on the details, I'm sure."

He handed her an envelope. "Two pages of the *Maleficum Maleficum*. This particular tome is one of the more difficult to acquire, and still more difficult to master, but I consider it one of the essentials. It will be crucial for your development."

"Uh, what's this for?" Her words were hesitant, but she took the envelope with all due alacrity. "I mean, thank you, but we're even, right?"

"These two pages are gratis. However, I have twelve more for you if you can perform an extra service for me during the theft."

The shock on her face was surprisingly rewarding. It also meant she understood the significance. For someone with her relatively limited contacts and resources, this would shortcut years of scrounging. He did appreciate a sharp pupil.

"Twelve? Oh my God. Okay! What is it?"

"The object belongs to a woman named Mona Gorow, and I believe she keeps it near her person at all times. She has considerable occult knowledge and skill. As a result, you will be needed to handle any magical defenses she may have erected. I can offer you some advice on that account."

"Easy enough."

"You will get inside with the help of your associates, get close to her, and kill her."

Genevieve's poker face was considerably poorer than Ruiz's had been. She froze, her mouth hanging open slightly, eyes fixed on nothing in particular, as if her whole system had locked up. Given the nature of the directive and its likely conflict with her existing structures of morality and whatnot, it probably had.

She thawed, slowly, her mouth working for moments before the words finally came. "I—I don't think I can . . ."

"Let me make myself clear." He lowered his voice to a warm, sincere murmur, leaning closer and projecting just enough to be heard over the locusts. He wished for a table in a comfortable room, a place where he could face her that wasn't so tightly constrained and awkward. It would make this easier for her. She'd feel less threatened. And if wishes were horses . . . He suppressed a sigh. "It's very important that you understand this. I am, today, in somewhat constrained circumstances. I can't simply ring up one of my usual contractors and get this job done." He paused. "I trust you, and I find you a very capable student and assistant. I need this, Genevieve, and there's nobody else I can task with this in whom I have more confidence than I have in you."

"I—look, I appreciate that, and, and, I'm honored, but I—I'm not a hit man. I can't just . . . I can't."

"It won't be as horrible as all that. You'll meet with Erica here in a day or so. She'll give you an object and some instructions on how to use it. All you'll have to do is get close. The dirty work will virtually handle itself."

"Enoch, I can't."

Well, even the best employees sometimes needed the stick as well as the carrot.

"I am given to understand that you and Ms. Ruiz have become close," Sobell continued.

"What?"

"I will not always be under such constrained circumstances. When my situation is better, I will make every effort to reward those who have helped me." He reached across to her and gently turned her face to his. Her cheek was smooth, and cool to the touch. "Do you understand?"

"What?" she asked again.

He made a pained face. This would irreparably damage his relationship with his pupil and surely put a sour note of resentment under all her interactions with him in the future, but what choice did he have? "Under normal circumstances, I much prefer not to insult the intelligence of my trusted employees, and I *detest* being so gauche as to make threats where implications suffice. These are not normal circumstances, are they?"

"No."

"Then listen: carry out this task, and you will be rewarded, richly, in both wisdom and treasure. Fail, and of course our current arrangement will come to an end. I will make it known in the underground that anyone helping you is accursed in my sight. And one day I will lay waste to everything you care about. *Now* do you understand?"

She nodded. He took his hand away from her face.

"Good. Then go."

She left.

Erica turned around in the front seat and gave Sobell a worried look.

He responded with a smile. "That went well, don't you think?" he asked.

Chapter 11

Traffic was worse than Anna had ever seen it. It took over two hours to go just six miles, because every damn thing was covered in locusts. Some were still flying, obscuring the road and bringing traffic to a crawl. A small proportion had spontaneously died and were piled up in awful crunchy drifts that Anna had no choice but to drive through. She kept the windows rolled down and the heater on, because the car kept trying to overheat. Locusts had clogged up the air intake. She and Genevieve stopped and cleared them out every so often, but more were always lined up behind the ones they got rid of.

"I think I might want to kill him," Anna said.

Genevieve had been quiet for most of the ride, which Anna didn't regard as a healthy development. After Anna'd gotten the instructions for the next job and left Genevieve with Sobell, she waited a long time, long enough for the locusts to thin out enough that she could make out the Prius's shape. When Genevieve had returned, she had been distracted and impatient to get moving.

Now Genevieve pulled herself out of her thoughts. "Van Horn?" she asked.

"Sobell."

Genevieve gave a weak smile. "I think everyone wants to kill him eventually."

"What did he want with you? You were in there awhile."

"Magic stuff," Genevieve said. "Honestly, I'm not sure I followed it all, but he was getting pretty tired of repeating it by the end." Her voice was flat and lifeless. Drained, Anna thought.

"Hey, uh, about the magic stuff . . ."

"Please don't, Anna. Now is not the time."

"It's never the time, you notice that?"

"Can't it just wait until we finish the next job?"

The locusts swarmed thicker—*a gust of locusts,* Anna thought—and a few dozen came in the window before Anna could get it rolled all the way up. They settled on the floor, on her lap. One in her hair. She did her best to ignore them. It was amazing what a person could get used to.

"There's always going to be a next job. That's why that shit is so dangerous. Always one more reason to reach into the bag of tricks. Until one day—poof. You make yourself disappear."

"Yeah, okay. Whatever."

Rather than fight, again, Anna put it out of her mind as best she was able. She needed to concentrate on her driving anyway. The pile of bugs had gotten so large ahead that traffic narrowed to one lane to go around it.

"Yay, magic," she muttered.

"Here's the job," Anna said. She, Genevieve, and Nail sat near the center of the ruined building they currently called home, far enough away to be out of earshot of Van Horn. Anna had taken a seat on a short stack of pallets, Genevieve sat on a clear space on the floor, and Nail stood. "The swag is a tooth. Incisor, he says, root and all."

"What's he want it for?" Nail asked, surprising Anna. He never used to ask that question, but she supposed the last job had changed that.

"I don't know," she said. She looked to Genevieve, who didn't notice. Genevieve had been checked out since meeting with Sobell, her mind wandering, and every new statement seemed to interrupt her anew, except the ones she missed entirely. It made Anna want to kick something.

Anna waved a hand in front of her face. "Any idea?" she asked.

"Huh? The tooth? No."

"'Kay." Nail didn't look too happy about that, but he inclined his head in a way that said, *Go on*.

"It is currently," Anna said, "in the possession of a woman named Mona Gorow. Know her?"

Nail shook his head. Genevieve said, "Not really. Heard the name around."

"Evidently, she is an Enoch Sobell–class pain in the ass, so I guess we can expect all the fun and excitement that goes with that." She waggled her fingers to suggest otherworldly powers and whatnot. Genevieve's expression soured further. At least she'd been paying attention.

"Pays sixty," Anna said, "divided up evenly. Who's in?"

Genevieve nodded, of course. Nail, too, after a moment. Anna would have liked to tell Sobell he could go piss up a rope, and with all the skulduggery around even setting up a meeting, she had begun to suspect that he wasn't in a position to insist. Then the man had released a biblical fucking plague on Los Angeles just to ensure that he could have ten minutes of conversation unobserved, and Anna realized that both Genevieve and Van Horn were right: this was not a guy you wanted to cross, even if he looked as if he couldn't really argue at the time. He would remember. There were a lot worse things in the Bible than a few oversize grasshoppers.

"Okay. Guess we're all in, then. The only other thing I've been told is that the item in question is very important to Mona Gorow, so she will likely keep it close." She tried on a smile. "The rest is just business as usual."

Nail hiked a thumb toward Van Horn's room. "What are we supposed to do with him?"

"Hang on to him. Apparently, Sobell thinks there's

too much heat for him to risk being nailed for kidnapping on top of everything else."

"I ain't excited about getting popped for kidnapping, either."

"Yeah. Well, we can either hang on to him or let him go. I don't feel great about that second one."

"Me neither."

"All right, then. We start the new job in the morning."

"I want to sleep in a bed," Anna said. She rolled over again. From her new position she could see the vague gray shape of the pile in the corner, the one that she suspected harbored creeping things. How had she not cleared that goddamn thing out of here yet?

"Am I bothering you?" Genevieve asked. She'd been sitting in the corner for the last hour, paging through a handful of yellowed old papers over and over again by the low light of a lantern, writing in her journal and generally looking angry enough to kick a hole in the wall. At least she'd rejoined the land of the living.

"No. I just want to sleep in a bed."

"What do you want me to do about it? I can't fucking disappear Van Horn, can I? Remember why we're here in the first place? None of that's changed."

"Maybe if he promised he'd be *real* quiet, we could take him back to civilization."

"Jesus Christ, is she *ever* going to shut up?" Genevieve said. She hiked a thumb toward the wall, through which Karyn's faint murmurings could be heard.

Anna sat up. "What? If you got a problem—"

Genevieve held up her hands in total surrender. "I'm—I'm sorry. That was uncalled-for, I know." She rubbed her eyes. "I'm just fucking frustrated. Sometimes I want to burn the whole lot of this shit." She picked the stack of papers off her lap, hefted them, then put them to the side.

"What is it?"

"This? This is a fragment of a late-seventeenth-century

grimoire, written in Latin and what I'm guessing is some
screwed-up dialect of French." She gave a bitter laugh.
"Did you take trig or anything like that in school?"

"Algebra."

"Yeah, okay. Imagine trying to learn algebra, only you
can only find a few pages of the book at a time, they're
not numbered or in any particular order, and they're in
goddamn French."

Anna chuckled. "Sounds tough."

"Oh, and one more thing: if you screw up your home-
work, it could kill you."

"Tommy never made it sound so dangerous," Anna
said. Tommy had treated the occult like a cool set of toys
he'd found lying around, disassembled, and he could
hardly wait to put them together and see what they did.

"Tommy was lucky he didn't blow his own balls off, or
worse."

"He wasn't that lucky."

Genevieve looked down and wiped something invisible off her pants. "No, I guess not."

The pause that followed was punctuated only by
Karyn's murmurings. These moments of connection were
rare lately, and Anna found herself casting about for
anything to continue the conversation. She pointed at
the pages. "Why don't you just get a translation? As
much occult crap as we traffic in, there's gotta be one
available."

"That was one of Hector's first lessons to me. You
learn from original pages only." She grinned. "I remember asking him about that. I was like, 'Why, because copies lose the magic?' And he looked at me and laughed
and laughed, and he finally said, 'No, you idiot. Because
copies are *dangerous*.' He said hand-drawn ones might
have mistakes, and even with photocopies there was no
telling what the original had actually been. Whether it
had been tampered with or anything like that.

"I thought that was so much windy bullshit, and I
went straight to the Internet to see what I could trade

with some friends. One of the guys I knew online swore he'd gotten hold of a legit scan of the last chapter of the *Infernal Dominion*, and he forwarded it to me." Her forehead tightened, and she looked away from Anna. "I didn't have time to dig into it right away, which turned out to be just as well, since poor stupid Wei made local news when he was found with his fucking head on backward and a gigantic bite taken out of his pelvis."

"Shit," Anna said.

"Yeah. That was the end of looking around online for that kind of thing. Some of those fuckers out there take trolling to a whole new level.

"The only way to go is to find a good mentor, but even that's risky. Lots of self-proclaimed mentors are parasites. Get somebody else to do as much of the easier stuff as possible and you burn down less of your own life, you know? And that's if the acolyte is lucky. It can get a whole lot worse."

"Do I even want to know what could actually be worse?"

"Blood's important in magic," Genevieve said. "Human blood especially. Human blood given willingly even more than that. It's messy business. I got lucky with Hector."

"Before a demon ate him."

Genevieve nodded, and Anna thought she saw genuine sadness there. "Moved in for good, anyway. You know, I saw him? After he, uh, turned or whatever. He didn't show up to meet me for, like, a week, so I went to his place. Three-room apartment, part of this old, creaky house. Sticky wood floors. I found him in the bedroom, hunched in the corner, bare-ass naked. Skinny, like gross skinny—ribs and vertebrae all sticking out. Looked like the fucking alien."

Anna fumbled for a reply to put in the pause, if only to keep Genevieve from drifting off into her head again. "Gross."

"No, the really gross thing was when he looked up. Beard all wet, dripping—I didn't know it was blood until

I saw the gutted rat corpse in his hands. He *grinned* at me. I will never forget it. Red teeth, shiny and dark. Goddamn horror show."

"Damn."

"Then he said, 'Genevieve.' Just that. One word, his voice with this . . . this crazed edge to it, like everything was just perfectly delightful and he hated every last bit of it. I can't even really describe it." A shiver ran up through her shoulders.

"What did you do?"

"I ran. What else? I don't even know if he got up to follow me. Went straight home, grabbed a few books and things, and abandoned my apartment." The corners of her mouth pulled down in revulsion. "Because, you know, He *recognized* me. Whatever he'd become, he still knew me."

There was a moment of hesitation before Genevieve continued. "I guess I was lucky, in a way. I mean, that that all ended and I moved on. Sobell's twice the teacher Hector was, and he's got access to more and better stuff. I've learned more in the last six months than in the four years before." She shook her head. "Bad for Hector, though. Fuck."

A question jumped to mind—the same one, from the same conversation, but Genevieve's mood had softened, and it felt natural to ask now. "If it's so dangerous, why keep doing it?" Genevieve cast a sharp glance at her, and she held up a hand. "I'm not accusing, really. I just want to understand."

Genevieve gave her a wry, weary smile. "Sometimes I wonder."

"Come on, I'm serious."

"All right. You remember the first time we went out? You said something like, 'Either I steal arcane crap from rich occult wannabes, or I work the Home Depot checkout counter the rest of my life.'"

"Did I say that?" Anna said, though she smiled. She remembered.

"Something like it. Aside from Karyn, and the money,

it's pretty simple: you like your work, and you're good at it. But come on—it's not so different from the occult thing. One bad mistake, you end up in jail or dead."

It sounded so stupid when Genevieve said it, the parallel so obvious Anna couldn't believe she hadn't seen it. She felt like a hypocrite. It simply felt good to do something she was good at, and that was all there was to it.

"I—" Genevieve began, but Anna cut her off.

"No, I get it. I totally get it. I'm sorry." She scooted across the floor, over next to Genevieve, and put her hand on Gen's knee, her head on her shoulder, both taking and giving what comfort she could.

"I don't know if a person really can be 'made for' something, but I feel like I was made for this," Genevieve said, gesturing at the pile of papers by her side.

"I told you, I get it," Anna said, nodding her head against Genevieve's shoulder. "I just . . . I've never had much, you know? And now—these days—I feel like I'm standing right on the edge of losing every little bit of it."

Genevieve put an arm around her and pulled her close. "It's going to be a while before you lose me. It's not today's problem, I promise."

Anna nodded without speaking. Her eyes burned and she didn't trust her voice.

"Hey," Genevieve said after a few moments, her voice deep and serious. "Sobell wants . . ."

The words trailed off, and the silence stretched out to where it seemed she'd never pick them up again. "Yeah?" Anna prompted.

"He wants me to learn this stuff," Genevieve said. The sudden gravity had dropped from her voice, and the pitch of her voice went up. Anna wondered whether that meant she was trying to downplay the significance of her words or if something else was going on there. "He says it's 'crucial for my development,' but all it's really doing is pissing me off. I need his help, you know?"

"I know."

"I really can't do this by myself."

Anna snuggled closer. "I know. I get it. Don't worry."

"I'm worried. I mean, this isn't a one-way street. He's not helping me for free." She glanced at Anna, and it seemed there was something wary in her eyes.

"What's he want?"

Genevieve shrugged. "Same stuff."

"That doesn't sound too hard."

"It's . . . it's like the other odd jobs. One day you're dropping money off, and the next thing you know, somehow kidnapping made its way onto the agenda. I'm worried this is just going to get worse and worse." Another one of those wary glances.

"It probably will." Anna laced her fingers through Genevieve's, then put her other hand over both her hand and Genevieve's and squeezed. She felt better, surprisingly. She wondered where her fear had hidden itself so suddenly, and who was supposed to be comforting whom here. "But I guess, you know . . . we'll get through it."

"I hope you're right. I just . . ." That distant look returned, giving Anna the strange feeling Genevieve wasn't talking to her at all, but some other audience. "I just want everything to work out for everybody. You, me, Nail. Even Sobell."

"Is it ever even possible for everybody to get everything they want?"

Genevieve closed her eyes and leaned against Anna. "God, I hope so."

Nail's phone rang. He checked the screen, swore under his breath, and flipped it open. "It's about fuckin' time," he said.

"Bro, that's no way to answer the phone."

Nail gave himself a slow count of five. Sometime between high school and the end of his time with the marines, his hero worship of his older brother had tarnished and finally undergone some alchemical transition to a sort of constant anxiety combined with an intense, angry impatience. It didn't take a trained psychologist to figure out what was going on there. Nail spent a huge portion of his time keeping DeWayne's ass out of various fires, which was enough reason in itself, but even that was only part of the story. DeWayne was a fuckup, and it drove Nail crazy. He'd been a smart kid, and somehow all his talents had been turned to stupid ends. The waste pissed Nail off for its own sake, and it came with a sense of betrayal to turn up the voltage. Just talking to DeWayne, with the endless deflections and evasions and rationalizations and just pure *bullshit*, was enough to draw a red veil over Nail's vision. The counting had become his coping mechanism, the only method he'd found to keep from losing his cool and saying something he'd regret. Sometimes it seemed the only way to keep from outright murdering DeWayne.

... *three* ... *four* ... *five.*

"You don't like the way I answer the phone, don't call me." *See? That could have been worse.*

"You left me, like, six messages," DeWayne said. "What was I supposed to do?"

"You were supposed to call my ass back after the first one, dickhead."

"I had some troubles. All under control now, but you know how it is." He cleared his throat. "I get the feeling you're not happy to hear from me."

"I get the feeling you about to hit me up for some cash. Dodgers game this Saturday, isn't there?"

"Is there? I don't know anything about that."

Nail let the obvious lie slide. Nowhere to go with that that wouldn't just make him madder. "You been to see Clarence lately?"

"Matter of fact, I have. Just saw him this evening, and holy *shit*, man. I thought I'd call you up and say thanks." He laughed. "Another week, and I'd be walkin' real funny, you know?"

"Yeah. A man'll walk real funny when he got no fuckin' legs."

"But, damn, man. I thought you were going to pay off the month, not the whole damn thing. The whole thing!

That's kid brother Hall of Fame material right there." He delivered that last line as though he was awfully proud of it. "I owe you one, bro. I really do."

Goddammit. It happened every time. Nail's buddies in the service had thought he was one of the hardest motherfuckers they'd ever met. Anna and Karyn trusted him with their lives and thought he was damn near indestructible—it was Karyn who'd given him the nickname Nail six years back when he got shot after pulling a job. Six bullets, no less, and Karyn had visited him in the hospital, calling him Doornail, as in "You should be dead as a." He *was* a hard motherfucker, and that wasn't bragging—that was just fact. And still, every time DeWayne pulled this "Aw, man, you're the best" bullshit, he'd be damned if he didn't feel something loosen up in his heart, maybe a little softness around the eyes.

Fuckin' family, man.

"Yeah, you do," he said, but without any venom. Once again, his big brother had managed to pull his fangs.

"So, uh, spot me five Gs for the ball game?"

"I don't—"

"Just messing with you, bro."

"You're square with Clarence, right? He didn't give you a hard time?"

"Yeah. Squared up. He didn't look too happy about it, but he said we're square."

"All right." It was better than all right, actually. Clarence had followed through. That was the best news Nail had gotten since who the fuck knew when.

"Hey, so I do have something you might wanna know about."

The anxiety, loosened by the good news, clamped down again. "Yeah?"

"Yeah. I didn't even make it a block down the street from Clarence's before I got picked up by the feds."

"What? Feds?" A shiver of alarm went up Nail's back. "What are you into?"

"That's the thing, bro. Wasn't me they wanted to know

about. They showed me some wack-ass video and asked me what I knew about that."

"What video?"

"Three chicks and some skeevy white dude, hanging out in a parking garage. It got all weird, though, all these bugs and shit flyin' everywhere—like that crazy shit from earlier. Anyway, I saw your friend in the vid."

Oh, shit. "Anna."

"Yeah. They wanted to know if I knew any of those people, and how, and if *you* know any of them, and how, and all this other shit."

"What did you tell them?"

"Told 'em I never seen any of those people before in my short, beautiful life."

"You lied to them?"

"Hell yeah, I did. I don't even know what their angle is, but fuck those guys. I about shit myself when they took me in, you know?"

Nail had to concede that, although lying to the feds was not normally a great idea, this time it was probably the right approach. It'd keep DeWayne out of shit he had no business being in and deflect a little heat from Nail and the crew for a little while, too. He felt a surprising bit of gratitude. "What else they ask about?"

"Wanted to know if I knew where to find you. Told 'em the truth there, sort of. I mean, that I haven't actually seen you in two years."

"Good."

"Don't thank me or nothing, bro. All part of being family."

Nail let the silence spin out while he counted to five. Then: "Thanks, DeWayne. Do me a favor and keep your head down, huh?"

"Don't have to tell me twice. Keep it cool, bro."

"Yeah. Later."

He hung up the phone, thinking of the handful of times he thought he'd been followed over the last week or so. Maybe some of that had been paranoia, but no way all of it was. Not now.

Feds. Not good.

"He's dying," Van Horn said as Anna sat down across from him. An abrupt conversation starter, and a hell of a jolt in her current frame of mind. In the new calm after she and Gen had talked, the talking had turned into kissing, the kissing into urgent, sound-stifled sex, and the afterglow into— well, back into insomnia, but an insomnia several degrees more pleasant than the one before. Gen had gone back to her studies, and Anna had decided it was time to check on Van Horn.

He looked pathetic, and for the fifth time, Anna wondered if they could take him to a motel somewhere, get him a shower, find him a hot meal. That wasn't the kind of thing you were supposed to think about the people you kidnapped, was it? It was like some kind of upside-down Stockholm syndrome.

"Yeah. Right. Dying," she said, sure that no such thing was possible. During that last big job, Sobell had been shot in the head at point-blank range, and he'd survived. Somehow the bullet had merely grazed his skull, plowing a gruesome furrow in his scalp, and she didn't think luck had anything to do with that. "If he's dying, he's got a funny way of showing it."

"No, he is. Did you see the way his hands shook? His skin, it's become papery and translucent, like he's had one too many face-lifts."

"We don't exactly go way back, so I don't have a 'before' picture."

"He's nervous."

"I'd be nervous, too, if I had six million cops crawling up my ass."

Van Horn shook his head. "Cops don't scare Enoch Sobell. He's dying. He's running out of time. That business with the locusts was pure desperation."

"Maybe you're right." God, if he'd just drop dead—what a load off her mind! "So?"

"Just . . . don't give me up to him. Please? Maybe you can wait him out."

Sure. No problem. When he calls, I'll just tell him you're out right now, and can he please call back later? "Yeah, well. We'll see how it goes." They sat in silence, the only light from Anna's flashlight, while she mulled Van Horn's words over and he awkwardly picked at his fingernails.

"Dying, huh?" she said after a while.

Van Horn nodded. "He's too old to keep living naturally, and he's too burned down to keep using magic to extend his life."

"Then what's he desperate for? What's with this tooth he needs so badly?"

Van Horn made a peculiar face. In the low light from the flashlight, she thought it looked like a cruel, cynical sort of grin, odd on the old man's soft face, but then it was gone.

"What indeed?" he asked.

Chapter 12

The beginning of a regular job was as comfortable as sliding into your own bed after a month in cheap motels, Anna thought. No kidnapping or any of the other shit Sobell had had them working—just a new place, like a present waiting to be unwrapped. *This* she understood, and she was good at it. She wished Karyn were with her, ready to drop a warning about any bad shit about to go down. It felt weird to do this without her, like it was her bed but somebody'd turned the mattress while she was gone, and it was ever so slightly unfamiliar.

It had taken less than three hours to get the basic 411 on Mona Gorow, and another thirty minutes to drive to the woman's street in Beverly Hills. Nail drove slowly down the street as Anna watched the neighborhood. It was, well, Beverly Hills. Nice lawns, carefully cultivated palm trees, old houses.

"They're gonna arrest us just for driving around here," Anna said, only sort of joking.

Nail nodded. "Yep. Be lucky if I don't get life."

"They'll fucking *deport* me."

Nail chuckled, but Anna couldn't even laugh at her own joke. *When did I get so anxious?* she wondered.

There wasn't much going on out here this afternoon. That seemed like a good thing at first, until the lack of other traffic made her feel conspicuous. She looked around, counting. She could see eleven houses from here, before the street curved and dipped down a little hill ahead. This wasn't like the Mendelsohn job, where he'd lived out in the middle of nowhere and all they'd had to do was show up. These houses were in the lower-rent section of the Hills, where the houses were huge but basically jammed together on lots barely bigger than the buildings. Mona Gorow had neighbors. Lots of them. This didn't look like the friendliest neighborhood right now, but nobody was home, so who knew? Maybe they all barbecued together on weekends. Maybe some hedge fund motherfucker who worked from home was looking out the window at them right now, taking down the license plate number.

Except . . . now that she noticed, there were a *lot* of For Sale signs up. Century 21 had claimed the yard just ahead and to her right, Re/Max the one next door and the one directly across the street. Of the eleven houses Anna could see, six of them were for sale. That was weird.

They crossed Ash Lane, took a rather sharp turn, and it was as though a switch had been thrown. Same neighborhood, just a different block, but it might as well have been on Mars for all the resemblance it bore to the last block.

"What the hell . . . ?" Nail asked.

Anna just nodded. It was cold here, for starters, easily ten degrees cooler than it had been just across the street, but that was the *least* noticeable difference. "Street sweepers didn't come," she said.

"Huh? Oh. Yeah. That, too."

"That, *too*?" The ground was covered with the bodies of dead locusts, piled over the sidewalks, strewn over the streets, filling the yards. Maybe it was just that the street sweepers hadn't got here yet—it was only the next day—but that seemed unlikely here, of all places. Moreover, there were no traces on the even carpet of locusts in the street. No cars had been through here since yesterday's locust Armageddon. Not a single one, it looked like.

"I mean . . . it feels nasty," Nail said.

She turned to look at him. The backs of his arms had bunched up in stripes of gooseflesh, and he was slowly shaking his head no.

"You okay?" she asked.

"Think I might be sick." He swallowed a couple of times and frowned.

"Sure you don't want me to drive?"

He stopped the car. A trickle of sweat wended its way down behind his ear, down into the collar of his shirt. His throat convulsed again, another thick swallow.

Anna looked around. Nothing jumped out as the source of Nail's anxiety, but she kind of got what he was feeling—a kind of metaphysical shove, a sense that she needed to be somewhere else. It was uncomfortable in the way that walking in on something very personal was, an internal sense that she had intruded rather than a sense of some external opprobrium.

I never feel like this, she realized. How many places had she broken into? How many bedrooms and bathrooms and private areas, without once feeling that she was invading somewhere she didn't belong?

"I'm good," Nail said. "I'm good."

"Drive."

There had been no vehicular traffic through the area, and the For Sale signs were up in force, but the area wasn't quite abandoned, Anna noticed. Somebody's porch light was on, and she saw a blond kid peek out through a big picture window before his mother pulled him away and yanked the curtain shut.

"Who would stay here?" she asked.

Nail didn't answer.

"There's the place," Nail said, pointing to a sprawling house ahead on the right.

"Keep rolling."

"I don't even know how we're gonna do basic recon on this," Anna said.

"Wanna try the old California Gas and Electric, or

should I go with Time Warner Cable?" Nail asked. "Pretty sure Tony's still got the van."

"Here? That'll stick out worse than if we camp on the lawn."

"Got any other ideas?"

Anna didn't answer. She was focused on trying to watch the house as they went by without looking like she was watching the house. She didn't see much. There was a blue-and-white sign, little more than a blur in her peripheral vision, that was almost certainly an ADT sign. No surprise there. Two-story house, oversize for the lot, maybe five thousand square feet. Every window curtained, every curtain closed. The neighboring houses crowded close, with too damn many windows on the adjacent sides. From here, the only promising thing was the cedar fence around the backyard. If it was fully enclosed, that would provide at least some protection from prying eyes once they got in.

What prying eyes? You're thinking about this wrong.

"Go around the block," Anna said. "I want to get a look at the alley."

Nail turned right four houses down from the Gorow place and rolled slowly down the side street. The alley behind the row of houses was a nearly straight shot, affording a clear view of the backs of the houses. Anna managed a little smile when she saw that the board fence continued around back.

"Let me out," she said.

"It's the middle of the day in the Land of a Million White People. You really want to go sneaking around back there?"

"Yeah. Park at the end of the block, and I'll meet you in five."

"Your call," he said.

She got out of the car, and Nail pulled away.

Several of the houses in this row had similar board fences, but most had fences built of metal bars. *Like cemeteries,* Anna thought. Inconvenient for her because anybody could see right through them. Presumably that was part of the point.

Given how dead the neighborhood was at this time of day, it seemed low-risk to take a quick walk through the alley. She put on a ball cap but otherwise walked with her head up as if she belonged there. If anybody saw her, hopefully they wouldn't think much of it.

She hadn't got fifteen feet into the alley when she started to get a real good idea of why the people who lived on this street were clearing out. There was something badly wrong here. No single thing was *that* bad, but lots of small details were just . . . off. At the first house she passed, the lawn sprinklers were running, and never mind that city ordinance forbade it at this hour, or that the grass in the entire backyard was a sun-bleached brown. Somewhere a bird sang two alternating notes, over and over again. It had decided on the two most dissonant notes Anna could imagine, notes that not only didn't belong together in any normal birdsong, but sounded out of tune and wavery besides, almost like a theremin or one of those weird singing saws. The second yard was fenced in, so Anna saw nothing of note there, but she froze, poised to run when she looked into the third and saw a body floating facedown in the swimming pool.

She kept herself from bolting just long enough for her brain to decipher what she was seeing. It wasn't a body at all, just a puffy jacket, arms stretched out to the side. *Shouldn't that have sunk by now?* Maybe it had air trapped under it. Or something.

The moment of panic passed, but her heart didn't slow as she walked by the fourth house and approached the open gate. The concrete of the alley was stained here in a series of staggered, elongated ovals. It took no imagination whatsoever to believe they were a set of bloody footprints. Going *to* the Gorow house.

Why am I not carrying? Anna wondered suddenly. The answer was obvious—the same reason she usually didn't carry a gun. Get pulled over and searched, and having a gun on you will make your day go from bad to worse in just as long as it takes the cop to yell for his partner and cuff you. Now she wondered if she should have made an exception this time.

She approached the gate, half convinced she needed to turn around and hoof it back to her ride already, right now, before *something* happened. The bright daylight now seemed like it was on her side rather than a liability, yet it was a poor sort of defense. Now maybe somebody could be a witness to her upcoming homicide. Not much consolation there, and it didn't ease her nerves any.

About ten feet back from the gate, she stopped. There was no denying now that the red marks on the pavement were bloody footprints. Dried blood, but heavier here and now accompanied by little round dried spatters. She couldn't help it—she thought of Tommy, of trying to hold his guts in while he hyperventilated, and it was easy to picture some poor bastard, hand in his jacket, the blood flow getting worse as he tore the wound open with every step and got too weak to keep pressure on the wound.

She shook her head. Where had that come from?

The footprints went inside, but Anna wasn't about to follow them. She hung back, inspecting the gate. Its top hinge had torn loose from the cedar post. The screws still hung loosely from a couple of the holes in the hinge. There was something unsettling about a door hanging in that way. It spoke of destruction and neglect, like a house with a smashed window nobody had bothered to board up.

There were marks in the gate, she realized. On the inside-facing surface. A series of them, seven or eight sets of four parallel scratches. Deep scratches, with splinters jutting from their sides. The wood in the scratches was still a lighter color than the rest, so they hadn't been there long enough for the sun to age them. Dark spots, undoubtedly more bloodstains, flecked the wood in some spots, stained it heavily in others.

They weren't from a dog. Too high, the individual

marks in each set too far apart. It was impossible not to imagine a person clawing at the door in some frenzied desperation, fingers bleeding, a little at first, spots and specks, and then more and more as the pads tore away. In Anna's mind's eye, she saw yellow-white bone protruding from the ends of a crazed man's fingers, and he still kept clawing, mad to get away from— from what?

She didn't want to be here, not this close, not until they'd watched the place a little while. She traced her steps back out of the alley. It was all she could do not to run.

Chapter 13

Sheila followed the gray thing through the night, down badly lit back streets and through sullen, stinking alleys, and the Chosen followed her. Sheila went first, nearest the thing. The others kept a healthy distance, fifteen feet back or so. The gray thing barely tolerated her, and it seemed to get agitated when too many of the others got close. They remained fascinated with the thing, but Sheila had ordered them back.

A single car turned onto the desolate side street down which they walked, yellow streetlights tracing its contours. Sheila ducked into a doorway. Behind her, the Chosen made themselves small in the mouth of an alley. Weak hiding places, and even the need to hide disgusted Sheila, filled her with the urge to tear flesh—but she felt it necessary. Sheila had been worried at first about the gray thing provoking some kind of response, like somebody calling the cops on them (*to report what, exactly?* she wondered), but it hadn't happened yet. It seemed people had an aversion to the gray thing. Drivers hit the gas, punks hanging out on stoops went inside, and the occasional person walking the street crossed to the other side and turned at the next opportunity. Did they remember it? Did they even see it at all?

The hiding wasn't for the gray thing's benefit—it was pure paranoia, a burgeoning fear even stronger than her rage and her hunger. The gray thing didn't seem to care who observed it, but Sheila didn't have that luxury. Every corner was a hiding place for enemies of the Chosen, every window a vantage point from which those enemies could gaze down upon them, every building a shelter in which they could lurk and wait for the opportunity to attack.

It was funny. When Van Horn had been in charge, Sheila didn't worry about this stuff. That had been the old man's job. She'd been vaguely aware that they had enemies, and there had been a couple of fights, even, but she hadn't wanted to focus on that. Van Horn's problem.

Then Van Horn had been taken, and the problem had fallen to her. Denial vanished as an option. She didn't care about the other Chosen, as such, but she recognized the safety in numbers, and it was clear they were being hunted.

Another reason to find Van Horn.

The car slowed as it approached the group and then, like all the others, abruptly sped off. The gray thing slid to the end of the block, then into the intersection. *Jaywalking,* Sheila thought, and a bubble of laughter escaped her. She walked faster, not wanting to let the thing get too far ahead.

"I could take a turn," Rain said, approaching from behind.

Sheila jerked her head around. "What?"

"Your fingers," Rain said. She pointed at Sheila's left hand, where three fingers were gone, one for each time she'd called the gray thing. The stumps sang a constant refrain of pain. It had become an exciting sort of background noise. "There's only so many of them. I could call the . . ." She tipped her head toward the gray thing. "That. Next time."

Sheila cast a sharp look at Rain, looking for signs of treachery, but Rain's face was guileless as ever. "It's mine," Sheila said.

"Okay."

Kind of silly for her to assert ownership over the thing, but that was how she felt. Sometimes she even thought of the thing as a dog, because that was its function in some sense. It snuffled around until it picked up the trail, and it brought her a little closer to her quarry each time. Other times, she thought of it as a sort of giant slug, because it looked like one.

"I would have named it, once," Sheila said.

"Like 'Fido'?"

"No. Its species. If you discover it, you get to name it."

"Does it even *have* a species?"

"I don't know. I'd sort of like to find out." Rain was looking at her as if she'd gone right off the deep end, but instead of feeling angry, as she did so often these days, she smiled. "I used to be an entomologist. Professor, actually." That part of her, though muted, still found the gray thing endlessly fascinating. Not long ago, she would have liked nothing better than to study it, watch it eat, sleep, and reproduce, and eventually dissect it. Another part of her found it utterly repulsive. Not because it was like a slug—she quite liked slugs and was fond of pulmonates in general—but because it wasn't, exactly. It was nearly featureless, with no eyestalks, no eyes, and no mantle. Moreover, its slime trail stank of rot, and ragged white chunks hung suspended in it, looking like nothing so much as bleached, waterlogged hunks of flesh.

And there was the fact that it quite clearly understood human speech. It followed commands, and despite its having no features, Sheila got the very clear impression it followed them because it wanted to, not because it had to. That was mildly upsetting, when she thought about it. What if it changed its mind?

All things considered, she would just as soon have left it alone to sleep and feed in whatever unthinkable place it called home, but each night the trail went cold. They'd go as far as they could, then fan out, looking for more clues, and find nothing. Then she'd call it back.

"I used to have a garden," Rain said. "I probably liked slugs a lot less than you did."

"Do. We're not dead."

"My dad used to kill slugs. Leave beer out for them. They'd find it and drown."

"He'd have a harder time with this one."

"You think we'll find him? Van Horn, I mean."

Sheila fought down a flash of annoyance. "I wouldn't be doing this otherwise. You might have noticed, it takes a hell of a toll." It did, didn't it? It must. She looked at the stumps of her fingers again. The blood was exciting, even dried, but she thought she should be more concerned about the gross violation of her person.

"I can wrap those, if we can find some gauze. Or even clean rags."

"What?"

"Your injuries. I can wrap them. I used to be a nurse."

"I thought you used to be a gardener."

"I used to *have* a garden, I used to *be* a nurse. Among other things."

That was what you did, didn't you? Wrap wounds? Cover them? Intellectually, Sheila understood that, but emotionally, it was . . . uninteresting.

"They'll get infected if we don't do something about it," Rain said.

Sheila shrugged. "If it makes you feel better."

Rain pulled a mostly clean T-shirt from her bag and began tearing it into strips.

"Give me your hand," Rain said.

The gray thing turned, slithering down a trash-strewn alley, and Sheila followed it in. "Not now," she said to Rain.

"This will just take a minute. We'll catch up."

It was more out of some misplaced sense that she *should* bandage the wounds than any desire to do so that Sheila stopped.

"Quickly," she said. She put out her left hand. Only the index finger and thumb remained, and the stumps of the other fingers were an angry red. Rain stared at them, swallowed, and bit her lower lip. Sheila heard her stomach rumble.

"Rain . . ."

"You should have some antiseptic," Rain said, but she hurried to cover the wounds, her eyes flashing guiltily to Sheila's. The first pass was too tight, sending a bolt of pain up Sheila's arm. Again, there was that intense double sensation—insane, electric pain, combined with a near-orgasmic rush of pleasure. She shuddered.

As Rain worked, the others edged by them, single file through the alley, following the gray thing. Sheila looked after them. She hoped none of them would do anything stupid.

"Maybe antibiotics, too," Rain added. She finished winding the bandages around and rummaged in her purse. She came up with a handful of oversize bobby pins, which she used to secure the bandages in place.

"I'll be fine. It looks good," Sheila said. "You really were a nurse, huh?"

Rain nodded.

"I had tenure," Sheila said. "It was really important to me. I can't remember why."

"I can't remember lots of things. No, that's not really true. I can remember most things. I can't remember feelings. Sometimes I wish they'd warned me about that, but mostly I don't care." She rubbed her arms. "I was going to be a healer. That's what he told me."

"Mendelsohn?"

"Belial."

"And you believed him?"

"You must have believed him, too."

"No. It was Mendelsohn who got to me. Nate. We met at a fund-raiser, if you can believe that. I drank too much, and next thing I knew, it was four in the morning and he was showing me the most amazing things. Creatures I'd never seen before. I was going to be famous. Discover a hundred new species."

"Did you?"

"I lost interest. Other things seem more important now." Like her constant hunger, and the constant need for stimulus. Even now, she felt an urge to jam the stumps of her ruined fingers into the wall. Not a strong urge, not enough to actually do it, but it was there, nagging at her.

A droplet of blood trickled from the corner of Rain's eye. She wiped it away with the back of her hand and stared at the dark smear.

"We'll find Belial," Sheila said, and she put her arm around the other woman. "We'll find him, and he'll make it right."

"I don't—"

A shriek of car tires came from ahead, followed by a shout and the report of a gun. Sheila broke into a run, the syllables of a chant already forming in her mind, flowing out through her throat and lips.

She burst from the mouth of the alley, skidding on grime from a ruptured trash bag. Before her, the Chosen had been scattered. A silver car, the same one she'd seen earlier and dismissed, had screamed to a stop, cocked in the street with black arcs of smoking rubber laid down behind it, and the Chosen lay to the left and the right. Raul clutched a bleeding arm, and Deanna sprawled in the gutter to the right of the car, and to the left, Maurice and Antawn scrambled over each other to get up from where they'd fallen. Between them and the car, Don, the former banker who'd fallen in with the Chosen, sat on the curb wearing a look of stupid surprise.

The back doors of the car were open, the stunted wings of an insect that evolution had rendered flightless, and a man sprang out from each side.

Don lurched to a standing position, his right foot flopping on the end of his ankle, just as one of the men from the car reached him.

Sheila recognized the man. Not one of those who'd taken Van Horn, but another, from the group that had shot at them outside the run-down dance club over a week ago.

Rain rushed forward. The driver, a woman, fired her gun through the open passenger-side window. Some vestige of survival of instinct dropped Rain to a crouch, and she covered her head.

Sheila's voice rose as the chant took hold of her. One of the men, the one who'd grabbed Don, looked up with big, frightened eyes. He was young, Sheila now noticed. A college kid, maybe, not too dissimilar from the grad students she'd taught. He probably didn't need to shave more than once a week.

The last words of the incantation fell from Sheila's lips.

With a deafening scream, a gale wind tore through the alley behind her. It swept up dirt, fragments of pavement, paper cups, aluminum cans, even a trash can. It shredded the trash bag and pulled its contents out, then blasted forward, dividing into two as it swept around Sheila, leaving her untouched. Her hair didn't even ruffle.

Debris pelted the car. One of the back doors swung violently, clipping the man who was fighting Don in the chin. He swore and shoved it away. Don gave him a feeble, ineffectual swat.

The other man braced himself against the wind, put his head down, and walked into the gale, presumably coming around to help his friend. A rock blew through the car's back window, spraying pebbles of glass across his face.

Beyond the fray, the gray thing turned. Despite its featurelessness, Sheila got a clear vibe off it: it was annoyed. It turned, unseen, and began to slide back across the street toward her.

The second guy reached Don and helped heave him toward the backseat of the car. More kidnappers? Why didn't they just kill him?

Ten or fifteen feet behind the men, the gray thing reared up, exposing a mouth that gaped along almost the whole length of its underside, ringed with fleshy tendrils. Sheila stared. It no longer resembled a slug so much as some kind of hellish Venus flytrap. More tendrils shot out of the mouth, long ones, that slashed through the air and grabbed the second guy's head, arm, throat. His scream was cut short as the tendrils wrapped his face and jaw and he was yanked backward. He slipped, fell, and was pulled headfirst toward the monster.

Through some superhuman effort, the other guy had managed to grab Don in an unwieldy bear hug and throw both himself and Don in the back of the car.

The driver looked back out the destroyed rear window at the gray thing, shouted, and floored the accelerator.

The car sped off just as the gray thing stuffed its captive inside itself. Sheila watched with something like her old avid interest as the gray thing flopped back down to the pavement, hiding its mouth again. The muffled screams from within its body went on for almost a minute, presumably about the time its dinner ran out of air.

Slowly, the Chosen got their bearings again and picked themselves up from the pavement.

"Are you all right?" Sheila asked Rain, vaguely surprised to find she sort of cared about the answer.

Rain nodded and stood.

The gray thing rippled along its length, and a hideous crunching and crackling sound came from inside it. Sheila hadn't seen any teeth in that yawning hole, but perhaps they were retractable. Or maybe it just squeezed very hard. The thought made Sheila feel sick to her stomach, but it gave her a thrill at the same time, one that shot through the center of her body and made her shudder with joy.

Rain surveyed the remaining Chosen, then met Sheila's eyes. There was fear, however muted, written in the wrinkles in her brow and the set of her mouth.

"Only seven left," Rain said.

Chapter 14

"This place is fucking wrong," Genevieve said.

Anna nodded. "This whole street is fucking wrong." She was standing at the second-floor window of a house two lots down and across the street from the Gorow place, looking out through the sheer curtain. It was only about nine at night, but the street below was abnormally dark. Most of the streetlights were dead gray spheres, and lights illuminated only a handful of windows down the entire street. It might be thought a neighborhood with an unusually early bedtime, if so many of the houses hadn't been abandoned.

After her and Nail's initial concerns about the difficulties inherent in performing recon on one of the only occupied houses on the street, they'd hit on a great solution—steal a house. The mass abandonment actually made the surveillance job easier than it would have been otherwise. The house they were in now was empty of occupants, staged with inoffensive furniture by the real estate agent who, if Anna was any judge of these things, would be waiting a long, long time for her commission. This room looked like a kid's bedroom, painted in a cheery blue that had faded to dull gray with the waning of the day, and equipped with an immaculately made-up single bed. A framed poster of a cartoon rocket hung on the wall, which looked like an act of anachronistic desperation. *See? This is a great room for children! Please, please, please buy this house!* Were kids even into that stuff these days?

Anna and Genevieve had broken into the place hours ago, right in broad daylight. The security system was either broken or off, and it had taken Anna all of six seconds to jimmy the lock on the back door. To anybody watching, it might not have been obvious that she wasn't using a key. Not that anybody was watching. Even without the For Sale signs, you could tell the empty houses on the street because they were the ones with their curtains open. Any house with people still living in it had the curtains shut tight, probably because the occupants didn't want to look out at the street.

Nonetheless, that was what Anna was here for, so she sat in the darkness with Genevieve, watching. It wasn't just the empty houses, dead lawns, and overall air of desolation that was wrong with this nice neighborhood. The rhythms were all off, too. People got up at weird times, wandered out of their houses, and went back in. One guy had started mowing his dead-as-shit lawn fifteen minutes ago in the dark, churning up the bodies of dead locusts. He went at it for about ten minutes, then left the riding mower in the middle of the lawn, still running, and went inside. Hadn't come back out yet.

Also, the squirrels were out at night. She'd only seen one at first, standing under one of the few functioning streetlights, nibbling at something in its paws. She hadn't immediately registered anything explicitly wrong with that, but it gave her this undefined sense of unease. Then she realized she'd never once seen a squirrel by streetlight. Not ever. Now that she looked around, she could see a dozen of them from here, dark spots moving erratically across the street or up the sidewalk.

The whole scene reminded her of a painting she'd seen one time in school. She couldn't remember the artist's name, but the name of the painting had stuck with her. *The Empire of Lights*, she was pretty sure. A normal house on a dark street, the porch light on, all of it painted in immaculate detail. You could imagine yourself on that street, maybe coming home after a late night partying or something. Yet the sky was bright blue, daytime sky, complete with puffy white clouds. It had given her nightmares.

"Anything in your stash of secret dark knowledge to account for this?" Anna asked.

"No, but it's not a very big stash. At a guess, I'd say it's probably safe to assume that the source of all evil is on this street."

"In that house," Anna said. "Unless there's another house on this street with some terrible occult shit in it."

"Yeah."

"Probably it's the thing Sobell wants us to steal. That's how this kind of thing works, isn't it?"

Genevieve turned her face away. "I don't really know."

She'd been preoccupied ever since meeting Sobell, and more so since catching up with Tran earlier that day. Supposed to get any new info, more occult junk from Sobell, and she'd returned hangdog and bleary. Jumpy, too. It wasn't like her. "This job bothering you? Like, more than the kidnapping one?" Anna immediately wished she hadn't added that last.

"Hey, come on. I wasn't happy about the kidnapping thing, either. I told you that."

"I know. I'm sorry." She wasn't quite sure that was true, but she left it at that. "Seriously, though. You seem . . . nervous."

Genevieve turned and gave her a deadpan stare. "We're breaking and entering on a street that looks like, I dunno. Fucking Roanoke or something. Why wouldn't I be nervous?"

"This stuff doesn't usually bother you."

"Well, it bothers me today." She sat on the bed, mussing up the picture-perfect setting. "We just going to squat in this house until the time comes? What if they come back to show it?"

"Yeah, because what nice couple with a ten-year-old

wouldn't fall in love with this neighborhood, right? Relax, huh? Nobody's coming." She put a hand on Genevieve's shoulder, but it felt perfunctory even to her. She supposed that Genevieve wasn't the only one who was preoccupied these days.

Genevieve made a noncommittal noise that sounded vaguely like agreement, covered Anna's hand for half a second with her own, then lapsed into silence.

Anna said nothing. This place bugged her, too, but it wasn't that bad. If she was on edge, it was because of every other damn thing. Karyn was getting worse instead of better, and the only lead she had on that was a certifiable nutcase. She still wasn't sleeping, still enjoying dreams of the final showdown after the Mendelsohn job interwoven with Tommy's bloody end. Oh, and they had some dude kidnapped and stashed in a condemned building. It was too much.

She'd stay here until morning, trade up with Nail back at the school, then do another eight hours of combined guard/babysitting duty. Then, when Genevieve got back and spelled her, it would be time to hit up a couple of contacts she knew. No point in putting all her eggs in Guy's weird basket, especially now that two-thirds of every day was accounted for with shit she absolutely had to do. Any progress on Karyn's situation would be paid for with lost sleep, hour for hour. She supposed that was the upside of not sleeping worth a damn anymore.

Genevieve put her boots up on the bedspread and watched out the window. Anna sat closer to the window, in a chair she'd appropriated from the downstairs dining room. They waited, watching.

Time passed. Thirty minutes, an hour. Anna zoned out in front of the window, half-hypnotized by the still scene. When the movement across the way finally registered, she wondered how long she'd been seeing it.

"Check it out!" she said, turning to Genevieve.

Gen looked up suddenly, and Anna got the strong

sense that she hadn't been paying attention at all. She hid something in her palm, quickly, but not so fast Anna didn't see it.

"What's that?" Anna asked.

Genevieve opened her hand real quick. A small, round object, like a tiny, striped brown button rested in her palm. "Just a . . ." She shrugged. It looked about as casual as a kid caught shoplifting porn. "Magic stuff."

Whatever.

"Look," Anna said, pointing out the window.

There was a car rolling along the back alley with its lights off. She saw it for just a few seconds as it moved into the open space between one house's fence and the next house. Details were impossible to make out from here—all she could tell was that it was a sedan, not a truck, creeping along the alley. Then it was gone, behind the house.

"Is somebody already on this job?" Genevieve whispered.

Anna thought back to the bloody footprints she'd seen the day before. "No," she said. "I don't think so." Coming for help, maybe?

On the other side of the house, there was only a thin sliver of alley visible between the house and the fence around the Gorow place. The vehicle rolled quickly through it, then was gone.

"Keep watching," Anna said. "I'm gonna go check it out."

"Wait—" Genevieve began, but Anna was already in the hall. She descended the stairs three at a time and dashed out the back door a few moments later. She took the alley on this side of the street, past two houses, then three, then four. A raccoon hissed at her from a toppled trash can, and she thought that goddamn dissonant bird from earlier shrieked a two-tone warning, but she kept going. At the end of the street, where Ash cut over, she stopped.

She checked down the street. To her right, across Ash, the streetlights were humming and even now lights shone from windows and the flickering blue glare of television played on shutters. To her left, the dead zone. From here it was even more striking, and the handful of lights, rather than sticking out even more clearly against the darkness, seemed muted and somehow stifled.

There was nobody in the street, though. She crossed and headed to the alley. The house on the end of the street was another fenced-in deal, so she crept around and stopped at the edge.

She peered around the corner. It was impossible to see anything from here, with the trees hanging down and the trash cans in the way.

Screw it, she thought, and she slipped into the alley. One house down, then two. She looked from her peripheral vision. Nothing seemed to be moving down there.

She started again, past another house and another couple of trash cans. Car doors opened, then slammed. Then a voice cried out, "I'll kill you!"

She ducked down. She was two houses away now, pressed against a chain-link fence that must have been grandfathered in against the wishes of the neighborhood homeowners' association. She made it to the edge of another board fence and peeked around.

"You're dead!" the voice shouted again.

There were three people. A blond woman and a white guy in a suit shoved a third along. A smear of dash light splashed across the third guy's face, and Anna's breath caught. It was the lawyer guy, the one who'd almost bought it by pissing off Van Horn and the entourage several nights ago. He was wild-eyed and furious, swearing and spitting, but for one terrible second she thought his eyes locked on hers. Then the woman shoved him, hard, and he stumbled and smashed into the fence.

Anna pressed back against the fence, willing herself not to hyperventilate. *What the hell?*

The sound of hinges creaking. More shouting. Then the gate slamming shut.

There were more fading sounds of struggle, and then another door, and the house swallowed the whole mess.

Chapter 15

It took a moment for Anna's eyes to adjust to the inside of the building, and it took another full minute to find Guy in the sea of sport coats and blazers. The place was a trendy café downtown, a seething sea of lawyers and private equity douche bags splattered in the middle of a collection of bullshit contemporary abstract art in what she guessed were supposed to be soothing earth tones. She and Karyn had had a fair amount of upscale clients—most of them, actually—but this kind of place always put her back up. It was all she could do not to bare her teeth as she picked her way between the tables toward Guy.

"What is this shit?" Anna asked. She hauled a chair out from the table and sat. Guy had replaced his jacket, she saw.

"We met where you wanted last time. I'm more comfortable here."

"You serious? We're way outclassed by the criminals in this place. At least you know where you stand with the Mongols."

Guy smiled neutrally. "The clientele here is less likely to push my face in."

"What is it you want?"

Guy glanced to the tables on each side. He didn't have anything to worry about, Anna thought. The nearest tables weren't all that close, and anyway, the occupants were busy. The ones on the left were deeply engrossed in a conversation that prominently featured words like "leveraged," and the ones on the right were loudly comparing sexual conquests.

"You had a vision," he said, smooth cheeks pushed up in a smug smile.

"I didn't have shit. But if you've got more of those little sticks, we have something to talk about."

"But . . . *He* spoke to you?"

Didn't take much to figure out what "He" Guy was referring to, and Anna thought back to the one-sided conversation she'd listened to when Karyn was holding the toothpick. Something had spoken to Karyn, but Anna had her doubts about whether it was the Lord. God might have triggered some of those looks of fear, but outright revulsion seemed a little less Godly, at least as far as Anna was concerned. She wished Guy were a little more . . . stable. It would have been nice to get an unbiased take on all this. As it was, though, she thought it best to tread lightly. "Not to me. To a friend."

"Oh."

"So, what do you want?"

"I told you, I need you to bring the woman in the picture and meet someone with me."

"Not gonna happen. You get me, or nothing."

"I don't know . . ."

His hands twisted together as he spoke, and he kept chewing at his bottom lip. At first she'd thought it was nerves. Some of her clients were like that. They'd never done anything illegal before, but they wanted something so bad that it pushed them over the moral hurdle. They still felt uncomfortable about it. The more she watched him, though, she didn't think this was that kind of anxiety. He wasn't looking up every time the door opened, and after the initial glance around, he'd totally forgotten about the people around them. This was more like junkie anxiety. Need-a-fix anxiety.

"You don't actually have any more of those little sticks, do you?" she asked.

She saw denial flash across his face—tightened brow, open angry mouth—and then it was gone and he slumped, deflated. "No. Mona has the reliquary."

All at once, the background noise faded to nothing, and Guy stood out in sharp relief against the crowd. "Did you say Mona? Mona who?"

"Mona. Just Mona. I—I don't actually know her last name. I mean, if she even has one. I guess she does."

"I'll be right back," Anna said, pushing back from the table.

"Wait! Where—"

"Bathroom." She stood. The bathrooms were in back, which was perfect. She brushed past a few tables full of excited yuppies and went into the ladies' room. She busied herself washing her hands while she thought. This might be a setup. Some kind of loyalty test from Sobell? That didn't seem too likely. Surely they'd proven their loyalty by now, and anyway, Guy was nobody's idea of the kind of smooth operator you'd want to draw somebody out. This wasn't coincidence, though. L.A. was just too goddamn big for a coincidence like that. She thought of the lawyer guy being disappeared into Mona's backyard. Did that mean they were on the same side? Or was this too fucked-up to worry about things like sides?

She dried her hands on her pants and went out. From the back, she could see the whole room, and she scanned the faces as she walked. Nobody familiar, nobody paying her any attention aside from the occasional brief glance, nobody hiding conspicuously behind a newspaper or any bullshit like that. If this was a setup, it appeared that Guy was the only one in on it.

"Mona," she said as she sat. "Everything you know, right now."

"She speaks to God," Guy said, his voice edging up past plaintive into whiny.

"Then what the hell do you need us for?"

His face was bland as he studied her. Coming up with a lie, or deciding whether to tell the truth?

"We're at war, you know. The real deal—good versus evil. Maybe this is really the end times, I don't know."

Now Anna felt like looking around to see who was listening. "The end times."

"Well, I mean, I don't really know about that. But the war is real." He leaned as far over the table toward her as he could and whispered, "Demons walk the earth."

"'Walk the earth'? Are you serious?" Funny enough, the demons part she had no trouble believing. That anybody would talk like Guy, though, was a hell of a lot to have to swallow.

"It's true," he said. He spoke calmly again, all trace of his earlier whine gone. It was the voice of someone speaking in undeniable certainties, so sure he was correct that he didn't care whether you believed him or not. Maybe it was inconceivable to him that you wouldn't.

"No argument here," Anna said. "I mean, really—I know."

"Mona's a saint. A miracle worker. I'm just a soldier." His face softened, and Anna thought she saw the slick glimmer of tears welling up in his eyes. "She can save us all, if we serve her."

"Save us from the demons."

"Yes."

Anna had never felt the urge to pistol-whip somebody just for being infuriating before, but it was coming on strong now. "What does that even mean? Are you being literal?"

"A great enemy has risen against us. Mona can save us—but she needs help. She needs an oracle."

"Oh my fucking God." If not for Karyn, for that tiny shred of hope, there was no way she would have had the patience to drag all this out of him.

He nodded. His cheeks were now wet with tears, but he didn't wipe them away. "And you can bring her to us."

"That's the part I don't follow." *Well, one of them.*

"We've seen you, in the visions. And the other woman. What is her name?"

"None of your business."

"The visions were clear. We need a prophet. She is one."

"What do you need a prophet *for*?"

Puzzlement pulled Guy's eyebrows together. "We were told to find her. You don't question the will of God. You simply obey."

"Tell me about Mona."

"Get the prophet, and we'll go meet her."

"Not a chance. I meet her first. Then we deal. Let me give you a hint: I'm gonna want more of those black toothpicks. A lot more."

Guy did a lousy job covering up his wince. "Mona will dispense some from the reliquary." He licked his lips. "Maybe not a *lot* more, but some."

"Yeah. Okay."

So there it was. If this was for real, she had options. Deal directly with Mona for more of those sticks, maybe get hooked up with a steady supply. Failing that, maybe she could steal this reliquary and get the tooth at the same time. She'd have to play it by ear, and the situation was tricky. If she *could* get hooked up with a steady supply, that might mean fucking Sobell over—after all, if Mona became her new hookup, it would really screw things up to get caught stealing from her.

"Let's go," he said. "Right now."

"Can't. Got places to be." And, more to the point, Genevieve would be watching the place right now.

"Then tonight."

"That doesn't work, either." Her next shift wasn't until tomorrow. Changing shifts was a possibility, but she'd need a reason for that, and right now this didn't look like anything she wanted to try to explain. Maybe it would all go smoothly and she'd walk away with everything—and maybe she'd come out with Sobell as an enemy. She couldn't risk telling Genevieve. There was no telling if Gen would tip Sobell off or not. "Tomorrow. Ten p.m."

"Not sooner?"

"No."

"All right. I guess."

"See you then," she said.

Chapter 16

Nail slammed on the brakes and skidded to a stop, his pulse pumping so loud in his ears it drowned out the traffic. The light was green, but some dumb kid had gone wandering out into the street anyway, and Nail had been so preoccupied he hadn't seen her until he damn near mowed her down.

"Get the fuck out of the road!" he yelled. He balled up his fist to keep his hand from shaking.

The kid gave him the finger and ran the rest of the way across the street. "I gotta get my head in the game," he muttered. He'd thought this latest job would be more straightforward, like the old days. Go in, steal some shit, get out without anybody being the wiser. It was looking less like that all the time.

He didn't know how many people were holed up in the house, but it was at least four, of that he was sure. He'd seen two, and Anna had seen another two. He'd seen them come back from a supply run, and either they ate like a platoon of marines or there was a hell of a lot more than four. They came and went at irregular hours, and as near as he could tell, there was never a moment when all four were gone.

The light turned yellow, and he drove through the intersection, shaking his head. He'd sat there the whole time it was green, head in the clouds. Bad sign.

Somebody honked, and he checked the mirror. Shit. The sight of the red bubble flashing on the dash of the car behind him sent a sick jolt through his gut, and he almost floored the accelerator. Instead, he guided the car to the curb, swearing under his breath the whole time. The car was unmarked, sure, but he should have seen it.

The guy who got out didn't look like a cop so much as a sales guy or someone belonging to a related category of empty suit. Off duty, or what? He rolled down his window and waited.

"Mr. Owens, I'd like you to come with me."

Even better. This son of a bitch knew who he was. Not a good sign. He knew a couple of corrupt cops who worked for various arms of organized crime, and they'd do you just like this. *Come with me*, and next thing, you were lying in back of a warehouse somewhere. "Aren't you supposed to ask for my license and registration?"

"This is a little more informal. We just want to talk with you." The guy grinned humorlessly. "Scout's honor."

"Talk."

"We should do it at headquarters."

"We should do it right here."

"Do you know why I stopped you?"

Nail gave him a bland look.

"It's because you sat at a green light for two minutes, then ran a red. That gave me probable cause. What do you suppose I'm going to find when I search your car?"

"Not one goddamn thing."

There was real humor in his smile this time. "Want to bet?"

"It's like that, huh?"

"Just like that."

A battered Taurus rolled by, close enough to the cop to ruffle his hair. "Can I see some credentials?"

The guy flipped open a wallet. Not a cop. FBI. The bands of tension squeezing Nail's chest actually loosened a notch. Corrupt city cops were a dime a dozen, but an FBI guy was another thing entirely. He checked the mirror again, saw another guy sitting in the car. *Two* FBI guys. Maybe legal trouble, then, but the odds he was about to end up facedown in a field seemed a hell of a lot smaller.

"Let's go," he said.

He spent the ride in the back of the car, watching the two guys. Nobody said a word until they got to the municipal building. "Come on," the first guy said. Then it was up the stairs and into a small, dingy elevator. *Walking into the municipal building with a couple of cops and not wearing handcuffs. What's the world coming to?* On the fourth floor, the cops—agents, he supposed—led him down a hallway done up in industrial beige. They knocked at the door. A black woman, similarly attired in a suit, dark hair pulled back in a severe bun, opened it.

"Hi," she said, offering her hand. She smiled pleasantly. "I'm Special Agent Elliot. Come on in and have a seat."

"I got a choice?"

"Of course. But I think you'll want to hear this. I really do."

Nail's first impulse was to answer, *Well, in that case—* big dramatic pause—*fuck you*, but he stayed quiet. Maybe she was right. Given all the shit they were in, maybe he'd pick up something useful.

He stepped through the door. The room inside reminded him, oddly enough, of the teachers' lounge at his high school. A couple of cheap, long tables were set up in the middle of the room, a flat-screen TV set up on one of them. A closed door was in the center of the wall at the far end of the room. Cinder block wall to the right. Corkboards on the walls to the left. He saw his picture on one. Anna's, too. And Karyn, Genevieve, and Tommy. The sight filled him with a sudden anger. Who were these people to be messing with his? He ground his teeth and said nothing.

Behind him, the door closed, leaving the two guys who'd picked him up out in the hall, so there was that to be thankful for.

"I want to show you something," Elliot said. "Have a seat."

"Think I'll stand."

"Suit yourself." She picked up the remote control and pointed at the TV.

The scene was a parking garage, shown from a slightly shaky handheld video camera. A man got out of a parked SUV.

Sobell. Shit. Way too close to home. He was carrying something in both hands. It was tough to make out, and his body was in the way most of the time, but it looked kind of like an urn. He walked around the vehicle.

Nail recognized Anna's car in front. This was the meeting that was supposed to be the drop, then. Just as DeWayne said. They must not have anything else, or they wouldn't still be barking about this. In the video, Anna parked the car and got out.

Sobell greeted them. "Ms. Ruiz, Ms. Lyle. I suggest you remain in your vehicle for a few more moments. Be sure to roll up the windows." The audio was amazingly good—no way it came from some crappy video camera mic. Somebody'd been there with something a lot more sophisticated.

Anna: "Why?"

"Exodus, chapter ten."

Anna and Genevieve got back in the car and, following instructions, rolled up the windows. Then Sobell bent down out of sight. For ten seconds, Sobell was blocked entirely from view by the vehicle. And at the end of the ten seconds, fifty zillion locusts came pouring up out of somewhere, creating an explosion of sound that dissolved the audio feed into deafening static.

Elliot stopped the film and studied Nail's eyes. "I've watched this thing a hundred and fifty times, and I *still* can't figure out what happened there. Got any ideas?" She smiled all the way to her eyes, as if there was real humor in it.

"Great special effects. ILM?"

She chuckled. "No, it's the real deal. Good audio, huh? I keep listening, wondering if I'm hearing it wrong, but I don't think I am."

"What's that?"

"Exodus, chapter ten. It's from the Bible. I actually went and chased the reference down. Exodus, chapter ten, is the bit where Moses unleashes the wrath of God on Pharaoh in the form of a plague of locusts. I memorized verses fourteen and fifteen." She cleared her throat, then held out her arms as though addressing a huge crowd. "'And the locusts went up over all the land of Egypt, and rested in all the coasts of Egypt: very grievous were they; before them there were no such locusts as they, neither after them shall be such. For they covered the face of the whole earth, so that the land was darkened; and they did eat every herb of the land, and all the fruit of the trees which the hail had left: and there remained not any green thing in the trees, or in the herbs of the field, through all the land of Egypt.'"

"That's all kinds of fucked-up." It was, too, but Nail didn't see what it had to do with him.

"We sent a team in afterward to figure out just what happened in there. They had to clean eight inches of dead locusts off the floor of the garage to even get started. I thought they were going to find some kind of, I don't know, drain or hatch or something that Sobell let all those bugs come in through. But no."

Elliot paused, seeming to wait for some kind of acknowledgment. "It's a weird old world," Nail said.

"I am one hundred percent sure a crime was committed in that parking garage, but I'm stumped on exactly which one. Littering? Vandalism? Oh, I know—maybe I can charge Sobell with ten million counts of malicious mischief." She sat upright in her chair, hands holding the edge of the table. "None of those count as RICO predicate crimes, though."

Nail let the words bounce off as though they meant nothing to him, but now he got it, the reason he was here.

All they needed was to prove a pattern of illegal activities, and prove Sobell was in charge, and they could bring Sobell down even if he hadn't lifted a finger himself. Somehow they'd tied Nail and the crew to Sobell, and they thought they could get him to put Sobell on the hook for them. "I hope you get him. That shit with the bugs fucked up traffic something fierce."

Elliot's smile didn't diminish a bit. "Look, we've got your crew on video talking to the guy. We know you're working for him."

"I musta missed where I showed up on that video. Maybe we can watch it again, and you can point it out this time."

Elliot waited. The urge to take a closer look at the photos on the wall nagged at Nail like something caught between his teeth, and it was all he could do to keep his eyes trained on hers.

The stare-down went on for long enough to become mildly ridiculous, and finally Elliot looked down at her hands, grinned, and looked back up. "Mr. Owens, I'm with FBI, NSIB. Do you know what that is?"

"No. That's a lot of alphabet right there."

"Not many people do. It stands for 'Non-Standard Investigations Branch.' We handle events of an . . . unusual nature."

"Like bioterrorism and shit?" Nail said.

"More like generally weird shit," Elliot said. Her smile turned somewhat apologetic.

"Weird shit. Like *X-Files* shit?"

"Last year, in Bakersfield, there was a very bizarre murder. The—"

"You didn't answer the question."

"I'm getting to it. The victim was a burglar, a pretty accomplished second-story man. They found him in the middle of a bank vault, near the safe-deposit boxes. How he'd gotten in was anybody's guess. Half his body was severely burned. The fire was so hot that the last two inches of the fingers on his right hand had actually burned up in their entirety—instantly vaporized. The burns got less severe radiating from there. The left third or so of his body was basically untouched. The vault was completely undamaged."

"Aliens got him."

"Not exactly. They were going to file it as an accident. There was no murder weapon, so how could they call it a murder? I never would have heard about it except the burglar was wanted on racketeering charges, and the FBI was already watching for him."

"Okay."

"The murder weapon was a safe-deposit box."

"On fire, I guess."

It seemed Elliot's grin wouldn't go away, no matter what Nail said to provoke her. "Not exactly. The only part of the box that showed any evidence of fire was in the inside on the bottom, where somebody had drawn a very particular diagram. They'd done some unusual things to prepare it. Most of it had burned away, but there was enough left to get a match."

"A match on what?"

"Another diagram, one I know well."

"A diagram can't kill a man." For the first time in this meeting, Nail was beginning to get genuinely nervous. Bad enough the FBI was involved at all, but that they'd brought in a division he'd never heard of that dealt with precisely the kind of shit the crew trafficked in was even worse.

Elliot leaned forward. "Yes. It can."

"I don't follow."

"I'll be blunt, Mr. Owens. The occult. The box was set with what was basically a very nasty sort of magical trap."

"Now I know you're messing with me. You're wasting my time. Come on."

"I get that everywhere I go." She didn't look concerned. "The box was traced to a man who we believe worked—off the books, of course—for Enoch Sobell."

"That's great. So you got your case, then."

"The box's owner has disappeared. We can't find that poor bastard anywhere."

"What makes you think he's a poor bastard?"

Elliot tipped her head forward so that she could give Nail a mock-incredulous look under raised eyebrows. "Even going along with the fiction that you don't work for Sobell, surely you've heard some of the rumors. If somebody working for him drew attention in such a high-profile way, don't you think he'd have them disposed of?"

"I got no idea."

"Somebody in your crew's going to get hurt, Mr. Owens. It's only a matter of time."

"Oh. So this is, like, a public service thing here. You lookin' out for me. You got my back, is what you're sayin'."

"Exactly. Almost nobody understands what the man's really capable of. I do. If you help us get Sobell, we can protect you."

"That don't sound like you got my back. That sounds like you chargin' a protection fee."

Elliot gave him a faux-helpless smile. "The bureau's got a lot of priorities, and my division in particular is very small. We can't help everyone."

He wasn't really tempted, but he was in shouting distance of it. Sobell's money was good, but, as Anna kept saying, shit was getting out of control. How long before he just wanted them to outright start capping people? Nail was already worried it would come to that with Van Horn. Bad habit to get into. Maybe sometimes you did what you had to, but making it into a full-time paying gig sounded like a bad, bad idea. If he could get the same kind of protection for Anna, Karyn, and Genevieve . . .

Nah. Didn't make sense. He wasn't sure whether to bet on Sobell or the FBI, but he didn't want to outright bet *against* neither one. And anyway, the FBI wouldn't kill him. Plus, you didn't rat. Those were the rules.

"Sounds like you can't help me," Nail said. "Appreciate the offer. We done?"

"We could arrest you right now," Elliot said.

"Not unless you want a lawyer so far up your ass he could wear you like a suit." Nail was all ready to go another ten rounds of stare-down, but he flinched when Elliot tossed a folder on the table in front of him.

"Wha—?" He stopped when he saw his idiot brother staring up at him from the front of the folder. What was this new bullshit?

"Would you believe we got your brother on possession with intent to sell?"

That surprised Nail. DeWayne had gotten into a lot of trouble over the years, but as far as Nail knew he'd never sold drugs. It sounded fishy, but he wasn't about to give Elliot the satisfaction. "Yeah. So?"

"He's looking at five to ten."

"Probably do him some good." There. That ought to cut off any talk of some stupid deal. Nail didn't care for the smug look on Elliot's mug, though.

"Would you believe he might actually walk on this?"

"Anything's possible."

"We're going to cut him a deal."

"That's pretty stupid."

"It turns out your brother has an awful lot of info about a known bookmaker and loan shark, one Clarence Wilkinson. We drop the charges, DeWayne testifies. We think we can put Wilkinson away for a good long time. Pretty tidy, huh? Justice will be served."

Nail's heart pounded so hard he thought Elliot must be able to see his pulse in his temples, at his throat, his wrists. "You motherfucker."

"Me? I'm doing your brother a favor."

"Clarence will cut him into a hundred pieces and eat the fuckin' pieces." Nail bit down, squeezing his jaw muscles, crushing his molars together before easing up. "But I guess you know that. Probably countin' on it, huh?"

"What do you say, Mr. Owens?" Elliot put in. "We could get those charges to go away, if you can help us."

"Is this even fuckin' legal? I never heard of a deal to reduce someone else's sentence before."

"It'll be fine."

"What do you need from me?"

"We just need you to testify that Sobell gave you the orders to commit a crime."

Nail considered that. "You mean directly?"

"It doesn't have to be direct, as long as you witnessed him giving the orders to somebody."

"Uh . . . I'm not sure I did."

For the first time, Elliot frowned, frustration drawn in the lines of her forehead. "What do you mean?"

"I mean, I spent all of ten minutes in the same room with the guy, and in that time, I don't think he told us to do anything illegal. You want the dirt, you gotta dig somewhere else." Anna would be the best place, but he wasn't going to tell them that. No reason to drag her into this shit. He thought about the video, and the photos. They would have already got to her if they had any leverage, he realized.

"Are you still working for him?"

Nail shrugged. "I don't know."

"Can you get close to him?"

"I don't know. Maybe."

"Are you willing to wear a wire?"

"Yeah, if I want my guts unzipped clear up to the bridge of my nose. Are you nuts?"

Elliot folded her hands again. "What *can* you give us?"

"I can look for a chance. See what I find out. But you gotta kill the deal with DeWayne. That shit will get him killed if you let it happen."

"We can put it on hold and give you a chance to come up with something. Probably push it back a couple of days."

"Days? What am I supposed to do in a couple of days?"

Elliot's smile was a thin, acid-etched line. "Figure it out."

Chapter 17

For the seventh time, Sheila gathered the Chosen together for the ritual. She looked down at her bloody, unwrapped hands. It would have to be an index finger this time. *This is horrible,* something inside her said, but she merely laughed. The only horrible thing about it was that it might slow her down, make it harder for her to complete the task. Even the pain felt good, kicking off an endorphin rush every time she brushed the raw stumps against something. The same distant part of her that thought this was all very horrible had noticed a creeping redness radiating up from the stumps of her left pinkie and ring finger, but even that wasn't of much concern. Maybe it would spread, but the hand was almost useless now anyway. No reason not to take it at the wrist, or the elbow.

The ritual was routine by now, and she didn't even really need to concentrate to finish it. She shuddered with pleasure and agony when she cut off her finger, and then the creature appeared, just as it had the last six nights, heavy and gray, slick with mucus. It no longer bothered waiting for her instructions. It knew she was looking for Van Horn, as she had on the last several nights, and it immediately pivoted toward the mouth of the alley. The Chosen had stopped *ooh*ing and *aah*ing on the third or fourth day. Now they just followed wordlessly.

Tonight was no exception. The Chosen followed the creature. Sheila trudged after as well, trying to focus through an interior haze of pain and weariness. One of the others passed her, then another. The gray thing and the others receded ahead of her. She sped up as much as she was able. Block after block, she walked as the night ground on, passing by darkened doorways and barred windows. Before long even those stopped registering as her world narrowed to one step and then the next. She staggered. She put her right arm out, caught herself against the pole holding the traffic light, and slid up against it. *Dizzy. Why am I so dizzy?* The gray thing was somewhere ahead of her, but she couldn't quite see where, and the world felt as if it had tipped on one side, then the other, like it was trying to shake her off. She slid farther down the post, reached for it, and bumped the end of one of her fingers. Screaming pain shot up her arm, delicious in its intensity.

The world came back into focus.

Rain was standing a few feet away from her. She'd stopped at the curb and turned around, and now she was staring at Sheila, her lips parted, tongue at the edge of her teeth. She wasn't staring at Sheila's face, though. Sheila followed the line of her gaze, saw red, red everywhere. Her stomach grumbled again.

My hand. That's my hand. She blinked. Yes. It was her hand, her left hand, leaking blood all down her pants in a sloppy red stream. Dimly, she understood her sudden dizziness. Did it really matter, though? All that blood . . . Her mouth watered.

Van Horn. We need to find Van Horn.

With an effort, she lifted her bleeding hand to her shoulder and, with an awkward motion, wrapped the wound in the collar of her shirt. Red flowers bloomed in the fabric.

"I'm hungry," Rain said.

Sheila looked up at her. "Me, too."

"I'm always hungry now."

"Me, too." She wondered just how hungry Rain was.

If the younger woman thought Sheila would make a good meal, she'd have an ugly surprise coming. Sheila might have been weak, but Rain was barely five feet tall and slight. Her waist-length hair would provide ample handholds, and Sheila had a sudden vision of strangling the other woman to death with it. Somebody might end up a meal, but it wasn't sure to be Sheila.

"He did a magic trick," Rain said wistfully. "A blue light, like a circle."

Van Horn. She was talking about Van Horn. "I know," Sheila said. "He did it for me, too."

Rain said a few words, waved her hands. A glowing blue sphere of light appeared in front of her, bobbing slowly at chest level. "It's not as good when I do it."

"It's beautiful," Sheila said.

"It's not as good. I thought it would be good, but it's not."

Sheila pushed herself upright. The dizziness had passed, mostly. She thought she could walk now, anyway. The others had already followed the gray thing down to the end of the next block, where an art deco gallery with bars on the windows sat, dark.

"Everything's good now," Sheila said. "Everything is . . . better. Brighter." She smiled. "Magical."

"Did you ever break up with somebody? And then, like, one night it's late and you're lonely, and they call you, and you meet, and next thing you know, you're screwing underneath the kitchen table?"

Sheila nodded. Part of her felt a low, building thrill at even the mention of sex, but the other part thought of an afternoon on a hillside off the PCH, a long time ago, and that part was . . . confused. It hadn't been a good experience, had it?

"And, like, you're thinking this is not a good idea, he's gross and mean and he ditched you all the time and never called and treated you like shit—you're thinking this *while he's inside you*, but right then it just feels so good you can't stop yourself."

Sheila nodded, the details of that long-ago afternoon coming into clearer focus. "And you just want the sex to last forever, because it's so good."

"And because, you know, as soon as you're done—the very second after you come—you're going to regret it. All of it."

"Yeah."

Rain threaded a hank of her own hair through her fingers, then suddenly gave it a vicious yank. Her head whipped sideways, and she grinned. "I think we've done some bad things, Sheila."

"I think so, too."

"But I don't care. I feel *good.*"

Sheila twisted her maimed finger in her collar, felt a spike of pain. Smiled. "Me, too."

"I don't think I'll feel good forever, though. What happens then?" She pulled harder. The handful of hair came free with a tearing sound, taking a piece of her scalp with it. Blood trickled down over her eye. "You wanna fuck?"

Sheila glanced down the street. The rest of the Chosen were barely visible beneath a streetlight a couple of blocks away. "We have to find Van Horn," she said.

She started walking before Rain could say anything else.

The next couple of hours were a miserable slog. Sheila's wound had stopped bleeding, but the blood loss was bad, and she wasn't going to recover from that right away. A couple of pints—that was the amount she had filed away in her brain somewhere. At somewhere around a couple of pints, an average person would pass out. Was that even real? Did it matter how long? She thought it mattered how fast you lost it, if there was a sudden drop in blood pressure. Regardless, she was still up, still walking, but it wasn't easy. She trailed the group with Rain sort of hovering around her, probably in case she fell. Rain would want to get there first, get a head start on dinner.

At first, it was almost fun, careening from one side of the sidewalk to the other, feeling light-headed and seasick as she lurched about. Exciting, kind of. Certainly interesting. But she couldn't keep up with the group, and she kept running into things. Fire hydrants, signposts. Buildings. Her breath came shorter and shorter. She lost track of where she was—only the gray thing's slime trail showed her where to go. She stayed close to it, slipping in it over and over, once falling to the sidewalk and banging her head. Was Rain even there anymore at that time? She didn't know. But the younger woman was certainly gone by the time she got up. Gone on ahead. Sheila supposed she should feel lucky—she hadn't become dinner after all. Instead, she wanted to lie down on the sidewalk and sleep.

Nevertheless, she got up. The gray thing wouldn't stay forever. It couldn't, she thought. The index finger was a big finger, though, and important, so she thought the creature would last awhile before going back. Not like with a pinkie. They might get five hours out of it. Maybe six. But the slime trail would fade, dry up in the heat. If she hadn't caught up to the group by the time that happened, she might never find them again.

She renewed her effort. One foot, then the other. Stomp, stomp, stomp, *squish*, stomp. Slipped. Didn't fall this time. She'd thought she was walking closer to the buildings—boarded-up retail, here, lots of brick—but she must have strayed back to the middle of the sidewalk. It wasn't wide enough, that was the problem. She pushed on. Made it one block, then two. Her feet dragged and stumbled over each other. Her head spun. Halfway through the third block, she slumped into a recessed doorway.

Just a minute. Just a few minutes.

They were getting farther away, but she was so tired. The last time she'd been this tired was when? Grad school? She was better able to handle it then, the exhaustion a burden to bear up under, not a soul-sucking force that hollowed her out and left her barely able to stand. She felt rough splinters against her face, warm brick against her thigh, the coarse, gritty texture of concrete under her thumb. It would be easy enough to stay here, revel in the sensations until she fell asleep. The others would find Van Horn. If they could call the gray thing. The thought was disturbing, but too bad. She'd had lots of disturbing thoughts lately, if she really considered it. Maybe Rain was right. Maybe there would come a time when they would look back, and all the actions they'd taken in the throes of hunger or lust or pure thrill-seeking would be appalling, a weight of guilt and grief she'd carry until death. Or maybe death would come first. That might be welcome.

She fell asleep, or at least drifted in some dreamlike place far removed from ordinary consciousness. Time passed in irregular, inscrutable chunks. It was still dark when she woke, though, her senses fully opened, her body tense.

What was that? she thought. Then: *what was what?* What had woken her? Nightmare?

No. A sound. The clicking of footsteps, of hard-soled shoes on concrete. She pushed back into her alcove. Moments later, a man walked by. He wore slacks and a nice blazer despite the heat, and he walked slightly hunched. He was watching the slime trail, she realized. He was *following* it. She recognized him now as one of the men who'd attacked the Chosen and taken Don a few days back.

She got to her feet, muscles protesting. A spike of pain rammed through her head, and she fell against the wall. She'd never catch him. Never stop him. Unless . . .

"Help!" she yelled. "Oh God, please!"

The man stopped. She pushed herself out onto the sidewalk. It wouldn't take much acting—she *had* been hurt; there was blood everywhere. She didn't think she could overpower him, not in her current state. But that wouldn't be necessary. Not if he'd just get close enough.

She started chanting under her breath.

"Ma'am, what's wrong? Are you—oh!" Maybe he saw

the blood, or just her general state of disarray, but he ran toward her.

He stopped abruptly two steps away. Yellow street-light fell across his face, and Sheila saw the shock of recognition there. Panic followed recognition, and he spun again, this time to flee.

She finished the words and lunged for him.

The sudden motion was too much, and a wave of dizziness crushed her to the sidewalk. The man was out of reach, fleeing frantically down the sidewalk, jacket flapping as he ran.

She heard a single word, a familiar word, and the back of the man's head exploded. A chunk of asphalt the size of her fist fell to the sidewalk, covered in blood and lumpy bits of tissue. The man's body hit the ground a moment later.

Rain stood at the corner, her right hand stretched out in front of her. In her left, another piece of ammunition.

"Come," she said, not taking her eyes from the corpse. "Eat."

Chapter 18

"You okay?" Anna asked. Three o'clock in the afternoon, Nail's downtime, and he wasn't sleeping. Just sitting out in front of Van Horn's room, staring out the nearest gap in the cinder block wall that passed for a window. Outside there was only broken brick and desiccated grass, dead and bleached nearly white from day after day of pummeling sun.

He swiveled his head away from the scene outside like it took a massive effort. Anna could imagine the bones in his neck creaking and grinding together.

"I'm just askin' because you look like shit," she said.

He put his tongue in his cheek and ran it over his bottom teeth, then exhaled heavily. "I'm fuckin' beat," he said. "I have just fuckin' had it."

"Pussy."

He didn't laugh, just grunted in a way that barely acknowledged the remark.

Anna sat on a camp stool across from him and lit a cigarette. "Need a smoke?"

"Shit no. You know, we get Karyn straightened out, she's gonna kill you for starting that shit again."

"She's not my mom."

"No."

She waited for more, but that seemed to be all he had to say on the subject. "I'm so tired all the time, and the buzz is nice." She drew air in through the cigarette. It tasted like shit, now that she was paying attention to it, but that wasn't the point. So did coffee. "Anyway, I'll quit again when this fucking job is over."

"Which fucking job is that? The thing with the house? Van Horn? Or getting Karyn straightened out?"

His tone sounded unusually bitter, taking her by surprise. "You think we got too much going on?"

"Yeah. Just a bit." He cracked his knuckles. "Be nice to get a break from Sobell's shit for a while, know what I'm saying?"

"Yeah. I do."

"What if he goes down?"

"Not sure I follow you."

"There's a whole lot of five-O up in his shit right now. He goes down, does he take us with him?"

Anna glanced at the plywood sandwich that served as Van Horn's prison door. She wasn't sure how much he could hear from in there, but he had to be looking for any scrap of information or anything else he could use to make himself more valuable to Sobell. She met Nail's eyes, jerked her head toward the far entrance, and got up.

Nail followed her halfway to the other end of the building, where she stopped. She looked up at him. He was worried. *Really* worried. She wasn't even sure quite how she knew. His face was its usual stoic mask, but there was something—a very faint tightening of his brow, a twitch at the corner of his jaw from clenching and unclenching his teeth, something. Not a state she'd seen him in a lot.

"It'll be cool," she said softly. "When they get the big guy, they don't ask him to testify against all the little guys. It's the other way around."

"Lotta people gonna get real fucked if they nail him," Nail insisted.

"They ain't gonna nail him. He's a slippery son of a bitch, and look—they haven't hauled him in. Haven't indicted him for anything. Haven't done anything more than ask a few questions." She took another draw off the cigarette. "Look, you know how it works. The big money guys never go down."

"I don't know. He drowned the city in bugs so he could have one conversation. That don't look like something you do if you got no worries."

"Three conversations," Anna said.

"Whatever. Just—if the shit hits, we oughta be thinking about how we're gonna stay clear of it."

She thought about Guy and her upcoming meeting. If this Mona person really had the goods, Anna would fuck Sobell over without hesitating. That would certainly split the sheets with him, though she didn't know if it would get them clear of any legal fallout. There'd be plenty of other kinds of heat to worry about besides.

"Hey, I need to tell you something," she said.

"Uh-oh."

"Yeah, well. Could be I'm about to get us in a whole lot of trouble with Sobell. You wanna know about it, or you wanna stay clear?"

A sketch of a grin appeared on Nail's face. "I notice you aren't asking me whether or not you should do it, just whether I want to know about it."

"That's right."

"I don't suppose he's the kind of guy who's gonna say, 'Oh well, you didn't *know*. That's all right, then.'"

"No. Probably not."

He looked out the entrance at the pavement, then crossed his arms and leaned back against a support column. "Lay it on me. We're all in this together."

Anna winced. "Yeah, about that . . . Maybe you shouldn't say anything to Gen."

"You asking me not to?"

"It's just—look, I trust her. Pretty much. Just not when it comes to Sobell." The words sounded uglier out loud. She wished there were some way around it, but that was the flat truth. "She's still convinced everything can work out for everyone. Me, not so much."

"All right. It's your call."

"Here's the deal: I think this Mona person can help Karyn." Nail's expression turned to one of surprise, and Anna talked faster. "I got hooked up with some guy who knows her — I mean, I didn't know it at the time — and he gave me a . . . a thing, and I gave it to Karyn, and it helped. It really did. I guess this Mona person is the source. She's got more."

Nail stood, contemplating the news or mentally condemning her, she couldn't tell.

"Anyway, it might all work — maybe I can get hooked up with her and steal that fucking tooth thing for Sobell, and nobody will be the wiser. But you know. If I have to choose one or the other . . ."

"You choose Karyn. I get it." He scratched his jaw. "Could make shit a lot harder for the rest of us, but I get it. I'd do the same thing." He stopped, frozen with a breath still locked in his chest. "Yeah," he said after a moment.

"What?" Anna said.

"Nothing. It's cool. Do what you gotta do."

"Thanks."

Nail checked the clock on the dash. Quarter after seven, the sun now well above the horizon. He'd be a little early, but Gen probably wouldn't mind. She'd probably appreciate the break, and hell, he wasn't getting much rest anyway. *Somebody* ought to get a break from this shit.

His phone rang. He checked the screen, swore under his breath, and flipped the phone open.

"What have you gotten into, DeWayne? Just what the fuck have you done?"

"Hey, relax. Just chill out."

"I'll chill out when you tell me what's goin' on."

"Nothing's going on. But, uh, you think you could maybe put me up for a bit?" When Nail said nothing, DeWayne kept talking "You know me. Can't quite keep my head above water long enough to get more than a breath or two, right?"

Eighty-five thousand dol—one. Two . . .

"Am I right?"

. . . Three. Four. Five.

"Can't you hit up Lisa or something?"

"Yeah, she's not really talking to me this month. Or last month, either. Been quite a few months, now that I'm thinking on it." He paused, swallowed, and then forced another laugh. This time it was so strained it came out like the word "Ha" repeated a few times. "And, uh, I don't think that'd really be all that good for her right about now."

"No? Why's that?"

"I'm, like, kinda out on bail right now."

So. That much was true. "So?"

"So, maybe I got some shit going on right now, you know? And maybe somebody said something to somebody, and I think Clarence got the wrong idea about some things. Like he thinks maybe I've been talking to some cops."

"Have you?"

Another phony laugh, this one the worst of the lot. "Shit no."

Oh, fuck.

"Goddammit, DeWayne. Just go to fuckin' jail. You fucked up, do your time. Keep your goddamn mouth shut. Clarence will ventilate you, you got that?"

"Hey, I don't know what you're talking about. My lawyer says we can beat this thing, that's all. I didn't know what was in the package—I was just taking a thing from point A to point B and making a few bucks on it."

The hell of it was, he might even have been telling the truth. It wouldn't have surprised Nail one bit if he'd just taken a package and pocketed a few dollars. It didn't matter. It would be good enough to convict, or at least to convince DeWayne it was good enough to convict, which meant Elliot had him by the short hairs. "One night. You can stay at my place one night. Then you gotta find somethin' else." Nail shook his head, half ashamed of himself. *King of the enablers, that's me.* "Might be a little while before I can get you a key."

"That's cool."

"You fuck anybody on my bed, I'ma kill you, you got that?"

"Wait, where you gonna be?"

"Not at home. Got shit goin' on."

There was a long pause, of a sort Nail had learned to recognize. Here came the rest of the hair on the deal. With DeWayne, it was never just one thing. Usually, it was money, but not *just* money. It was money *and* a ride. Money *and* a favor.

"There might be more than Clarence looking for me. He was just, you know. Point A. I don't think Point B is any too happy, either."

"Look, just crash at my place. I'll send somebody to meet you with a key. Lock the door and don't let nobody in, okay? I'll be there tonight. We'll figure shit out after that."

"Yeah. Cool. Later, bro."

"Later."

Nail pulled the car over. "Fuck!" he said, and he slammed his hands on the steering wheel. Elliot straight up had him by the balls. And if Clarence really thought DeWayne was talking to the cops, he'd be dead by morning. No doubt about it.

He had to get DeWayne's deal killed.

He reached for his phone. This would bring heat. But what was it Anna had said? If saving Karyn meant the crew took a little more heat, so be it. She'd understand.

"Fuck!"

He dialed Elliot.

"This is Special Agent Elliot. What can I do for you?"

"DeShawn Owens. I don't know how much I can help, but I'll do your fuckin' C.I. thing."

"I'm glad to hear it. When can you come in to talk?"

"How's tomorrow?"

"Fine . . ." She dragged the word out in a way Nail

didn't like at all. He thought there might be a " . . . but" waiting at the end of it.

He jumped into the pause. "One thing, though. I need you to arrest my brother, like right goddamn now. Get him in custody."

"I'm sorry, Mr. Owens, but we'll need to meet before I can take any action on your brother's situation."

"You need to get him in fucking jail. I'm serious." He was squeezing the phone so hard he thought it might crack.

"I can't do that."

"Dammit, can you cut me some slack on this?"

"No." She sounded cheerful, goddammit. Cheerful.

He thought furiously. DeWayne was too chickenshit to do time—he'd cut a deal, no matter what Nail told him, relying on his ability to fast-talk his way out of trouble. That was hopeless. Clarence already suspected something was up, or DeWayne wouldn't need to hide, and if he made the deal, no amount of bullshit would keep him from getting cut into tiny pieces. The only way out of this was to get the deal killed, make sure no information ever flowed from DeWayne to the cops, make goddamn one hundred percent sure he never testified, and then go see Clarence and try to get it sorted out. That looked just about impossible, but it was all he had.

The first step was to kill the deal, and that much, at least, he could control. He prayed it wasn't too little, too late.

"I can meet you at nine o'clock," he said. As soon as Genevieve was good and gone. It would mean abandoning his post for an hour or so, but fuck-all ever happened there anyway.

"I'll see you then."

Chapter 19

Anna stopped at the back door to the surveillance house, her hand resting on the knob. Every damn thing these days seemed to take a deep breath and more energy than she had, so, once again, she took a deep breath and forced herself to keep going. *This will get better when we get Karyn back.* God, she hoped that was true.

She let herself in and went up the stairs. Nail was sitting a few feet back from the window on a chair he'd brought up from the dining room, elbows on his knees.

"Anything?" Anna asked.

He shook his head. After a pause, he cleared his throat. "Gen said she saw somebody looking out the attic window, though. Said she thought it was a woman, though she couldn't be sure."

"Yeah. I heard." That had been just about all Genevieve said to her. A few curt words, and she'd seemed eager to get the hell away from Anna as soon as possible. She'd slept, or pretended to, until Anna "woke" her when she was ready to leave. It wasn't normal, and all afternoon Anna had sat with sour dread churning her belly. What did Genevieve know? "Hey, you didn't say anything to her, did you? About . . . you know."

"Huh? Oh. No." Nail got to his feet. Anna heard something in his hip pop. "You good?" he asked.

"Guess so. Beer in the fridge?"

"Yeah. Right. Water, though, and about a hundred cans of that Red Bull shit Genevieve likes." He made a puking noise. "Diet fucking Red Bull. Sign of the end times, you ask me."

Anna shrugged. "It was a handful of bennies in the old days."

"I ain't sure this is better." He yawned. "I'm out. Call me if the place blows up or anything."

"Roger that."

He lumbered stiffly out of the room and down the stairs. He must really be beat, Anna thought. She couldn't remember seeing him quite so worn down.

She settled in to wait.

The sun went down, though Anna could have sworn the street got dark first, as if its natural state was darkness, and it was eager to shed its daytime camouflage. Bullshit, she knew, but regardless it was the most singularly dreadful sunset she'd ever witnessed. Light and color *fled* the street, a draining tide leaving pools of black shadow behind, even while the sky was still a darkening purple. Things moved in those pools, things with glimmering eyes and shifting, furtive bodies. Rats, for starters, but she also saw something that might have been a ragged, patch-furred feral cat, and it seemed there were other things only glimpsed at the edges of her vision.

You're just freakin', that's all.

Maybe. She was certainly freakin', though whether she was *just* freakin' . . . Not here. Not on this street. This place was fucked. It would be a relief when Guy got here and they could get on with it. Be a further relief when they could wash their hands of the whole mess.

She checked her phone. Ten to nine. Guy was supposed to arrive at ten. It was gonna be a long hour.

The sun was gone. Not a single light was on in any window or on any porch across the way. If Anna got close to the window and looked down the street, she could see one porch light five or six houses down, and then a single streetlight another few houses past that, but when she sat back, they were gone. The half dozen houses she could see from her chair were dark. It seemed *unnatural*. The word itself made her grin—these were houses, for God's sake, on a paved street in twenty-first-century America; what could be less natural?—but the concept behind it wiped the grin away. People didn't live like this. Somebody left a night-light on for their kids. At nine, people should still be up and around. Television sets should be flickering in windows. Hell, some people would normally be eating dinner this late, or, in this neighborhood, walking their dogs now that the sun wasn't hanging overhead, waiting to cook them. Instead, it was as if one of those bombs had gone off here, the kind that was supposed to kill everyone and leave their stuff. Or maybe some kind of chemical or disease had been released. It was easy to believe everyone was dead or had left, but she didn't think that was the case. People still lived here, or at least they had last time she had a day shift.

She sat and watched. Nobody stepped out for a cigarette on the front stoop. No cars rolled through the neighborhood. Nothing happened. Instead of relaxing her, lulling her to sleep, it just made her more tense. This was the calm before the storm, a held breath before a huge, maybe final leap.

At nine thirty, she stopped putting her phone back in her pocket after checking the time and just kept it on her lap. At quarter till, she realized she'd been staring at the tiny LCD screen, willing the time to tick past, and she put the phone back in her pocket.

A big bird—a *huge* bird, like a big vulture or something, its ugly hairless head exposed and gruesome in the moonlight—settled on the grass of the Gorow place. It was a testament to how messed up Anna's head was, how twisted up her reality had gotten, that she thought, seriously, that maybe it was Guy. Like he'd changed shape somehow. You never knew, right? But it didn't stretch, growing into the shape of a man, and it didn't disappear.

It pulled a glistening gobbet of something gross out of a shadow, choked it down in a series of convulsing swallows, did an ungainly, shuffling little run, and took off again.

Jesus Christ, I'm losing my shit. She checked the clock again. Ten on the dot. Guy didn't materialize from the air.

She scratched at her thigh. Any minute now, that dumb-shit College Republican or whatever he was would get here and they'd get on with this. Any minute.

A minute went by. Another. She went out to the hall and lit a cigarette, then came back. Somebody across the street might see the cherry, but probably not. Nobody seemed to care anyway.

The cigarette burned down, and she lit another from its last ember. Then another from that one. Halfway through the third, she felt kind of sick, and she put it out.

Five minutes until ten.

What if he stands me up?

At last, a question she had an easy answer for. If he didn't show, she was going in. Period. Maybe he'd flaked out, or his car broke down, or the goddamn Rapture took him—it didn't matter. If he was a no-show, she wasn't going to rely on him to get this done.

A man walked into view. Visibility wasn't great, but he was clearly wearing a suit, and the stiff posture was instantly recognizable.

Am I really gonna do this?

She picked her gun up from the bed. Pepper spray was all well and good for staying out of some kinds of trouble, but as rotten as this neighborhood was, and that house at the center of it, she wasn't going in without something lethal. She just wished she had some silver bullets.

The gun went in her waistband.

Anna went downstairs. She came around the side of the house, crunching through dead locusts on the lawn, doing her best to ignore the dozens of beady little eyes on her and the sense that the house across the way watched as well.

Guy smiled as she crossed the street and approached him. "Good to see you," he said. "I'm glad you could make it."

"This isn't a fucking dinner party. Let's go."

"Stay close."

"Or what?"

"I told you, we're at the center of a great conflict. We have many enemies. With me, nobody will mistake you for someone who doesn't belong."

He walked up the path to the front door. She followed half a dozen steps back, watching. Not a twitch from the windows. No sound from the street, or from inside, for that matter.

Guy opened the door.

Anna stopped. The smell rolling out of the house hit her like a slap, and she fought back a gag. There was something dead in that house, yes, something large and dead, but it was worse than that. Rot mingled with an eye-watering burned metal stench and—what the hell?—lavender? And something else, too, like gasoline or fuel oil. Anna opened her mouth to breathe through it instead of her nose—and then, crazily, thinking that the stench itself might somehow settle on her tongue, might somehow get inside her, infect her, she closed it. It triggered a memory—a dark room, something horrifying and invisible in a cloud of blackness. Tommy taking a bullet in the guts.

"I'm not going in there," she said.

He gestured toward the black hole of the doorway. "It's okay."

"It's not okay, Guy. There aren't any damn lights on, and it smells like Hell's back porch."

An expression of discomfort briefly disturbed his bland features, and then it was gone. "The forces of evil are pressing in on us."

"That's one way to look at it. Another way is that all

the bad shit on this street is radiating from this house, and you want me to come inside and have coffee."

"Please," he said. "It's important."

There were two options, she thought. Get the hell out of here and come back later, with help, to get what she needed. She'd be going in blind, though. No clue of the layout, very little idea of who or what was in here, or how many. The other option was to go in now, with a guide. Maybe get what she wanted the easy way.

Maybe get killed.

She pulled her gun. She kept it by her side, pointed at the ground, but Guy's eyes still bugged out.

"You first," she said.

He hadn't taken his eyes from the gun. "I don't think *that's* necessary."

"I do. Take it or leave it."

"Have it your way," he said, and he put on an unsteady smile.

He went in. After a moment's hesitation, Anna followed. The stench enveloped her as she crossed the threshold, and a weird thought formed: *this isn't a house, it's a coffin.* Random, and obviously inappropriate—a house was a house, even if something dead was in it—but unshakable. This place was a box for dead things, a burial container, a place where the once-living made their last transition.

"Close the door," Guy said.

"No fucking way."

He flipped on a flashlight. A blue-white beam threw a distorted oval across a scratched parquet floor.

"What's wrong with the light switch?" Anna asked.

"Nothing, but the power is out."

"Did you try paying the bill?"

"Will you please shut the door?"

Anna didn't move. Guy made an exaggerated sigh—*good*, Anna thought—and went around her.

She pulled her own light, the small one on her key chain, and shone it around the room while Guy closed the front door. It was a big room, and her flashlight did little to clear away the darkness, the beam becoming far too diffuse by the time it reached the far walls, and even the ceiling. Twenty-foot ceiling, she judged. On the right and left edges of the room, a pair of wide staircases led up to a balcony and the second floor. Directly ahead, on the ground floor, a pair of double doors guarded the way deeper into the house. A panel had been knocked in on one, exposing splintered wood.

No furniture, wall hangings, or decorations of any kind livened up the room, as far as Anna could see. *Kinda like home.*

Behind her, the lock on the front door clicked home.

"Afraid something's going to get in or out?" she asked.

"We're doing God's work here. You'll see."

"Mm-hmm."

"Come on." He headed right, toward the stairs.

Anna went up and followed Guy through the depths of the house. The place was big, too goddamn big, the kind of place she imagined you needed to have an army of servants to maintain, and anytime you wanted a damn sandwich, you had to get on the phone. That was no big deal by itself, but it was dark, and before long Guy had taken her up some stairs and down some others and all over the place, and while she normally had a pretty good sense of direction, she was beginning to wonder if she'd lost her bearings.

Seemingly forty minutes after coming inside, Anna followed Guy into what looked like a game room. By her flashlight, she saw that somebody had upended a billiards table, and somebody else had shot about fifty bullets into it, shredding the red felt to tatters. The plaster had rained from the walls, revealing skeletal ribs of lath, and a potted plant had been sprayed over one corner.

"This looks like a war zone," Anna said.

"Yes. It is."

"That's what you got? 'Yes, it is'? This is some lady's house, not goddamn Fallujah."

"You don't think there's somebody's house in Fallujah?"

"You know what I mean."

He walked around the table and cracked open the door to the next room. "Come on," he said, and he went in.

"Sure, why not?"

She heard voices from the other side of the door, more than just Guy's. She readied her gun and flashlight, and then she walked to the door and shoved it open with her foot.

Three people, clustered close together, stood in the beam of her flashlight. Guy and a shorter Latino guy to his left squinted. The woman standing in the room behind them held up a hand to block the light.

"That's not necessary," the woman said. Anna looked her over. She was in her mid-forties, Anna guessed, and she had a soft-looking pale face and copper-colored hair that had to have been dyed. She stood leaning against a desk, wearing a maroon robe or nightdress. The only note amiss was a deep hollowness around her eyes. Anna could relate.

"Mona Gorow," Anna said.

"Yes. Can you point that somewhere else?"

Anna moved the light around the room. It was a library, of sorts, or had been. The whole room was lined with shelves, but the shelves sported as many curios as books—candlesticks, figurines, a silver bell, an ugly porcelain duck. A dozen or so candles illuminated the room, and moonlight came in through a couple of small windows.

The smell in here was eye-wateringly strong, so powerful Anna half expected to see a wavering in the air, like that above a pool of gasoline. Not death or rot, but that pervasive burned-metal smell. Nobody else seemed to give it the slightest notice.

If the men were armed, it wasn't obvious. Anna lowered her gun but kept it in hand. The flashlight she switched off and put in her pocket.

"Thank you," Mona said. "Guy tells me you have some concerns about bringing the prophet to us."

"And I can't say this visit has made me feel a hell of a lot better about the idea so far." Three people, no obvious weapons, she reminded herself. Windows. Anything got weird, she had an escape route, and probably enough time to get to it before they could do much.

"My home. It . . . bothers you."

"Your agenda bothers me. Your home grosses me right the fuck out."

Anna'd said the words to provoke the woman, but Mona's expression didn't change. "Does that matter?" Mona asked.

"I don't know. I guess not."

"Not if I can give you what you want."

"Pretty much, yeah." Almost exactly what Anna had been thinking, in fact. "Only thing is, this looks like it might not be something I want."

"Why not?"

"You might have these jackasses fooled, but I don't think you and God are on speaking terms, let alone a first-name basis."

"Hey!" the Latino guy said. Guy, as usual, ignored the gibe.

"Also, you want to drag Karyn into the middle of some shit I don't understand, and I don't like that at all."

"Shouldn't Karyn get to make that decision?"

Oh, shit. Names. Jesus Christ, I'm getting sloppy. "No." She stifled the urge to elaborate.

"Why not?"

"None of your business."

"She's already in the middle of it," Mona said, words firing back before Anna had gotten her entire sentence out. "You, too. You wouldn't be 'dragging' her anywhere."

"You need to be more respectful," the Latino guy said.

"You need to go fuck yourself," Anna said.

"Terry, Guy—can you let us speak privately for a moment?" Mona asked.

Shock on Terry's face, fear on Guy's, but neither one hesitated. They went straight for the door. Ten seconds later, Anna and Mona were alone in the room.

It would be so easy, Anna thought. She was armed, and Mona was not. She could simply force the woman to hand over her toothpick stash at gunpoint. Being a stick-up guy was repellent, but she wasn't sure she had any other good options. *What if she screams? What if she won't give up the goods and insists I shoot her? Could I even get out of here with the damn things alive?*

"Of course God doesn't talk to me," Mona said. "I don't even believe there *is* a God."

"What?"

"Let's put our cards on the table, shall we? Guy and Terry are useful idiots, and if they've drawn some conclusions about the nature of our patron, who am I to tell them otherwise? Lots of people have concluded they are working God's will on a lot less."

"Uh. Okay."

"Now, the rest of the cards. What about *your* agenda? Why are you really here?"

"Guy brought me. I want more of your magic toothpicks. That's why I came."

"You've been watching my house since before Guy told you where to find it."

"Guy found me," Anna said, trying to keep her voice even rather than shout over the sudden pounding of her heart in her ears. "I don't know what you're talking about."

"Are you here to kill me?"

"What? Jesus, what is *wrong* with you people? You brought me here, Guy practically dragged me inside, and now—"

"You've thwarted Belial's will. I've seen it."

"I don't know any Belial."

Mona watched her face and waited.

"Really," Anna said. "I don't know anybody called Belial."

"That's too bad, because you're on the short list of people it would like to squash like a cockroach. Probably not before pulling your legs off, though."

"'It'? I don't like the sound of that."

"There are demons and there are demons, child, and they all have different goals, when they can be bothered to focus on them. One wants to wipe you out. Another, however, might be the best friend you ever had."

"I like to think I got a better class of friends than that."

"Better than what? 'Demon' is just a word, just a name for something powerful we don't understand. There is no 'evil.' There's simply functional, or not. Antagonistic or not. Surely you've figured this out by now." She grinned, and a silver crown glinted somewhere toward the back of her mouth. "'Demon' is just a word. 'God' works just as well. Ask Guy."

Anna said nothing.

"Cards on the table, then," Mona said. "I've put mine down. Now you: why are you here?"

All the cards, Anna thought. Something inside her shouted that this was not the way to do business. She ignored it. Business was fucked these days. At least Mona was being straight with her.

"I've been hired to steal some kind of bullshit magic tooth. That's why I've been watching the house. That's it. The whole thing got all fucked when I met Guy. I didn't know he had anything to do with this. With you. I just want my friend to get better. I don't even give a damn about the tooth anymore."

"Who hired you?" Mona asked.

"Your turn. Belial. How does it know me?"

"It used to run a little cult. You and your friends, according to rumor, wrecked its day a little while back."

"You mean . . . Hector?"

"Your turn."

"What's the real cost?" Anna asked. "That's all I want to know."

"Of what?"

"Of using those . . . things. The relics. I saw Karyn's face. She was suspicious at first. Then something scared the hell out of her. It helped break through the visions, but if it's doing so out of the goodness of its heart, I'm the undead corpse of Elvis. So. What's the cost? What's she getting into, if I hook her up with you?"

"You never answered my question. Who hired you?"

"Enoch Sobell, the motherfucking Prince of Darkness."

For the first time, Mona looked genuinely surprised. She broke eye contact and stared at a spot a few feet to Anna's left, eyes unfocused while she thought. "What does he want out of all this?" she said after a while.

"Hell if I know. You wanna call him?"

"What does he want it for?"

"I don't ask those questions. It wouldn't be the first time I've had a buyer order up some useless bullshit." It wouldn't, but she didn't believe that was the case this time. Not for an instant. Not Sobell.

From the look on Mona's face, it was clear the other woman wasn't buying it, either.

"What else did he say?"

"I . . . Nothing, I don't think. I mean, he moved Heaven and earth to set up that meeting, but all he wanted was the damn tooth, I swear."

"He's playing you."

Anna said nothing. Seemed like everybody thought she was being played these days.

"Why?"

"I don't know." Anna shifted uncomfortably. "What is it *you* want, lady?"

"I told you. I want a prophet. Seems there's a lot of that going around lately."

"I don't know anything about that."

"You want to know the cost? You're looking at it wrong. For my patron, it's no hardship to help your friend—the help is a benefit in itself. It can see what she sees."

"The visions."

"Yes. Helping your friend is quite literally its own reward, for my patron."

"Your patron. A demon."

Mona shrugged. "If you have to attach a name to it."

"How do I know you're telling the truth?"

"I'm telling you more of the truth than Enoch Sobell is. Isn't that much obvious?"

Anna nodded. "I'll bring her."

Chapter 20

Anna paused outside the room she shared with Genevieve. There was no way around it, now—they had to
talk, the three of them. Nail nodded at her. She wished
they could have this conversation after she'd had about
ten hours of sleep. Her eyes felt gritty, and she knew her
patience was a single thin filament on the verge of snap-
ping, but there was no way to put this off.

She opened the door. Genevieve rolled over and
groaned. "Oh my God, what does it take to get a nap
around here?"

"Get up," Anna said. "We need to talk."

Genevieve looked from her to Nail, face bunched up
in confusion. "Who's watching the house?"

"Nobody. This is more important."

That seemed to clear some of the fog away. "Okay.
Come on in."

Anna came in, stepped over Genevieve, and sat
against the wall. Nail followed suit, sitting with one leg
stretched in front of him, his back to the corner.

"What is it?" Genevieve asked.

Anna gave her the short version: Guy, toothpicks,
Mona. Mona's offer. It took surprisingly little time, and
as Genevieve's expression curdled, Anna found herself
wondering if she could string it out longer, keep the
eventual explosion at bay. But there was only so much

story, and anyway, she was tired. "She can fix Karyn, maybe. The toothpicks can, and she has them."

"What the hell are you saying?" Genevieve asked, and Anna flinched from the jagged tone of rage in her voice. "What were you *thinking*? You just went in there, by yourself, without a word to anyone? You didn't—you *don't* know if the guy's a psycho or what, but you know there's all kinds of shit wrong with the house, and you just walk in? What if you hadn't come back? They could be cutting you into tiny pieces and serving you for hors d'oeuvres right now."

"They didn't. It doesn't matter."

"Something's fucked here, something isn't right." Genevieve's eyes were wide, her face pale in the dim room—almost panicky, Anna thought. "Aren't you the one worried somebody's going to get hurt all the time? What about us, huh—we're worried, too!"

"Mona's got something that can help Karyn. That's all that matters."

Genevieve shook her head. "You want to—to what? Take Karyn back there? Form some kind of alliance?"

"No," Anna said. She surveyed Gen's face, then Nail's. "I'm not getting Karyn near those people. I'm going to steal those toothpicks."

Chapter 21

The street was dark, and it looked to Anna as though more of the streetlights had died even since the night before. All things considered, that was probably good. She looked down the street from the corner where it intersected with Ash, willing the Gorow place to become clear in the murk. It remained stubbornly hidden in a pocket of darkness.

She looked at Genevieve. The other woman's face was a sickly orange-yellow under the last streetlight for two hundred yards, and she was pushing at the stud in her bottom lip with her tongue.

"You okay with this?" Anna asked. "I could go in alone."

"You're not going in there alone."

Anna just nodded. The argument had been bitter back at the school—Nail had insisted that he be the one to go, and Genevieve had done the same, and it just wasn't possible to take both. Not with Van Horn there. Genevieve had insisted, with fervor that bordered on panic, that Anna wasn't going in without some occult support, period. After about an eternity of bickering, Nail had grudgingly conceded the point. Anna had taken more convincing, but she'd finally given in. Gen didn't look so good, though, and that made Anna nervous.

"If you're gonna puke or something, you might want to sit this one out."

"I'm fine."

"You sure?"

"Yes! Jesus!"

She let it drop and turned back to the street. There were a couple of ways she could go here, she thought, as she tallied up what she knew about the house. Yeah, there was an ADT sign out front, but that didn't worry her much. There were a million ways around an alarm, for one thing. Probably more important, most people didn't set their alarms when they were actually in the house. There was also the fact that nobody had paid the electric bill for some time, and the batteries wouldn't have lasted forever. And last, what if it did go off? That might even be useful. Get everybody running one way while she and Gen went the other. Odds were good they didn't have it police-monitored, and even if they did, again, so what? It might not be a bad thing for some cops to show up here. An odd thought struck her—what if she just called them? Tell them she heard a domestic disturbance or a gunshot. See what they flushed out.

Yeah, and maybe get some cops killed. They got no idea what's in there.

Okay, so that hadn't been one of her better ideas. What else did she know? Well, there was the alley approach. The problem there was that the alley saw more traffic than the street, and she didn't want to get stuck back there.

No, the right thing to do was something she'd never even contemplate at a normal place—go at it from the front. It was an utterly ludicrous, risky approach that would practically guarantee her getting caught on any street where the inhabitants didn't seal themselves in their houses after nightfall. Here, she thought the chance of anyone seeing was slim, and the chance of them *doing* something about it if they did essentially nonexistent. She thought there was an approach that would keep her and Gen out of sight of the windows, for the most part, and she could even see how she'd get in—up the trellis, over the fence, and in through any window she could find. Cake.

Nonetheless, her feet stayed planted right where they were. She checked down the street, thinking maybe she'd catch sight of someone before she committed herself to anything. No such luck. She wondered if she ought to head down the alley anyway, get a more thorough look at the other side of the house. There might be something better from that angle.

She was stalling, she realized.

Come on. This is what I do. She had actually lost track of the number of places she'd broken into. Big houses, little houses, apartments, movie studios, toolsheds, machine shops, museums, department stores, boutiques, gas stations, restaurants—too many to remember. When she was younger, she'd done it for kicks sometimes, between jobs, just to see if she could. Karyn had given her a hard time for taking extra risk, to which she'd always replied, "Thanks, *Mom*," and gone right back to it. Compared to the usual business they got up to, taking a stroll through somebody's living room while the owner was out wasn't shit. No risk at all. The thrill had worn off, she supposed. She couldn't remember the last time she'd rifled through a nightstand or a desk to see what it said about the owner.

Still stalling. Just move!

She squeezed Genevieve's hand, gave her a thin smile, and crossed into the neighborhood. The hairs on the back of her neck stood up as she imagined all the eyes of the neighborhood turning to her, but nothing moved. Locusts crunched underfoot, sending up the stink of decay.

Anna and Genevieve passed in front of one house, then two, then a third. Nobody looked out the windows. Nobody opened a door to ask them if they were lost, or what they were doing here. Anna looked over her shoulder. Behind, the light across the street seemed dimmer, the receding exit of an endless tunnel.

A squirrel dashed through one of the lawns, sending up a sound of dry rustling among the small insect corpses. Genevieve jumped.

Anna sped up. Walking quickly now, too fast to pass for nonchalant, Genevieve almost jogging to keep up.

The house came into view. Dark, as always. Windows curtained and impenetrable.

Anna stopped in front of the next house over. The approach would be simple from here. The fence on the Gorow property blocked most of the ground-floor windows on the east side of the house, save one, and the curtains were pulled shut there. She led Genevieve up almost to the front door of the house on this lot and moved west, watching that single window. Once she reached the property, she hugged the fence—now she was hidden from view from the second-story windows as well. She didn't feel hidden, though, and she had to fight an urge to stop, look around the neighborhood, and see if anyone was watching. This spot was incredibly exposed, the whole approach the antithesis to her m.o. Nonetheless, she didn't slow. Once you were committed, second-guessing yourself was a good way to screw up.

She gestured to Genevieve, who followed quickly, also keeping pressed to the fence. *Don't panic,* she thought, willing the words to reach the other woman. *Just keep coming.*

Genevieve reached her, and she set off again, this time with Gen close behind. They got to the house without any sirens going off, or anybody shooting at them, or the house opening up to vomit bat-winged horrors at them. This time, back pressed against the stucco, Anna did take a moment to check the neighborhood. As before, nothing gave any indication that there was human life on this street.

"Sit tight a sec," she whispered.

Anna ducked under the window and went around to the front corner of the house. The vines weaving their way through the trellis were dead and withered, their leaves fallen to the ground. Easier climbing. She hung on to one of the crosswise pieces of wood and slowly gave it her full weight. Steady. She checked the top, remapping her route. From here, it would be a quick climb up, drop over the fence, and they could get in through the ground-floor windows in back. Should be no problem, if nobody was around.

So quit thinking about it.

She hauled herself up the trellis. Once the top of the fence was about waist-high, she leaned over and braced her hands on the top. Then she swung her body over and balanced there, one leg over the side and braced against the fence's support pole.

There wasn't much to see in back. A swimming pool took up a third of the yard, as expected, and most of the rest was concrete and tile. A low flickering candlelight briefly lit up the window above her, but the bottom windows remained dark.

Perched on top of the fence, she gestured to Genevieve.

After a pause that seemed unduly long, Genevieve came over and started up the trellis.

Was I that loud? Anna wondered.

Once Genevieve got to the top, Anna helped her over, and the two of them dropped down to the other side of the fence.

Anna pointed to the window. "Anything?"

Genevieve took a white grease pencil from her backpack and drew a bunch of symbols on the window, a couple in each corner. There was some mumbling, and then she shrugged. "Don't think so."

Anna listened for noises or voices coming through the window. When she heard nothing, she got the glass cutter from her pocket. She traced a quick, erratic circle with the cutter. There was no guaranteed quiet way to do this next part, at least not with the tools she'd thought to bring. She hit the glass with the fleshy part of her fist. The piece popped loose, fell inside, fluttering the curtains, and landed softly on a fold of excess curtain. Lucky.

She'd half expected it to smash on the floor—probably not *too* loud, but still not good.

With the hole there, it was easy to reach through and open the latch. Once that was done, she opened the window, holding her breath for the shriek of an alarm.

Nothing.

She grabbed the top of the bottom window frame through the hole and pulled. It stuck, then abruptly jerked free. She felt a sudden bite as the edge of the hole in the glass cut the back of her hand, but at least the window was open. She pushed it the rest of the way open. Then she slipped inside.

Once she extricated herself from the curtains, she pulled them aside to get a good look at the room. The moonlight coming in through the window at least sketched the outlines of objects in the room—a set of chairs, a bulky black rectangle that was probably a dresser or cabinet of some kind, stacks of books, and, closer to the window, a pile of thick magazines that had to be the inevitable collection of hundreds or thousands of *National Geographic*s. The air was thick with a musty unused smell, like an attic, underlaid with a wet, mildewy odor that made Anna wonder if water wasn't leaking in somewhere. It wasn't too different from most of the other residences she'd broken into, either for exploratory or business purposes. Just a room for storage of excess, useless shit.

Genevieve crawled through the window behind her, sounding like somebody kicking a box full of wrenches down a flight of stairs.

That's not fair, Anna thought—but *Christ*, the woman was loud. This wasn't her thing, Anna had to remember. Probably another good reason she shouldn't be here, but it was too late to worry about that now.

The walls of the room were too far away to see in the dimness. Anna walked through the piles of stuff, looking for anything that might be a door or a hatch, wishing that the moonlight were stronger or that there was a damn streetlight outside. God knew what she might run into up here. She imagined knocking over a crate of wineglasses or something like that. Even better than a straight-up alarm to get everybody running. She had a pair of Nail's thermal-imaging goggles in her satchel, but everything in here was likely the same temperature, at least as far as the goggle resolution was concerned. Not to mention they wrecked her peripheral vision.

"Stay close," she murmured. Not really necessary, given that Genevieve had practically glued herself to Anna's ass, but it couldn't hurt.

At the back end of the room, they found the door. She listened at it, heard nothing, and tried the knob.

The stink hit her in the face, and she reflexively brought up a hand to cover her face. It didn't help. The stench was so bad that even breathing through her mouth didn't make a dent. It was overpowering, gut churning, like the worst public outhouse she'd ever been in, only this wasn't human waste. At least, not in the usual sense. It was meat, rotting meat, the smell so bad she could imagine hundreds of pounds, a whole side of beef, slick with gray-green slime, coated in flies, teeming with maggots.

It was a human body. It had to be. What else?

She opened the door wide and stared into the blackness. She couldn't see a thing in there, not even vague outlines. Maybe her eyes hadn't yet adjusted, but it wasn't as though the moon had blazed down like a spotlight in the last room. She waited, hoping she was wrong. After a minute or more, the room had become no clearer. She couldn't even tell how big it was. She imagined floundering through the room, feeling along the walls for a door, and stepping in the still-wet remains of a person. Or worse, pushing her questing hand into a hanging corpse. *Why hanging? Why would they be hanging?*

She got out the goggles and tried them. Nothing but a black wash with vague suggestions of lines in it, devoid of context or sense. Back into the backpack with them.

Fuck this. I need a light.

"Come on," she whispered. She pulled Genevieve

into the room and pushed the door shut. "I'm going to turn on my flashlight."

"Okay."

She put her tiny key chain flashlight in her closed left fist and switched it on. Red light bloomed between her fingers, and her breath froze in her chest as she waited for somebody to shout.

Nobody did, but while she waited, her eyes began to adjust. The edges and planes of the room acquired a soft definition. She was glad she hadn't moved far from the door, since this room appeared to be just as much a mess as the previous one. She loosened her fist and let more light into the room. This room was twice as big as the last, and, as near as Anna could tell, done up in Mid-Nineteenth-Century Old. Massive dark trim along the edges of the walls and ceilings, dark wood cabinets—*wainscoting*, for Christ's sake. A black rectangle blocked out a swath of the far wall. A painting, Anna guessed, probably of some foreboding old white dude with ridiculous facial hair. Boxes of useless shit were stacked in ragged rows between Anna and the door. She shone the light over them. A stack of LPs with some archaic fare by Peter, Paul and Mary on the top. A box of plates in varied pastel shades. She walked forward and found an aquarium full of animal skulls. Something moved, a spider or cockroach skittering back into the depths of an eye socket.

"Fuck me," Genevieve said. Anna nodded.

At the door, Anna stopped again, trying to ignore the nagging sense that, at this rate, it would take days to get through the house. They'd have to find a place to hole up and sleep during the day. The thought made her queasy.

She killed the light. No sound through the door, no light leaking around the edges. One more time with the goggles.

She listened one more time. Hearing nothing but Genevieve's breathing, she opened the door.

Another pitch-dark room. The goggles would have told

her if there was anybody here, would have lit up with their body heat, but again there was nothing. The faint click of the door latch echoed, suggesting a big space.

She took a step and put her foot on something rough and slick. It squished. Carpet, she thought from the texture—a relief. But it was covered in something. Blood, rot, some gruesome bodily fluid she didn't want to think about. She stared down, willing the scene to become clear. Nothing.

Goggles off, light on.

She was right—it was a big room. A big room with a staircase running up against the far wall, and in front of that—

"Christ," she muttered.

"Tell me those aren't bodies," Genevieve whispered.

What else could they be? Oblong shapes lay scattered at the base of the stairs, a dozen or more, all the right size.

"What happened?" Genevieve asked.

"How should I know?" But they had to go up, so it was either keep fumbling through the house to find another staircase, or pick through the corpses. And besides, it would be a good idea to get a closer look, as much as she hated it. See if there was some indication of what had happened here.

Anna took a step forward and Genevieve grabbed her shoulder. "What the hell is going on here?" Gen asked.

"I told you, I don't know. Let's just get what we came for and get out, okay?"

"Yeah. Okay."

They crossed the room slowly, more slowly than was warranted, Anna felt, but she couldn't make herself go any faster. The darkness, usually her ally, now seemed to hide glaring, hateful eyes on all sides, and she felt funneled, pushed down a narrow tunnel of light toward the pile of bodies. She wanted to look away, wanted to keep

scoping out the surroundings, keep watching for enemies. It was impossible. The light stayed fixed on the
corpses.

One on the end caught her eye, something seeming
suddenly familiar about it. She tried to ignore the feeling, but her eye kept coming back to it. What was . . .

"Blond dreadlocks," she whispered. "Remember him?"

"Yeah," Genevieve said. "From Mendelsohn's cult."

"Uh-huh."

"Why?"

"I don't know."

They reached the body, and now Anna had no doubt.
She'd seen this man before, right at the beginning of Sobell's first job. Oddly, she remembered him shopping for
groceries. Pushing a cart back to a big SUV with some
other guys, laughing as they loaded the back. Like they
were in a college fraternity instead of a liar's cult. Now
he was lying on his side, dreadlocks draped across one
outstretched arm. A small hole in his throat and a large
one in the side of his face. Entry and exit wound, Anna
thought, as she tried not to gag. He'd been here awhile.
His skin had gone gray, and an erratic line of what looked
like blue mold crept down from his hairline.

No flies. Why no flies?

"This isn't . . . decent," Genevieve said.

"No shit?" Anna moved the beam of the flashlight
over the other corpses. More gunshot wounds, a few horrible gashes, a couple of bodies with no sign of what
killed them. Some new, some desiccated and half-eaten
with rot.

And one more.

"Oh no." She stepped over the blond guy, stepped *on*
another corpse's hand, and stumbled, catching herself on
the rail.

A body lay facedown at the bottom of the stairs, half
on the carpet and half on the lower two risers, giving the
unmistakable impression of having been thrown down
the stairs like so much refuse. It was the body of a small

woman, wearing a dirty white shift, her spindly arms thrown out to either side.

Anna stood and looked down at the body. The room seemed to rock, adrift on an angry sea, and Anna's own rage swelled as if in response.

"What?" Genevieve asked.

"It's Adelaide."

"Shit. Why?"

"I don't know." She hadn't gone easy, though. Not from the look of the bruises and the burns. "They wanted something from her. Just like they want something from Karyn."

Poor Adelaide.

"Hey, uh . . ." Genevieve paused, her voice so tight it was as though her throat had seized up and cut off the words. "I don't know. Maybe we should get out of here. These people are insane."

"Go if you got to. I ain't leaving without those splinters. Not now. There are no other options left."

A long silence. No footstep or creak of beam interrupted. "Let's get moving, then," Genevieve finally said.

Anna edged around Adelaide's outflung arm, the curled fingers on the end somehow adding a pathetic note to the whole scene, and started up the stairs. She wasn't entirely clear on what was going on in this place, but she had a handle on this room: it was a body dump. Why they couldn't get the corpses out some way or bury them, she didn't know—had a suspicion that maybe this was something she really, really didn't want to know—but the fact that Mona had turned her downstairs living room into corpse storage was undeniable. This hadn't happened yesterday. Anna was no expert, but some of those people had to have been dead for weeks, maybe longer.

She'd just as soon forget about it, or at least lock it away in the back of her mind, but she doubted that was going to be possible.

As she ascended, the scent of rot was pushed to the

background by that other smell, burning metal and fucking flowers. She thought again of the monster at Mendelsohn's.

Is it here?

The stairway ended at a wide hallway, surprising Anna. The ground floor was so dark and silent that it felt subterranean, like it must be a basement or a cave, and the pile of corpses seemed like something that even somebody psycho enough to have would still want to keep behind a locked door, separate from the space where they lived and slept.

Maybe it's food, Anna thought. *Not for the people here, but for the source of that stink.*

She stopped at the top, and once Genevieve joined her, she killed the light. The hall had gone into darkness, but she'd thought there had been a couple of doors on the left and at least one on the right. Best she could figure, if she hadn't got turned around on the ground floor, she wanted the last door on the left. That ought to take her to the northwest corner of the house, more or less. Mona's rooms.

If her eyes had adjusted, she couldn't tell. Everything was still an undifferentiated black. She put the goggles on again. She still couldn't see a damn thing. Her feet lit up like the Vegas strip, but the whole rest of the hall was a blob of black and blue with the occasional stray line or shape that suggested nothing in particular.

With the goggles still on, she walked slowly down the hall, keeping a finger on the left-hand wall. She found the trim of the first door after a few steps and stopped to listen. Nothing beyond the slight shuffle of Genevieve's shoes on the carpet.

She kept going. No sound at the second door, either, and the hallway ended shortly after that. She turned around and listened at the door again. To her left, Genevieve was the sole bright shape in the darkness, white on black, her face an eerie skull.

No light from below the door, no sound from beyond.

She crouched and slowly turned the doorknob. The door swung quietly open when she pushed.

Only darkness in the next room.

Good. Means nobody else is in here. Probably. It wouldn't do to get too cocky. Nail had warned her that the infrared couldn't see through things or around them. Maybe, if she was lucky, it could pick up a sort of heat halo around somebody who was hiding behind a couch or something, but she'd have to be pretty damn lucky. These just weren't precision instruments. In retrospect, they probably weren't even the right tool for this job, but they were what she'd had handy.

She pushed the goggles up on her forehead and counted to sixty while her eyes adjusted. Moonlight leaked around the curtains on the far window—light that was *almost* useless, but a shade better than she'd seen through the goggles. At least she could kind of tell what this room was. Some kind of lounge, she thought. A handful of big dark lumps were arranged around the floor, and the faint light reflecting off them suggested leather. Couches, chairs. The dim sparkling to the left seemed like it might have been a row of glasses behind a bar.

This was going to be slow going, she realized, even slower than she'd thought. She couldn't navigate with the goggles on, but if somebody were hiding in one of these rooms, she'd never see them without the goggles.

These are people, she reminded herself. *They need to see, just like I do. They talk. They move. They sleep and snore. And they probably don't know I'm here. I have the advantage, dammit.*

She made her way across the wood floor to a dark rectangle on the right, which had to be a door or a doorway. A door, it turned out, in some dark wood. She listened at it, heard nothing, and with a barely audible sigh, put the goggles back on. Then she opened the door.

Again, nothing. No—wait. That wasn't quite true. There

was something ahead of her, maybe fifteen feet away at the level of her thigh, the size of . . . A glass. A glass full of some warm liquid, sitting on an end table.

If the liquid was warm, somebody had been here recently. Maybe they'd be back.

She went toward the table, sliding her feet slowly a bare inch above the floor. She found the edge of a chair that way, skirted it, and got to the table. She touched her hand to the glass. Fairly warm. Had to be recent.

Somebody had just been here. Her heart rate kicked up a notch. Where had they gone? She couldn't see the damn exits.

One more time, she took the goggles off and waited. This was maddening. It helped, though. There was only one way out of this room besides the direction she'd come in—straight ahead. She opened another door and went into another room.

At last, light. A trace of moonlight came from a doorway across the room in the right-hand wall. She thought she remembered windows from before, so she walked around the room, hugging the wall to her right. The candle wasn't much, but her eyes drank in the light, and the details of the room began to resolve. It was a mess. The door on the left-hand wall had been smashed to the floor. Ahead, a pile of sticks looked like the remains of a destroyed kitchen table. Bullet holes pocked the wall next to her. There'd been a showdown of some sort in here. She wondered who won.

She approached the doorway and, keeping low, peeked around the corner.

This was it, the library Guy had taken her to meet Mona in. No candle here, just the moon through diaphanous curtains. Once Genevieve had followed her in, she closed the door.

Anna flicked her light back on. This part was old news, though she hadn't often performed it with the owners in the house. Even so, her hands were quick and sure as she took books down from shelves and checked drawers.

Nothing on the first set of shelves, nor the second. She wasn't exactly sure what she was looking for. The picture in her mind was a sort of tarted-up toothpick container, like the little plastic jars you could get at the store, only with a pentagram painted on it in red nail polish. Ludicrous, and she had to consciously try to keep the image away so she wouldn't focus on it. The fact was, she didn't know what she was looking for, but she had to be open to finding it.

"She, uh, she comes in here a lot?" Genevieve asked.

"What? Yeah, I guess. Shhh."

Genevieve stood to the side, hands in her pockets, musing as she surveyed the room. Anna found that irritating as hell—she could at least help, though Anna supposed she'd probably be noisy if she did, so maybe that wasn't a bad thing after all. It was still irritating.

Having cleared the books off two shelves, she started pushing at the back panels on the bookshelves, hoping for a false back or something. The toothpicks—the *reliquary*—might not even be here, she realized. Her instincts were usually pretty good about this kind of thing, but nobody was perfect. She'd go room to room if she had to. Even if it took all night.

"To what do I owe the pleasure of this visit?"

Anna spun, and Genevieve dropped the figurine she'd been holding. It smashed with a sound so loud it seemed it would wake the whole block.

Mona stood in the doorway.

Chapter 22

Everything hurt. That was the core truth of life that had evaded Sheila for thirty-nine years, a truth masked by a thousand other distractions, and it had taken this latest immense, crushing agony to finally crowd out the rest to the point where she couldn't ignore it anymore. Life was one long lesson in pain, physical and emotional, and even the most sheltered and cushioned accumulated aches of the body and soul over time, ranging from the slow breakdown of knee and spine to the cumulative guilt of wrongs inflicted and humiliations suffered. She thought maybe that was what really killed you, eventually. All that weight of suffering. Surely if you lived long enough, it would drive you mad otherwise.

She followed behind Rain, each step a shock that rippled up through the webwork of bloody slashes that now covered her torso. Rain had put them there, she remembered. Sheila had collapsed, feverish, her body no longer able to tolerate the blood loss and infection, and even that last meal of blood and flesh had done little to help her recover. She hadn't lost consciousness, not exactly, but she'd descended into delirium. The brick of the alley she'd collapsed in oozed a black slime, anthropomorphic rats had paddled by on boats made of human skulls, and giant, angular jointed limbs, like those of a monstrous spider, protruded from every window and probed blindly around the alley.

Rain had stayed with her. Had tried holding her hand, even, though that had proven too painful, and so she'd stroked Sheila's forehead instead. Sheila remembered her smiling down, lips and cheeks still stained with blood.

Eventually, Rain had taken the knife from Sheila's bag and begun cutting. At first, Sheila had laughed, thinking Rain had gotten bored and had finally discovered a new diversion, and while the pain was horrible, there was a hilarious sort of irony in thinking Rain had stayed with her out of a desire to help. But as the blood poured, she realized that it wasn't boredom or bloodlust—Rain was working magic in Sheila's flesh. Painful, terrible magic—but somehow, crazily, healing magic, of a kind. The wounds in her fingers closed. The red streaks on her hands faded. The fever abated. The new wounds scabbed over quickly. Not healing, but not bleeding much, either.

She was going to live.

The truth of life was pain, but that core truth held a secret. Experiencing pain was living, truly living, and once you embraced that, it came with a euphoria greater than the pain itself. She had a memory of a place of darkness, where all sensation was mostly absent, muted when it was present, the senses straining for any kind of input at all for years, decades. It was insane, a false memory, nothing she'd ever experienced, obviously, but compelling nonetheless. Even pain was better than that nonlife.

She reminded herself of that at each step, and with each painful jolt, a comparable thrill ran through her body. It didn't erase the pain, didn't offset it in any way, but it felt *good*, and that was enough.

Rain looked back and smiled at her. She smiled back. Something bothered her about the exchange—it didn't hurt. It felt good, all by itself. What was up with that?

Just pain in waiting, she thought. One day, those good feelings would be swept away on a tide of loss and agony, and they would have only served to make the wave that much stronger. She felt relief at the thought. Better that than that she'd somehow misunderstood everything.

They followed the slime trail of the slug creature. Rain had called it this time, once Sheila had shown her how, and the fresh stump of her finger still bled. Not freely, though— Rain had had the presence of mind to bandage the wound, a concept that had somehow, horribly, been driven from Sheila's mind at the sight of red running blood. The red blot on the bandage still spread, though, and it was hard for Sheila to keep herself from watching it.

They trudged through still another section of town full of run-down buildings and wreckage, nearly devoid of people. Since joining the Chosen, it had been like this, as though the universe had opened a crack and Sheila had slipped through to an alternative dimension full of ruin. She knew better, mostly. The company she kept now wasn't fit for roaming the suburbs and holding office jobs, and they had relegated themselves to the cracks between ordinary life. They weren't cracks, though. She could see that now. They were craters, colossal, inescapable gaping mouths, even for the normal residents who hadn't taken up with otherworldly forces. Pits lined with downward-pointing spikes. Once you fell down here, it would take divine intervention or a near-miraculous cosmic accident to get you back out.

The apartment buildings thinned as the Chosen walked, and soon whole banks of windows were covered with plywood and danger signs.

"We could live here," Rain said. "Just like at the slaughterhouse."

The idea had a certain attraction. Spend their time sleeping, eating, and plumbing the strange mysteries that itched at the back of her mind. It wasn't realistic, though.

"No," she said. "We can't."

Rain merely looked at her, eyes wide in a question.

"What happened to Harriet?" Sheila asked.

"Died, I guess."

"While I was out?"

"Yeah."

Sheila nodded. "Accident?"

Rain's forehead wrinkled. "No. I don't think so. I didn't see it, but I think she just . . . gave out." She licked her lips. Sheila doubted she knew she was doing it.

"There's only six of us left, Rain. We really are all going to die." It was true, she thought, but the most unsettling thing wasn't the fact itself, but that it carried no emotional weight whatsoever. She expected her heart to pound, her stomach to get that queasy, acid-sick feeling, but there was none of that. Instead, it had the feel of a nuisance, or maybe the contemplation of the distant conclusion of a great party. One day the good times would stop, and that was it. It wasn't that distant, though, she didn't think. She just wished she could really *believe* it.

Rain nodded, her mouth drawn up small, her face serious, "I think so. Yeah." She looked around, gaze moving from the yellow sky to the decaying buildings to the four remaining Chosen who still walked with them. "We're damned, you know," she said. There was no particular concern in her voice—it was just an observation, like "Hey, it might rain later."

"I know."

"All I can think about is how hungry I am."

Sheila knew what she meant. "And how much I'd like to get fucked right about now."

"Fuck *yes*."

It would be easy. Turn around, grab Antawn or Raul by the balls, and do it right here, or maybe go into one of the buildings. Maybe get everyone to go.

The gray thing turned. It picked up the front end of its body and pointed it back at her, giving the exact impression of studying her over its shoulder, never mind that it had neither eyes nor shoulders.

Van Horn. It was supposed to take them to Van Horn, and it occurred to her for the first time that, having been tasked, it might not be receptive to distraction. She thought of the crunching sounds it had made when eating, shivered, laughed, and walked faster.

Ahead, the apartment buildings opened onto a wide plaza of cracked concrete, surrounded by a rusty chain-link fence. The building beyond was a sprawling disaster of cinder block, broken glass, and collapsed walls. A fragment of smashed plastic sign reading MENTARY SCH still stood out front.

The creature led them straight toward it. It slithered across the road, up the curb, then through a break in the fence.

Sheila stopped at the fence. The creature hadn't gone off easily trod paths before, whether that meant sidewalks, alleys, or streets.

"Here?" she whispered. "Is he here?"

Once again the creature made as if it were looking back at her. It paused for a nerve-racking moment, then continued.

"Shouldn't we have a plan?" Sheila asked. The other Chosen looked at her, but the creature kept moving.

She looked to Rain. "Take Raul. Go around the back." She smiled. This might actually be fun. "We'll go in the front. If you see anybody besides Van Horn, kill them."

The others nodded, mouths solemn, but gleeful anticipation dancing in their eyes.

They moved in.

The scream sent a sickening spike of fear right up the center of Nail's body, and he was on his feet before his head had even cleared.

The sound stopped. He paused, wondering if he'd really heard it, or if he'd finally fallen into that half space between sleep and waking and he'd imagined or dreamed it.

"Hurry up!"

Karyn. Nail moved. He threw the door open so hard it banged off the wall and rushed in, lighting the room up with his phone as he came in.

Karyn's eyes were wide and fearful, unfocused on Nail, unfocused on anything. But either she'd heard him come in, or she was pretty good at guessing. "Somebody's coming. Somebody's coming *now*. We need to run."

"What about Van Horn?"

She gave no sign that she'd heard him, and for a moment he thought maybe *she'd* been having a nightmare. She wasn't exactly in the here and now these days anyway.

The hesitation lasted a few seconds before he tossed it aside. He'd been at this way too long to ask questions. He chambered a round in his pistol. "Come on," he said, again with no effect.

He took Karyn's hand. Karyn obligingly stood, just as if this were one of her usual walks, but Nail could hear her rapid, frightened breathing. "It's gonna be okay," he said. He ducked into his room, grabbed his emergency pack, and led Karyn out to the main space.

Now what? He couldn't see anything to the left or right, and gazing across the main area through the blown-out windows of the old cafeteria didn't reveal anything, either. Moonlight coming through the distant holes in the wall made it worse, creating threatening patterns of light and shadow where it was just as likely that no real threats hid.

Maybe she's just freaking out. Maybe that's all this is.

Something cracked across the way, a sharp sound that echoed in the hollowed-out space.

"I can't . . . ," Karyn said. "I can't . . . I can't *see*!"

"Shh, shh." Nail took Karyn's hand once again. How was this going to work? Somebody was out front, blocking the main way and probably coming toward them. It didn't make sense to leave Van Horn, not after all this shit, but it was gonna be hell getting both him and Karyn out of here. Probably have to get Van Horn to move at gunpoint, hoping his sense of self-preservation was strong enough. Then maybe hug the wall and take the long way out to where he'd parked his car at the side of the building.

It might not even be that bad. Maybe I ought to just fight it out.

Nonetheless, he headed toward Van Horn's cell, Karyn in tow. Somebody was coming; he had little doubt of that. Best be ready.

The thought was interrupted when a line of fire bloomed into existence, cutting across the open space behind him. Nail pulled Karyn forward with him, then dropped to one knee. Two figures stood at the source of the fire, details lost in the flickering light. He squeezed off a couple of shots at them, then pushed off again, half blinded by the sudden brightness, eager to get away. The heat dried his skin and sent searing blasts of air into his lungs at every breath.

Get Van Horn and . . .

He pulled up short. There was a thing in front of Van Horn's cell door, not ten feet away, a glistening, gray, undulating mass about the size of a couch. Firelight danced in reflections down its length. For a moment, his mind flailed for an explanation, substituting and discarding a rapid series of absurd possibilities. It was a big sack of garbage. A water bed. An inflatable raft.

The gray thing suddenly reared up, pulling the top two-thirds or more of its body off the floor. The entire bottom side of the thing was a huge mouth, surrounded with dozens or hundreds of slimy gray tendrils. Nail forgot about Van Horn, pushed off to start running, slipped on dirt and pebbles—

Half a dozen long tendrils shot out and grabbed him, wrapping around him at ankle, thigh, waist, and left arm. He fell, landing with a heavy thud that smashed his breath from his body.

The thing started to reel him in. He braced his feet against the floor, but he might as well have put them on a sheet of ice for all the good it did.

Finally, he remembered his gun. He pulled the trigger

three times, scored three hits, and at each one, he saw a ripple go through the creature's body, blue-white goo pouring out of the bullet holes. They didn't seem to faze the creature at all.

Five feet. Less. From here, the smell coming off the creature was overpowering, a heavy, nauseating stench of decay and corruption and something that smelled a lot like semen. Nail screamed and scrabbled at the concrete floor. No good.

He pulled the trigger again and again.

Two more tendrils whipped out of the creature's maw and wrapped around his legs.

Two more shots, three, whitish goo flying in sticky, sloppy streams, and now Nail was screaming at the top of his lungs.

The thing slopped forward, covering his feet with its mouth. *Dozens* of the tendrils wrapped around his legs and pulled him in farther. It moved up to his knees. His waist.

He dumped the pack on the floor. A concussion grenade rolled loose of the pile. He scrabbled for it, knocked it away, lunged, and finally grabbed it. Then he pulled the pin, tossed the grenade over to the far side of the thing, and covered his ears with both hands.

The detonation was huge. Waves rippled through the creature's gray, gelatinous bulk, and it tipped over, curling up on its side. A shock wave that felt like a three-hundred-pound hammer swung by a pissed-off giant slammed into Nail's body and smashed his head into the floor. He screamed, or at least he thought he did. Everything in his vision went fuzzy. Distantly, through a haze of pain so immense he had nothing to compare it to, he heard laughter.

"Grab her!" somebody said. Van Horn, it sounded like.

"Karyn!" Nail shouted.

A cry of pain or fear came from nearby. Nail forced himself to pull the world into focus, though mostly he just wanted to black out. There were four or five figures arranged in an irregular line, maybe twenty feet off. One of them had Karyn.

Van Horn pointed at Nail. "Please kill him."

The man on the end began chanting and waving his arms. Nail thought of a trash can lighting itself on fire from even farther off.

His gun was still in hand. The guy was blurry, doubled, and Nail's hands none too steady, but he fired before the guy could finish working whatever horror he was preparing to unleash. One bullet, high in the belly, and the guy went down shrieking.

Sorry, guy. Meant to aim a little higher.

At the realization that maybe Nail's stinger hadn't been pulled quite yet, Van Horn stepped back behind Karyn. "On second thought, let's get out of here," he said.

Nobody moved for a moment; then Nail squeezed off another shot. The group fled, laughing, pulling Karyn along behind them. She yelled once, and then was gone.

I'm fucked. I'm so fucked. Karyn, too. He pushed with his arms, trying to get to his feet, but barely managed to lurch forward. A convulsion racked his guts, and he vomited.

He tried again. Put one foot on the floor, tried to stand—

And fell over.

Concussion. Bad one. His gut spasmed again, not quite hard enough to cause him to puke. His head swam. *What if I black out? What if they come back?*

Anna. Focus on that. He had to talk to Anna, let her know what happened. He managed to fumble his phone out of his pocket. After what seemed like twenty minutes of concentration intense enough to split his head open, he even managed to dial. A tinny ring came from the speaker.

The call went to voice mail. He tried Genevieve. The phone rang once. Twice. By the third ring, he was having difficulty remembering who he was trying to call. Anna? No, that wasn't right. He'd already called Anna. He shook his head to clear it, triggering a surge of nausea.

Voice mail again. Genevieve's.

This was bad. He tried to get up, made it to one knee, and a new wave of dizziness collapsed on him, crushing him back to the earth.

He was fucked. Karyn was fucked. Anna and Genevieve might be fucked, too. He needed a plan, something. He tried to get his mind together, dragging shreds of thought in one after another, slowly, like hauling in fish that might slip the hook.

Somehow, after what felt like an hour of idea-fishing, all those pieces added up to something.

"Fuck," he said. He had no other plan, though, and no hope of generating one.

He dialed DeWayne.

"'Sup?" DeWayne said. "You on your way? Or just checkin' to see if I burned the place down?"

"I need a favor."

Silence on the phone, so total that Nail checked to see if the call had been dropped. It hadn't. "You there?" he said.

"Sorry—I passed out there for a second. Shock. Did you say *you* need a favor? From me? Because that shit is, like, against the natural order of things."

"Go to the closet in the bedroom." *Oh, shit, am I really gonna do this?*

He closed his eyes and thought of Karyn's cry as she was hauled away. Yeah, he was gonna do this. "There's a safe."

"Sure is. Big motherfucker, too."

"The combination is forty-one, twelve, nineteen. Open it."

"Oh, let me see here. Forty-one. Damn, you got some small numbers on here. Where the hell is forty-one?"

Jesus. This was going to take an hour. Nail felt drowsy. It'd be nice to take a quick nap and let DeWayne get his shit together. That was a dangerous thought, though. He forced himself to focus.

"Okay. Forty-one." Sounds of movement, a grunt, presumably as DeWayne sat down in front of the safe. "Twelve."

"I don't need a play-by-play. Just open it!"

"Relax, man. I'll get there."

One . . . Two . . .

"Mother*fuck*er! You paid Clarence off and you still have *this* lying around? You rob a bank or what? Nice piece, too. Three-eighty?"

Three . . . Four . . . "Get the keys to the car. They're on the bottom, in front of the money. Hard to miss. Don't touch the gun. Don't touch the cash."

"You need somebody to hold some of this for safe-keeping, you just let me know, huh?"

"The car keys. Get the car keys."

"Key, bro."

"What?"

"It's just one key."

"Are you seriously fuckin' correcting my fuckin' grammar right now?"

"No, man. Just makin' sure. I mean, what if there's supposed to be more?"

"There's just one goddamn key. Do you have it?"

"Yeah. I got it."

"Great. Get my car and come pick me up. And move your ass. Don't dick around here, DeWayne."

"I got it. Where you at?"

"East of Doyle Gardens. Pico and High Street."

"Damn, man. Even I don't go down there."

"Just get here quick, okay? I'm hurt, so don't screw around." Maybe if he repeated it enough, it would sink into his brother's thick skull. "See you in twenty."

"Cool."

Nail hung up. His head swam, and his surroundings seemed viewed through a thick, swirling liquid. His earlier thought, that of taking a quick nap, returned, this time followed by alarm bells and klaxons. You didn't go to sleep after a concussion, right? That was bad. He'd had two in high school, when he played football, and they'd always warned him about that. Neither had been anything like this, though. This was like being drunk, having the flu, and having somebody turning the crank on a clamp positioned on his skull, really leaning into the fucker, all at the same time.

He took a long, deep breath.

To his right, something moved. He turned his head, fighting off another wave of dizziness.

A woman, clambering awkwardly over the remains of a shattered wall. Something was odd about it—her arms were bent, curled inward, and she seemed to be using her wrists to brace herself against the wall as she came over.

Nail panicked for a moment when he couldn't remember what he'd done with his gun, then found it down by his leg. "Don't move," he said, hauling the weapon up to level it at her. His hand shook, but he thought he had six bullets left. Lots of chances.

She was one of Van Horn's—Nail remembered her, though she hadn't been in the lineup he'd recently been shooting at. Hair a limp shock of blond that had once been bleached, dirty jeans, and a blouse that might have been blue under layers of bloodstains. Her skin hung loose as though she'd lost a lot of weight in a very short period of time. Reminded him of his grandma, how she'd wasted away before his eyes like an ice cube in a fry pan. He didn't know how much longer he could hold the gun on her, didn't know how much longer he could hold the gun at all. He wanted to rest so bad. Sweat ran down his face in cold rivulets, dripping steadily off the end of his nose, and he was breathing way too fast. He became aware of other pain, in his shoulders, his back, his ribs. Might be more than his head was fucked-up, he realized.

The woman stood uneasily, and she stepped forward into the faint glow of the distant streetlight. Blood pumped slowly from a wound on her head. Nail got a better look at her hands now, and *everything* was wrong there. They were a mess of bandages, crusted with dried blood, and he was pretty sure she was missing most of her fingers. They curled inward at the wrist, as though she was unconsciously protecting the wounds.

"Get the hell out of here," he said. "And do *not* come back."

The woman grinned at him, stumbled, and caught herself against part of the wall with her maimed left hand. A shriek of agony and laughter sent gooseflesh all the way up Nail's back. She found her footing and pulled her hand in, cradling it against her belly.

"Where's Van Horn?" she asked.

"I will shoot you dead, lady, you come one step closer."

"Will you?" She said something he couldn't make out, and a fragment of brick the size of his fist slid down a pile of debris, then floated into the air near her shoulder. "Where's Van Horn?" she asked again.

He could shoot her, he thought—but if he missed, he had a pretty good idea where that brick would end up. The thought of it hitting him in the head almost made him throw up again.

"Where's Rain?" she asked.

"What the hell are you talking about? Just get the fuck out of here!"

She stepped forward again and staggered, clutching her wounded hands. Drops of blood hit the pavement. The whole time, the brick didn't so much as waver. When she straightened, she looked him over. Her tongue flicked out and licked the corner of her mouth. Saliva glistened on her chin. *Jesus, I got a live one here.*

"You throw that brick, you best not miss," Nail said. "What are you still doing here?"

Confusion washed over her features. "I ran into a post."

"Maybe you should watch where you're going."

"It's dark, asshole."

"Get the fuck *out* of here!"

"Or what? You gonna put me in a cell, too?" the woman asked. "Make me do tricks?"

"Jesus," Nail said. This was bullshit. This was all bullshit. His head was throbbing, crying on its own behalf even as it compiled complaints from the rest of his body, and he was arguing with somebody who wasn't on speaking terms with reality.

She just stood there, either awaiting an answer or simply looking for an opportunity.

Headlights sent shadows swinging through the school, then stopped moving, sending blazing rectangles of light through the windows, sending rats scurrying for their dark warrens. DeWayne, Nail prayed, not somebody else wanting to crash the party tonight.

A car door slammed.

"Yo!"

DeWayne. He'd actually come. Unbelievable.

"Hold up!" Nail yelled.

The woman didn't take her attention from Nail, despite the glare of the headlights raking her face. Not for even half a second. She shuffled backward to get out of the light.

The sound of quick footsteps and DeWayne, never one to listen to goddamn instructions, came running up and skidded to a halt. "What the fuck?" he said, staring big-eyed at the scene. Oddly, Nail's first thought was that DeWayne had shaved his head since the last time he saw him. It had been cornrows before, for years. Also, he'd grown a seriously ugly mustache, a ratty thing that Nail guessed was supposed to be a handlebar but wasn't quite up to the job.

"Where's Van Horn?" the woman asked again. "So help me, I'll kill you both."

DeWayne looked as frightened as Nail felt. "What in the hell is going on here?"

"She's insane," Nail said. He thumbed back the hammer on his pistol.

The brick rotated slowly. "Don't," the woman warned him.

"Holy shit, is that a flying brick?" Then, without waiting for an answer or even pausing for air, DeWayne continued. "Okay, look." He held up both hands, palms out, presumably to show just how harmless and reasonable he was. "This shit doesn't need to get all crazy. We're all friends here, well, maybe not yet, but we could be, I guess. I don't know what the misunderstanding is, but we can get this all worked out. Hey, sweetheart, what's your name?"

"What?" the woman asked.

"Your name. I'm DeWayne. This here's my brother—he's a tough guy, so you can call him Nail. What's your name?"

Oh my God, Nail thought.

To his amazement, the woman answered, "Uh . . . Sheila."

"Okay, see, that's better? Bro, you wanna lower the gun?"

"You want me to shove it up your ass?" Nail said.

"I guess we're not ready for that yet," DeWayne said, unfazed. "Look, I don't know what's going on here, but we'll figure it out, huh?" He looked uneasily from Sheila to Sheila's brick to Nail and back. "Is this a money thing? He owes you some money or something? We can get that straightened out toot sweet."

I'm gonna kill you next, Nail wanted to say, but Sheila was already talking.

"It's not money," she said. "I need . . . I need help."

"I can see that," DeWayne said, his voice mellow and reasonable. "Maybe we get you to a hospital or something, then you can settle your beef with this asshole later?"

"A hospital can't help me. I need Van Horn. Belial. I need Rain. Something."

"It's August, baby," DeWayne said. "It's not going to rain."

"Not . . ." Sheila gestured skyward. "Rain. She's . . . a person." A rivulet of blood trickled from her nose. She extended her tongue to a point, curled it, and licked the redness from her upper lip. It left a wide smear.

"You know this Rain?" DeWayne asked Nail.

"No. I know Van Horn, though. He left with the rest of your fuckin' people," he said, directing the words at Sheila.

"Hey, no need to be a dick about this," DeWayne said. "He's alive?"

"How should I know?" Nail asked. "He was when he left, but you fuckin' people mighta ate him or something by now!" *Or Karyn. They mighta eaten Karyn.* "Fuck!"

"Calm down now, okay?" DeWayne said, actually taking a step closer to the line of fire connecting Sheila and Nail, if not actually getting in it. "Hey, how about you two put down your, uh"—he glanced at Sheila's brick, and quickly away—"weapons, and we just talk through the rest of this? This is all pretty heated, huh? Lots of grievances on both sides. I never seen a situation like that get better with a gun, you feel me? Or a, or a—um. You know."

"I don't have time for this," Nail said. "I got friends in trouble. We gotta get moving."

Sheila glanced toward the front of the building, shading her eyes, and for one moment her attention was completely off Nail. Maybe he could make the shot, maybe . . .

The click of a cocked weapon stilled his hand.

Sheila's attention snapped back. DeWayne was training a pistol on her.

"Hey!" Nail shouted. "That's my three-eighty!"

"Drop the brick, sweetheart," DeWayne said. To Nail, he said, "Sorry. Sounded like you were in trouble." He looked back at Sheila. "I'm serious, though—we can work this out. You want to find this Van Horn guy, and I guess my brother's girlfriend is with him, so how about you just put that thing down, and we'll talk this through? Otherwise . . ." He shrugged. "You're outgunned."

A snarl contorted Sheila's features, and for a split second Nail was sure she was going to explode in rage, hurl the brick and God knew what else—and then the brick dropped to the ground.

"Mona," Sheila said.

"What?"

"They're going to her. Van Horn hates her, and Belial says she must be destroyed. Van Horn says Belial will help us, after." Anger—*hatred*—flashed in her eyes.

"They goin' there right now?" he asked.

"I guess."

"Shit," Nail said. "DeWayne, help me up. And you—you're coming with us."

Chapter 23

"This isn't her," Mona said. One finger poked out from her crossed arms and pointed at Genevieve. Mona spoke calmly, but when she stopped, her mouth was small and tight, her eyes bright with fury. Just behind her stood two men Anna hadn't seen before, both with pistols already in hand.

"I can explain," Anna started, though she had no idea how.

"Don't." Mona strode into the room, the two men after. Guy, previously hidden from view, came in last, looking as if he'd just received a shock he'd never recover from.

Four of them, at least two with guns. Anna thought about going for her own weapon, but there was no way she'd take enough of them down. She might not take any of them down—she was a decent shot on a target range, but this wasn't a target range, and she'd have to pull some unlikely quick-draw bullshit besides to even get caught up to these guys.

"I'll have your prophet whether you want to cooperate or not."

"Whether she wants to cooperate or not."

"Yes."

"Just like Adelaide."

"Here's what happens now," Mona said. "You and

Andy are going to go to get the prophet. If you're not back within two hours, I'm going to hurt this woman here. If you're not back in three, I'm going to kill her."

"And throw her on the pile?"

"And throw her on the pile," Mona said, accompanying the words with a trace of a smile. *I'm glad we have an understanding,* it said.

"Why?"

"Go. You've wasted any goodwill you had here. You don't get to ask any more questions."

"Fuck you. I ain't doing this without answers," Anna said.

Mona gave a slight nod, and the bigger of the two guys—Andy?—stepped forward and grabbed Genevieve.

"Wait!" Anna shouted.

Too late. The guy spun Gen around and cranked her arm up behind her back, pulling a cry from Genevieve that was half pain, half indignation. She bent at the waist with her left arm twisted behind and the other stretched straight, fingers trembling.

"Please," Genevieve said. "Don't hurt me. We can work something out."

"We *are* working something out," Mona said.

Anna raised her hands in front of her. "Don't do this," she said. "I'll get Karyn, okay?"

"Now you've got an hour."

Anna nodded, trying to avoid looking directly at Mona, as though making eye contact would only enrage her further. In her peripheral vision, Genevieve twisted around. Something dropped, a little thing, like a little brown, striped button. It bounced a couple of times, then rolled across the floor, finally toppling a few inches from Mona's foot.

Guy picked it up.

"I'm going," Anna said.

Mona stepped aside.

"Ow!" Guy shouted. He stuck his finger in his mouth. The button fell from his hands.

It had legs, Anna saw. A cluster of spiky black legs, sprouting from the underside. It hit the floor, and an instant later it leaped. A little black star appeared on Mona's hand.

"Shit!" she said.

Then she swayed, staggering back into the doorframe.

Andy—or whoever—was frozen in shock and confusion, and there wouldn't be another chance. Anna pulled the gun from the back of her jeans. Andy figured things out a moment too late and started to turn.

She pulled the trigger. The round caught him high in the neck, and he dropped to his knees, hand over the spurting wound.

"Run!" Anna yelled.

Guy fell to the floor with a thud as Anna and Genevieve charged the door. The third guy made as if to intercept, and Anna waved the gun at him, shooting wildly. He threw himself to the side.

Anna glanced back in time to see Mona collapse.

"Go!" Genevieve shouted. The last guy got off a few shots, punching holes in the plaster past Anna and blowing a piece of trim off the door casing, and then they were in the next room.

Anna cut left, trying to remember the path to the front door. Going back through the bodies was unthinkable, as was trying to escape out a window with somebody following her. She ran through the room with the billiards table with Genevieve so close she was worried Gen was going to step on her heels. Then through the next doorway.

More gunshots, bullets blasting through the wall, and she flinched. Her flashlight bobbled and skewed in front of her, light fracturing off an elaborate light fixture, off a shelf full of crystal. Then they rushed out into the main hall, and it was all Anna could do to stop running into the balcony. She shoved off it and dashed down the stairs. She stumbled at the bottom, but Genevieve grabbed her, the momentum pulling her up and forward before she could fall.

Another missed shot, and the shouts of at least two men.

Then they were out, bursting out the front door into—?

"Ohhhh, fuck!" Anna cried. There were half a dozen people out here, including one very familiar face—a man in a worn pin-striped suit. He'd recovered his hat, and he was grinning like a fiend.

Anna cut left just as Genevieve, to her left, cut right, and they fell all over each other, going down in a mess of bruised knees and swinging elbows. Something bony—chin? elbow? head?—rammed into Anna's jaw, sending her reeling.

A number of people rushed out the front door in pursuit—Anna couldn't see how many, could barely keep from falling off the world, she was so dazed. All she knew was that there was a scream, and somebody caught fire, and then Van Horn's entourage rushed them. The screaming got a whole lot worse. Anna tried to get to her feet, but somebody pushed her back down. She tried to haul her gun around to shoot the bastard, but the weapon was easily slapped from her hand.

"Shhh," Van Horn said. "Just wait."

She tried to roll away, but Van Horn planted a foot on her chest.

The screaming stopped, but the tearing sounds went on for a while.

At last, Van Horn took his foot off her. "Okay. Can you stand?"

She lifted her head from the roach-strewn grass. Genevieve was lying on her back a few yards away, still breathing hard from the run. She seemed okay. Anna looked the other way, then wished she hadn't.

"Yeah, I think so." She got up. That dazed feeling had dissipated some, but her head wasn't totally clear yet.

"How many more?" he asked.

"I—how many more what?"

"Men. In the house."

"Mona's dead," Genevieve said.

"She fell down," Anna said. "I don't know if she's dead. Where's Karyn? Nail?"

Genevieve shook her head, rolling it on the disgusting, locust-covered lawn. "Mona's dead. The other guy, too."

"That's six, then." Van Horn's voice oozed smug satisfaction. "Bastards. How many left?"

"Where are Karyn and Nail? Are they okay?"

"Sit up," Van Horn said.

Anna did. Karyn, she saw, was right next to Van Horn, some guy holding her by her upper arm. She looked okay. Out of it, but okay. Anna's first response was relief, but it was quickly flushed away as she appreciated the situation.

"Where's Nail?"

"Back at your lovely base of operations, I suppose. How many men are left inside?"

"Is he okay?"

"He's alive, or was when we left. How many men?"

"I don't know." She caught another glimpse of the aftermath of the feeding frenzy, and her stomach roiled. She wanted to turn away but feared presenting her back to the blood-streaked psychos now lounging on the lawn. One of them tossed a fragment of bone in her direction. It fell short and skittered along the sidewalk.

"Rain, Antawn, Jude—come with me. The rest of you, throw these bodies inside. We need to get out of here as soon as I take care of something. Ladies," he said, gesturing at Anna and Genevieve. "Take me to Mona."

"Nail might need help."

"Too bad for him. Now, Mona."

Anna could resist, she supposed. Make it as hard as possible. Make a run for it. And then what? Even if both she and Gen got away, somehow outrunning the mob and their twisted magic, Karyn would be stuck here. And if they *didn't* both get away, the outcome would be even worse. Mona had been willing to make an example of Genevieve. These people would probably just eat her and make Anna watch.

"Can I have my gun?"

Van Horn gave her a deadpan look. "Oh, you won't need that. You'll be quite safe with us."

Anna led them back into the house. The stink seemed less severe now—she was actually getting used to it, as unlikely as that seemed. You really could get used to anything, she supposed. Van Horn propelled Karyn along behind Anna. At first, Anna thought that was just to remind her that he was in control, but she wondered about that. Van Horn was solicitous with Karyn. Careful. Gentle, even. Maybe he was afraid to leave her alone with his guys, in case they got hungry.

The trip seemed shorter, now that she knew where she was going, but at every new room, she was acutely aware that she entered first, that anybody who remained would have to shoot the others through her, and they'd be only too happy to do so. She briefly entertained a grimly satisfying fantasy—she would duck a bullet, a miracle of reflexes, and it would blow the top of Van Horn's head off.

No such luck. They reached the back rooms without seeing a sign of another living body. Mona lay just inside the doorway she'd collapsed near, unmoving. Van Horn regarded her still form for a moment, then rolled her over and started checking her pockets.

"Seriously?" Anna said.

"Be quiet." He stood, empty-handed, a frown creasing his face. Then he started rifling through the shelves.

"I've been through the shelves," Anna said.

He whirled on her, teeth bared. "And what did you find?"

"Nothing."

"No?"

"Really. Just a bunch of shit. You wanna go through *my* pockets?"

Van Horn made a disgusted noise in his throat and kept searching. Anna shone the light around. What had killed Mona? Genevieve had done . . . something. It was creepy. She thought of Gen's insistence that she come with on this trip, and pulled her thoughts back. There would be time to consider that later. Right now it was too upsetting, and she needed to concentrate.

Mona looked peaceful, so there was that.

Movement caught Anna's eye. *There.* A wet black splinter stuck out from under the dead woman's thumbnail. As Anna watched, it pushed itself out and fell to the floor. It was covered in blood, though only a drop or two had fallen on the floor nearby.

What the hell?

Van Horn gave up on the shelves. He turned a slow circle, scanning the room. Finally, he plucked a short gray hair from his head. He held it between his left thumb and forefinger and said a few words over it.

"More light," he said.

Anna held the flashlight on his hand, desperately wanting to shine it back over at the toothpick on the floor, yet terrified to draw attention to it. The hair was a tiny silver filament in the beam. As she watched, it bent over.

"Come on," Van Horn said. Somebody shoved her. Van Horn followed the direction the hair was leaning, through a doorway into the next room. Raul pushed Karyn after.

What the hell? Anna mouthed to Genevieve. Gen tightened her lips into a line and just nodded after Van Horn.

Behind them, somebody dropped on all fours to Mona's corpse.

In the next room, Van Horn was already pulling a little glass vial out of a jewelry box. He held it up to Anna's flashlight. Inside was a blackened incisor, root and all. The hair in Van Horn's other hand, Anna could see, was pointed right at it, quivering.

"It's *your* fucking tooth?" Genevieve said.

Van Horn's eyes darted toward Genevieve. "That'll be our little secret. If you don't mind."

"Whose side are you on?"

"I'm on my side. You should probably take a lesson from me. Now, Anna. I need you to call Enoch Sobell."

"No."

He rolled his eyes and sighed dramatically. "Call Sobell, or I'll sew a weasel up in your belly. Or Karyn's. Or whatever threat you find motivating."

"I can't just call him. I don't have his number."

"Contact him. You must have a contact."

"Yeah, fine." She bounced a sullen glare off him. Might as well have kissed him on the cheek. "What do you want me to tell him?"

"Tell him Forcas would like a word with him. Or just give me the phone."

"I told you, I can't just call him. All I can do is pass the message along."

"Do it."

She flipped open her phone, squinting at the light from the screen. The others around her stirred restlessly, grumbling to themselves.

She dialed Nail. He picked up halfway through the first ring. "Jesus, Anna, I'm glad—"

"I need you to get a message to Mr. Sobell," she said, voice carefully neutral.

"Uh, what? Hey, we got problems here. Van Horn's loose with his army of freaks, and he's got Karyn—"

"Tell him Van Horn would like a word with him. Right now. Have him call my cell."

"Forcas," Van Horn said. "Forcas would like a word with him."

"Right. Sorry. I meant Forcas would like a word with him. Have him call my cell, please. I'm sure he has the number."

She hung up. Nail would get the message, she was

sure. Whether he'd be able to do anything about it before Van Horn's traveling circus needed a midnight snack was another issue.

"Now what?" she asked.

"Now we move." He clapped his hands together. "My friends! Let us seek out our companions elsewhere."

"Uh, shouldn't we wait? Sobell might call back."

"I hear you can take your phone with you these days. Now move."

She walked back into the library. Two of Van Horn's psychos had been at Mona, but they rose now. The black toothpick would have been just to the right. All she had to do was get to it, maybe fake a fall and palm it. Get it to Karyn later.

She took a few steps and then lurched forward. Her knees hit the floor; her hand fell forward. The toothpick was right around here somewhere. She reached out for it.

So did Karyn.

Karyn didn't know where she was. Somewhere different, she thought, if only because much of what she'd seen lately had taken place under open sky rather than inside, and because she'd been standing in the same place for a while. Usually, they sat her down if they weren't directly exercising her. She tried to enjoy this now. It was different, after all. She had friends here, in some of the visions. That was nice. Nail. Genevieve. Anna. Good to see them, even if it was impossible to interact with them in any meaningful way.

She was watching the demolition of a sprawling two-story house, when an image flickered to life in her mind. It was unclear—fuzzy, in a way. It had the same feel as a TV screen covered in snow and flickering lines, though it didn't look that way at all. It was out of focus. It had pieces missing.

For all that, the vibe it gave off was familiar, and the object of the image itself *very* familiar. A toothpick, black. On a wood floor. Next to something that might be a body. She put her hand out, saw movement, an irregular shape that *could* be her hand.

She went for it. Anything was better than this. Dropped to her knees, reached her hand out, and—

"Shit!" Just as before, she'd been reaching for the thing when it stabbed her. Her left thumb this time, and right under the nail.

Instantly, the image became clear. Awesomely, 1080p H.D. clear, right down to an arc of light reflected in the bead of blood flowing over her lifeline.

"What's going on?" she asked. Nothing good, she knew that much. The scene earlier, all the violence—it might not have gone down exactly the way she'd envisioned, but it had happened. Something had. She had a memory of being urged to move, a sense of acceleration. Car, almost certainly.

For an answer, she got another image: Anna, getting to her feet in a dark room. Behind her, a couple of people Karyn didn't recognize. There was something odd about the image, and it took her a moment to figure it out—ghostly traces framed it. Her nose and eyelashes, eyebrows at the very top edge. This was happening, she thought. This was what she'd be seeing, if she were seeing normally.

"What's going on?" she asked again.

She couldn't hear the answers, not clearly. There were words, lost in an overlapping flood of sounds that matched the scene of the demolition before her eyes. Anna said something, though, and she didn't look happy. She was baring her teeth and breathing heavily through her mouth. From experience, Karyn took that as a very bad sign.

Rough hands grabbed her at the elbows and pulled her up. Anna, too. Okay, they were in some shit, then. These people weren't friendly. Somebody pushed her forward—not hard enough to make her stumble, but enough to get her moving.

She dropped her hand to her side, not wanting to draw attention to it. In her mind's eye, the splinter was burning down, just like the last one. In a minute or two, she'd be dropped back into her shifting world of useless information, incapable of doing anything to help herself, let alone Anna or the others. The demon's offer—for surely the creature in her head was a demon—was ugly, but not as ugly as sitting, powerless, while Christ knew what happened to her friends. It occurred to her that she might never actually find out what happened.

Okay. What do I have to do?

No response. Either it couldn't hear her thoughts, or it was screwing with her.

"Fine," she muttered, trying to keep her voice low enough to avoid being overheard. "What do I have to do?"

The next image was a single, very clear instruction.

"Are you kidding me?" she asked.

The old man came over and, at least in the image, put a hand on Karyn's shoulder. He had the expression of a tired orderly in the psycho ward. Karyn shrugged him off and took a step backward.

"Chill," Karyn said.

The old guy gave her a worried look, but he stayed back. The procession started moving again.

"Is this for real?" Karyn asked quietly.

The old guy was gone. In his place, a willowy woman in a blue gown. She nodded once, then vanished.

"Great," Karyn muttered. She watched as she walked through one room, then the next. Anna kept glancing over at her, trying to make eye contact, maybe trying to convey some kind of message.

How much time did she have?

There was a millennia-long tradition of suffering being a spiritual thing, or good for the soul, or what have you. Righteous in some way. Karyn thought of monks flogging or starving themselves, of Puritans and Victorians condemning sex as sinful while they went around with their libidos cranked to eleven, dreaming up crazy

Freudian crap because all that pent-up energy needed somewhere to go. She thought of the Inquisition, and witch trials, and those modern-day motherfuckers who thought that the poor could join the righteous if they'd just suffer a little more.

A long tradition. An *enormous* tradition and, as far as she could tell, one of pure bullshit. A way to protect the hierarchy, nothing more. Pain was pain, privation was also pain, and little good came from either, most of the time. Fetishizing it sickened her. When somebody said the pain was for your own good, nine times out of ten your pain was for *their* good. Words to live by.

So here she was. The instructions had been very clear. This was a small thing, but would likely hurt more than anything she'd experienced in her life aside from taking half a blast of buckshot a few months back. She was sweating, she realized, and her heart was pounding in her temples.

Take this cup from my lips, somebody had once said, but that was naive. The cup never went anywhere. It was there, waiting for you to drain it to the dregs. Even if it killed you.

She held her hand flat, straight to the bent elbow, and then tucked her elbow in to her body. Then, before she could talk herself out of it, she ran the end of her thumb into the next doorjamb she came to, putting all her weight on her elbow. The weight drove her hand forward.

The splinter slid in under the entire length of her thumbnail, sending an electric bolt of pain up her arm. She didn't scream—she froze, her mouth open, her mind shocked at the wound. She closed her eyes tightly, pushing tears from their corners, and she cradled her left hand in her right.

"What the hell?" she heard from somebody, though she didn't recognize the man's voice. "Is she okay? What did you do?"

I can hear! she thought. It was enough to get her to rock back on her heels and open her eyes.

No. The world beyond was still crowded with vehicles and people, many overlapping in disturbing ways, and the noise of dirt movers and construction workers still swam in her head. If she looked inward, she saw Anna arguing with the old man she'd seen earlier. A moment later, she felt hands. She shook them off once more.

"I'm ready. Let's go." She pushed herself to her feet.

"—bleeding," she heard.

"Let's *go*."

The image of Anna and the old man disappeared. She saw two men shake hands. A woman at a car dealership putting a signed contract in a drawer. Two kids pushing bloody cuts together.

"Yeah, great," she said. "Just you and me, baby."

Anna walked toward the front of the house, flanked by Van Horn's mob. *Something* had happened with Karyn, that was certain. It had been confusing and dark, but it looked as though Van Horn's guy had steered her into the side of a door by accident. There was more to that story, Anna thought, especially when Karyn looked her way. Made eye contact.

She got shoved to one side, tried looking back over at Karyn without being too obvious, got shoved again. Got separated a little.

That was real. Please. That had to be.

Down the stairs and out the front door, and the night air felt positively frigid against her skin. It smelled good, too—or maybe not good, but in contrast to the stench of the house, it was flowers and perfume.

"Let's go," Van Horn said. "Anna, give Jasper your car keys."

"I don't think so."

Van Horn's dull-eyed stare bored into her skull for about five seconds before she sighed and gave the keys to the naked guy, who was standing there with his hand out. She wondered where he'd keep them. What he'd say if he got pulled over.

Then she was shoved over to Nail's van. Van Horn and one of the others got in front, and Anna was jammed in the middle between Karyn and a big guy who took up a seat and a half by himself. Genevieve was shoved in back with another guy.

Van Horn hit the gas. Anna felt none of the usual sense of relief for getting off this awful street, probably because she was bringing the awful with her.

"Are you all right?" Karyn whispered.

Anna checked Karyn's face. Eye contact again, and tracking her, not lighting on her and slipping past to follow something invisible. "I, uh, yeah," she said with a nod. "Yeah, I'm good. The situation could use a little help."

"Where are we going?"

Anna sent another prayer out to the universe: *let this be real, not some fucked-up cosmic joke.* "I don't know. Are *you* all right?" Anna asked Karyn. "You're bleeding."

There was an odd pause as Karyn gave her a blank look, then followed Anna's gaze down to her hand. "It's not bad," she said. "I'm fine."

Holy shit. This looked as though it might turn into a real conversation. All this bullshit might actually have been worth it. She thought the pounding of her heart might actually be more excitement than fear. Here she was, crammed in a van with a bunch of demon-worshipping psychos, en route to some horrible unknown destination, and she felt happier than she had in literally months.

"What happened to your hand?" Anna asked.

Another blank look, just like when Karyn had gotten that first splinter. Karyn pointed at her ear. "I can't hear everything," she said, "and what I can hear is pretty hard to follow."

"It's fine, it's fine," Anna said. "Anybody got a pen?" Genevieve handed forward one of the Sharpies she always carried, along with a folded piece of paper. The guy next to her reached for it, but Van Horn said it was okay.

"Just don't you *dare* try to stab me with that," Van Horn said.

Anna took the marker without looking at or acknowledging Genevieve. She wrote in big letters: *Seeing any threats?* She showed it to Karyn.

"I can't really tell—I'm seeing a lot of everything right about now." Her smile lit up her whole face. "It is *so* good to see you."

"It's good to be seen," Anna said. Karyn gave her a sheepish grimace that said, *I didn't quite follow that.* Anna scribbled the message on paper. *Good 2B seen.* She started writing faster, hoping to convey their situation as quickly as possible. Let Karyn know what was going on, and maybe give her some framework to evaluate whatever crazy shit she saw. And hell, because it simply felt good to communicate with her friend.

She'd covered about half of the page when Van Horn glanced in the mirror, then over his shoulder, and frowned. "That's probably enough of that," he said. "Put the pen away."

"Go to Hell."

"I'll get there soon enough. Put the pen away *now*, before I have Raul confiscate it."

Anna put the pen in her pocket. She pointed at Van Horn for Karyn's benefit. "Sorry," she said. "This guy's an asshole."

Genevieve leaned forward from the backseat. "Is she going to be okay?"

"I don't know," Anna said. "But better, maybe." Her mind pulled back from the moment, casting back to Mona's sudden death. That whole scene left a bad taste in her mouth, the more she thought about it. "What did you do back there?"

"She was like a rabid dog, Anna. Did you see that? Out of her mind. She would have killed us." The words poured out fast, one running into the next until they were almost incomprehensible.

"I get that. Sure am glad you just happened to have something handy. It's just . . . all I can think of is how eager you were to come with me. How mad you were when

I went without you the first time. Were you planning for this? Was this always part of the job?"

"Yes," Van Horn said. "And believe me, I appreciate it."

"Don't lecture me," Genevieve said. "You have no idea what you're talking about."

"Are you working for this asshole?" Anna asked.

"No! Sobell."

"Oh, right. Sobell. I should have guessed. It's always Sobell."

"Just like all of us," Genevieve said.

"Not quite."

"You have no idea what he's capable of," Genevieve said, "the kind of shit he'd do if I fucked him over. To me. To you."

"Oh, so this was a, what, then, like some kind of self-less act?"

"Not ex—"

"Fuck you."

"All right, that's enough," Van Horn said. "Do you want me to turn this van around?"

Anna looked up at the rearview mirror and caught Van Horn grinning.

"In all seriousness, I'd appreciate a little quiet for the rest of the ride. All this squabbling makes me tense."

"I don't care—"

"I'm not above having you gagged."

Anna turned back around in her seat and glared at the road.

Karyn reached over and squeezed her hand, though, and while everything wasn't quite right in that department yet, it sure seemed one hell of a lot better.

Chapter 24

"What do we do?" Erica asked.

Sobell set his glass down. Ice water, which was a shame. He had a craving for tequila, for some odd reason, and he wanted nothing more than to down half a dozen shots, sit back, and enjoy the buzz. Too bad he'd cut himself off from even that small pleasure. Erica had impressed upon him how important it was not to draw any more attention from the police, and prudence dictated that the act of lowering his inhibitions was to be avoided. He thought of himself as a pleasant drunk, and not prone to taking additional risks while under the influence, but these days he was better safe than sorry, distasteful as it might be.

"I'm sorry. What?"

He didn't miss the moment of alarm on Erica's face, though she smoothed it over almost instantly. She thought he was slipping. Maybe he was slipping. She tended to be right about these things. That should worry him, he supposed.

"About the message."

Ah, the message. Something must have happened with Mme. Gorow, because one of Ruiz's accomplices had left Erica a message on her burner, invoking both Van Horn and Forcas. Probably best to move on that right away. "Oh, right. Have you got a secure phone?"

"Secure? No. Unidentified burner cell, yes."

"I'll assume the two are roughly synonymous for our purposes."

Erica scowled. "Not if the phone you're calling is tapped."

"Ms. Ruiz changes phones like lesser women change their undergarments. It's a risk I'm comfortable with."

"I'm not sure I am."

Sobell paused in the act of reaching for his water. "Excuse me?"

"I'm in this almost as deeply as you are, Enoch. If you go down, I'll end up going down with you."

"Nonsense. That's why they invented attorney-client privilege."

"The FBI will kick the privilege to death in a case like this. It's not designed to cover up actual criminal activity. And you damn well know it. That's what gets me. Do you think this is amateur hour?"

He touched his fingertips to the glass and rotated it on the desk. When he spoke, his voice was low and soft. "I need this, Erica. It's not a matter of going to prison. It's life or death. If you get me through this alive, I will buy you an island. From prison, if necessary."

She smiled sadly. "You can't afford an island."

"Small island. Collection of rocks and seaweed, really. Somewhat connected to the mainland when the tide is out."

"You'll buy me a peninsula."

"If that's what we can get. I need to make this call."

"All right." She pulled a phone from her purse and handed to him, along with a Post-it note with a phone number on it.

He dialed.

"Hi." A woman's voice, over road noise.

"Ms. Ruiz?"

"Yeah. Sobell?"

"*Mr.* Sobell will do fine. Thank you."

"Right."

"You said somebody wanted to speak with me."

"Yeah. Uh, here he is." More road noise, followed by a loud burst of static as the phone mic brushed something.

Then Van Horn's voice: "Enoch."

"Edgar."

"Your thieves came through."

"I'm not so sure about that. Had they delivered properly, I would be holding the item in my hand. Instead, I'm speaking to . . . you."

"There's been a change in my fortunes."

"So I gathered. Has there been a change in mine?"

"Looks like you did quite a number on Mona," Van Horn said. "My friends ate her, you know."

"That's particularly unpleasant, if not surprising. I was told Forcas was ready to speak with me."

"He is. But you're not exactly in his good graces, you might remember."

Sobell looked at Erica and rolled his eyes. "I assume there's a price for that."

"We need a sacrifice."

"Oh, is that all? Virgin or otherwise?"

"Different kind of sacrifice. The Pharaoh's Chalice should do nicely."

"That is . . . no longer in my possession."

"Anything of roughly that caliber should work. St. George's sword, that grotty old torc we found."

Sobell nearly laughed aloud at the man's insouciance. The torc he referred to, an ancient ring of bronze and gold large enough for a big man to wear around his neck, was priceless. "That 'grotty old torc' is twenty-eight hundred years old and has killed fourteen kings."

"It ought to work nicely, then."

"Not really a sacrifice, though, is it? Not in the classical sense."

"It will be."

"Very well. I can accommodate that."

"We'll also require your kit for greater workings."

"Are we performing a greater working tonight?"

"And eight hundred thousand dollars."

"Not very mystical, that."

"A man's gotta eat." Van Horn sounded peeved. Nice to know he could still get under his skin, Sobell thought.

"I see. Are you coming here, or shall I meet you?"

At this, Erica became so agitated she stood up and whispered, "What?"

"The latter." Van Horn gave an address, which Sobell dutifully copied down.

"Give me an hour. I don't think the ATM will accommodate this evening's requirements."

"Sure." He hung up.

Erica exploded. "Where are you going? Who are you meeting? And what was that crap about an ATM?" Her mouth tightened into a small angry slash.

"You need to move quickly," Sobell said. "Get eight hundred thousand from one of the caches and meet me back here in forty minutes."

"Absolutely not."

"Erica, if I have to get it myself, what do I need you for?"

"Is that a threat?"

He frowned. "A threat that I'll have to terminate your employment if you can't handle the most basic of tasks, yes."

"Fifteen years, you've followed my counsel and stayed out of prison. I don't like this, Enoch. You're becoming . . ." She paused, her mouth turned down in disgust. ". . . erratic."

"I prefer to think of myself as whimsical. Now, I don't have time to faff about with this, particularly if you're not going to help. Are you going to get the money, or do I need to handle this myself?"

"I'll go. What are you going to be doing?"

"Assembling high explosives."

From the shock on her face, he realized he'd gone too far. "I kid, Erica. Just a joke. I do need to put together the most basic of occult defenses, though. Forcas detests

me, and while he might be able to stave off his worst
impulses long enough for us to work together, I'd be a
fool not to take some precautions."

"We'll be followed," Erica said.

"And if they pull us over, the worst they'll find is a bag
full of cash, and you and an army of the best criminal lawyers money can buy will exhaust them and finally bury
them over the issue of probable cause. I am a millionaire,
remember, not some street-level dope pusher." He laughed
as a surprising thought occurred to him. "Incredibly, we're
not actually doing anything illegal tonight."

"No explosives?"

"Sincerely. I promise, no explosives. You're losing your
sense of humor."

She bit back a retort, Sobell was surprised to see. He
wasn't the only one wearing down, it seemed.

"Fine," she said. She got up to leave.

"Before you go . . ."

"Yes?"

"Leave the phone."

She took it back out of her purse and hefted it, as if
she might just throw it at him. "Don't do anything stupid,
okay?"

"Erica," he said, dropping any pretense at jocularity.
"Take a moment to remember to whom you are speaking."

She met his gaze and held it, and once again he thought
she was about to open up and give him both barrels. At
last, though, she put the phone on the desk and walked
out.

He picked up the phone and started dialing.

Chapter 25

"Would you look at that?" Nail said wonderingly.

Up front, in the driver's seat, DeWayne made a show of looking out the windshield and side windows. "I don't get it. It's fucking *dark*. These people don't believe in streetlights?"

Nail glanced to his left, where Sheila sat beside him, covered by the gun he wasn't sure he could even shoot straight. She watched the street, her expression going through a discomfiting sequence of alternating detached curiosity and fear.

He looked back out the windshield. "It's not all dark, though." It was just one porch light, two houses down from the Gorow place, but the effect it had on the street—and on Nail's mood—was huge. It was like the sun had come up on this miserable little street for the first time in centuries, chasing away all the creeping and scuttling things, burning away pale sickly fungus and cobwebs alike.

"Well, hell. Neighbors gonna fuck that guy up. Breakin' the rules." DeWayne made a clucking sound. "And frankly, I gotta tell you, this doesn't even rate on the scale of shit I don't believe tonight. You sure you doin' all right?"

Nail turned his head left, then right. He wasn't yet a hundred percent, still dizzy and sometimes disoriented or confused, but he hadn't felt like throwing up in the last twenty minutes. He knew DeWayne wasn't asking about that, though. He was asking about everything else. He'd asked if Nail was in a cult, if Sheila was in a cult, if the both of them were in a cult together, what was up with his girlfriend (Nail had had to disabuse him of the notion that he and Karyn were involved, and who the hell knew where he'd gotten *that* idea?), who this Van Horn guy was and was *he* in a cult (Nail had simply said yes, because it was easier than trying to explain, and not all that far off), if it was true that cults were heavy into S and M sex parties and if so could he get an invite, and every other question that had popped into his head, since he had no filter between brain and mouth. If he thought something, he goddamn well said it.

"I'm good," Nail said. "Feeling like a badass."

"Uh-huh."

"Head on into the alley," Nail said. DeWayne obliged. A cat ran for cover as the lights swept over it. The place seemed free of its weight of foreboding, a perfectly ordinary alley.

"No car," Nail said.

"Huh?"

"Go down to the end." Sometimes Anna parked the next street over, but Nail didn't think that was the case this time. Sure enough, down at the end of the alley, there was no car.

Fucking Van Horn.

"Turn around. Take the main street," Nail said.

DeWayne turned back on to the street. Still no squirrels or creepy birds or legions of rats—turn the lights back on, clean up the yards some, and things would be back to normal.

"Stop here."

DeWayne stopped the van in front of the house and twisted around in his seat.

"Now what?"

"Hang tight for a sec. Keep an eye on her. I gotta go check on something."

He got out and stepped onto the sidewalk. Be nice if

he had some light. Better than a flashlight. If the house was empty . . .

He heard car doors open behind him as he walked up to the house. He'd thought the place had lost much of its malevolence, but dread kindled in him as he approached. Dark, wet smears stained the sidewalk, the front step, even the doorknob. He pulled a handkerchief from his pocket and tried the door. It opened easily.

He reached around the doorjamb, feeling for light switches. He found three, flipped them all, and got not a flicker for his trouble.

He got out his flashlight and went in.

The place stank, but no worse than any of half a dozen places Nail could think of off the top of his head. Mostly those were combat zones, so it was pretty goddamn weird for an upscale place in Beverly Hills to have that tang of corpse and gunpowder hanging in the air, but at least it was familiar.

He did a quick search of the place. There wasn't nearly enough time to go through room by room, but the blood trail led him to the important parts. Mona was dead, and nobody else was around. Not Van Horn, not any of his crew. They'd been here, though.

He found DeWayne and Sheila back in the main entry room, both staring at the body there, presumably for different reasons. "I know that guy," Sheila said.

"I just, uh, wanted to get off the street," DeWayne said.

"Come on. Out."

Outside, Nail tried to pull enough of his concentration together to take stock of the situation.

"Now what?" DeWayne asked. "Ain't shit in there but dead people, and I gotta tell you, I never seen anything like that in my whole life. That is *fucked-up*." He kept talking. Nail, at a loss for anything else to do, dialed Anna again. No answer.

When he put his phone away, Sheila was standing on the sidewalk, staring at what was left of her hands. She turned the left one over and looked at the back, then turned it again to inspect the front. The whole time, she shook her head.

"Your people were here," Nail said.

She nodded.

"Where'd they go after that?"

"I'm thinking."

"Think faster."

She spat, thick and red, and whether it was directed at him or not, he couldn't tell.

"There's blood," she said.

"Yeah. Fuckin' everywhere."

"No. Here. And here." She pointed with the remaining finger on her right hand. Nail came closer. The locusts here had been kicked away in patches, and sure enough, there were scattered drops of blood on the sidewalk. Might have been somebody from the house, but as he looked at the parallel trails of crushed locusts on the street, he thought it more likely that somebody had gotten in a car here, either wounded or covered in the blood of the dead.

Sheila crouched next to the drops, studied them, then stood again.

"I can find them," she said.

"Yeah?"

"Maybe. What if I do? What happens then?"

Nail mulled it over. "You think Van Horn will trade for you?"

"I don't know." For once, she seemed neither bloodthirsty, demonic, nor an alien in her own skin. She just looked weary and afraid. "It's worth a try. I'll need some help." She held up her hands. "I can't do it myself anymore."

Nail looked quickly away from the tears that suddenly shone in her eyes. "Yeah. Okay. What do you need?"

It didn't take long. At her direction, he got some string—a spare bootlace, in fact, at which DeWayne exclaimed, "You keep spare shoestrings?" and Nail replied,

"Doesn't everyone?" After that, she did some simple preparation, writing symbols awkwardly on the back of an envelope that contained the van's registration, and Nail helped her with more manual details.

At the end, she held up a simple little contraption, and DeWayne snorted. "Look at that. You got a cigarette tied to a piece of string." The bootlace looped around the middle of the cigarette, holding it roughly parallel to the ground. It wavered gently, as though stirring in a light breeze.

She touched the filter end of the cigarette to one of the drops of blood on the sidewalk. "And the end with the blood on it points toward the others, probably."

Nail groaned. "Jesus Christ, why is it always blood? Can I tell you how tired I am of blood?" He let the "probably" slide. Just didn't have the energy to go into it.

"It works, that's all, and it's what I have. Are you ready to get us out of here or should we talk about it some more?"

Nail headed toward the car.

Chapter 26

The elevator to the garage stopped. Sobell got out, but to his surprise, Erica did not. "I can't be a part of this," she said.

He put his hand in front of the elevator door to keep it from closing. "I'd say you're fifteen years too late to make that decision, wouldn't you?"

"It's one thing to be at arm's length, but this is something else entirely. Enoch, listen to me: I am no good to you in jail. If I'm implicated in any of this, I can't be your counsel."

"Implicated in any of what? We are meeting with a former business associate of mine, as investors."

"Investors don't hand over suitcases full of cash at two o'clock in the morning."

The doors tried to close again, and Sobell pushed them back. "And yet there's not a single law on the books preventing it. Curious, wouldn't you say? What you're about to be 'implicated in,' if anything, is conducting a cash transaction for information or goodwill. Perfectly legal. The only conceivable issue is if Forcas fails to report the income to the IRS. I suspect he very well might—but that will be his problem. Now, enough is enough. Let's go."

The elevator tried to close once again. This time, when Sobell stopped the doors, the elevator began to shriek.

Erica stepped out. The doors closed. To Sobell's relief, the shriek stopped.

"It doesn't matter if it's perfectly innocuous," Erica protested. "It looks bad. It connects you to whatever this Forcas character does next. You make it sound like he's unstable. If you give him some cash, then he goes out and breaks the law, they're going to try to tie it back to you and use it as a RICO predicate."

"Only if they witness anything."

Revulsion flickered across her face. "Don't tell me you have another jar of bugs."

"Sadly, no. I do have another solution, though. Don't worry." He tried on his best charming smile. "Think fondly of small tropical islands."

She made an exasperated noise and began walking toward her car. A few minutes later, they pulled out onto Figueroa.

Erica was stressed to the point of losing her cool, a thing Sobell would have regarded as unthinkable until recently. He didn't know anybody more capable of taking care of business, except maybe the late, lamented Joe Gresser, and Joe had handled a different kind of business entirely. Sobell watched Erica's hands as they continually clasped and reclasped the steering wheel, like if she just got a firm enough grip on the thing, she'd be able to steer a course through this shit.

Sobell thought that was simultaneously rather humorous and deeply worrisome. "Turn left."

She rolled up to the next light, slowed, and turned left.

Sobell checked the mirror. There wasn't much traffic at this hour, so the white Impala trailing half a block back could hardly have been more obvious. Sobell had Erica take a couple more turns, enough to prove to his satisfaction that the Impala wasn't an unlucky wanderer. He took out Erica's burner phone and sent a quick text message.

"What are you doing?" Erica asked.

He put a finger over his lips. "Shhh." Not talking in

the car had been her admonition to begin with, and it
was a good one. "Right on McKenzie."

Another car, a blue rust bucket, joined the Impala behind them. A little while later, a newish pickup truck
turned onto the street, cruising up the lane to their right.
By the time a fourth car pulled in close, Erica looked
panicky. She barely watched the road anymore, she was
so busy checking the mirrors.

Sobell nodded at the man driving the pickup truck. A
few seconds later, there was a screech of tires as the guy
apparently lost control. The truck dropped back, weaved
across the road, and T-boned the Impala.

"Next right," Sobell said.

Erica gave him an incredulous look, but she didn't say
anything. Good. He gave her instructions, one word at a
time, occasionally even pointing one direction while saying another, just to be safe. Who knew what kinds of
trickery those FBI types had gotten up to with their surveillance tools?

"Here," he said. "Pull over right here."

Erica stopped the car. There was nothing here—a
chain-link fence in front of a weed-choked lot on the left,
a concrete slope down into a drainage ditch on the right.

Sobell got out. "Go home," he said.

She didn't even try to argue, just stepped on the gas.

Once her taillights had disappeared around a brick
building, the blue rust bucket pulled up. The driver was a
grinning Latino guy with what appeared to be gang and
prison tattoos down the length of his arms and covering
most of his neck. "Mr. Sobell," he said. "Toomey sent me."

Sobell got in, kicking a crumpled white bag over to
the driver's side. "Enoch Sobell," he said, holding out a
hand.

The guy grabbed hold and squeezed once, hard.
"Rhino."

"That's the name your mother gave you?"

"Naw, man. She calls me Enrique."

"Are you armed, Enrique?"

The guy pulled up his shirt, revealing the grip of a fearsomely large revolver.

"You still use revolvers? I'd expected some kind of intimidating rapid-fire weapon."

"Kill ya just as dead," he said.

"Word up."

Enrique gave him a dead-eyed stare, probably trying to figure out if Sobell was messing with him. "Where we goin'?"

"Forward, for now."

More directions, more miles gone. It seemed like hours since getting the money together and leaving the office, but barely forty minutes had gone by. Somewhere, some angry cops were doubtless still having a heated argument with a couple of beefy gentlemen who had run their car off the road. Risky, Erica would have said, and she would have been right. Sending semireliable accomplices to take out law enforcement officers was not an action a prudent man would take. He'd sent *good* accomplices to do it any number of times, but those days had passed with Gresser, and with the FBI's mapping of his usual network of contacts. He was cashing in favors now, relying on a friend of a friend—rather, minions of a distant business associate—and flying on hope. If the guys in the truck escalated the situation to violence, or, God help him, had outstanding warrants, it could get bad.

So be it. It was out of his control now.

He guided Enrique down a few more streets. He was surprised at the contempt he felt for the places they passed, boredom combined with a weary disgust. This was his kingdom, and Enrique and those like him were his vassals. It wasn't what he'd envisioned. He'd never been idealistic about it, but he'd harbored a secret thought that he'd rule over a league of honorable criminals, blue-collar and white-, Robin Hood's Merry Men without the altruism. It turned out there really *was* no honor among thieves, and the street corners he'd once dreamed of ruling were miserable places where miserable people went for goods or services that had slid down between the iron rails of the law. He'd never allowed himself to completely romanticize these places before, but he'd never felt like taking a flamethrower to them, either. Now, though, he felt he'd be happy to napalm all of L.A., if he could just get away from the place.

Getting a shade maudlin in here . . .

By the time they reached the address Van Horn had provided, he felt as if they'd crawled through every rat hole and back alley in Los Angeles, and as if many of the worst bits had stuck to him.

"Follow me," he said to Enrique.

"Wasn't part of the job."

Christ. It was hard to believe he'd fallen this far. "Five hundred dollars."

"A'ight."

They got out. Sobell stood by the car, looking over the place. From the fences, graffiti, razor wire, and layout, he guessed it was an abandoned jail. Not large enough to be a full prison, but it definitely evoked correctional facility.

"Don't shoot anybody unless I say so," he said.

He headed toward the front door.

Van Horn pulled the vehicle to a stop in front of a foreboding gray building, surrounded by fences and covered in graffiti. He had everybody get out of the van. One of his entourage had some candles, which he distributed to the others and lit using a borrowed lighter. The group surrounded Anna, Karyn, and Genevieve and herded them inside.

Anna knew of the place. A women's correctional facility that had been shut down sometime back. Rumors were, appropriately enough, that the place was haunted. "Infested" might be a more accurate word now, she thought, but regardless the place was pretty spooky. Block walls, heavy rusted doors with—strangely enough—the knobs removed. Stolen? Salvaged? Who knew? There were no windows. No lights other than a handful of candles Van Horn's entourage held. Abandoned or no, the oppressive aura of despair clung to the place.

Anna leaned toward Karyn. "I guess I always knew I'd end up in a place like this," she said.

At her other side, Genevieve cast a glance and a nervous, conciliatory smile in her direction. Anna ignored her.

The group stopped in a sort of waiting area, a bench-filled anteroom between admitting and the depths of the jail proper. It felt like being in some kind of poisonous air lock. The door to the inside of the jail was held shut with a loop of chain that went through the knob hole and disappeared inside. Locked from inside. A series of symbols was drawn in a spiral on the door. *Probably nothing bad in there.*

They sat on the benches at Van Horn's instruction and waited.

"We're gonna get out of this," Genevieve whispered. "He's working with Sobell, he's gotta be."

Anna gave her a skeptical look. "I don't know what to believe right about now."

"Give me a fucking break, would you?"

"Hey!" Van Horn barked. "Do I need to separate you two?"

They lapsed into sullen silence.

A short while later, the chain on the inner door jangled. Then a clanging slap as somebody let the heavy length fall slack against the metal door.

The door opened on darkness.

A cracked voice, hoarse and unstable with some unidentifiable emotion issued from the blackness. "Edgar."

Next to Anna, Genevieve startled. Anna looked over despite herself to see Genevieve's eyes wide, her face pale, and small beads of sweat fattening on her forehead. A droplet slid into the lower orbit of her left eye, pausing before free-falling down her cheek.

"It's Hector," Genevieve whispered.

Hector Martel, former leader of the Brotherhood of

Zagam. Presumably the guy who'd murdered Nathan Mendelsohn. The last time Anna saw him, she'd been shooting at a monster, and he'd been standing at the edge of the fray, howling his rage.

Anna thought she might be sweating a little, too, now.

Hector walked out of his den into the candlelight, and Anna knew there was something wrong with him, something terrible. In just the two months since the showdown at Sobell's, the man had undergone the kind of transformation she associated with terminal illness. His flesh had melted away, and his arms, protruding angularly from a dirty white wife beater, seemed little more than bone, with prominent knobs at shoulder, elbow, and wrist. The beard had gotten wilder, as had the hair, draping his head and neck in a black shroud. Even by candlelight, Anna could see that his skin had become blotchy. Somehow the bare feet below stained gray sweatpants only served to accentuate the sense that this man was gravely, gravely ill.

"Mona's dead," Van Horn said.

Hector's face contorted in a sneer. "Poor Mona. Poor Mona. *Bitch*. Eat her corpse."

"Ah, Antawn and Jude did an admirable job of that."

Hector smiled, showing his teeth.

"Sobell is on his way with most of what we need," Van Horn said.

"The oracle?"

"Dead. I got us a new one, though."

Van Horn pointed toward Karyn, at the end of the bench the three women sat on. Hector's gaze swept past Anna and Karyn and locked on Genevieve.

"Genevieve," he said.

"No, no, no, no," Genevieve whispered. The word faded in volume, but her lips kept moving, and she shook her head in tiny, rapid denials.

He approached, and Genevieve stood. Anna could see the curve of her spine where the sweat-soaked T-shirt clung to it.

"Did you miss me?" Hector asked, echoing a moment later with a whisper: "Miss me?" The whisper thing was deeply creepy, more so because she got the impression he didn't know he was doing it. He stopped in front of Genevieve at a distance that was just a hair too close to be comfortable for normal conversation. Genevieve stood stiffly, and it looked to Anna as though she strained not to lean back, like trying not to show fear to an angry dog.

From this viewing distance, it was obvious there was a lot more wrong with Hector than she'd even thought at first glance. Dark lines ran up and down his arms in parallel tracks, as though he'd been scratching himself rather viciously. The stink coming off him was weeks of sweat, dried blood, and rotten meat. Anna had no idea if those latter two were from things he'd eaten or rubbed on himself or if they were coming from some horribly damaged, festering part of his person that had remained mercifully covered.

His skin was twitching, she now saw. Pushing up in little tented points, as though somebody were pulling on little hairs, stretching the skin out. A wave of the points rippled up his arm, over his neck, along the side of his face.

Revulsion wrote itself all over Genevieve's face. She coughed. "I killed Mona," she said.

"You're quite the killer these days. Killed my brother, too. Our brother. One of the great ones."

"I don't know what you mean."

She must, Anna thought—even Anna had a pretty good guess. During the catastrophe at Sobell's, Genevieve had been the one to swing the sword and destroy that jawbone thing.

"You know. You know. You know."

"That was . . . a misunderstanding. I'll . . . I'll make it up to you, I promise."

"Oh? Then I shall put you at my left hand. You will rain fire upon our enemies. We will smear ourselves with their ashes, drink their blood from wineglasses. Glasses. Wineglasses. Blood."

Anna couldn't tell if he was mocking her or being sincere. Given the erratic changes in tone between each word or phrase, she wasn't even sure if he knew. Maybe both. What the hell was wrong with him? Was this what happened when you'd been host to a demon for too long? Was the demon itself insane?

"Great. So, uh, what's next?"

The door swung open, and a dozen people turned their heads to see. Enoch Sobell walked in, strutting like he owned the place and he'd come to demand back rent. Just behind him, a cholo in the obligatory khakis and tank top carried a briefcase and did his damnedest to look tough.

"Let's talk business, shall we?" Sobell said.

Sobell made a quick assessment of Hector—Forcas whatever he was calling himself these days—and fear seized him by the base of the spine. It wasn't the man's physical transformation. He looked gruesome, yes, but he'd obviously deteriorated, not grown more fearsome. It wasn't the look in the possessed man's eyes, either, though the last time Sobell had seen that look, Hector had shot him in the head. It was mostly, as best he could assess with the old hindbrain machinery broadcasting *Run, you idiot* directly into his motor system, the horrible sense of vitality the man exuded. Sure, he was breaking down, but it typically took demons a matter of weeks, sometimes days, to destroy their hosts, usually as a result of insane, insatiable lusts combined with no impulse control whatsoever. Forcas had been running Hector's equipment now for, what? Eight months, maybe? More? He had no right to look even this hale, no right to be ambulatory. No right to the gleeful sneer on his face.

For the first time, Sobell wondered just how badly he'd missed in his evaluation of the situation. He put on a smile, though, and forced himself to take one more step toward the man.

"It's not like you to hide, Forcas," Sobell said.

"It's not like you to ignore what's in front of your face." Hector made an odd swallowing noise, then repeated "Your face."

"Can't spot everything. You could have said something before you shot me in the head. Had the common decency to gloat a little."

"You and your women killed my brother. Our brother. My strong right arm."

The amplifications and amendments were delivered in a jerky, hitching cadence, interspersed with convulsive swallowing. It reminded Sobell of fishing with his grandfather as a young boy. The old man had caught a too-small fish and thrown it down on the beach, watching it flop and gasp in the sand before finally kicking it in the head and killing it.

"They're, ah, not actually *my* women. Free agents. And just in case you find yourself in polite society, that sort of language went out of fashion five decades ago." Hector made no response, so Sobell continued. "In any case, rock and a hard place. Believe it or not, I am here to make amends, just like I told Edgar."

"Good. Good. *Fuck you.* Good."

Even his communication had deteriorated since Sobell last spoke with him, and it had been erratic before. His brain was probably little more than neuron soup by now, held together by malign demon will. "Since you called me, can I assume that you have some idea of how my atonement should take shape? Or is this simply for making threats and other social overtures?"

"Kill him," Hector said. Nearly everybody in the room jumped to their feet.

"Stop!" Sobell yelled, voice reverberating back to him from the hard walls. "If anybody moves, shoot *him*," he said, pointing to Hector. Enrique dropped the case and pulled out an enormous chrome revolver.

Sobell dropped his arms to his sides, palms facing front. "Last time you tried to kill me, it didn't work out so well. Do you really feel like trying your luck again? I had a much more profitable relationship in mind."

"You fucked me," Hector snarled. *"Fucked."*

Sobell knew he'd have to deal with this. Demons held *such* grudges, and he'd really screwed Forcas back when. It must have been humiliating back at the demon social club, but it wasn't Sobell's fault the demon had negotiated like a neophyte. "I exchanged three lives for one hundred years. That was the deal."

"I don't give a shit about your deal."

Sobell paused, his head slightly cocked, eyebrows drawn together in puzzlement. *"Our* deal," he said.

"I made no deal with you."

"Is your memory going, Forcas?"

"I ate Forcas. I chewed it, swallowed it, digested it, shit it out."

Sobell's bad feeling soured further. "That's, ah, charming," he managed to say.

"I am large. I contain multitudes. But Forcas no longer."

Sobell tried on a smile, but as his stomach sank through the floor, dragging his heart with it, he felt sure it looked more like a nauseated grimace. This was beyond bad. Was Forcas here? Truly dead? Could demons actually die? With whom was Sobell now conversing, if not the demon he sought? "Shall I just call you Legion, then?"

"I am Belial."

There suddenly seemed to be no air in the room. "I . . . see."

Then, whispered: *"I am Malphas, I am Amon, I am Volac, I am Orias, I am—"*

Hector laughed wildly, then said it again: "I am Belial."

Sobell had set a rat trap and caught a Gorgon, a titan, a colossus—something awful and terrible that could smite him so thoroughly that there wouldn't even be atoms left, erase him from existence, or Hell knew what else. Belial, Prince of Hell. The name was unmistakable. Was there another demon that showed up more times in the literature, that was responsible for more atrocities, whose name was linked to more terrible magic? If so, Sobell couldn't think of one. And it appeared that Belial was not alone in there, not by some distance. A Prince of Hell and a dozen or a hundred other demons, crowded into one man's body until it was fit to burst. What in the world was going on here?

If anybody could help him, though, surely, *surely* Belial could. That hope, however bleak, was worth clinging to.

Hector pointed. "Kill—"

Sobell recovered his wits quickly. "Rhino here is an excellent shot. Fancy a trip back to Hell?"

The expression on Hector's face was fascinating to watch, twisting through rage to hilarity to rage again, sweeping through indecipherable intermediate emotions on the way. He didn't give any orders, though, merely stood with his face doing its unnerving thing.

"Listen to me, Belial." Sobell looked to each side of the room and frowned. "Actually, would it be possible to speak in private?"

A wild, hectic laugh burst from Hector's face. "No. It would not."

"All right, then. You have my sincerest apologies for our earlier misunderstanding. *My* earlier misunderstanding. I had Mona killed as a gesture of goodwill, at Edgar's suggestion. I brought the torc and the cash by way of atonement, though I shudder to think what use you have for them. I have one more thing you want, besides the cash. You have something I want. I think you know what it is."

"You have nothing more that I want."

"I have an army," Sobell said.

Hector pouted, though Sobell saw, or hoped he saw, avarice in his eyes. "I *had* an army."

"Yes. Well, that turned into a complete cock-up, didn't it? I've brought you a new one."

"How many?"

"Thirty or forty. Hoodlums, parasites, and highwaymen, to be sure, but I suspect you're disinclined to be picky." To underscore his point, he made a show of looking around the room.

"And you want what?"

He leaned forward, close enough for Hector to bite his throat out if the whim took him, and he whispered, "I'm dying. I need more time."

Hector nodded, then shook his head and sneered. "*I* can't help you."

There had been emphasis on the pronoun there, and Sobell was sure he hadn't imagined it. "Don't play word games with me. Maybe you can't help me, but somebody in there can, or you know someone, some way. Something."

"Someone. Some way."

"You make an introduction, I'll hand over my legion of loyal followers."

"You first."

"It appears trust will be somewhat hard to come by. Halfsies?"

Hector nodded convulsively.

"Seal it in blood?"

"Of course. *Blood*."

Sobell wasn't sure how haggling with demon lords was supposed to go, so he opted for the old standby. He produced a piece of paper, dickered over the basic terms, and then they drew up a short contract. Sobell played no games with it. Forcas might have been easily fooled, but it would be insane to try that sort of thing with Belial.

Finally, Hector drew some kind of figure over the words, they each cut a finger and smeared some blood on the paper, and then Sobell burned it.

"Bring them," Hector said.

Chapter 27

Sobell's gofer brought a couple of guys in, a heavyset bruiser and a reedy-looking guy with a sparse beard and a big hole where one of his front teeth had been. They didn't look like Sobell's usual class of criminal, and Anna wondered where the hell he was coming up with these people.

Van Horn's creatures moved subtly around them, and without making a big thing out of it, they quietly cut off the path to the door.

"I'm Jerry. What do you need?" the skinny guy asked, grinning widely.

"Are you with us?" Van Horn asked. "Are you truly one of us?"

"Uh, yeah. I mean, I guess."

Van Horn's forehead wrinkled in grandfatherly concern. "Are you sure? There will be an initiation. Nothing painful, I promise, but you will be tested. You are among the elect now."

Jerry's grin became cockeyed and uneasy. "The elect, huh? I like the sound of that."

"Your new family awaits you."

"This is, like, some kind of Mafia thing?"

Van Horn gave him a kindly smile. "Yes. Just like that. Nobody messes with a made man—isn't that right?"

"Fuck yeah. Uh, I ain't gotta whack anybody or nothin' like that, right?"

"No. Nothing like that."

Van Horn stepped aside, exposing Hector to view. Jerry's smile faltered.

"I am the way, the truth, and the life," Hector said. He spread his arms, palms up, and cocked his head. As his smile spread across his face, Jerry's withered.

"Hey, I was just looking for a little action. I don't know about all this." The guy looked around the room, his eyes saying, *A little help please*, and noticed that the door was now blocked.

"Just ritual, Jerry," Van Horn said. "You'll be fine."

"Now kneel before your lord and savior," Van Horn said.

"Been a while since I been to Our Lady of the—"

"Please," Van Horn said. "Are you with us?"

"Yeah, just—"

"Then kneel. When you rise, you will be greater than you have ever dreamed."

Jerry lowered himself shakily to the floor. He lost his balance and tipped forward, catching himself on his arms. Then he got himself back into a kneeling position. "Now what?"

"You, too," Van Horn said, gesturing at the heavyset man. That guy obliged without any hesitation. From the gang tats, Anna guessed that initiation was old news for him.

One of the entourage, the one called Raul, Anna thought, came up behind Jerry and tied a rag around his head, making a crude blindfold. Another performed the same service for the second man.

Van Horn handed Hector a little folding knife, blade no longer than a couple of inches. In Hector's hands, it took on a sudden menace. A machete would have been no more frightening, Anna thought.

Hector approached the kneeling man, flicking the edge of his knife with his thumb.

Anna couldn't look away.

Hector stopped inches from Jerry's body. The knife

grew to enormous proportions in Anna's mind, taking up all her attention.

Hector pulled up his own shirt. As Anna stared, he pinched a fold of skin above his hip and cut off a slice of skin about the size of a quarter, his face betraying no more pain than if he'd been idly scratching an itch. Blood ran into the waistband of his sweatpants. He spoke an incantation in low, incomprehensible words.

Hector finished his chant and held out the slice of bloody flesh. "This is my body," he said. "Take it. And eat."

"Open your mouth, Jerry," Van Horn said.

"And what?"

"It's like Halloween. You put your hand in the box and—"

"And, like, feel the eyeballs and stuff," Jerry said.

"Exactly. If you're brave enough. Open up."

"Jesus Christ," Anna said. Van Horn shot her a warning glance and put his finger over his mouth.

Jerry opened his mouth. Hector put the skin on his tongue.

"Swallow," Van Horn said.

Jerry closed his mouth. He gagged, cheeks inflating, but to Anna's surprise he didn't spit Hector's grotesque communion wafer out. He swallowed it.

The process was repeated for the second guy, who slurped down the gobbet of flesh without the slightest hesitation.

Raul took off the blindfolds.

"That's a trooper," Van Horn said, extending a hand to Jerry. Confused, Jerry hesitantly reached up and took it. Van Horn helped him to his feet. "You will be rewarded for your service."

Jerry made a sound lodged somewhere between a gag and a cough. "Man, that's—that's fuckin' great, man." He cleared his throat. "Warm in here."

Van Horn patted his shoulder. "Turn, and greet your brothers and sisters."

As Jerry turned, Van Horn took his hand and raised it

in victory. The entourage cheered, and damned if a hesitant smile didn't appear on Jerry's mug.

"Bring me more," Hector said.

Sobell's lackey went out. Van Horn sent the two new initiates behind him.

Moments passed. Genevieve looked over at Anna, an idle glance, probably just to get a quick read on how she was doing. Whether it was the glance or simple sadism, Hector pointed at Anna.

"You," he said. "You will take communion."

Anna ran her options as she fought down terror. She could run and get caught. She could fight and take a beating. Maybe get killed while Karyn and Gen watched. If there were other options available, she couldn't identify them.

"I don't wanna be in your fuckin' club," she said.

"Heretic. Heathen. Blasphemer. You'll eat, whether you will or no. Or be eaten."

"Please don't," Genevieve said. Her tone was even, try as Anna might to read some desperation there. "Anna's my friend."

Hector didn't look at her. "Good." His tongue darted from his mouth, then pushed at his lip and cheek rapidly, seeming to move of its own accord. Drool oozed into his beard.

"You don't have to do this. She'll cooperate. We'll all cooperate."

"I *want* to do this," he said. He looked over his shoulder at her. "If it's so important to you, make me stop."

"This is stupid," Genevieve said. But she didn't move.

"Stop this," Karyn said. Anna had no idea who the words were directed at.

Hector didn't look over. "We'll get to you," he said. He stopped in front of Anna and sliced a thin strip of skin from over his hipbone. The knife missed the last bit, but he simply tore it away. He said his incantation again.

"Take this and eat," he said, proffering the strip, which lay flat, leechlike and oozing on his palm.

She could shove him, knock him down, run for it. And even if she made it, Karyn would be left there. Genevieve, too.

Anna picked the strip of flesh up between thumb and forefinger and put it in her mouth. The rubbery, wet texture made her want to gag, but she chewed slowly, grinding it between her teeth as she stared a silent *Fuck you* into Hector's eyes. Finally, she swallowed it.

Anna caught Genevieve's gaze. There was nothing there, no expression at all. She'd shut down, her emotions gone on vacation.

Hector put a hand on her forehead, almost as if he was checking her for a fever, then leaned forward. He stank so badly it curdled Anna's guts, and when he exhaled it was the breath of a dog that had just eaten five pounds of roadkill. His eyes wouldn't leave Anna's. "Bless you, my child," he said.

Sobell's guy came back with another couple of crooks. Hector winked at Anna and turned away to attend to that business.

A strange heat burned in Anna's gut. Warm, like bathwater, or a candle held several inches away. It moved up through her chest and down through her legs, spreading through her body. It felt . . . corrupt. Not the heat of bathwater at all, but the heat from a rotting garbage pile. She wanted to tear her flesh away everywhere she felt it.

She felt feverish now, as though she ought to be shivering under a blanket and sweating, body aching from head to toe, but she wasn't sweating, and she wasn't in pain. She was just warm. Really, really warm.

This can't be good for me, she thought, and she nearly laughed aloud as she understood. Hector was a contagion, an infection in human guise. A little fever was the least of her problems right now.

"We're gonna figure this out," Genevieve said quietly, sidling over to her. "It's going to be okay, I promise. We'll figure it out. Somehow. I promise."

Anna laughed. "Everything's gonna work out for everyone, right?"

"Wait. You," Van Horn said, crooking a finger at Genevieve. "We require your services."

Genevieve paled. "I don't—"

Van Horn scowled. "Not like"—he waved his hands at the room—"all that. We need your expertise. Come here."

Genevieve gave Anna a lame pat on the shoulder, then walked to the corner of the room and started talking in a low voice with Van Horn. Anna cast a disgusted look in her direction.

"Are you all right?" Karyn asked.

"I don't know."

A few minutes later, the naked guy sitting on the bench on Karyn's other side started fidgeting and mumbling. Anna tried to ignore him, but he got louder and more agitated. When she glanced over, she saw something dark move at the corner of his left eye. Before Anna could say something, he reached up to touch it. When he pulled away his fingers, a dark red clot about the size of a pencil eraser tumbled down his forearm, leaving red traces the whole way down. He watched, bemused, and then tumbled forward. Anna thought that the flat whack of his face hitting the concrete floor might keep her awake nights for a long, long time.

Across the room, another low-rent thug took infernal communion.

Near Anna, nobody moved. The pool of blood widened around the naked man, and nobody cared. There were maybe nine people total, four holding candles, most of them seated. One or two gave the dead man a hungry look, but for once it appeared they were waiting on word from the boss before chowing down.

Eventually, Anna couldn't stand it anymore. "Is somebody gonna get rid of him?" she asked.

Van Horn shrugged and waved at the body. "Raul,

Deanna?" The two dragged the body out. Judging by the short time they were gone, Anna supposed they'd dragged him to just the other side of the door and called it good.

"What's wrong with your guys?" Anna asked. Van Horn scowled, but didn't make eye contact with her. He angled his body away, in fact, so he couldn't even see her by accident.

Anna couldn't leave it alone. "They're all dropping dead."

Van Horn took Genevieve's arm and walked to the other side of the room, still without making eye contact. He did it casually, as though it had just occurred to him that maybe it would be more comfortable over there. Like he needed to stretch his legs.

Damn, it was hot in here. For a moment, Anna wondered how that was even possible—it was night, and this deep in a concrete building, in a room with no windows, it probably would have been reasonably cool even at midday. It wasn't the room, she finally understood. It was her, still running hot from whatever Hector had done to her.

She thought about the guy who'd dropped dead. A contagion.

Somebody came back and opened the door, poking his head in. He said something Anna didn't hear. Hector and Van Horn started conversing in low voices. Once, they even paused to ask Genevieve something.

"It's the magic," the woman to her left whispered. Her name was Rain, if Anna had heard correctly, and she creeped Anna out, partly because her recently maimed hand made Anna imagine all the bad things that could have happened to her, but mostly because, unlike most of the others, she wore a haunted, haggard look. She, at least, had been thinking about her situation. Yet she was still here.

"Say what?"

"The magic. It's killing us."

"Which magic is that?"

"We thought it was a gift. Maybe it was. Some of the others think Belial can fix us, but I don't think he knows how. Doesn't care. We're waiting to die."

Anna glanced around the room. The others didn't seem to care about Rain's loose lips. They were each tracking their own obsessions, holding conversations with themselves, or assisting with the latest iteration of Hector's grotesque ritual.

"Who's Belial?"

"Hector, Belial. He has other names, I think."

"He gave you magic," Anna prompted.

"He gave us something. Magic comes with it." She looked down at the bloody rag wrapping her hand. "Or maybe magic is only the side effect, and we — I — mistook it for the whole point."

"So, can I do magic now?"

"I don't know. Can you?"

"How the hell should I know?"

Rain shrugged. "You'll know. First you get really warm. Like a fever, only you feel okay."

"Yeah," Anna said, and despite the warmth, she shivered.

"Then you start having really strange thoughts."

"Like what?"

"Like you'll suddenly think car exhaust smells amazing. Or that sunlight is like being in the light of God — awesome, but too intense. Or that it would be a really good idea to shove a kid out into traffic to see what happens."

"You didn't —"

"Other thoughts will come after that. Not impulses or sensations, but *strange* thoughts. Really, really weird stuff. Geometry. Songs in languages you don't understand." Her face softened into a forlorn smile. "That's the magic. If it stopped there, it might have all been okay."

"I feel warm," Anna said.

Rain nodded.

"What happens after the magic?" Anna asked, because she couldn't bring herself to come outright and ask how much time she had left.

"You get numb. Then it's like you develop a tolerance. Like a drug addict who needs more and more after a while just to get a lesser high. It's like that."

"I don't get it," Anna said, though she was afraid she did.

"You can't feel anything, so you cut yourself. You can't taste anything, so you eat flesh. Raw. You can't really taste that, either, but—but it's a thrill. Rats, birds. People, eventually. Biggest thrill of all."

Anna wondered if Rain knew she looked as though she wanted to throw up.

"And meanwhile all the thoughts keep getting weirder, and you keep trying stranger and stranger things. I don't know why everybody's dying, but I guess they're not made for this. None of us are."

"And Hector? He gonna die, too?"

"Not in a million years. He's the Devil."

Anna had nothing to say to that.

"Slow down," Nail said. "You ain't gonna do anyone any good you crash this thing. Or get us arrested."

"You in a hurry or what?" DeWayne asked.

"We almost there?" Nail asked Sheila. He couldn't keep the frustration out of his voice—not knowing what the hell was going on, or why, combined with that awful sense of everything happening outside of his control was making him nuts.

"I don't get distance, just direction," Sheila said.

"Great."

The next ten minutes passed with agonizing slowness as Nail alternated between worrying they'd be too late and that DeWayne would get pulled over. Finally, they came to a T in the road and DeWayne slowed the vehicle.

"Now what?" Nail asked. The cross street ahead had

a whole caravan of vehicles parked on it, fifteen or more, all with their lights on, idling. No blue and red, though, so it wasn't cops. "Any chance we can back up and go around this?"

The cigarette pointed straight through the middle of the vehicles at the squat concrete compound beyond. Nail didn't like the look of it.

"Really?" Sheila asked. "Is that how you think this works?"

"A guy can hope. They're not in that mess, are they?"

Sheila said nothing. Nail considered the options, which all looked terrible. After a few minutes, DeWayne slapped his shoulder and pointed at a couple of men emerging from the building. "Know that guy?"

"Yeah," Nail said. "Enoch Sobell."

DeWayne laughed. "No shit? Huh. I meant the other guy. That's Rhino Vasquez. Hangs with the Ninth Street Pinheads. Big-time banger. Breaks knees for Clarence on the side, too. You never heard of this guy? You ever get outta the library, or what?"

Rhino went to one of the cars and motioned to the people inside. Two men got out, one tall and skinny, the other tall and damn near as wide.

"Check out the ugly one."

"The ugly one?" Sheila asked.

"Point. The one looks like a dump truck. Thaddeus Winchell. *He* breaks knees for Johnny Flathead."

"Do you know every knee-breaking lowlife in California?" Sheila asked.

"If they run sports book, he does," Nail said.

"Yeah, well. You know how it is," DeWayne said. "But I'da thought it'd be a cold day in Hell before Flathead's boys would sit down with Clarence's. Something must be cooking here."

They watched for a while longer while Nail tried and failed to come up with any kind of plan. Rhino moved to the next vehicle and sent those guys inside, too.

"Li'l Rodge Hastings," Nail said.

"Yeah," his brother added. "Breaks legs for Jimmy the Fence."

"So not only do you know every knee-breaking low-life in California, but they're all here."

Nail nodded. "Yeah. Tell me that shit's a coincidence."

A drop of blood spilled from Sheila's nose. She wiped it off with her finger and stared at it, her expression veering suddenly from excitement to melancholy and back in an erratic way that made Nail uncomfortable.

He stared at the building again. "I don't even know if this has anything to do with us, though."

"This is the place," Sheila said, though how she knew was anybody's guess. "Let me out."

"I don't think that's such a hot idea," DeWayne said.

Nail tended to agree with DeWayne on this one. "I don't see Van Horn here, or any of my crew, either. That was the deal, remember?"

"They're in there," she said to Nail. "And you owe me. You'd still be at Mona's without me."

"What if you're wrong?" Nail asked.

"I'm not." Another drop of blood, then several more, spattering her lap. "If I don't get help, I'm going to be dead very soon." Her deadpan tone created an eerie contrast against her words, further unsettling Nail. "The only people that can help me are in there. You can come in with me, if you want. I don't care."

"That's not—"

Three sharp taps, metal on glass, and Nail swung his head around to look out the driver's-side window.

"I know you," a man said. Big guy, shaped like a fire hydrant, rocking a poorly fitting suit jacket like a bad disguise. The kind of guy with a permanent squint, as though he had to concentrate like hell just to stay upright and keep from dragging his knuckles. He tapped a nine-millimeter Browning against the window again. "Get out the fuckin' bus, DeWayne."

"Hey, Stevie, how's it hangin'? Me and Clarence, we're square. You didn't hear? Paid up, paid in full, uh, think I got a receipt around here somewhere." Still talking, he patted his pockets, either pantomiming the search for a receipt or going for his gun. Nail never found out, because Stevie hauled the door open with the hand holding the gun, grabbed DeWayne's collar in his other fist, and threw him bodily onto the pavement.

Nail moved before DeWayne's "oof" had finished sounding. Threw open the sliding door on the passenger side and, weaving a little, came around the front of the car.

Stevie brought up the gun, and Nail brought up his hands. "Hold up there, man," Nail said.

"You wanna stay out of this. Ain't none of your business."

"What are you doin' here, Stevie?" DeWayne said from the ground. "I got the feelin' this is not a good place to be tonight. Hey, how's your nephew? He gonna play football this year?"

Stevie took his attention off Nail long enough to plant a foot on DeWayne's wrist, eliciting an indignant squawk.

"Hey, what are you—don't, man, just let's be cool about this—"

Nail saw the man shift his weight, putting more pressure on DeWayne's wrist. "Shut up."

DeWayne shut up.

Stevie returned his attention to Nail. "Get the fuck outta here." He gestured with the gun. "You don't wanna die for this idiot."

"This idiot is my brother," Nail said.

"Oh, goddammit," Stevie said, rolling his eyes.

DeWayne moved, faster than Nail would have thought him capable, and suddenly the three-eighty was in his hand.

Oh, shit.

DeWayne pulled the trigger.

A dry *click* echoed off the concrete of the building.

Stevie's eyes went wide, and he whipped his gun around toward DeWayne's prone form.

Nail charged. He slammed into Stevie, shoulder down, catching the big guy right under the ribs. The gun went off as the air blasted from Stevie's lungs, and a fraction of a second later, Stevie hit the pavement with Nail on top of him. The gun went spinning away with a clatter.

The earth seemed to tilt under Nail, and his gut clenched again. He swung his fist, connecting with Stevie's neck or collarbone or some damn thing, even though he'd been aiming for the face, the force of a useless impact traveling back up his arm. Thick fingers grasped his face, pushing his head back and away as he scrabbled for Stevie's throat.

There was a flash like the sun going nova as Stevie's fist collided with Nail's head. The force was unstoppable, like a goddamn truck rocketing down the highway, and Nail was thrown to the side. The earth did that uneasy dip thing again, and it seemed as though Nail took half an hour to find his bearings, but it must have been a hell of a lot shorter, because he was on his back, some big fucker practically lying on top of him, choking the shit out of him. Black fluttering shadows moved at the edges of his vision. He was going to lose consciousness, and this fucker was going to kill him. He swung wildly, connecting with implacable shoulders, immovable arms.

One of the shadows resolved itself into a moving form—DeWayne, rushing toward the fight.

DeWayne's foot swung forward in a swift, vicious arc. His Doc Marten connected with Stevie's head with a sound like a baseball bat hammering a triple deep into left field.

Stevie's eyes rolled up in his head, and he collapsed.

Nail gasped, pulling sweet air into his lungs, his chest heaving. When the world seemed in no danger of permanently receding again, he shoved Stevie off him and sat up.

DeWayne stood a few feet away, stooped over with his hands on his knees, breathing almost as heavily as Nail himself. His face was practically gray. "Clarence is gonna kill me," he said.

"You didn't load the fuckin' gun?" Nail asked. "How you gonna shoot a guy with an empty fuckin' gun?"

"I just figured you kept it loaded. At least it wasn't a fuckin' *fork*."

Nail laughed. He glanced over at Stevie's prone form and saw the slow rise and fall of his chest. "He ain't dead." Probably better this way than if the gun had fired, actually. There was still at least a chance they'd be able to patch this shit up with Clarence, however small.

DeWayne straightened, grinning. "Lucky him." His grin didn't fade a bit as he looked at the car and announced, "Hey, what's her name's gone."

Chapter 28

After the endless procession of thugs had taken communion, Hector did . . . something. Karyn couldn't quite tell, because the demon in her head was apparently a little sensitive where Hector was concerned. When Karyn had first seen Hector come out of the back, the images went berserk. Dozens had flashed through her mind, too fast to follow, and when they'd slowed, Karyn wished they'd speed right back up again. They were all death—execution, in fact. Hector, with his neck under the heavy blade of a guillotine. Bound at hands and knees and kicked off a bridge. Tied to a post and burning. On his knees in an alley with a gun pressed to the back of his head. Karyn held the gun. Whenever she looked in Hector's direction, the demon went crazy, generating a frenzied and endless sequence of ways to off Hector and bouncing off the insides of her skull like a fly caught in a jar. It was hard to pay attention to anything going on around her. It had, in fact, taken her a few moments to even place the guy and link him back to the jawbone job. He'd deteriorated considerably since then. The tank top and sweatpants were particularly disturbing, for some reason. Before, he'd at least nodded toward normal dress, but now it appeared he didn't give a shit.

At any rate, Hector did something—waved, gestured, spoke, she wasn't quite sure—and the crowd gathered itself. Those seated stood. Somehow a selection process had occurred. Somebody moved to pull Karyn to her feet, and she stood before they could follow through. Anna did as well. In the end, ten of them headed or were shepherded toward the door from which Hector had emerged—Sobell and his new bodyguard, Hector, the old man who had apparently orchestrated this mess, the woman next to Anna and two of the others, and Anna, Karyn, and Genevieve. The others waited.

Karyn glanced at Anna. "How are you feeling?"

Anna held her hand out, flat, and wobbled it. *So-so*.

Karyn wasn't sure what to make of that. The demon had explained the communion episode with a single expressive, if awful image: Hector, jamming a tapeworm down Anna's throat.

Flashlights flicked on as Hector led them back into the depths of the jail. It amazed Karyn how easy it was to stop paying attention to the world she saw with her eyes and focus on the image in her mind. She was still getting this figured out, but it was vastly better than the lost existence she'd had before, and she'd already learned a few tricks. In particular, the image, when not screaming *homicide*, helped her focus on the sounds around her, helping her pick one stream of noise from the rest, like focusing on a single conversation in a crowded room. They went past some administrative area and into the cell block proper. It didn't look like maximum security to Karyn—decent enough rooms, enclosed rather than exposed, windows on the doors—but the feel of the place was still institutionalized despair and wasted lives. Some of the walls were tagged with graffiti, crude scrawling in black spray paint rather than anything artful. Lots of variations on "Fuck the police."

Minimum security or no, this was a sprawling complex, and with the block walls and no windows, it seemed as though it must be deep inside the earth. Karyn had to keep reminding herself that she was aboveground, not descending into some Hell-bound mine shaft.

They went farther into the building. When the demon images remained those of Karyn's surroundings, the flashlights played over everything in spastic trajectories, unpredictable and unmatched to her movement. Much of the rest of the time, the demon was bombarding her with images of Hector's execution, *Clockwork Orange*–style, like if she saw it enough times she'd decide to follow through on the suggestion.

"Shut up!" she yelled as they turned a corner. "Shut up! Shut up!"

The images cleared, briefly, showing mild amusement on the part of some of her captors, and a total lack of interest from others. Anna mouthed some words. Karyn nodded to make her feel better, having no idea what she'd said, but guessing it was some kind of status check.

I am officially a ranting crazy woman now, she thought, a private joke that lost all its humor before she even finished thinking it.

They went farther into the building. It split into a couple of main hallways. They hugged the left wall and, after passing yet another row of cells, entered a bigger room off to the side. The flashlights showed nubs of burned candles sitting in pools of wax, chalk in wide arcs across the floor, and rows and rows of chicken-scratched graffiti across the walls.

No. Not graffiti. These markings were the same kinds of symbols Tommy and Genevieve always used. Genevieve, in fact, had covered walls of Karyn's great-aunt's place with them, in an attempt to keep the crew hidden at one point.

Somebody shone a light into a corner, revealing a heap of colorless, holey blankets.

He's been staying here, Karyn thought. *Hiding.*

In her mind, Hector exploded into a million pieces, leaving a red soup in the middle of some noonday, western-town-looking street.

Thanks for that. Asshole.

Hector said something, and the man Anna had identified as Van Horn pointed to Karyn. The whole room turned to her, giving her the feeling she'd suddenly been shoved onstage.

Now Van Horn said something, and one of his minions began lighting candles. Two, five, ten—a dozen. More. In the center of the room, the candlelight revealed a huge occult diagram on the floor, much bigger than any Karyn had ever seen. You could park a pickup truck on it and not go outside its boundaries.

In the center was a five-pointed star, and in the center of *that* was a star-shaped arrangement of what looked like pine two-by-sixes, lying flat on the floor, and gang-nailed together. Karyn had the sudden grim intuition that it would be just about the right size for a person to lie down on. Then she saw the restraining straps screwed into the boards.

Sobell stepped forward. He gave her one of his supposedly charming smiles, and said a bunch of shit, not a single word of which she heard.

In her mind, the surroundings were replaced by a massacre. Bloody bodies lay scattered around the room, chopped and shot up and who knew what else. Only Anna was left standing. *Kill them all* being the subtext, she imagined. Just how the fuck was she supposed to do that, if she even wanted to?

Sobell was back, brow furrowed in concern.

"I can't hear you," she said. "Not a single word."

He said something else. She guessed from the tilt of his head and the cocked eyebrows that it had been a question.

"I'm alive. More or less undamaged. What do you want from me?"

Sobell said something and looked to Hector. Another image of blood and pain blotted out the scene briefly.

Hector walked a few steps around the perimeter of the drawing, coming closer to her. She fought the urge to lean away. He said something else and pointed at the wooden frame.

The next image Karyn saw was unbelievably strange — a series of vaguely human-shaped creatures in a burning cloud, each creature with four faces. Human, lion, eagle, and something that looked like a cow or maybe a water buffalo. "What the hell?" The image vanished, replaced by a woman in a robe standing in what Karyn supposed was a Greek temple, a line of people waiting in front of her. Then a man on an island. Hovering above him, an angel broke a seal.

The first image was utterly incomprehensible, but the second and third at least suggested something. "Prophecy," Karyn guessed. "You want to speak to the oracle."

Hector nodded, a grin seaming his face.

"Too bad. I can't hear a thing. Your oracle is deaf as well as mad."

Hector merely grinned wider, exposing his teeth, his hand still pointed at the frame. He didn't come closer, though, and he made no move to coerce her.

"If I do this, we walk out of here," she said. "Me, Anna, and Genevieve, unharmed."

The demon images erupted in her mind, the shock of them like a blow, and she staggered. Hector, lounging on a pile of skulls, flies buzzing around him. His minions chopping down men, women, and children with knives and axes while he pretended to conduct them like an orchestra. Torture in back alleys, mutilation in half-lit warehouses, worse. Was that what Hector wanted? What she'd enable him to do with her prophecy? Some other, inadvertent consequence? Or just demon fun and games from her temporary resident?

"Not my problem," she whispered, looking from Hector to his thralls to Anna, standing by the wall and watching, her expression locked down in the robot face she made when she was particularly stressed. "Not today."

Hector pointed to Anna and Genevieve and nodded, then to Karyn and shook his head.

"You'll let them go, but not me."

He nodded again.

"Are you going to kill me?"

He shook his head.

Movement stirred at the edge of Karyn's unnatural vision. She ignored it and focused on Hector. "Is *this* going to kill me?"

Again, he shook his head, looking decidedly annoyed with this exchange. The movement grew more agitated, and Karyn glanced over. Anna, waving her arms and saying something, gently restrained for the moment by a hand on her shoulder.

"But you just can't give up your own personal oracle. Is that it?"

He gave her a phony-looking sheepish grin, as if to say, *Hey, can you blame me?* Then his face twisted in a snarl; then the snarl was gone.

She looked at Sobell. "If I make a deal with this guy, can he cheat?"

Sobell shook his head firmly as Hector looked at him. The second Hector looked away, he gave a shrug. Karyn wasn't sure how to interpret that. No? Probably not? I don't know, but I don't really want to say that very loudly?

What choice did she have? Nobody was coming to help them. She wondered if Nail was hurt. Or dead. And the others sure as hell weren't going to fight their way out. Hector had made some kind of alliance with Adelaide before, and while that had surely been a terrible arrangement, Adelaide had been happy enough to screw her over and go along with it.

And Anna would come back for her. She knew that, as certain as breathing.

She glanced back toward Anna, for whom gentle restraint would no longer suffice. Anna thrashed and shouted, her face racked with fury and pain, and two of Hector's minions held her back. If Karyn concentrated on Anna hard enough, some of the words came through, and she could guess at others. She got "fucking martyr," "don't," "again, goddammit," and a whole lot of profanity that didn't seem to be attached to any other particular phrase.

Sobell's bodyguard hefted his gun and pointed it at Anna's head, looking at Sobell with a question on his face.

"Put it down. Right now," Karyn said. "She gets hurt, and I'm done here," she said to Hector. "You *will* have to kill me, too, I fucking promise you."

Hector nodded. Sobell waved at the gunman, and the guy lowered the gun.

"Please don't do this," Anna said. Through some hateful trick of the cosmos, the words came through perfectly.

Karyn tried to smile at her. "Don't worry. This'll be just one more jam for you to get me out of." Before she got an answer, before she could even read Anna's expression, she turned away. She couldn't look at Anna anymore. It hurt too much, and right now it was bad for both of them.

She looked to Hector. "Yeah, okay. Fine. You got a deal. Let's get this over with." One of Hector's minions reached for Karyn's arm, and she stepped away. "I think I can walk over there myself, big guy."

She stepped through the diagram, taking care not to smudge any of the lines. Tommy had always been obsessed about not breaking the lines, and whether that was correct or not, she didn't figure on taking the chance.

She paused at the central star. "Let's do it."

"Gotta be at least twenty," Nail said, tallying up his best estimate of the number of guys he'd seen go into the jail. "Might be thirty or more."

The two men stood back by the car, side by side, staring at the jail. Stevie was in the back of the vehicle, trussed like a hog and gagged, still unconscious. Out of the way for now, but Nail sure wished they knew what to do with him.

DeWayne shook his head. "Yeah, and what's her name already in there, I bet. Tellin' everybody the party crashers are here. Man, I think we're shit outta luck. Maybe we just call this off, huh?"

"Maybe there's a back way in," Nail said. "Must be, this place is huge."

"I don't know. Want to spend an hour dicking around to find it? Maybe call ahead, see if they'll prop the door open for us? Anyway, the longer we screw around here, the more likely it is that your lady friend gets them to send out an army of pissed-off guys to rearrange our faces."

"You got another suggestion?"

DeWayne just shrugged.

"Never thought I'd do this," Nail said. He pulled out his phone and dialed. It rang twice, then three times, and just when he was afraid he'd have to leave a message, he heard the click of connection.

"Hello?" The woman on the other end didn't sound tired at all, but she was surely pissed off.

"Special Agent Elliot?"

DeWayne's eyes widened. *What?* he whispered.

"Owens? Is that you?"

"Yeah. You want Sobell, or am I interrupting something?"

"I'm checking one of my guys into the hospital. He got T-boned by a couple of bastards trying to follow Sobell, so you better have something."

"You mean like a RICO predicate? 'Cuz I got him on a RICO predicate. Right now, in fuckin' progress."

DeWayne was shaking his head, like one of his core beliefs had evaporated. Like gravity had turned out to be a mass delusion after all this time.

"Don't fuck with me, Owens," Elliot said.

"I don't even wanna take your ass to dinner. Think I'd be doing this if you hadn't fucked me first?"

"What's the crime?"

"Kidnapping, three counts. If you don't hurry up, it's gonna be murder, I guess."

"Where?"

Nail gave the address. "Old prison," he added. "Bring the SWAT team or whatever else you got. He's got twenty guys or so with him, maybe thirty. Not too many armed, I don't think, but I don't really know."

"I can't mobilize a SWAT team on your say-so."

"Mobilize what the fuck you got, then, because I'd guess you got a short goddamn window here. Three hostages, all women. Two Caucasian—"

"Ames, Ruiz, and Lyle."

"Yeah."

"What does Sobell want with the hostages?"

"Don't know. But how long you wanna screw around before he does whatever it is he's doin' and gets out, leavin' you with three dead bodies on your hands?"

"Dammit. I'll send local P.D. and follow up as soon as I can."

"Are you not hearing me, lady? *Kidnapping*. Two counts, *red-fucking-handed*. He's there, right now, and you are gonna get people killed you don't get here with your best, like yesterday! I'm not talkin' the county sheriff with his thumb up his ass. I mean professionals!"

There was a pause, during which Nail thought he heard distorted speech over a hospital intercom. Then: "I'll get my best team there as fast as I can. We're some distance out, though. Might be thirty minutes. Maybe more."

"Shit. Hurry the hell up."

"Stay put. Don't mess with these guys."

"Yeah, yeah." He hung up the phone and stuck it back in his pocket.

DeWayne was staring at him, mouth hanging open. That almost made it all worthwhile. "Okay, great. So the feds are on their way. Now what?"

Nail considered. No telling how long it would take Elliot to get her team together. No telling what would happen between now and then. Impossible to know whether Anna, Karyn, and Genevieve were even still alive. Their odds had to be getting worse by the minute.

"Now we go find the back door."

*   *   *

The others—the *new ones*—had given Sheila a hard time
at first. Raul had recognized her and let her inside the
front door of the old prison with a smile, but the others
hadn't recognized her once she was inside. One told her
to fuck off, another to beat it. Others, more than a couple,
eyed the bloody wrappings on her hands and licked their
lips. A few made faces of pity or disgust and kept their
distance or looked away. She'd felt her blood rising, that
killing urge sending strength into her arms and jaws, and
only Deanna's arrival and an intense exercise of will had
kept her from trying to tear somebody's head off.

"Who are these people?" Sheila had asked.

"More of us," Deanna had answered. "New brothers
and sisters."

There were a lot of them, Sheila noted. That was the
dawning of her suspicion. So many, and all at once. No
care had been taken in selecting them—Belial and Van
Horn had simply rounded up and given the blessing—
curse—affliction to any warm body they could find.

"Replacements," Sheila had said. The first thought
that had jumped into her head. It made sense. She'd
looked at her hands, at the fresh spots of blood that had
leaked from her nose onto her arms and shirt. The old
ones were wearing out, so replacements were of course
needed.

She had to find Van Horn. Had to find Belial. They could
help. She'd clutched at the idea with desperation, trying not
to think that replacements wouldn't be necessary if the first
of the Chosen could be made well again. Perhaps they were
just *more*, not replacements at all.

Deanna had only shrugged. At Sheila's insistence, Deanna
told her where Belial and Van Horn had gone, though it
hadn't been particularly helpful. "That way. Inside."

She'd gone into the darkness. Weakening. Taking slow,
staggering steps through the depths of the building. She
ran her bloody hands across the concrete walls. Her
body was hot, boiling, and the cool touch of the concrete

felt good even as her nerve endings screamed at the affront.

It was dark. She stumbled and nearly fell down a flight of stairs, catching herself on the cold steel pipe of the railing. Crying out and laughing at the pain.

She kept moving. Exhaustion dragged at her feet, trying to draw her down into the earth. She lifted one foot, dropped it heavily to the ground, then followed with the other. Over and over. There seemed to be noises coming from ahead, though she wondered if those were lies, products of a delirium brought on by her fever.

She stopped at a corner, pressing her forehead to the gritty wall. Belial couldn't help her, she thought with a sudden certainty. Had he ever? All his gifts had come with a price far exceeding their value.

Rain, then. Rain had healed her once.

Somebody.

More noises—voices, she thought—and she pushed herself from the wall and trudged onward.

She walked a thousand years or so before the orange flicker of candles drew her out of her pain and back into the world. She could see, and now the voices were clearer than ever.

She approached a doorway and entered.

A ritual had begun, or preparations, and even now that stirred excitement with her, however weak. It was vast, much bigger than anything she'd done. The impulse was to become overawed by it, but as she picked out the figures around it, she remembered her purpose.

"Belial!" Sheila said.

Belial ignored her, continuing to draw at the edge of the diagram, but Van Horn stopped in the middle of pouring a fine white powder. One of the men near him held a flashlight on the work, and the beam illuminated a curl of fine dust floating in the air like smoke. "Now is not a good time, dear," Van Horn said.

"I'm dying, Edgar."

"Aren't we all? It's hell getting old."

"I need help. Where's Rain?"

Van Horn gave her an ersatz smile that didn't touch the hardness around his eyes. "After. We'll know what to do after. Just hold on, dear. It'll be fine."

Sheila paused, mouth open in the act of making a response. *There isn't time,* she was going to say. Instead, she exhaled, letting her original words dissipate. "I see."

"I'm here, Sheila," Rain said. She got up from where she'd been sitting, unseen, on the floor. "Come. Come here."

Sheila's feet obeyed her long enough to haul her over to Rain. She searched the other woman's eyes and had no idea what she found there.

"Sit," Rain said. "You're bleeding."

"Can't you do something? Please?"

Blood spilled from the corner of Rain's eye. Rain wiped it away with the heel of her hand and showed it to Sheila. "I don't know how."

The strength left Sheila in a rush, and her knees buckled. Rain caught her under the elbows and lowered her slowly to the floor. She saw Van Horn watching her as she sat. There was something speculative in his eyes. Sheila wanted to gouge them out.

The moment passed, and he went back to pouring salt.

This is fucked, Anna thought. *This is all wrong.*

After the new woman's arrival and the odd exchange with Van Horn, work on the spell or ritual or whatever had continued. Van Horn had restrained Karyn, the whole time offering up reassurances that the straps were so she didn't accidentally erase one of the lines. Anna didn't think Karyn could hear any of it, but Van Horn kept chattering nonetheless. He seemed happy, buzzing about from place to place, lighting candles, pouring out neat little mounds of yellow, white, or red powder.

Anna couldn't remember the last time she'd felt so wretched, so suffused with fear. They'd said they wouldn't hurt Karyn, but what if they lied? And what happened after this? And would they really let Anna and Genevieve go, or was that a lie? The fear took on a bloody tinge of rage.

"What's it going to do?" Anna asked.

"I don't know," Rain said. She had one hand on the newcomer's back. Sheila, that was what Rain had called her. Sheila was in rough shape, leaning against Rain as though she'd fall over otherwise. "I don't recognize it, but I—I'm new at this."

"Will it hurt her?"

"I don't know."

Anna closed her eyes and rested her head against the wall. Her body felt as if it was warm enough to catch fire, and now she was nauseated, too. She wondered what it would be like to tear out Van Horn's throat with her teeth. Hot. Bloody. Like a rare steak. The thought calmed her stomach some. She thought she ought to be worried about that.

"I'm hungry," Rain said.

Anna's stomach grumbled in answer. "Don't even talk to me about that."

"I'm always hungry now. I think I've eaten parts of six people." Matter-of-fact. Like she thought *she* ought to be worried about that, but it was academic, like maybe eating people was bad for your cholesterol and one day that might be bad for you.

"They're never gonna let her go," Anna said.

"They're never gonna let you go, either," Sheila said, her voice cracked and quiet.

Anna opened her eyes. The other woman met them. Anna recognized her now—one of Van Horn's entourage, Sheila had been there the night they kidnapped Van Horn.

"Karyn will fuck them up if they don't." Anna didn't know if she really believed that, but at least Karyn had leverage. Even simple refusal to cooperate might be enough. Might be.

"Oh, they'll probably let you walk out of here. But they have you now. Just like me." Sheila looked down at the bloody, dirty bandages covering the stumps of her fingers.

"And me," Rain said.

Anna felt the urge to move away from the two of them—the newcomer, Sheila, was freaking her out. It was her facial expressions. Like Hector, they veered from one extreme to another, many of them wildly inappropriate. There was a muted tenderness in her eyes, sadness pulling down the corners of her eyebrows, yet her gaze kept flicking to the blood, and she pulled at her lips with her teeth and kept swallowing. Anna couldn't tell if she wanted to hold the other woman or eat her.

Van Horn glanced over, catching Sheila's attention. Maybe it was too dark, or Van Horn was too far away, but he didn't act like he saw the hatred pouring off her. Anna was too close to miss it. He went back to work. Sheila watched him like if she stared hard enough he'd catch fire.

This is a tinderbox. How many factions are represented in here? There was Hector and Van Horn, who seemed like they were on the same team, and they might even be. Sobell was not, though he might find it temporarily convenient. Genevieve? Who could tell? Anna wasn't sure if she and Sobell had fucked her over or not, wasn't *quite* sure they wouldn't pull some clever trick and walk out of here with Anna and Karyn, the four of them fighting off all comers, but if Sobell was making the call she thought it more likely that he'd walk out of here and feed the two of them to the dogs the moment it looked as though they were getting too close to his heels. Then there were Hector's minions—and Sheila. The others seemed loyal enough, but Sheila was obviously cracking.

The right catalyst could blow this room apart. If Sheila sided with Anna and Karyn, and Sobell threw in with them, the fight would be even. Too bad Anna couldn't count on either Sobell or Sheila. She made a frustrated noise.

There had to be an opportunity here. Somewhere.

Van Horn took a thick gold hoop from Sobell, arranged it carefully on a set of intersecting lines at Karyn's feet, and then retreated to the outside of the circle, above Karyn's head. Hector went to the position opposite him across the circle. Sobell took the spot to the west, if the Van Horn/Hector axis was considered north/south, and Genevieve took the spot to the east.

Hector raised his hands and opened his mouth to speak, but before he could say anything, a couple of his new disciples rushed into the room.

"We got a problem, boss," one of them said.

"What? What the fuck is it that's so goddamn important?"

"Cops," the guy said. "A whole lot of cops."

"Kill them."

"It's . . . It's a lotta cops."

"A thousand?"

"I dunno. I mean, not that many."

"Then kill them. Draw them away from this room, and kill them. All of them."

"Uh . . . okay."

"If we are interrupted, I will personally seek you out. Do you understand?"

The man nodded. "Yessir."

"Good. Go."

In Sobell's experience, there were few things that would bring the wrath of God down on a man like murdering a police officer. He supposed that circumstances warranted it this time—he might not get another shot at this, after all, and he was painfully aware of how little time he might have left—but Belial's manner in giving the order gave him pause. There wasn't a flicker of hesitation or even a moment of consideration. No thought of consequence, only of what he needed right now.

Fucking demons. He'd essentially thrown in with them for his whole life, but after all this time, they had become

a tiresome lot. And the fact that either Van Horn had
bait-and-switched him, or Belial had simply tossed old
Forcas back into the abyss, was worrisome. Trucking
about with garden-variety demons was bad enough, but
Belial's name was written throughout a dozen or more
occult texts, usually in reverent or terrified tones. En-
countering it in the flesh was like running into Jehovah
at a bakery one morning. It was one of the ones you
didn't mess with, not ever. Sobell felt as if he'd gone trout
fishing and somehow ended up with a great white shark
on his line.

Maybe it's lying, Sobell thought. But it had been his
experience that demons didn't lie. It was said they
couldn't, but he didn't know if it stretched that far, just
that he'd never known it to happen.

There was nothing to be done for it. Not now. Just
proceed, and hope he got the answers he needed.

Once the peon had fled to either take on the cops and
die, or more likely hide somewhere and wait until it was
over, Belial started up again. He held his hands over his
head and intoned some ominous-sounding words in a
language Sobell didn't recognize at all. Not Greek or
Latin, those old occult staples—likely it was no human
tongue at all.

For the first time it occurred to him to wonder: if hu-
mans entreated demons to work magic on their behalf,
to whom did demons turn? Why couldn't Belial just *do*
whatever it was he was trying to do, rather than go through
all the occult negotiations? Was he hampered in some
way, bound in human flesh?

Van Horn nodded at Sobell and knelt. Sobell and
Genevieve, having been instructed to follow along and
do exactly as they were told, also knelt. Van Horn held a
candle to a pile of yellow powder that flared up in front
of him with a bright yellow flame. Once again, Sobell and
Genevieve followed suit.

More chanting from Belial. More nonsense. Ordinarily, Sobell would have paid close attention to every

particular of the proceedings, but ordinarily, they would have made at least a shred of sense. The diagram would have had some familial relation to others he was familiar with, or at least some of the same components, and the incantation would similarly be constructed of borrowed and repeated phrases, and it would be possible to divine, if not the exact nature of the working, at least some general idea of its intent. This, though, was nonsense. Only the star in the middle and the circle at the outer edge were familiar diagram components to Sobell, and they were so generic as to be useless. The rest was incomprehensible. Alien magic.

What, exactly, am I participating in here?

The others began walking around the circle—widdershins, of course, Sobell noted wryly—at least that much was typical. Once more, he followed, lagging a little. They stopped at a quarter revolution, each taking up the station formerly held by the last person, so that Sobell now stood at Ames's feet. The subject of this whole experiment waited patiently in the center. No struggle, no noise. The restraints seemed superfluous. She'd said she would cooperate, and she was doing just that. If this didn't kill her, and Belial had said it wouldn't, Sobell would have to throw her a bonus. Provided, of course, he got the answers he needed.

Belial started another verse. An unsteady keening noise, like one of those monstrous singing saws, or a wet finger along an edge of finest crystal, filled Sobell's head, seeming to originate somewhere just above his back teeth. The sensation was beyond unpleasant. His eyes watered, and he swore it felt as if the crown was going to vibrate right off one of his molars. He kept his teeth clamped shut, but he wasn't sure how much good that would do as the sound got louder.

Is it just me? he wondered, but the question was answered immediately. Tears shone on Van Horn's face, and Belial had begun chanting louder.

Another sound intruded, a muffled short bang, like

somebody slamming a car door or a firecracker going off in a barrel. A gunshot, surely. How far away? How long did they have?

Van Horn lit a pile of red powder. Sobell nearly toppled over as he knelt, but he steadied himself with one hand and lit the red powder with a candle held in the other.

More gunshots, a whole fusillade of them.

Belial sped up his chant. The four men stood again, and Belial began moving once more around the circle.

A hot trickle of blood spilled from Sobell's nose and dribbled over his lips.

"They're killing her," Anna said.

Rain, transfixed by the ritual in front of them, didn't look at her. "No."

"They're killing *us*, then." The noise was going to vibrate her head to pieces. On balance, she might be grateful for that. "We're not getting out of here alive, anyway, and Karyn's not getting out at all."

Rain nodded. Her mouth hung open, and a sticky strand of spit depended from her chin. Slumped against her, Sheila moaned and held her head with both hands.

"Look at me," Anna said.

Amazingly, Rain did.

Now what? They could take Hector, probably. Maybe kill Sobell or Van Horn. Not all three of them though, and there were still two of Hector's faithful minions standing by the door, watching. Attacking Hector might stop this shit, but so what, if it got them all killed and eaten?

The idea of being killed and eaten, repulsive as it was, actually made her stomach growl. *What the fuck?*

"Hey!" she said. "Magic!"

"What?"

"You said I'd get warm—I'm warm. You said I'd start having gross thoughts—Jesus, am I ever. But you said I could do magic, too. Can I?"

"Maybe. Probably. Do you have any ideas?"

"Ideas? No. But you can, right? Teach me something? Anything that will help?"

Rain's face was still and blank, and Anna saw her head slowly rotating back toward the ritual.

"We have to stop them, Rain! We have to stop this. We have to *hurt* them."

Rain didn't acknowledge this, but the smile that spread across Sheila's face was truly chilling, a hungry, feral grimace coupled with a sudden glee in her eyes. She lowered her hands and touched Rain's shoulder.

When she had Rain's attention, she pulled a marker from her pocket and began drawing on the floor. The dance out on the main floor continued another step, and blue flame flared up. The tone in Anna's head took on a second pitch at some god-awful dissonant interval with the first. Blood dripped from Sheila's ear.

One of Hector's minions by the door fell down, convulsing.

"Gather in a circle," Sheila said. "Take my hand in your left, Rain's in your right. Repeat after me."

"Wait, what are we doing?"

"We're stopping this," Sheila said. "We're hurting them."

The sound of a gunshot echoed off a nearby structure. Before the echo could die out, a dozen more followed it. "You hear that?" Nail asked.

"What, do you think I'm deaf?" DeWayne asked. "Your cops. Hope they don't get anyone killed."

This side of the building, much of the foundation was exposed to provide access to what looked like a loading dock. Stark concrete retaining walls held in the mounds of dirt to either side of the dock. A pair of heavy steel doors had been put in place back here next to a giant overhead door. As Nail and DeWayne approached, Nail saw a heavy chain and padlock holding the doors shut.

"Don't suppose you got any tricks up your sleeve for that?" DeWayne asked.

"Not handy, no." He walked up the stairs to the door and inspected it.

"Can't you just, you know, shoot it?"

"If I wanna blow my own balls off, yeah. Maybe. Not sure it would work anyway, but even if it did, with a steel door and concrete everywhere, one of us might catch a ricochet. You in a hurry to get shot?"

"Fuck," DeWayne said.

"Yeah."

Nail looked at the chain again. It was wrapped around the door handles three or four times, and—

"Oh, that's cute."

"Huh?"

"Somebody already took some bolt cutters to this thing." Nail unwound the chain. It fell into two pieces, linked by the padlock. He pulled the door open. Beyond, the inside of the loading dock was a dark, dry space that smelled of motor oil and detergent. At the far end, he could see a faint suggestion of stairs in the gloom.

"All right," Nail said. He checked his weapon. One in the chamber, safety off. "I'll go first."

"Hey, man, I don't know."

He looked back at DeWayne, who was standing at the base of the stairs, shifting his weight from one leg to the other like he had to piss. "Don't know what?"

"Man, you got the cops on this. We ain't gonna do shit in there but get in the way, fuck things up. Maybe get shot. Which, like you said, I ain't exactly in a hurry to do. And, you know, there's, like, maybe a dozen of Clarence's guys in there, which if we meet one is not gonna do good things for my life expectancy."

"God—" Nail cut himself off. Yeah, this was chicken-shit, but DeWayne didn't know Anna and Karyn. Had no idea what he owed them. It didn't matter, he supposed. Anna and Karyn were family, but not DeWayne's family.

"You ain't gotta be the hero here," DeWayne said, a pleading edge to his tone. "That's what cops get paid for."

"Get outta here, man. Take the car, get rid of Stevie somewhere. Then get out of circulation, for fuck's sake."

"Hey, I—"

"No, it's cool." He looked DeWayne in the eye and gave him a single curt nod. "For real. You did good tonight."

"All right, man. Watch yourself, huh?"

"Yeah."

Nail went in. He heard DeWayne's footfalls recede behind him.

Chapter 29

An unearthly peace had come over Karyn, not at all like what she had expected from the sort of magic she'd seen Tommy perform, where blood and pain too often seemed integral components. First, the strange cacophony she'd been hearing for weeks quieted, driving home just how bad it had been, how much she'd grown accustomed to. Other sounds intruded—sounds with a different quality, less muted and more immediate. Chanting. Gunfire and screams. The low whisper of flame.

None of it was *present*, though—it was like traffic noise when she was trying to fall asleep. Easily ignored, but easily picked out if she paid attention. It had little weight or consequence.

The visions did a similar trick—fading just a little, retreating nearly into the background even as they multiplied. Perhaps that was because she was in a place that was dark much of the time, perhaps not. They didn't *demand* her attention in the same way they usually did, though.

She felt calm. Happy, though not in any exuberant way. Content, as though nothing was wrong in the world, though nothing could be further from the truth.

Hector traversed the circle, finally crossing from the outside to the interior. He produced a knife, a tiny thing about the size of a paring knife. *Now he kills me.* The burst of panic that accompanied the thought surprised her, as did the sudden movement of her limbs. The restraints held, though, and before she could do anything else, Hector cut the ball of his thumb.

Ah. There was the blood. He leaned over and smeared it across her forehead, then extended the knife in Sobell's direction, hilt-first.

Sobell approached. His nose was bleeding, Karyn saw. There was a smear on his lip where he'd wiped the blood away, but a fresh trickle ran down and dripped slowly from his chin.

He took the knife from Hector. He paused then, turning to each of the faces around the circle. The hesitation was odd, Karyn thought, but there was something on his face—fear, or confusion, it was hard to tell, masked by the flickering light. Neither Genevieve nor the old man did anything more than stare back at him. Hector crossed his arms and waited.

Sobell cut his thumb. Karyn wondered if that was really necessary, given the blood on his face, but he went with the program. When he smeared it across her forehead, making an X or a cross with Hector's blood, it was hurried, as though he wanted to get it over with.

Then he retreated to the circle's edge.

One more revolution, and the players stood back in their original positions. Blood now streamed from both Sobell's nostrils, and he no longer bothered to wipe it away. He and the old man weaved on their feet—one of them must collapse soon.

Hector pronounced a final syllable and dashed Sobell's torc to the floor inside the circle. It smashed apart, fragments flying everywhere.

All the lights in the room went out.

There was a moment of complete darkness, and then a diffuse blue light began to fill the room. It grew in intensity until Karyn could make out Sobell's awed expression, Hector's avid greed.

It was coming from her, she realized.

The visions, the images swelled and bloomed, filling her head, enveloping her, sucking her in as the blue light blazed and a crazed vertigo spun the room around her.

One image in particular grew in front of her, blocking her entire view.

She began to speak.

There had been shooting, of that Anna was sure. After that—she had no idea. Each time the circle rotated, a new tone at a new dissonant interval joined the others keening in her head, until she thought her skull would shake apart. If there had been gunshots when the circle turned for the fourth time, Anna hadn't heard them. She couldn't hear Sheila, chanting three feet away from her, was only keeping up her end of the chant by repeating what Sheila had said before, watching Sheila's lips, and hoping. Had she mangled the words? How would she know?

Sheila and Rain were shouting now, and Anna tried to raise her voice likewise, just to hear it over the noise in her head.

The circle rotated one more time, and the lights went out. The noise stopped, too, leaving Sheila and Anna screaming into the void.

Blue light shone—Karyn. It came from Karyn's body, limning her in foxfire. The sight tore Anna's concentration away from the task at hand, almost caused her to fumble the chant.

A voice, loud as the amplified vocals at a rock concert, ripped out across the room.

"*Life, you seek life, one reprieve from the abyss, the other escape.*"

That, too, came from Karyn. Her eyes were rolled back in her head, her body stretched taut.

"*In the valley of the garden, here in this Gomorrah—*"
Sheila spat out another line, then released Anna's hands.

"*—a man, naked, bound, and shot through with arrows, in dying finds salvation.*"

Anna tried to keep up the chant, but it was nearly impossible with the noise and Karyn's gigantic, eardrum-crushing voice.

Sheila got out a knife.

Oh, Jesus, don't—

"In his salvation you will find yours."

Sheila cut off her thumb.

Anna scrambled back as a huge, terrifying gray *thing* filled the space between her and Sheila.

"Kill them all," Sheila said. "All save the women."

She fell over. Rain collapsed.

The gray thing reared up.

Anna saw the creature for a split second before the light vanished, saw it reach out and destroy Van Horn like she'd brush lint off her shirt. Van Horn made some kind of gurgling, strangling noise and then collapsed. In the darkness that followed, there was a single deafening gunshot, and by the time Belial—Hector—whoever—conjured up more light, Rhino was dead, too, crushed to a pulp, and the slug thing was still squeezing his corpse.

"Anna!" Genevieve yelled. She stood close to Sobell's side, the bulk of the gray thing and its flailing tendrils between her and Anna.

Anna's eyes locked with hers. Genevieve's distant, disengaged expression had vanished and been replaced by a twisting visage of pure emotion. Terror and regret, desperate need combined with emotions Anna had no name for and couldn't read from the others. Tears glimmered on her cheeks.

"Run!" Genevieve said. "Get out of here!"

Run where? The gray thing was between her and the door, too close to Karyn. She couldn't leave Karyn here, and she dared get no closer to the creature's questing arms. She had no idea if the thing would follow Sheila's instructions to the letter, or if it was about to go on a killing rampage, and she wasn't about to test it.

Everything, Anna was now quite sure, was not going

to work out for everyone. She felt no vindication at the thought, no triumph, only a sick sort of emptiness and disappointment. She supposed she must have expected something different after all.

The slug thing turned toward Genevieve. Gen's face contorted with horror. Sobell broke and bolted for the door.

The creature lurched forward. Tentacles lashed the air.

Genevieve cast one last miserable look Anna's way, and she fled. The creature followed her.

Anna had no time to think about what had just happened, only thoughts for getting Karyn the hell out of here.

Anna snatched up Sheila's knife and ran to Karyn.

The restraints came free easily. Karyn pushed herself to a sitting position, and Anna hauled her to her feet.

"What the hell was that?" Karyn asked.

"Don't know. We gotta go."

"I'm not sure I can—"

"You can. Come on."

Anna half dragged a stumbling Karyn over to Sheila. "Come on," she said. "We have to *go*."

"I don't think she's getting up," Karyn said.

There was a lot of blood, Anna now saw, a dark pool surrounding Sheila's hand and head. It hadn't come just from the knife wound, but from her nose and ears as well. Her eyes were open, unblinking. Rain was curled next to her, trembling.

"Come on, get up!"

Rain closed her eyes.

Anna looked down, helpless. "Damn."

"Now would be good," Karyn said. "Sooner than now."

They ran out.

Chapter 30

"There was something else," Sobell said, gasping. He pulled Genevieve forward and shoved her down the hall in front of him. She'd been quick about catching up with him, but apparently her self-preservation instinct was flagging. "There had to be more."

"There was nothing else," Belial said.

"Anna!" Genevieve shouted.

"Keep moving, dammit! You can't help her." Sobell shoved Genevieve forward again. Obstinate pupil.

Belial didn't even slow to look at them. He went through the next doorway. Sobell pulled Genevieve along. The only light came from Sobell's borrowed cell phone, barely enough to keep Belial in sight, and Sobell wondered how long before the battery went dead. It hadn't seemed to take quite so long to get in here as it was to get out.

"Whose question did she answer?" Sobell asked.

"Shut up," Belial said.

Belial stopped at the next doorway. Beyond, flashlight beams careered around the large room they'd come through on the way. Armed men, and not friendly. They wore black with tall white letters printed on the uniforms or suits, and while Sobell couldn't read the words from here, he was moderately certain they all spelled some variant of LAW ENFORCEMENT.

"Here they come," he said.

"What are we doing?" Genevieve whispered.

A flashlight swept past another doorway, stopped, then returned to it. A mostly naked man leaped out, held up a strip of paper, and shouted something. Sobell recognized the words partway through, and got his hand up in time to shield his eyes from a brilliant flash of white light. Somebody shouted, and somebody else fired off a few rounds. The naked guy hit the ground, full of freshly minted holes, so either he'd fucked up the blinding spell or the LAW ENFORCEMENT guys had better gear than Sobell thought. Or there was one lucky, stupid, blind bastard out there shooting, he supposed.

A dozen other remnants of Belial's army rushed out of other doorways, screaming at the top of their lungs.

Belial started to go forward, and Sobell grabbed him by the shoulder.

"Are you insane?" Sobell asked. "Why does everybody around me have a death wish today?"

Belial spun around. In the blue-white light from the cell phone, his eyes were overlarge, face twisted in a snarl. "Fuck yourself, Enoch."

"I can help you, Belial, but not if you're dead."

Belial hesitated. His face worked in that peculiar way it had, the various bits moving with no particular relationship to each other.

The screaming started. Somebody started shooting, regardless of whether they could see or not; then somebody else joined him.

Sobell yanked Belial back through the doorway and to the side, before one of them caught a stray bullet.

Above the screaming, there came a *shriek* so awful it caused the hairs to stand up on Sobell's neck.

"I hate to say this, but we need each other," Sobell said.

"You need me. Us. You need us."

"I have money. I have people. Your people have a nasty habit of dying, even when they're not getting mowed down by law enforcement." He peeked around the edge of the doorway—impossible to tell what was going on out there, bodies swarming everywhere, flashlight beams bobbing, muzzle flash and flame adding to the chaos. "The oracle said there's one solution to both our problems." *I think. I hope.* "We just have to find it. But to do that, we need to get out of here."

Belial looked back through as well. Was he actually loyal to that collection of morons out there, or was he struggling to overcome the twin temptations of bloodshed and chaos?

"Fine," Belial said. "*Go fuck yourself.* Fine. Let's go."

"Glad you're all in agreement in there."

The noise was dying down. Sobell couldn't tell if Belial's mess of an army had won, but even if they had, they wouldn't for long. The thing about the law was that it was effectively bottomless. You couldn't go toe-to-toe with it and win. You needed to obfuscate, lawyer up, cover up, be unbelievably careful, and, when you'd exhausted all of the above, run.

"There a back way?" Sobell asked.

"Yes."

"Lead on."

They retreated from the battle, going deeper into the building. Sobell wondered what his chances were for successfully pinning this whole mess on Belial, if they got caught.

Not terribly good, he supposed.

Finding the way toward the front of the building was easy, even if Nail had gotten a little turned around inside—just head toward the noise. He had climbed up to the ground floor, taken a few dead ends, but now he was headed toward the front, where this shit show was likely reaching its conclusion. Maybe the cops would rescue Anna and Karyn before Sobell and company did something horrible to them, but Nail kinda doubted it. Any sort of hostage negotiation had obviously failed, but

Sobell's legion of doom had an entrenched position and fuckin' voodoo or whatever on their side. They'd lose in the end, but it would take a while.

The sounds of battle echoed through what looked like a long row of cells. The noises were much louder when Nail got to the end. There was a slight turn, then another long hall. The noises were getting closer now, and he killed his flashlight.

Yeah, footsteps.

Keeping low, Nail looked around the corner. Couldn't see shit—whoever it was wasn't carrying light. He readied his gun.

Genevieve stepped right out into the hall. "Who's there?"

"Gen? That you?"

Genevieve flooded the area with light from her phone. Two figures stood at her sides. Sobell, and the crazy cult leader who'd shot Sobell in the head a couple of months back. "What is going on here? Where's Anna?"

"This is all terrifically touching, but we need to be moving," Sobell said.

"Where's Anna and Karyn?"

Genevieve shook her head.

"What's that supposed to mean?"

"Means I don't know," she said tonelessly. "You should get out of here. There's nothing but bad shit that way."

"How, exactly, did you get in here?" Sobell asked.

"I gotta go," Nail said, walking forward.

"Good luck, Marine," Sobell said.

"Fuck all of you." Nail shouldered past them.

"Nail—I mean it. That is not a good idea," Genevieve said.

"Tell me about it. Now get outta here."

"Be careful," she called after him.

"Right. Sure. No problem."

She walked away, in line behind the cult guy. He knew it was stupid, but he felt a pang anyway, way worse than when his brother had split. He and Genevieve should have been on this together. She was really gonna leave him here, let him do this one by himself.

He headed away from the them, deeper into this burgeoning clusterfuck. He used no light, hugging the wall for navigation. It wasn't like he had any better ideas. Shouting and gunfire echoed through the hall, diffuse and distant, and he moved toward it as rapidly as he dared, sliding his feet softly across the floor so as not to suddenly step forward and fall in a hole.

The hall either took a right angle turn to the left or opened out into a wider space—he couldn't tell which. From the sound, it was probably the latter, but the echoes did funny things in here, bouncing around off the hard concrete surfaces and never seeming to come to rest.

He could call out, he supposed, though that might be a good way to get shot or incinerated. Yell for help, maybe—though it was impossible to know who'd show up. The police, maybe, or maybe some crazy-eyed fire-slinging motherfucker who had an endless list of imaginary scores to settle.

This sucks.

A scream, a real bad one, echoed up the hallway, and Nail paused. Bad shit, that. Last time he heard something like that, a guy had stepped on a land mine and blown most of his leg off. They'd pulled him out of the mine field with a charred black bone sticking out of the end of his thigh.

Was he really going to go toward that?

He exhaled. He literally could not see his hand in front of his face. Somewhere dozens of people were fighting and dying over a hostage situation that, for all he knew, wasn't even a hostage situation anymore. Well, half of them were fighting over that, and the other half were fighting because they were crazy. He had the funny feeling he'd been here before.

Whatever. Family's family.

He kept going, one slow step at a time. After a few minutes, he realized that light, however faint and tenuous, had sneaked up on him. He could see the outline of a doorway and the flat gray plane of the wall beyond.

Something moved behind him, and a light threw his shadow down in front of him.

"Freeze, motherfucker!"

That sounded awfully coplike. He held his hands up, keeping his finger off the trigger of the gun as obviously as possible.

"Put the gun down! Slowly!"

He lowered himself to one knee, turning as he did. The flashlight beam was like a hammer to the forehead, and he couldn't see shit past it.

He put the gun on the floor and his hand back in the air. "I'm on your side," he said. "I need to talk to Special Agent Elliot. It's important."

"Push the gun over here."

What if these weren't really cops? he wondered, then decided that was too much paranoia even for him. Again, careful not to move suddenly, he shoved the weapon toward the cop.

"Facedown. On the ground."

"I really need to talk to Agent Elliot."

"Now!"

He lay down. Footsteps approached, at least two sets. Somebody knelt and pulled one of his arms behind his back. If he was going to move, it would have to be now. Two guys, one probably with a gun at the ready, Nail himself lying on his belly with one of the dudes practically sitting on him.

DeWayne was right. I'm fucked.

The cuffs went on.

They'd long since left the sounds of fighting behind, and now that safety seemed more or less in hand, all Sobell wanted was out. He wanted to get out into the light and lay eyes on his new partner, and take the demon's measure. It looked like they were in it for the long haul together, an arrangement Sobell had deep misgivings about, especially now that Belial had taken to mumbling to himself. At first, Sobell had thought the man was talking to him, and he'd tried to listen more closely, but he knew now that, whatever Belial was saying, it had nothing to do with him. Sobell got the impression that the man was conducting a dialogue with himself. Was the body's original owner still in there, talking to Belial? Sobell had never heard of such a thing, but he supposed it was possible. Hosts didn't usually live this long, so clearly something unusual was going on here.

They found light before too long, in the form of a spotlight trained on the doors to the back loading dock.

"They have the place surrounded," Sobell said. "We're fucked."

Belial shook his head in a rather overly violent expression of denial. "No. *No*. Come with me."

For a moment, Sobell thought Belial was about to take a second crack at his earlier blaze-of-glory suicide run, but the man—demon—whatever—turned and led them back into the cell block.

"I hope you know what you're doing," Genevieve whispered.

"That makes two of us," Sobell said. He pointed at Belial. "Also, I hope *he* knows what he's doing. Our fates are likely in his hands now."

"God help us."

"I doubt he'll be so inclined."

Belial led them to the first cell on the left. "Ink," he said.

Genevieve handed over a marker. Belial scrawled some symbols on the door. This time, Sobell was glad to see, they were actually recognizable.

"Inside," Belial said.

The three of them went in. Belial shut the door.

"What's going on?" Genevieve asked.

"Now we wait them out."

"Most people won't notice the door," Sobell added. "All we need to do is be patient."

Belial smiled.

Anna and Karyn emerged from the back of the prison right into the glare of a blazing spotlight.

"Down! On the ground, right now!"

Anna held up her hands, and Karyn wasted no time doing likewise. A handful of men in SWAT gear, FBI written in huge letters across their chests, stood a hundred feet or so away. One brought a second spotlight to bear on the two women.

"Come on," Anna said. "We're the good guys here!"

"On your knees! Hands on your head!"

She knelt. Karyn, for her part, followed, slowly. She was there but not there. More "there" than she had been, Anna thought, but still . . . not vacant, exactly, but more than preoccupied. *Call it progress.*

The SWAT guys approached, patted them down, and somebody gave the okay. One of the guys helped Anna to her feet.

"My hero," she said.

Chapter 31

"What the hell happened, Owens?"

Nail put his hands flat on the table in front of him and tried to ignore the cuffs. If he looked at them, he just got angry, and he didn't want to join Special Agent Elliot in that department. She looked *furious*, like she'd had gasoline and rusty nails for breakfast, and she was looking for somebody to unleash hell on.

"Like I told your guy—I don't know what happened. I was worried about my friends, so I went looking for them."

"You said kidnapping. You said, and I quote, 'red-fucking-handed.' Now you're not so sure?"

"I saw Sobell go in."

"Alone?"

"With Rhino Vasquez."

"And . . . ?"

"And nothin'."

"I've got ten agents down and my ass in a sling, and you saw *nothing*?"

"He was there. What about my girls?"

Elliot fiddled with her shirt cuffs before answering, "Two out of three."

Nail felt his stomach drop to the floor. "Which two?"

"Ames and Ruiz."

"And Gen? You—you find her body?"

"Nothing. She's gone, just like that bastard Sobell."

Nail was so worried about the first half of Elliot's statement that the second half took a moment to sink in. "Wait, you didn't get Sobell?"

"We're looking. Meanwhile, anything you can tell us about him or where he might be could help."

Oh, this was bad. Sobell was loose. *At large*, as the cops liked to say. Nail felt stupid. How had he thought this would go down? Somehow he'd convinced himself Sobell would end up dead or in custody, caught "red-fucking-handed," and with himself in the clear except as an anonymous informant. Now Sobell was running around out there somewhere, and they were trying to get him to straight-up rat on the guy. This shit was bad for Anna, bad for Karyn, probably bad for DeWayne, and certainly bad for Nail himself. So this was what cold sweat felt like.

"Sobell who?" Nail asked.

"Do not get smart with me, motherfucker. Not tonight."

"You mean Tyrone Sobell? Yeah, we go way back."

"I got you on a gun charge."

"I will personally buy you a fuckin' Mercedes if you can find a single bullet on the scene fired from that gun."

"The gun had no serial numbers. It had a high-capacity magazine. You don't have a carry permit. With your record, that probably means five to eight."

"A pillar of the community like me? Five to eight months of probation."

"You called me. You damn well know you told me Sobell was on the scene."

"Got a recording? That might refresh my memory."

"Put Sobell on the scene for me. Give me *something*, and I can get rid of the gun charges."

Much as Nail wanted to, he'd seen how this went down. "You already played that game with my brother, and you played sloppy. Damn near got him killed. Might still."

"I'm trying to *help* you, don't you get it?" Elliot

kicked the table leg, then slowly got control over herself. "I want Sobell," she said.

"You ain't got him. You might be able to see how that's a problem for all of us."

"I saw the remains of a greater working at the correctional facility. Do you know what that is?"

"No."

"Very serious occult business. It also bears no resemblance to anything I've seen before, or anybody in my office has seen before. I think your buddy Sobell has gotten into some very bad shit, probably with some very unpleasant allies."

"I believe that."

"Whatever he was doing, his activities resulted in ten casualties. Additionally, your friend Ames seems to have been struck deaf, though our physicians can't find any damage, and Ruiz has no memory of any of the events that wound up with her down there. I need you to tell me what Sobell wanted them for. It's important."

"I don't know."

"I'm not certain, but I don't think he got to finish whatever it was he started down there. Do you think he'll be content to leave them in peace now?"

Nail chewed on that. "Doubt it."

"We're not going to hold you," she said. "But I need you to go to Ames and Ruiz. See if they want protection. Failing that, see if they want help. There are things we can do off the books."

"I can't promise nothin'."

Elliot gave him a tight, humorless smile. "The three of you are short on friends right now, and I think you're going to need some. Badly."

"I'll see what they say."

Sobell brushed the dust off the edge of a cheap-looking plywood desk and sat. The room was small but adequate, an old bit of unused office space in a strip mall. He'd kept it off the books for just such an occasion, never really believing he'd be reduced to sleeping in it. Dining on Cheez-Its and soggy pizza from the corner 7-Eleven.

Belial stood in the center of the room, arms crossed, face working in its relentless way. The stink rolling off him could have stunned a polar bear. If they were going to be living in close quarters, the demon was going to need a primer in human personal hygiene.

Genevieve sat in the corner, her expression slack and exhausted. Not too different from how Sobell felt, actually. She was chewing gum. About once every minute or so, she'd chew a single time.

Lastly, Erica Tran stood just inside the door, looking like she might run out it at any second.

"They took nineteen men in," Erica said. Her face had taken on a greenish, ashen look. Possibly the fluorescents, but maybe she was simply going to be sick. "Seventeen others were hospitalized, including six federal agents. And eleven were killed. Including four federal agents."

"Shit," Genevieve said.

"So?" Belial said.

"There were actually very few gunshot wounds, according to my contact. Most of the men simply gave themselves up. The casualties came from—well, there are conflicting accounts."

"We know what the casualties came from." *Well, sort of.* "Have we been associated with this in any way?"

Erica frowned. "There's a lot of noise about you."

"What kind of noise?"

"Nothing specific. Just vague 'wanted for questioning' stuff."

"We could have worked something out," Genevieve said, looking up through her eyelashes at Belial. "Karyn was going to cooperate, and then you're all 'no, you can never leave, bwahahahaha.' You need to learn to take yes for an answer, you stupid fuck."

Belial's hands knotted into fists, and a sneer pulled at his lips.

"Calm down," Sobell said. "Now is not the time. You've squandered your army, Belial, and for a second time. You should appreciate your allies when you can find them."

"Don't presume to give me orders."

"No orders, just advice."

Belial's lip twitched, but he added nothing. Sobell turned back to Erica. "So we're in the clear?"

"Not exactly. What do you know about the FBI's Non-Standard Investigations Branch?"

"I can't say the name rings a bell. Is it safe to assume that's not the forensic accounting department?"

"They've issued a warrant to go through all the things in your office."

"Another one?"

"And all the things, in fact, in your entire building and in twenty-seven other properties you own or can be shown to own substantial portions of, directly or indirectly."

"On what evidence?"

"That part of the warrant is sealed."

Sobell raised his eyebrows. "That sounds rather illegal. I seem to recall there being some sort of constitutional amendment regarding that, in fact."

"The warrant has been issued. We can fight if something goes to trial, but the search is going to start regardless, if it hasn't already. There's nothing to find, is there?"

"That . . . depends what they're looking for. I'd have said no if you hadn't invoked the Non-Standard Whatsit. As it is, I'm not sure."

"I would guess that they're looking to tie you to the deaths of several federal agents."

"We should be fine, then. I don't have the faintest clue how to conjure up whatever the hell that thing was."

Belial grunted. "None of this matters. The oracle gave us direction. Instructions. We need to start work."

"On that much we agree. I'm just trying to figure out

if I need to keep my devilishly handsome face out of sight, or if we can work with relative impunity."

"Out of sight," Erica said. "No question. The FBI is working like crazy going through tonight's evidence. You need to clean up and stay down until we know what they find and whether they're going to issue an arrest warrant."

He looked at Belial, who was grinding his teeth together and flexing his cheeks in a way that was wholly unlike smiling.

"Wonderful," Sobell said.

Anna exited the police station, squinting into the afternoon sun and still fuming from the endless inquisition, and came to an abrupt stop at the top of the stairs that descended from the front door. Karyn stood on about the fourth stair. She faced out into the parking lot, and damned if she didn't have a half-smoked cigarette burning down between the fingers of her right hand.

Karyn turned and looked up at her. A huge smile formed on her face.

"Oh my God," Anna said. "This is, like, the first time ever you didn't have to bum a cigarette off me."

Laughter from the both of them, and then Anna rushed down the stairs. She hugged Karyn so hard it got a squawk out of her.

"Hey! You're going to squish this," Karyn said. Anna eased up a bit, and Karyn pulled another cigarette from her shirt pocket. "Bummed it off a guy just for you," she said.

"It's you, right? You're really in there?"

"Slow down—I'm still not getting everything. If I concentrate, sometimes I can follow, but mostly I get a mess. I'm still seeing all the same stuff I was before, it's just that I'm also seeing the normal stuff more clearly. It's . . . hard to explain."

"It's fine. It'll be fine. We're gonna be—hey, you got a light?"

Karyn lit the cigarette. Anna didn't even draw off it yet, just stood on the stairs, breathing. There was still so much to take in, and she'd had no chance to process anything while the cops went over and over and over her story. Karyn's return to the regular world was just one piece, though by far the best one. Genevieve was another, and Anna was still sorting through her anger over what was either a chickening out or a straight-up betrayal, and—

"Hey, what's going on?" Karyn asked, looking down at Anna's hand.

Anna followed the line of her gaze. Anna's left hand had curled into a trembling claw, and only now did she consciously register the urge to do violence. She straightened her fingers with an effort and held them steady.

And there was that.

"They demonated me," Anna said.

"I know. I got one, too."

"Huh?"

"This," Karyn said. She held up her hand. The splinter was a dark line under her thumbnail, clearly visible in the sunlight. "I don't know if it's the demon itself, or just some kind of, I dunno, demon telephone, but it communicates with me. It's also basically tethering me to reality at this point, I think."

Anna rubbed her temple. She felt the murder slowly drain from her face. "I think mine's driving me crazy." She paused, weighing her words. "I think I'm gonna kill someone real soon if I don't get a handle on this. I kinda don't even care who."

Karyn tapped ash from her cigarette. Anna wasn't sure if Karyn had heard her or not. It didn't much matter. A few words one way or the other were nothing compared to the situation they'd suffered during the last couple of months.

"We got played," Karyn said.

"I know," Anna said.

"I'm starting to think we got played right from the start."

Anna wiggled the cigarette between her finger and thumb, watching the ash flake off the end and flutter to the stairs. "Yeah? Why's that?"

"The monster in Mendelsohn's basement—it's the same as the demon helping me navigate. And it's, like, Hector's worst enemy."

"Belial," Anna said. "Sobell kept calling Hector Belial."

"Either way, the thing in my head *hates* him. It."

"What's that mean?" Anna asked.

"I don't know. But I'm tired of getting jerked around. Sobell used us. Belial used us. I don't even know what we're in the middle of now, and I don't know how we get out of it."

"I've got some ideas about that," Anna said. Lots of thoughts, none very well examined. Thanks to Van Horn, she knew Sobell was dying, and thanks to Karyn, they all had the same sketchy clues regarding whatever it was he needed to stay alive, as well as whatever it was Belial sought. Leverage on Sobell might mean freedom, and leverage on Belial might mean—well, *somebody* had to know how the hell to get rid of her demon. "Later, though. This ain't the best place to talk about it."

Karyn nodded. "Yeah. One way or another, I'm through getting played."

The door behind them opened and a cop walked by, killing the conversation for the moment. Anna studied Karyn's face, amazed at how happy something as simple as Karyn looking back at her made her feel. Almost everything was fucked. Sobell and Belial were out there, somewhere, cooking up God knew what. Anna had a murderous demon in her head, and if she didn't get rid of it, it would most likely kill her. Karyn harbored a demon of her own, it seemed, and there was no telling what it wanted from her. The situation with Genevieve was so far beyond fucked that Anna couldn't even think about it without getting pissed off all over again.

Yet, for the moment, she was content to stand here on the stairs with her oldest and best friend and just smile.

Her phone buzzed. She took it out, opened it, and read the short text message.

"That's Nail," she said. "He's out. On his way to pick us up."

"Good," Karyn said.

They stood on the stairs next to each other and waited.

Read on for a special preview of the next
novel in the Arcane Underworld series,
coming in July 2016 from Roc.

The alley stank. Best as Anna could tell, the people from the burger joint that let out back here had been dumping their grease into the storm drain. Had to be a health code violation or a violation of some other kind of city ordinance. There was a freaking horde of rats in there, squirming over the congealed, reeking mess.

Horrifyingly, Anna's stomach grumbled. *The demon,* she thought. *That's not me.* It felt like her, though, and it was getting increasingly difficult to tell where the line was. Not for the first time, she wished she could choke the living shit out of Belial, the demon that had afflicted her with her new live-in guest.

She approached the next door down. It was the back exit from one of the city's more eclectic pawnshops, a place where people dropped off the small and weird for cash. Rissa, like half the pawnbrokers she knew, was a fence, and if unusual goods were moving around, there was a fair chance Rissa had heard about them.

The door opened while Anna was still ten feet away, and Rissa froze in the opening. She was in rough shape, mouth pulled down in an anxious, squirming frown, and she had a set of blue-black rings under her eyes from lack of sleep. She'd let her hair grow out some, the gray tresses pulled back in a ponytail, which fell past her collar.

She was hauling a suitcase behind her.

"Hey, Anna," she said slowly, the words dragged out in trepidation.

"Hey."

"I'm closing up."

"I got that impression. For good?"

Rissa shrugged. "Don't know. But I'm sure as shit getting out of here for a while."

"Can I come with?" Anna said, smiling to let her know it was a joke.

"What in the world are you mixed up in? Actually, never mind. I don't want to know." Rissa came out, set the suitcase to one side, and locked the door.

"What's going on, Riss?"

The older woman searched Anna's face in the light from the window. She didn't owe her anything, Anna knew, but they'd done a lot of business over the years, and it had always been fair. Anna hoped that counted for something.

"This is a bad time for somebody like me to be around," Riss said. "It's . . . it's like the pillars holding up the earth are shaking."

"Huh?"

"The whole occult underworld—and the regular old criminal underworld—is a mess. Cops looking for Enoch Sobell, some kind of massacre or something at the old women's prison. I hear that was mixed up in the occult, too. Really weird stuff." She gave Anna a frank look. "But I guess you know about all that."

Not for the first time, Anna marveled at the sneaky, serpentine paths information took around the city. Who had been involved in the shit show at the prison who would have recognized Anna? Who would possibly have talked about it? But here she was, just days later, and word was out.

"None of that's got anything to do with you," Anna said.

"Four crime bosses got guys in jail," Rissa said. "People are gonna get squeezed. Word's gonna get out that I don't want getting out. Time for me to take a break, that's all."

"I ain't buying it," Anna said. "You're not mixed up in this. So the big guys throw boulders at each other awhile. Big deal. It happens."

"Those rocks gotta fall somewhere," Rissa said. She watched Anna's eyes again, then scowled. "I got a call from a lawyer. She had some questions about relics."

Anna's gut clenched. "A lawyer. She give a name?"

"Erica Tran."

"Fuck." Sobell's lawyer. Bad because that meant she was already making the rounds. Good because that meant they hadn't found whatever Sobell and Belial were searching for, which meant Anna and the rest of her crew might still be able to get ahead of them. Get to it first and then talk deals. Anna thought her life probably depended on it—her demon, she knew from experience, wasn't going to sit idle forever, and either Sobell or the demon Belial might have the key to getting rid of the damn thing.

"Yeah. I asked around. I know who her client is. You ask me, that's as close as I need one of them rocks to fall before I get the message."

"Jesus, Riss. It's the right call. I'd get out of town, too, if I was you." Anna paused, then, "What'd you tell Erica?"

"Told her I'd ask around."

Something about the way she emphasized the word "told" suggested there was more to the story. "And the truth is . . . ?"

Rissa said nothing.

Anna pulled a roll of bills from her pocket. "I think it's two grand. You won't buy a summer home with it, but it'll get you a hell of a long way from here."

Riss glanced at the bills, but that was it. She bit her lip, and shook her head ever so slightly.

"This ain't a regular job, Riss. If I don't get ahead of Sobell, I'm gonna be a very unpleasant person for a while, and then I'm gonna drop dead. Please. Anything you got could be a big deal for me."

"Don't mess with me on this, Anna. This for real?"

"Yeah."

"Oh, shit. I don't know about any relics, but it seems there's a hell of a market for them all of a sudden. Tran was the second person to come looking."

"Yeah?"

Rissa nodded. "About a week ago, a guy came in looking for relics. Not just any old relic, he said. Specifically body parts. Saint Christopher's walking shoes wouldn't cut it."

"That's . . . bizarre. And gross."

Rissa shrugged. "I get a lot of bizarre requests. I probably wouldn't have even remembered it if he hadn't offered to pay in gold."

"No shit?"

"None."

"He give a name? What did he look like?"

"Latino guy with a teardrop tattooed at the corner of his left eye. He gave a name, but had to think an awful long time about it, and then it was so obviously fake I didn't bother to remember it."

A pause. When Rissa added nothing else, Anna laughed. "Okay. That's about ten thousand or so guys in L.A. Got anything else?"

"He had a big Gothic number seven tattooed on the back of his hand. Some other gang tats, but I don't really remember."

"Gang tats? That's fucking weird."

"I don't even blink at fucking weird anymore."

"Did you have anything for him?"

"Hell, no. This isn't twelfth-century France. This side of the pond, we don't tend to have Saint Peter's knucklebones hanging from a sack in the nave."

"Well, it's a start." She tossed the cash to Rissa, who caught it neatly and made it vanish in a pocket in one smooth motion.

"Don't let this come back on me, Anna," Rissa said,

her voice low and serious. "I don't stick my neck out for people much. Don't make me wish I hadn't."

"I won't," Anna said. "Now get outta here before I get all weepy."

"Yeah, right," Rissa said, but she smiled. Then she hustled down the alley, leaving Anna alone with the stench of cold grease and the squeaking of rats.

ALSO AVAILABLE FROM

Jamie Schultz

PREMONITIONS

An Arcane Underworld Novel

Two million dollars. It's the kind of score Karyn Ames has always dreamed of—enough to set her crew up pretty well and, more important, enough to keep her safely stocked on a very rare, very expensive black market drug. Without it, Karyn hallucinates slices of the future until they totally overwhelm her, leaving her unable to distinguish the present from the mess of certainties and possibilities yet to come.

The client behind the heist is Enoch Sobell, a notorious crime lord with a reputation for being ruthless and exacting—and a purported practitioner of dark magic. Karyn and her associates are used to the supernatural and the occult, but their target is more than just the usual family heirloom or cursed necklace. It's a piece of something larger. Something sinister. Karyn's crew and even Sobell himself are about to find out just how powerful it is…and how powerful it may yet become.

Available wherever books are sold or at penguin.com

R0207